I0724456

The Flower Trade

ALSO BY LON OTTO

A Nest of Hooks

Cover Me

A Man in Trouble

*Grit: Bringing Physical Experience
Into Imaginative Writing*

The Flower Trade

A NOVEL

Lon Otto

Copyright © 2022 by Lon Otto
All rights reserved.
Printed in the United States of America

Brighthorse Books
13202 N River Drive
Omaha, NE 68112
brighthorsebooks.com

ISBN: 978-1-944467-36-4

Cover Art: Mola, San Blas Islands, Panama, 1989. Private collection.

This book is a work of fiction. The characters, incidents, and dialogue are drawn from the author's imagination and are not to be construed as real. Any resemblance to actual events or persons, living or dead, is entirely coincidental.

For permission to reproduce selections from this book for purposes other than review, contact the editors at info@brighthorsebooks.com. Brighthorse books are distributed to the trade through Ingram Book Group and its distribution partners. To learn more about Brighthorse Books, go to brighthorsebooks.com.

For Kathleen and Audra and Evan,
compañeros de viaje

Bothrops asper, the pit viper known to North Americans as fer-de-lance (spearhead), is the most frequent source of fatal snakebite in Costa Rica, where it is called terciopelo (velvet).
—*Snakes of the New World*, Gustav Herder

The Flower Trade

CHAPTER ONE

VIVA THE 15TH OF SEPTEMBER

THE HOFFMANS HAD BEEN LIVING in Costa Rica three weeks when the thunder of drums started. At first they thought it was real thunder echoing in the mountains around them, then found it was a percussion band from the high school down the road from their apartment, twenty-some drums, snare to bass, marching, shaking the air with their pounding. *Ra tu tu Ta tu tu Boom, Ra tu tu Ta tu tu Boom, Ra tu tu Boom, Ra tu tu Ta tu tu Boom Boom Boom*, every day, all morning sometimes. It was the same with the other liceo in town, it was the same with the schools in San José, seven kilometers away, it was the same, for all they knew, from the Nicaraguan border to the jungle frontier with Panama—drums beating furiously, practicing for Independence Day, September 15, 1989.

Close up, it was not all drums. In each band a few girls with glockenspiels tinkled melodies against brief silences of the drums. But the drums were what mattered, boys pounding them, thunder from taut skin overwhelming the nervous struck silver. A block away it was all thunder.

Every day Ted would run into the bands marching in Escazú's steep streets or see them on the razor-wire-guarded roof of one of the schools, practicing before the afternoon rains began. Even Saturdays the kids were in their school uniforms, navy and sky blue, navy and white, marching and drumming, young teachers drilling them with whistle blasts. Hour after hour, *Ra tu tu Ta tu tu Boom, Ra tu tu Boom Boom Boom Boom.*

Explosive and disciplined, it was the most nakedly warlike music he had ever heard, the hard throb of armies marching, in a country that had disarmed itself forty years before, outlawed its own military. ¡Viva la paz! paper banners in the shop windows urged. ¡Viva Costa Rica! *Boom.* And ¡Viva el quince de setiembre! The country was covering itself with flags, congratulating itself on the freedom handed over to it 168 years before (¡Viva la independencia!), neither asked for nor generally desired by Costa Ricans at the time, much less won in battle. ¡Somos libres! September 15, 1821: fed-up, exhausted Spain cuts loose her Central American colonies once and for all. It takes a month for the news to arrive from Guatemala, carried by a relay of messengers traveling not only by day but straight through the night, guided by lanterns. *Boom.*

Ted loved the violent, paradoxical music, monotonous and infinitely varied, numbing and intoxicating. He couldn't get enough of it, would stand on a narrow, broken sidewalk listening for hours if his wife or kids weren't there to drag him back.

"Aren't you going out to the farm?" Monica asked him as he and Valerie, their four-year-old, were about to leave on an errand that would draw him into the path of one of the bands. Monica had their four chairs upended on the table that separated the kitchen area of the second-floor apartment from the living room and was sweeping the mysteriously dented wooden floor with a broom they had inherited from previous tenants. The floor looked as if someone had beaten it with a ball peen hammer or danced madly in stiletto heels.

He stood in the doorway with Valerie tugging him toward the stairs. "It takes forever to get out there without the car," he said. "Anyway, Alejandro needs to feel he's running things now,

I'm not Cal Richardson." He saw something skeptical in the tightness of her shoulders. "What?"

She had her wild black hair restrained in a ponytail that hovered restlessly over her bent back as she swept. The handle of the old broom was too short for her, but she worked it doggedly, as if their lives depended on her cleaning up a mess she usually didn't even notice. "It's just that you maybe shouldn't take so much for granted," she said.

He waited for her to stop sweeping and look at him, but she kept working relentlessly around the table legs, pursuing cereal and toast crumbs from the kids' breakfast. She was still wearing the sweat pants and faded red T-shirt she slept in these days, and her bare feet were pale against the dark wood of the floor. Her breasts swayed against the fabric of the shirt. He said, "Richardson's problem was he didn't trust anybody here. Last thing he said to me before he left, he's standing right in front of Ana Rosa, he says, 'Teddy boy, you don't know what you're up against with these people. If it ain't nailed down or locked up, it's theirs.' Ana Rosa's sitting right there at her desk. Has perfect English."

Monica groaned, closed her eyes. Cal Richardson was an old friend of her father, who had invested a lot of money in a flower farm Richardson was starting in Heredia, a little north of San José. Checking on it during a family vacation in Costa Rica a few years later, Ted had found the business floundering, Richardson hostile and ready to throw in the towel. "You're right," she said. "You're probably right."

"I'll keep Valerie out of your way for a while," he said. "You can get some work done." Meaning work on her dissertation, though he didn't say so. She was looking around for the dust pan. He followed Valerie down the stairs to the garage, which had housed their battered Volkswagen Squareback during the seven days it had run for them after they had bought it for too much money, their worst mistake since renting an apartment too far from the flower farm. A load of laundry was chugging around in the old washing machine in a corner of the garage. Once it stopped, Monica would come down and start hanging clothes on the lines Ted had strung across their little concrete courtyard. He didn't think she would get to the file box containing her long-stalled dissertation. She would finish the laundry, then sit at the table and drink coffee. She might pull a chair out onto the balcony and read a novel she had picked up at the used goods store in San José where they had bought most of their furniture. He didn't know how to mention the dissertation without sounding pushy.

Clanging the garage door closed behind him, he took Valerie's hand and walked down the rocky dirt road that led to the liceo, where the band was already drumming. Beyond the row of red-roofed stucco houses on their right and a high concrete wall on their left, topped with broken glass glittering in the sun, they reached the place where a towering stand of trees threw the road into shadow and an overgrown coffee plantation stretched down the mountain foothills below them. A jungly house on stilts stood among the trees. It was built of bamboo and thick, raw lumber, and an open deck on the second story jutted out toward the road. Behind the deck was a screened and louvered tree-house-looking structure roofed with sloping panels of faded green fiberglass. Beneath the house, among the log stilts, a twenty-foot-long dugout canoe lay overturned, as if it had been dragged up from the brown rushing stream in the gorge just beyond the house.

Near the bridge that crossed the stream, Ted had noticed a pile of branches that might supply him with a suitable farol stick for Stephen, his nine-year-old, who needed it for an eve of Independence Day program at his school. Cutting the stick was all Ted was going to do. The boy would have to make the lantern himself.

The mimeographed assignment had come home with the usual splendid greeting, "Estimados Padres de Familias." Stephen hadn't been very helpful in explaining the project. Even back in Cincinnati, where he had finished fourth grade the previous spring, Stephen never talked about school. It was hard to tell how he was doing now, how much Spanish he was learning, whether he was resigned yet to being wrenched away from his home and friends. He went to school, came home at two-thirty, read again and again the superhero comic books he had smuggled down in his suitcase. So far, the only thing he seemed to have picked up at school was a breathy, maniacal laugh he must have learned from one of his classmates.

The laugh sometimes drove Ted a little crazy, but he tried not to be critical. It was he who had persuaded Monica that the boy should go to a theoretically bilingual Costa Rican school rather than one of the English-speaking international schools. "They don't *want* the kids to speak Spanish!" he had raged after an interview with the principal of one expensive academy. "They used to not even allow Spanish on the playground."

"She said they don't forbid it anymore."

"But why did we come down here, for Stephen to get to know a bunch of rich brats speaking the master language?"

Neither of them would have been able to say exactly why they had come. They had drifted into the decision in a mazy sequence of propositions, hope taking them by the hand, showing them where to sign their names. It was business, they would say, a chance for Ted to make a fresh start. Monica could get her dissertation going again. It was a favor to Monica's father, who stood to lose his hundred-thousand dollar investment unless Ted got the flower farm untangled from the mess Cal Richardson had made of it. It was an educational opportunity for Stephen and Valerie they couldn't pass up. A chance to rebuild their marriage, still cracked and precarious a year after Ted's affair.

Those were their reasons, what they told themselves. Yet rumbling beneath whatever they could say or think, crushed by depth into something like silence, a voice had murmured, *Save yourself, run, there's a sickness around you, greed, violence, desire, pride. Save yourself. Save yourselves and your children. Run.*

And they had run, though they never would have called it that, obeying a voice they didn't even know they had heard. And they were running still, though they thought they had settled down now, in this quaint mountain town, this peaceful country, safe as Switzerland.

At the jungly house, gawky turkey chicks pecked around in the gravel. Valerie yanked herself away from him and chased them back into the shelter of a bamboo shed. It was okay, there was little damage she could do to herself on this ridiculous road, full of ruts and potholes deep enough to slow down even the most lunatic driver. The steeply sloping field of coffee and plantain falling away toward the valley was protected by a wire fence. Monica sometimes complained about the steel bars and fences everywhere in Costa Rica, rejas guarding parked automobiles and second-story windows and balconies impossible to reach from outside. But Valerie's reckless energy made Ted grateful for them. He had seen her trying to squeeze through the bars over her bedroom window, hoping to retrieve a Duplo block she had dropped onto the tin roof below, during what was supposed to have been a nap. She liked to dangle her legs over the edge of their little balcony to tease Boby, the watch dog owned by two men who rented one of the apartments below them and used it on weekends for entertaining women. While Boby barked up at her from the enclosed parking area, she would climb the balcony grillwork like a monkey looking for a way out. Ted wished Stephen had more of this physical boldness, he wished Valerie had a little less.

He ran and caught her before she could mount the low guardrail of the bridge. Far below them, dark water foamed among the rocks and rubbish—old paint cans, bulging garbage bags, a child's red boot—and crashed on down the mountain slope past the mossy ruins of some sort of concrete abutment, blue-green in the perpetual shade of banana leaf and elephant ear. A stand of bamboo with trunks thick as a man's leg leaned over the stream, rattling in the morning breeze, and a vague smell of sewage hung in the cool air. He picked her up, her wiry little body electric in his arms, and walked on to the pile of branches, letting himself be caught up in the roll of drums beating against the roar of the stream.

Valerie insisted that he first cut a stick for her. While she put it to use slaughtering the creamy, pendulous blossoms of queen of the night plants that grew along the ditches, he searched through the pile of branches until he found one with a shallow *S* curve, thick enough to carry the modest weight of a cardboard lantern. Stephen had been worried that a wooden stick wouldn't be strong enough. "I've seen the right kind in stores," he had said. "Hook metal ones, like, you know, those shepherd things?"

"Crooks, shepherds' crooks. Come on, Stevie, I can cut a great stick, it'll be more traditional. Anyway, what kind of farol are you planning to make?"

He hadn't decided yet, or wasn't telling. Monica had suggested that they might want to just buy one of the commercial blue, white, and red paper and cellophane lanterns that were by now hanging in all of the pulperías and school supply stores, but Ted hadn't even had to argue against that idea. Stephen was what everybody called a creative child, and since kindergarten he had always received a lot of praise for his art projects. "I've got some ideas," he said. "I'll make it this afternoon. I just hope the stick isn't too cruddy."

Trying hard not to make a cruddy stick, his tongue clicking in counterpoint to the percussion band, Ted was working his pocket knife through the branch when Valerie wrapped her arms around his leg. A bearded, stocky man, 4' 8", 4' 9", was standing on the other side of the road, watching them. He was wearing a short-sleeved, orange-and-black-striped Bengals jersey that hung down to his knees, and he cradled a row of small green mangoes in his arms. After Ted waved to him, the man came over and started talking to him in rapid, slangy Spanish. Ted wasn't catching much of it, but when the man gestured toward the stick he was cutting, he tried to explain about the lanterns.

The man nodded as if he understood. Suddenly Valerie thrust her stick toward the man's chest and shouted, "That's *our* team, at our real home!" While Ted tried to explain about the Bengals, the man squatted down, bringing his broad, darkly bearded face close to the little girl's, and asked her if she liked mangoes. "Sí," Ted answered for her, though in fact he could not get either of the kids to eat the slippery, grainy fruit. Stephen claimed they tasted like gasoline, which, Ted had to admit, they sort of did.

The man handed Valerie one of the mangoes, then another. She didn't know what to do with her stick, handed it to Ted, took two more mangoes, stood there looking in pleased surprise at her armload of fruit. Ted thanked the man, wondering what to do with unripe mangoes, and prompted Valerie into saying gracias. The man smiled, patted her on the head, made the usual fuss over her white-blond, frizzy curls. He held two more mangoes in his left hand like tennis balls before service. Did he like mangoes? he asked Ted. Sure, he liked to eat mangoes, Ted replied. The man handed him the last two mangoes and stood smiling while Ted thanked him. The man gestured toward the jungly house, which loomed on its pilings on the other side of the stream. Did he know the people who lived there? he asked. Bolivians?

Ted didn't know them, though a busty woman in a short, tight skirt and low-cut blouse had waved down to him from its high balcony once when he was walking by. A man wearing a cowboy hat had come out and joined her at the flimsy railing and invited him, in good English, to come on up. "Another time," he had answered, thinking of the eighty thousand colones he was lugging home from the bank in his briefcase. The woman was a prostitute, he suspected, the man perhaps her pimp. He hadn't seen either the man or the woman again. He would see people drinking on the balcony from time to time, but nobody had ever spoken to him except that one time.

The Bolivians and he were like this, the bearded man said, extending two fingers pressed together. Did Ted want to visit them? Did he have any money? Ted shook his head regretfully, patting his pockets and cringing inwardly at the jingle of his keys. He had only his keys, he said, showing the man, wondering if he should offer to give back the mangoes. The man looked down the road for a moment, then shook hands with him again and walked away toward the jungly house. Ted saw him stop below it and call up softly, until a brassy-haired woman—not the one who had waved to Ted—came out onto the balcony and talked with him. Finally the man went away.

"Why did he gave us these fruits?" Valerie asked.

"He was just a nice man. I hope he didn't need them for something."

"I think he was a nice dorf," she said.

"No, he's just a short man."

She rolled her eyes at the lame distinction, and they walked on toward the percussion band. Ahead of the drummers now marched a squadron of school kids bearing long, empty flagpoles, and behind them other kids marched down the road with crude wooden rifles, more or less in time with the powerful drums. Valerie tired of it too quickly, and Ted walked home with her, conscious, as they passed beneath the cantilevered balcony of the jungly house, of the green abundance they carried in their arms.

When he returned from school that afternoon, Stephen set to work on his lantern, cutting up and taping together pieces of cardboard from a liter milk carton, losing his temper whenever Monica or Ted made a suggestion, taking pains to draw and color a bald eagle on one side and stars and stripes on the others, covering his mistakes with new layers of construction paper until the sides were thick and cushiony. He didn't seem to think much of the stick, even though Ted had nicely rounded the ends and peeled off the bark.

"How do we get the candle to stand up?" Ted asked when Stephen brought the finished product to be hung from the end of the stick. The boy's face went red with confusion. "And we'll have to cut some holes or something, for the light to shine through. It's a lantern, after all."

"A candle?" Stephen cried. "A candle? A candle's going to set the whole thing on fire! Cardboard's like paper, Dad, you can't put fire in it!"

"The faroles in the stores are paper," Ted pointed out.

"You want me to carry around a bunch of burning paper? Are you crazy? On that stupid stick?"

"We'll fix it so nothing gets on fire. Wait. *Wait*."

Stephen stormed out of the room, and Valerie shouted at Ted in fierce, unexpected solidarity, "Now just look what you made him do!" She ran off after him, only to have him slam their bedroom door in her face, sending her into outraged tears.

While Ted tried to soothe Valerie, Monica went in to the boy, and eventually they worked out a way to line the lantern with layers of aluminum foil, and cut slits all around the edges of Stephen's designs for the light to shine through. For good measure, Stephen covered the stick with foil, too, though Ted tried to argue him out of it on the grounds that the flame would never come close to it, and that he was making it look like something from outer space rather than a traditional lantern commemorating an event in 1821.

"I *like* space stuff," Stephen answered, and when he was walking away, mumbled, "I wish I was in space right now."

"Keep being a smart ass, buddy."

Monica laid her hand on Ted's arm.

"All right, who knows where they sell candles around here?" he asked. At Pulpería Zeta, the little general store a few blocks away from their apartment, he steered the kids away from the displays of bright paper and cellophane faroles and big plastic flags, and bought them instead a pair of paper flags mounted on what seemed to be bamboo sticks but turned out to be some kind of reed or thick straw, which collapsed when the kids waved them aggressively at each other like swords. "We have tape at home," he told them. "Stop whining."

September was the heart of the rainy season—the green season, travel agents had started calling it. The rain held off until late afternoon that day, but by 5:00, when the family walked down to the hulera road to catch the bus to Stephen's school, it was coming down hard, soaking their legs and seeming to drive right through the seams of their umbrellas. A plane had crashed in the mountains above them during a rainstorm like this, a couple days before. They still hadn't recovered the bodies.

By the time the bus came, Ted's shoulders ached from carrying Valerie's wriggling weight in one arm and trying to keep the umbrella over them with the other. Monica, elegant in a black dress and gray silk scarf, carried the farol onto the bus. Stephen had decided he hated the lantern and wanted nothing to do with it. They had ruined it with their suggestions, he said. He still thought the candle inside it was a terrible idea.

Stephen got on the bus last, scrubbed and serious in the short-sleeved white shirt and navy trousers elementary students in Costa Rica were required by law to wear, whether attending public or private school. It was a democratic leveler that Ted approved of, though Monica had pointed out that embroidered school emblems sewn on chest or sleeve still served to differentiate the students according to social class. Ted was glad that Stephen hadn't had to wear the national uniform for pre-school and kindergartners, the light blue smocks—gabachas—which he thought made the children look like little Walgreen's clerks.

The bus dropped them off in front of the school's iron gates and continued down the mountain toward San José as they fumbled open their umbrellas in a haze of fumes. A few parents and children were standing around in the shelter of one of the porticos that ran the length of the school's low, stucco buildings, but it was clear that nothing much was going to happen by the announced 5:30 starting time. Ted sat down on a bench in the portico to furl his umbrella, and Valerie darted out into the rain and up a little hill in the school yard toward a swing set. She slipped and skidded down, plastering her legs with the slimy brown clay they could never get out of the children's clothes except by boiling on the stove and scrubbing with a stiff brush. He tried to quiet her—she was screaming as if she had really hurt herself. He looked around for Monica, hoping that she would take over. She was as self-conscious as he was about the effect their kids' uproars had on a people whose children stood quietly beside them for hours in lines at banks, bus stops, government offices, not fussing, never fighting with each other or running off or hanging by their legs from railings or queue divider chains or knocking over racks of brochures reaching for the ones on top.

Monica was apparently off somewhere with Stephen. She had wanted to talk with his teacher. Ted's dark trousers were already smeared where he had reached into his pocket for a tissue to wipe the mud off Valerie, but he still had hopes of saving his white shirt. He remembered a pair of little toilet stalls and a trough sink off the courtyard outside Stephen's classroom, got lost looking for it, found another bathroom off a different courtyard. When he had cleaned most of the mud from her legs with wads of toilet paper, he found that she actually had hurt herself. Tiny pebbles of blood welled up on her knee where the skin was scraped rough. "I'm sorry, sweet girl," he said, lifting her and hugging her tight, though by then she had stopped crying and was interested only in rejoining the others.

When they found Monica and Stephen, Valerie showed off her wound to Stephen, who acknowledged it without enthusiasm. He looked tired and glum in the dim light of the portico and had stuck his lantern under the bench where he sat slumped against Monica. Other parents were arriving now, in big cars, Ted was surprised to see—Volvos, Mercedes Benzes, luxury Japanese cars filling the asphalt portion of the school yard—and were starting to crowd the long porticos to stay out of the rain. Their children were lugging huge, elaborate faroles that must have taken weeks to make, beautifully painted lanterns in the shape of traditional campesino houses and ox carts, ornate geometrical forms, enormous doves and flowers fringed all over with crêpe paper like piñatas. No kid could have had a hand in making them. The average adult couldn't have executed some of them, company graphics departments must have labored on the projects. Delicately-cut-out letters glowed with colored cellophane—"VIVA 15 SEPT," "100 AÑOS DEMOCRACÍA," "PAZ," "VIVA COSTA RICA," "SOMOS LIBRES."

Ted felt Stephen's humiliation and sense of betrayal rise in his own throat as a chunky, slick-haired boy stood in front of them with his hand in his pocket, switching on and off by remote control wires the lights inside a glowing mountain village he carried on a six foot pole. "You made yours yourself," Ted reminded Stephen. "I'm proud of you. I love your farol. Let's get it out here where people can see it."

Reluctantly Stephen hauled it out and Ted took it from him. It really did look pitiful compared to the works of art bobbing around them now in the increasingly crowded portico. It was a fraction of their size, and it looked like what it was, the afternoon's work of a nine-year-old boy. "This is a terrific job," Ted insisted. "Look at how the foil wraps around the inside, Monica, isn't that great?"

"That was Mom's idea."

"Well, you drew this eagle, I know that. When the candle's lighted behind it, it's going to look incredible."

Mention of fire got him red-faced again, seeming about to cry. While Ted and Monica tried to encourage him, Valerie ran over to a window looking into the school's assembly hall and started shrieking with pleasure at a television set flickering up on the stage, the mouse Gigio dancing and singing. They were waiting for some sort of national patriotic broadcast celebrating the eve of Independence Day. The Directora, a large, severe-looking woman, kept adjusting the television and checking her watch. Stephen joined his sister watching the puppet's antics.

"Since when is he so afraid of fire?" Ted asked Monica. "If I had carried on that way when I was his age, my father would have killed me."

"Your father. The gold standard."

A boy ran by with a big, crudely-made, papier mâché airplane swinging from a farol stick. The plane was painted dull black and was warty with ball turrets and bristling machine gun barrels—clearly a bomber. A votive candle stuck up from its cockpit. Ted laughed and tried to get Stephen's attention, but other kids pressed between them, and then the bomber was gone, a knot of boys running after it, admiring the audacity of its maker.

"I'm not sure it's so bad, a little discipline."

"Cut it out, Ted, he used to beat you up. The man abused you."

It was more complicated than she could ever understand, and he wished he had never told her about it. He had brought it up once after his brief affair had come to light, thinking it might explain something, but instead she seemed to expect him to do something about it. What can you do about the past? You move on.

He looked around at the parents shepherding their children into the crowded shelter of the main portico, some starting to filter into the assembly hall. Mothers outnumbered fathers by a considerable margin. The women were well-dressed, most of them young and attractive, relaxed, chatting with each other while their children milled around, faroles swaying above the crowd. Stephen was still staring through the window with his sister, lulled by the first television he had seen since they moved out of the housekeeping hotel in San José and into their Escazú apartment.

Ted worried that they were too indulgent with Stephen, tolerating tantrums and moody obstinacy that would make it hard for him to get along later in life. Costa Rican kids were well-behaved, stoic in the face of boredom or discomfort. He hoped it would rub off on Stephen and Valerie.

At some signal, everyone started moving into the assembly hall, where folding chairs were set up facing the stage. Ted managed to keep the family together as they edged down a row toward some empty chairs on the far side of the room. Stephen kept making little disgusted noises as his farol stick bumped and tangled against his legs. "Watch it, pal," Ted murmured.

When they were all settled, Monica whispered to Ted, "What if Valerie wigs out on us? She didn't take a nap, maybe you should sit where you can get out with her."

"I've been dealing with her all day," he said. "I'd like to stay with Stephen."

"You're already muddy," she said. "I'd never get that junk out of this dress. Sorry, Ted." She smiled apologetically, the glossy red of her lipstick making the expression unexpectedly dramatic, even glamorous. She didn't often wear lipstick these days.

He picked up the little girl again, heedless now of his clean shirt, and carried her around to the back of the hall. He found a seat at the end of a row, close to the door, and settled down, while Valerie accepted as her due the adoring pats and ¡qué linda!s from the women and older girls sitting near them.

Perfume floated in the warm, moist air. He looked around. There were almost no other men in the hall, as if Costa Rica's Independence celebrations, for all the testosterone-driven drumming and marching, were essentially a feminine concern, after all. A grandfather or two sat toward the front, and the few other men at the event lingered in the portico outside.

Ted liked being among women, breathing their rich evening fragrance. Elaine's scent was what he remembered most vividly whenever he thought about her, something with vanilla, but animal, too, musky. Met first as a tax client, she had become his partner in a solar energy company he was trying to get started, and they had grown close during the long lunches and evening meetings, first wreathed in the excitement of their shared vision, then trying to find ways of accessing energy conservation grants that shimmered in the distance like mirages, finally struggling to get out from under as much of the failing company's debt as they could manage. It had taken him by surprise, the frank touch of her perfume one night as they were wrapping things up, and their affair, their brief affair, had somehow seemed to him as much a matter of chemistry—chemistry in the literal sense—as moral choice. He knew it *was* moral choice, and that it had almost cost him everything he cared about, might still cost him that, if Monica couldn't finally get over it. It just felt like something else on some level—brute atmosphere, the air he had had no choice but to breathe in a country that he had now safely escaped. That they had all safely escaped. He had gotten them all to this safe, peaceful place, he deserved some credit for that, along with the blame crouching on his heart.

A woman in the row in front of him turned around and smiled at Valerie, reached back and stroked her light frizz of curls. He noticed a smear of mud and perhaps blood on the cuff of his shirt and rolled the sleeves up to his elbows. He felt thuggish in his soiled clothes and tried to relax back into cool fatherhood, tried to enjoy the admiration generated by his beautiful little girl.

After all the seats were occupied, parents and children still kept crowding into the hall. The Directora stood on the stage and signaled for silence. Over the continuing noise of the crowd, she made a speech of introduction that Ted, sitting so far back, could probably not have understood even if his Spanish had been better than it was. Everyone rose, lights dimmed, parents and children fumbled for matches and began lighting or switching on the lanterns. Some of the bigger ones had as many as six candles inside. The television volume rose. A resonant male voice made another speech and a symphony began to play what Ted assumed to be the himno nacional that the school program mimeograph had mentioned. Led by the guitar-playing music teacher, the crowd joined in, lustily at first, then more raggedly as the song proceeded through later verses.

Standing with Valerie in his arms, Ted could see Monica and Stephen toward the front, looking tall and out of place, though with their dark coloring they blended in better than he and Valerie did—blond, fair-skinned, and now muddied. Monica had her black, unruly hair secured in a bun that always took her a long time to get right and had only been achieved tonight with the ruthless application of bobby pins and a tortoise-shell comb. It left her slender neck bare, except for a few stray curls that had already escaped in the humid air. When she turned to say something to Stephen, the curve of her nose in profile and the heavy lids of her eyes made Ted's heart ache.

Stephen's lantern had gotten lighted somehow—Monica didn't smoke anymore, and Ted had forgotten to leave her the book of matches he had brought for this purpose—but the boy was holding the stick low rather than raising it overhead like the other kids, and he seemed to be bothered by the smoke, kept twisting and jerking his head back. Raise it up, Ted urged silently. He felt his own father's hand reach out and smack the boy upside the back of his head, ringing some sense into him.

When the televised program was over, the Directora led the assembly through a pledge of allegiance, then the music teacher joined her again at the microphone, strumming his big acoustic guitar, and they began some more patriotic songs.

The room was hot, the singing went on and on, and Ted was actually relieved when Valerie started squirming. She whispered to him that she had to pee. They found the bathroom easily this time. Afterward, rather than pushing back into the hall, he decided to wait out the program in the cool darkness of the portico, which also was crowded, but more comfortable than inside. The asphalt portion of the playground was jammed with cars now, and people were still arriving, parents holding umbrellas over their children's lanterns, calling out to each other, in no hurry. That's it, he thought, get there when you get there.

A man lounged against a wall opposite him, elegant in gray linen suit and silk tie, Burberry draped over his shoulders like a cape. A beautiful, well-dressed woman was speaking to him in low, respectful tones. He made Ted feel like a street person. Ted wondered which kid belonged to the man, what splendid farol he had commissioned.

Valerie tried to get away and join some kids playing on the swings in the rain, but he grabbed her in time and brought her back to the assembly hall window, where they could watch what was going on inside. They looked for Stephen. The teachers seemed to be trying to herd the children into a line, presumably for the desfile de faroles, the procession of lanterns that was supposed to be the centerpiece of the program. Ted saw Monica, carrying Stephen's farol, working her way toward one of the doors, a resigned look on her face.

"I hate this. Let's go." It was Stephen, who had come up behind them.

"What's the matter? We went to all this trouble to come down here in the rain. The program isn't over."

"All right, I'm walking home then."

Ted had just grabbed him by the arm when Monica reached them. "What's going on?" She looked at Ted as if he had done something to Stephen.

"He doesn't like the program," he said. "He's decided to walk home by himself. What do you think, good idea? You know the way in the dark, Stevie?"

"Ted." Turning her back to him, she crouched before the boy. "We'll all go home, if you want," she said. "It's your school's program. If you decide to stay, we should light your farol again. They want all the kids to file around the hall and out here and back in again for the judging."

"The judging—for prizes. I almost forgot about that."

"Maybe we *should* leave," Ted said. "Val's getting antsy."

"I guess I want to do this thing," Stephen said. "They showed us the prizes this morning. They're medals, made out of real metal. Maybe I'll win one of them."

"How can he think he has a prayer?" Ted asked Monica after

they had lighted the lantern and sent him back in to join the others. "He despises his farol, he knows what the competition is. It's just another chance for him to be crushed."

She shrugged. "He wants to do it. Think how brave he's been, starting a new school in the middle of the year, hardly knowing the language. How would you have liked it?"

Ted's stomach tightened with the knowledge of how profoundly he would have hated it. He would have run away from home, as he had in fact done many times, sometimes with less provocation than this. But where could he go, alone in a foreign country? Where *had* he gone? To city parks at first. Later, down along the river. Always running out of food, always found—caught.

Two by two, their lighted faroles dangling from the ends of sticks or mounted on poles, the children began pushing their way out of the front door of the hall, along the portico between lines of applauding adults, and back again into the other door. When Stephen passed his family, he had a strange expression on his face, dark, resolute, his sad lantern held reasonably high. Monica and Ted cheered and clapped.

Without seeming to acknowledge them, Stephen gestured with his head for them to notice what was following him a few kids back. Ted looked. It was the papier-mâché bomber, candle burning now in the cockpit, soaring as high as its maker's stick could raise it, black and ominous among the glowing doves and flowers and decorated ox carts and pretty white and blue campesino houses—a warplane, lumpy with menace, thundering silently through the night sky, delivering destruction to the world of parents and teachers and politicians and patriotism and prizes and liberty and democracy and the flimsy, self-flattering lie of peace.

It was such an exact embodiment of the planes Ted remembered obsessively drawing on notebook covers and in the margins of his textbooks when he was the boy's age that he could almost see dotted lines of machine gun bullets blazing from its bulging gun turrets, bombs pouring from its belly. Here, anyway, was a project no adult had co-opted.

When the children were all packed once more into the assembly hall and the judging was about to begin, they saw through the window that Stephen was mouthing something to them, and Monica decided to shove her way in to him and give him some moral support. Ted and Valerie watched as she joined him and let him draw her forward until they stood near the inner ring of kids and parents crowded around the judge's table, which was piled with medals and blue, white, and red ribbons. Maybe there *were* enough to go around. It would be typical of them, as worshipful of democracy as Costa Ricans were.

Each time a prize was announced, the children near the winner would yell and hoist their still-lighted faroles high above the crowd. While the ceremony crept along, Ted was distracted by a whining and stamping behind him in the portico. At first he thought it was Valerie, but she was still standing on the bench, face pressed against the window. In the middle of the portico crowd, somebody else's kid, for a change, was throwing a fit. He saw a woman grab the crying child, maybe a year or two older than Valerie, and pull him to her side. The boy screamed and struck at her with his free hand. In a movement almost too quick to see, the mother gave him three hard cracks on his bare legs with the whippy metal farol stick that she had evidently just yanked out of his hands. The little boy cried out, then subsided into muffled sobs and let his mother lead him away through the crowd. Ted never saw the woman's face, kept seeing the cheerful, red and blue plastic-covered wire make its brief sharp arcs against the boy's thin legs, felt the humiliating burn in his own calves.

There was a flash of light from inside the hall, and Valerie shrieked in delight. The crêpe paper streamers on one of the big faroles had caught fire, and the lantern now blazed on the floor while children and adults circled around it, laughing and shouting. And then somehow Stephen was inside the ring, screaming, jumping toward the fire in his panic, whirling finally, and breaking into the excited mass of spectators as other boys danced around the already-shrinking flames.

He was sobbing and out of breath when he reached Ted, who hugged him until he was able to talk. "Dad," he said, "there was a real fire, right on the floor, and everybody was laughing! How could they laugh when a real fire was burning in a building?"

"It's okay now, look, the fire is out."

Stephen looked through the window, saw that he was right. "But how could they laugh?" he demanded, more angry now than frightened. "The grownups too. They laughed at a real fire. They didn't even try to put it out."

"Well, it's a concrete floor," Ted observed. "They knew it wouldn't catch fire. Besides, they must be used to this sort of thing. Come on, kids with candles burning inside paper lanterns? It must happen all the time."

"That's exactly what I said!" Stephen shouted. "I kept trying to tell you it was dangerous. Jesus Christ!"

The guy with the Burberry draped over his expensive shoulders was watching them with amusement. Ted crouched beside the boy, put his arms around him, protecting or concealing him. "You've got to keep yourself from panicking that way, Stevie," he said in a low, calm voice. A good father's voice. "You've got to be brave."

Monica came up to them carrying Stephen's farol and began scolding him. Ted interrupted her. "It's okay, I already chewed him out."

"It's not okay, he ran right toward the fire, he could have hurt himself."

"He knows. He's sorry. He'll do better next time, right?" It was not at all clear that he would do better. Indignation still mottled his face and he only accepted the farol stick from Monica when she shoved it at him.

People were starting to filter out of the hall. Kids with medals and ribbons exchanged congratulations with their classmates, and one by one, families made dashes to their cars, glittering darkly in the heavy rain. Ted carried Valerie under his umbrella as they splashed through the playground parking lot between the rows of automobiles and across the road to their bus stop. A dozen people were already waiting there, some under the corrugated tin shelter, others standing with umbrellas or bareheaded in the downpour, talking quietly, ignoring the rain. There were no buildings on this side of the road, only a steep slope rising above them, dense with brush and trees, and it was very dark.

No one else came across the road from the school. The luxurious cars rolled out of the school's gates, headed uphill or down. Confronted with the two hundred percent automobile import tax, Ted had opted for the ten-year-old Volkswagen that was in a repair shop now, something wrong with its transmission. Even Stephen and Valerie knew not to mention the car to him.

The school parking lot across the road was almost empty by the time a bus appeared out of the glistening darkness, heading up into the mountains. It was the Mercedes Benz micro to Belo Horizonte de Escazú, which would pass within a block of their apartment, but it was jammed. When it stopped, passengers already standing in the door well jumped off, let several of those waiting squeeze on, then swung back in again themselves.

"Should we take it?" Monica asked. "Should we try to get on?" The micro was just starting to roll again. Most of the people waiting had stepped back, either hoping for a larger bus with more room or waiting for one that took a different route. Ted wanted a Belo Horizonte or a Santa Teresa. The other buses, including those that only went to the central plaza in Escazú, would leave them with a kilometer hike the rest of the way up to their apartment. They would be drenched.

Before he could make up his mind, the little bus was gone, disappearing up the hill in the slow stream of traffic. "We should have tried to squeeze on," he said to no one. Before holidays, the buses were always jammed like this, and there was no reason to suppose the others would be any better. It had taken them most of their first few weeks in Escazú to sort out the bus routes that were available to them there. The different buses felt to him like members of a big, temperamental family in which everyone fiercely guarded his individuality and kept his own secret but emphatic agenda. You never knew when one would refuse to let you jump on even a few feet past the stop, or when another would slow down in the middle of the block and wait to see if you wanted a ride.

After a while, when one of the smallest micros, little more than a van, passed them without stopping, they watched it in silence. They waited, holiday traffic streaming by monotonously in the rainy darkness. Valerie fell asleep on his shoulder. Stephen leaned against Monica on the narrow bench under the shelter, too tired even to complain. Red taxis periodically drove past, but they always were occupied, whether going up the hill or returning down toward San José. Rain drummed steady and businesslike on the shelter roof. Headlights of big trucks tricked them into false hope. Two buses, close together, came down the hill, heading toward San José. Then, suddenly, a bus was slowing in front of them, one of the big old Blue Birds, like the school buses Ted had ridden when he was growing up in Ohio, though instead of yellow this one was painted white, with blue and red-faded-to-orange trim, "El Calypso" in large ornate letters on its sides, a macaw clutching a banner in back. The little, hand-printed sign behind the windshield was turned to "Sta. Tere."

"Move! Move!" he shouted, getting a fresh grip on Valerie's limp body and urging Monica and Stephen toward the waiting bus. Uphill traffic streamed around it, heedless of oncoming cars. While Monica fumbled for the change she had long before sorted out and then absentmindedly dropped back into her purse, he lugged Valerie up the steps, collapsed the umbrella awkwardly, and pushed through the turnstile. Most of the seats were taken, but a man near the front of the bus at once stood up and gestured him into his seat. Ted shook his head, but the man insisted. He dropped to the seat beside two middle-aged women, who cooed and fussed over the sleeping child. He watched four or five new passengers push down the aisle before Stephen and Monica finally came through the turnstile. Stephen must have fallen asleep before the bus arrived, for he had the bewildered expression on his face that he often woke with. He looked blankly at Ted when he passed him, pressed by Monica and the other boarding passengers toward the back of the bus, farol seemingly forgotten in his hand, and Ted wondered whether he would survive the ride home without some sort of hysteria. When the boy was exhausted, when he had been woken prematurely, he could be like a delicate explosive, any odd jar might set him off.

The bus lurched into motion. Ted turned around as far as he could and saw that a couple five rows back from him had squeezed over so that Stephen could perch on the edge of their seat, leaning on his silvery farol stick for balance. Monica must have been somewhere farther back, he couldn't see her. The little overhead lights blinked on, then off again.

Swaying in the rain and darkness, the old bus lumbered up the hill. It stopped for a few minutes at the plaza of the old town, where some passengers got off and more crowded on, parents furling umbrellas, laughing kids carrying lanterns from the public school's Independence Eve ceremony.

He leaned back in the seat, adjusting Valerie's sleeping head on his shoulder while the new passengers pressed toward the back. Suddenly he smelled burning candle. A boy in a rain-wet slicker was edging past him, carrying a lighted paper lantern into the middle of the packed bus. Ted tried to remember the word for dangerous, but the bus lurched into motion, giving the mass of standing passengers an extra jolt toward the back.

He couldn't see the boy anymore, but the smell of the candle burning in its shell of paper and cellophane remained in his nostrils. As the crowd in the aisle edged slowly back, the live flame would swing past Stephen's face and he would go crazy, trapped in the darkness and pressed in on all sides by strange bodies. If Ted could get to him, he would grab him like someone drowning, he would smother the fear like fire. But he was out of reach. Shoving back to him, shouting to him over the roar of the bus as it labored uphill, might make things worse.

"¡Con permiso!" he said, and slid Valerie off his shoulder into the arms of the startled but pleased matron beside him. He twisted around in his seat, half-rising, trying to see what was going on. The boy with the lighted farol must have almost reached Stephen, but Ted couldn't see past the passengers who pressed against him, clinging to the rod overhead.

He stood awkwardly. The bus jolted in a pothole, the mass of bodies shifted for a moment, and he caught a glimpse of the boy with the lighted farol in the aisle beside Stephen. The tiny yellow lights along the roof of the bus flickered off, then on again. The word for dangerous came to him uselessly. And then the smell of candle smoke grew suddenly sharper—the odor of birthday wishes. Lights flickered, rain beat against the windows. He settled back into his seat and took the sleeping girl's damp weight onto his lap again, as if nothing had happened.

Nothing had. Nothing had happened yet.

CHAPTER TWO
CASA PICKETT

IF THEY DIDN'T LET HIM GO, what would he do? He felt as if he would just vanish, blasted into vapor by the unfairness of it. If they made him lose this chance. He packed grimly, jamming blue jeans and sweatshirt and underwear and comic books into a backpack already heavy with the books and supplies he had to haul back and forth between home and school each day. They had never heard of lockers down here. But why couldn't they just leave the stuff inside their desks? He yanked viciously at the zipper and didn't even bother trying to overhear the discussion of his fate going on in the next room. If they didn't say yes to this, he would turn to nothing right in front of their eyes. This was his chance. He had had friends in Cincinnati, but never a brother. This was his chance to have a brother. If they—

They said yes. His father came in to give him the word, and he almost vaporized anyway, the permission was couched in such insane reluctance. "I'm still uncomfortable with an overnight. People we don't know. You sure you couldn't come home after supper? Couldn't Ray come over here?"

He worked at the zipper. "I told you, their car is broke. *Like* ours. Ray's dad needs their truck or something, so they can't drive back. Isn't that what the note says?" Ted looked at the note Ray's mom had sent home with him, studying it as if it contained some secret message he couldn't decode. Stephen felt betrayal seep into the air like poison gas, his chest grew tight. He fought the zipper. Frustration boiled up behind his eyes. "So, I *can't* go?"

"You can go, I said you could go. I just wish we knew something more about them. We don't have a phone, they don't have a phone. We don't even know what his dad does for a living."

"What do *you* do? *I* don't know what *you* do."

"Yes you do, I'm an accountant. And an entrepreneur," he added after a moment.

"Yeah, right, what's that?" There was always an odd shift in his father's voice when he said the word.

"Okay, fair enough, but—"

"Shit!" He shoved the jammed backpack away.

"Hey." Monica was standing in the doorway of the children's bedroom. "We're not trying to back out of it, it's just scary for us, it's hard to get used to the idea of your being away all night."

He wiped his nose with the back of his hand. It wouldn't have been a problem back in Cincinnati, where he had been having sleepovers for years. The past summer especially he had often been at friends' houses overnight, his parents happy enough to indulge him during the furious weeks of their preparation to leave, the long talks with people who might rent their house, the trips to the storage locker, the endless packing. Down here they clung to him, everyone was a stranger. Yet Ray was already more than a friend.

"Ray's mom owns that bakery down by the ice cream place," he said, shuffling once more through the thin deck of what he knew, all he needed to know. "He goes to International Academy. He's a fifth grader. The bus picks him up and drops him off at the bakery."

That was how they had met, in the microbus van that took Stephen to Saint Mary's every morning and brought him home again in the afternoon. The morning ride especially was a long one, the microbus winding around in the foothills for forty-five minutes sometimes, picking up grownups as well as students going to several different schools. "Ray has his own horse," he said. "His family's him and his sister and his mom and dad. They live in Santa Ana, on a finca. That's like a ranch. They're Americans."

"North Americans," Ted automatically corrected, "estadounidenses," wading through the ridiculous word. It was something his mother and father said. "Costa Ricans are 'Americans,' too," one or the other of them would say.

Stephen said nothing for a moment. He knew who was an American and who was not. Americans spoke English, regular English, not like his English teacher here. "He's my best friend."

Ted sank down, folded him in his arms. "I know, Stevie, that's why we're letting you go. I'm glad you have a best friend."

He looked over his kneeling father's shoulder and saw Valerie in the living room, getting away with eating her cereal on the sofa. He waited for Ted to release him. It was hard to predict when these surges of emotion would seize his father, and he knew that it did no good to squirm in his grasp. It was love, he understood that, and even if it embarrassed him to be held that way, he had learned not to be afraid of it, he had learned to accept it like weather.

Valerie lost control of the cereal bowl, crashing milk and Zucaritas (the Frosted Flakes they had rarely been allowed to have back home) onto the wooden floor. Monica ran to mop it up before the milk leaked through the cracks into the apartment downstairs, and Ted stood up, his hand still trembling a little on Stephen's shoulder.

"I know you'll be okay."

"Sure."

"You'd better be."

"I know."

•

AT THE END OF THE CLASS DAY, when the microbus pulled into the paved playground of his school, Ray was sitting in the front seat as usual, next to the driver, and as usual he moved back to a seat where they could be together when Stephen got on. It felt great to settle onto the seat beside him, to look out and see the kids climbing the thick, low branches of the schoolyard's ancient mango tree and not to need them. He had tried to tell some of his classmates about his sleepover, but nobody had seemed to understand.

"How do you say 'sleepover' in Spanish?" he asked Ray.

Ray didn't know. He didn't think there was such a thing in Spanish, had never heard of a Costa Rican kid spending the night at a friend's house. "They won't even come out to the finca for the day," he said.

Stephen was glad they didn't. Ray had been born in Costa Rica, and his sister apparently teased him about the way he pronounced some English words, but he was American, all right. He had a silver tooth, which Stephen had never seen on a kid in Ohio, but he was still an American. They had established that the first time they talked together. After Stephen had been riding the bus for a week, Ray had turned and said something in Spanish to him, who always sat in the back. When he didn't answer, Ray had said, "You're American, right?" and broke into a wild, strange laugh. "Me too," he had exclaimed. Stephen had felt foolish that he hadn't known it. He *had* known it, he decided then. Ray had sandy hair, glossy and slicked back in the morning, falling into his dark eyes in the afternoon. But there was an even blonder Costa Rican kid in his class who spoke no more English than the rest of them—*hello, goodbye, how are you, my name is*—and he had learned not to trust that clue. Ray just looked American, he told Monica when he got home that day.

As the bus turned around to leave the school yard, Ray shouted back in Spanish to a boy who had called out something to him from the top of a slide. "I think I know that kid," he said.

"He's not in my class," Stephen said. "I don't know his name."

"He used to go to my school, I think. Diego!" Ray shouted out the window, and the boy waved. Stephen was glad when they left the school behind.

It was strange driving past his house. Valerie was on the balcony, watching for him as she always did in the afternoon, but he didn't wave. "Estefan," don Santos called back over his shoulder without slowing down. Was he sure that it was right? Yes, it was right, he answered, though it didn't exactly feel right. He wished his parents had been out on the balcony to see him go past. He wished he had waved to his sister.

They got off at the bakery, and Ray introduced him to Ivana, the woman working behind the counter, and to Katya, who was in a back room scouring cookie sheets. "¡Ay, qué guapo tu amigo!" Katya exclaimed. She bent over and accepted a kiss on the cheek from Ray, then motioned to Stephen. "Un besito, guapo," she coaxed, turning her cheek to him. He hung back for a moment. He had gotten used to kissing older women, but Katya was young and very pretty. Ray was watching, so finally he gave her the dutiful peck on the cheek. He felt himself blush hotly at the softness of her skin, but she didn't tease him, merely brushed her palm lightly over his hair.

He followed Ray to the front of the bakery, where they sat at one of the tiny tables and ate cookies and waited for Ray's mother. "She's always late," Ray said. They slipped out of the front door while Ivana was busy with some customers and walked down the hill a few blocks to the ice cream place. Ray had money. They bought cones and ate them sitting on the chopped motorcycle that would vibrate and rock back and forth a little and rumble and play "Rudolph, the Red-Nosed Reindeer" if you wanted to invest twenty colones—about a quarter—for the necessary tokens. Three boys about their age, whom Stephen had seen hanging around the ice cream place and who some- times asked his father or mother for money, approached them and looked as if they were thinking of challenging possession of the motorcycle, but instead they climbed onto the swan and the horse and played around on them for a while, then went up to the counter and undertook what seemed to be some sort of negotiations with the woman who ran the cash register. They weren't in school uniforms, never were. If he had been with his family, he would have been a little frightened by the boys in their dirty T-shirts and shorts, but with Ray he felt brave, he felt he had a right to be there.

By the time they got back to the bakery, the big red pickup truck that Ray had described was parked at the curb, and Grace Pickett was inside the building, talking on the phone. She smiled and waved when they came in, and didn't seem to have been worried about them, though they had told no one where they were going. She seemed about as old as Stephen's mother. Her long, smoothly waved blond hair was lighter than her tight, tanned face.

When she was done with her call, Grace introduced herself to Stephen in the heavy Texas drawl he had never encountered except on television before coming to Costa Rica. "I'm so glad to meet you, Stephen! Ray's told us all about you, we're pleased as can be you're honoring us with a visit. And how are your momma and daddy and baby sister? I'm dying to meet them! Soon as we get things straightened around, we'll have you all out to our place, how do you think they'd like that?"

"Fine, I guess."

"Ray, honey, have Ivana get you boys something to eat while I make a few more phone calls." She looked at them. "You been down at Mon Piks, having an ice cream, haven't you? Well, play out back or something, darlings, I'll be done here in a flash."

The boys hung around while Grace spoke with her employees in Spanish too rapid for Stephen to follow it, paged through a thick notebook full of columns of figures, made more phone calls. The last of the calls took a long time. He expected her to be upset afterwards, for she had raised her voice again and again, sometimes almost screaming into the phone, oblivious of the customers who came and went a few feet away. When she was finished, however, she winked at the boys and directed them out to the truck as if absolutely nothing were the matter.

"That was ICE, right, Momma?" Ray said, sliding over on the bench seat toward her to make room for Stephen. "Those sons of bitches."

"Ray!" There was pride and approval in her mild shock.

"We hate them too," Stephen said. His parents raged about it, "*ee say*," the government monopoly that controlled telephone and electrical service, doling out incomplete information and false hope to anyone trying to get a phone connection. "ICE," a curse word, like "Migración," "Aduana."

"They are an aggravation," she said. "Damn!" Leaning on the horn, she slung the truck around a jeep that had tried to beat her through an intersection, then swerved back hard enough to mash Ray and Stephen up against the passenger door. Ray laughed. Grace drove fast and with an air of complete authority, as if the traffic that had terrorized Stephen's parents during the few days they had had their car couldn't touch her. The high seat of the truck had something to do with it, he thought. You felt in charge up there.

When they reached the little village of Santa Ana, they stopped at a farm supply store so that Grace could pick up dog food. The boys studied the restless, overcrowded cages of chicks and pullets while she argued with the shopkeeper. The store smelled of bird droppings and ripe grain and was crowded with men and women who seemed to know Grace and Ray and teased them about the species of animal they were feeding with the huge bags of kibble the shopkeeper's son hauled out to the pickup.

As soon as they left the cluster of shabby little houses and stores, the road started to wind its way up into the mountains. It was so narrow, he felt a surge of terror when a car appeared from behind a curve, barreling downhill directly toward them, but Grace swung onto the far edge, the truck's outside wheel spraying dust and gravel into space, and the long black car slipped past as if it were sliding through water. Ray looked up at his mother, but she kept her eyes on the road.

No other traffic approached them. They could see the Picketts' house a long way before they got there, a blocky white building set into the side of the mountain. The steep road winding up to it was deeply pot-holed. In places it seemed to have been bombed. Boulders jutting from the side pushed the jolting truck toward the precipice, where he could look down and see the last three switchbacks of the road they had already negotiated and the dark car they had just met, tiny now, gliding out of sight.

It made him feel sick. He didn't do that well in cars under the best of circumstances. At the steepest part of the road, where the truck had to grind upwards in its lowest gear and it felt as if he were being jammed back against the seat by tremendous acceleration, there was a double track of ridged concrete, red sand and clay breaking away from its edges.

"*We* built this part of the road," Ray said. "Right that I helped smack down those tread things?"

"You sure did," Grace said.

They stopped in front of a heavy-looking wire and metal gate that blocked the road like a border crossing. Ray clambered over him, leaped down onto the road, heaved up on the end of the gate, and walked it out of the way, moving in short, shuffling steps, the gate was so awkward. Grace drove the truck through, stopped, and waited for Ray to close the gate again and catch up with them. Stephen had the door open for him, but he jumped onto the back bumper and clung to the tailgate while Grace jolted the last several hundred yards up to the house. "We're here, honey, Casa Pickett."

Turning away from watching Ray in back, Stephen screamed as a monstrous face suddenly reared up beside his open side window, slobbering and roaring at him. Grace leaned over and swatted at the huge wet mouth. "Track! Down!" she yelled, and the big dog dropped to all fours again and whirled and snapped at two other dogs that had just reached the truck. "He won't hurt you, sweetie, long as you're with us. He's just saying hello."

Stephen kept the door shut and watched the three Great Danes now surrounding Ray, the terrible scythes of their tails lashing with excitement. They were much bigger than Boby, and even Boby was always locked up. "That's Tracker," he managed to say, "the biggest one. Which one is Princess? The one with the bandaged ears?"

"You're absolutely right. The big bruiser is Tracker, the puppy's Princess, and that fat thing is Queenie."

"Queenie, I forgot her." Named, the dogs were less terrifying, though he still couldn't get himself to open the door. Ray had told him about the dogs, and he had convinced himself he wanted to see them, but the weight of terror their barking flung at him was something even his past frightening experiences with animals hadn't prepared him for. He felt flattened by it, as unable to move as a drawing on paper, you would have to wait for the next panel. "Tracker killed a communist," he said. "How does he know I'm not a communist?"

Grace put her arm around him. "He can tell just by looking at you, honey. Anyway, that was a long time ago, that old dog's forgot everything he ever knew about politics. Ray!" she shouted out the window, "Have Jorge pen up the dogs."

Ray ran up the hill toward the enormous concrete house, castle-like, with a tower and balconies and tall narrow windows. The dogs tore after him, flashing white shapes gaudy with splashes of black. Stephen watched them disappear around the side of the house. When Grace got out, he unlocked his door and climbed down from the truck.

The finca was not at all what he had imagined. Everything was vertical here, with mountains covered by forest or jungle— he didn't know what to call it—rising behind the house, and pasture sweeping in terraces into the valley below them. He looked down on the red corrugated tin roofs of some of the houses they had passed on the way up, shacks, mostly, though a few were built of the white-painted adobe that his father liked so much, the blue paint at the bottom usually flaked and eroding into mud, which was all it really was.

Then, on a terrace below him, he saw the horses, two of them, and a pony that must be Ray's Davy Crockett grazing in the shade of a low, enormously spreading tree. A thin old man came down from the house to get the bags of dog food from the back of the truck. He said something in Spanish about Ray, and Grace said to Stephen, "Come on, he's changing his clothes. I'll show you where his room is." That's what the man had said, for him to join Ray in his room.

A long stairs led up to the house. Inside, past the massive, dark-stained wooden doors, there was an actual waterfall trickling down two stories of boulders and ferns, *inside* the house, with a wooden staircase curling around it from a floor of gray stone to a sort of balcony overlooking the entryway, then corridors forking in two directions. He got to the top of the winding stairs and stopped, afraid to go any farther. Grace had sent him up with only the vaguest directions. "Ray?" He felt alone suddenly, homesick. Maybe his parents had been right.

But then he heard Ray's laugh. He looked up and saw Ray's red face, upside down, thrust out of an opening in the ceiling that Stephen hadn't noticed before, though now he saw metal rungs leading up to it. "I didn't tell you about this," Ray said after Stephen had climbed the ladder and pulled himself through the opening. "I wanted it to be a surprise."

It was the most amazing room he had ever seen—maybe ten feet by ten feet, with narrow barred windows piercing the thick walls on three sides. There was a bunk bed and dresser along the remaining wall, and the floor was completely covered with clothes and toys and sports equipment and comic books and food wrappers and a pile of blankets that had evidently been stripped off the lower bunk, which was bare.

"How do your parents let you have it this way?" he asked, once the extent of the squalor had sunk in. Since he had to share a room with Valerie in the Escazú apartment he had begun to keep his half of their room fanatically neat, controlling his own space and emphasizing Valerie's carelessness. There was something frightening about the intensity of this chaos.

"My mom can't get the maids to come up here, and she doesn't like to climb the ladder, either. Once in a while they make me clean it up. I was supposed to before you came over, but nobody checked. Got your stuff?"

Stephen realized that he had left his backpack at the bottom of the ladder. He climbed down, struggled into its straps, then climbed back up and changed out of his school clothes, folding his white uniform shirt and navy pants and stuffing them into the pack while Ray examined the comic books he had brought. Looking for a place to put his things, Stephen saw something half-buried under a pile of clothes that sent a jolt of heat into his chest—the black barrel and front sight and stock of some kind of gun. He gingerly peeled back a Superman pajama top and a tangle of blue jeans and a pair of underpants that sent a whiff of pee into the air as he lowered them onto the far side of the clothes pile. It was a gun, all right, full-size and entirely black—shoulder stock and pistol grip and trigger and trigger guard and protruding magazine and the parts he had first seen.

Ray reached over and grabbed the gun by a handle on top, flipped it around into firing position, and aimed it at Stephen's chest. Stephen made a choked noise and Ray lowered the weapon with a breathy laugh. "M-16," he said, and handed it to Stephen. Feeling now as if electricity were leaping through his body, Stephen accepted the gun. It was plastic, he could tell that right away, but solid and convincing. His finger found its way to the trigger—metal, colder than the rest of the gun. He heard a click and looked up. Ray had the drop on him with a pistol he must have pulled out of another pile. Ray fired three times, sharp cracks that added a delicious, biting smell to the sweaty must of the room. Then the gun just clicked a few times, and Ray tossed it aside. Stephen hadn't moved.

"That's the trouble with caps," Ray said, "they jam up. That baby you got is supposed to shoot caps, but it never did work. Looks cool, though, right?"

"What are caps?" Stephen asked, and Ray retrieved the pistol, broke it open, and showed him the little roll of red paper, perforated and dotted with gunpowder blisters, crinkled up in the mechanism. Stephen carefully laid the M-16 down on a cushion of dirty clothes. His parents refused to have what they called war toys in the house. He had played with some at friends' houses in Cincinnati, but none as realistic as Ray's.

"You like these babies?" Ray asked.

"Sure."

"You like *these* babies?" Before Stephen could figure out how to answer, Ray signaled for silence, then led him down the ladder and into a room at the end of the long balcony hallway, darkened by heavy curtains and full of massive wooden furniture, including a bed bigger than any Stephen had ever seen. Ray went to a tall cupboard and tried the door. "Shit," he whispered. "Sometimes he leaves it open. He's got a M-16, and an AK-47, and a 12-gauge, and a deer rifle, and pistols. I know where he keeps the key."

"No," Stephen said. "Let's get out of here."

"You sure?"

"Please. Please."

"One thing I *got* to show you." He went around to the far side of the huge bed and disappeared. Stephen followed and found him crouched in front of a shallow fabric box, like you would use to store shoes or extra blankets under a bed. He pulled back the cover, and that's what was in it, blankets, but then he reached under them and drew out an ugly metal thing that didn't exactly look like a real gun at all.

"Uzi," Ray whispered.

It had a trigger and pistol grip, okay, but the barrel looked like a piece of pipe, and where there should have been a shoulder stock was just some stamped metal.

"You want to hold it?"

"Put it back."

Ray hefted it affectionately, demonstrating with hacking machine gun noises how to fire it from the waist, spraying the bedroom with death. "This is the safety," he said, and clicked it off.

"Is it loaded?"

"Of course it's loaded. It's in case somebody busts in." He swung its short, brutal barrel around the room again. Finally he clicked the safety on, tucked the gun back into the blankets, and slid the box underneath the bed.

They returned to Ray's room and read each other's comic books for a while. Stephen couldn't concentrate, the guns filling his mind, and he wasn't sorry when Grace shouted up for them to go outside. Even aside from the guns, he felt uneasy in the big strange house, where nothing was regular. The Hoffmans' Escazú apartment, cramped and bare as it was, lacking the taken-for-granted amenities of rugs and lamps and television, was more like his real home in Cincinnati than the Picketts' was. The Picketts' was better, way better, he could hardly believe the luck of anyone with a waterfall inside and an almost unapproachable tower bedroom and a television big as a refrigerator (he hadn't seen this yet, but Ray had described it), but it would take getting used to. And guns. He wasn't sure if he would ever be able to get used to the guns.

At least there was only one family living here, not three apartments carved out of a house much smaller than this one. Not that you could call the party guys a family. Only Boby was there all the time, the men arriving on weekends with women dressed like movie stars. In the apartment, he sometimes couldn't sleep, bothered less by the music than by the cigarette smoke drifting up between the floor boards. He liked Pepe and Eva, the young couple who lived in the small apartment next to the party guys' big one, but he and Valerie had to be quiet early in the morning not to disturb them. Ray could make as much noise as he wanted in his bedroom. He could shoot off guns if he wanted.

When they went outside, Stephen had to worry about the dogs again, but Ray showed him the wire mesh kennel where they were locked up, barking their throats out. The boys slid down the hill to the fenced paddock where the horses were. Ray caught the long-maned, long-tailed pony, Davy Crockett, and rode it bareback until he had herded the big white mare into a corner where he could get a rope around her neck. "This is Mary. You want to ride her?"

Stephen shook his head. This was the part of the overnight he had been worried about. "I'm kind of allergic to horses," he said.

"Davy Crockett's not a horse," Ray said, "just a pony. Come on, he's real old and quiet, I'll ride Mary."

A third horse, the color of gold, eyed them from the far side of the paddock, pawing the ground, raising sharp puffs of dust. "How about that other one?" Stephen felt an insane recklessness sweep over him. Anything was worth delay.

"Only my sister can ride him, he bucks. You want to try?" There seemed to be real possibility in Ray's voice, though he couldn't have been serious. After a moment he said, "Here, let me help you up on Davy Crockett."

Lacking an alternative, Stephen squirmed himself up onto the pony's barrel back, grabbing fistfuls of harsh, blond mane, and waited while Ray maneuvered the mare close enough to the fence for him to use the gate as a ladder to get onto her. "Don't you have, like, saddles?" he asked while Ray settled himself.

"The tack's all in the barn, locked up. We'd have to get one of the muchachos to help us. It's easier to just go bareback."

Stephen had no idea how to make the pony go, much less go where he wanted, but once Ray popped his heels into the white mare's sides and headed through the gate, the pony lurched into motion and followed. His legs soon ached with the effort of clamping around the thick body. Finally he had to let them just dangle, depending on his handhold and concentration to keep him aboard. Ray kept the mare at a steady walk, and Davy Crockett followed with only an occasional disconcerting trot to catch up. It wasn't so hard, though by the time they circled the pasture, went a ways up a rutted dirt road, and returned to the paddock, Stephen had a headache from the tension of his clenched jaws.

"Tomorrow," Ray said, when they had released the horse and pony, "we'll ride up to my fort."

"Why not now?" Stephen asked, knowing why not, clouds piling up darkly in the northeast. It would be raining soon, he could afford a cheap bravado now, courage that wasn't quite bluff. He had ridden a horse, a pony, anyway; that was enough for one day. He was where he had never been before, in a fantastic place, far from his family, with his best friend. He had seen a real gun.

Ray's sister, Charlotte, was in the kitchen when the boys burst into the house. She was grown up and, according to Ray, treated him badly. Now, though, she was being nice. She gave them bags of chips and poured Cokes from a two liter bottle, then leaned against the counter and asked them how their day had been, what they had been doing, and how Stephen's family was. He wondered where Grace was. Charlotte was playing mother, he knew, that's why she was being nice, and because he was a guest there. Her hair was darker than Ray's, a brown that looked red sometimes. Otherwise, she looked a lot like him. They had the same short nose, for one thing, pointed up a little so you could see the nostrils. Dark brown eyes. Charlotte was a twelfth-grader at Lincoln School, in Heredia. She was going to get her own car, she said, but for now had to get a ride to school with one of her classmates.

"A boy," Ray said. "Ro*dolf*o."

"Yes, Rodolfo," she said, raising her eyes in pretend glamorousness. "Poor thing, he adores me. They all do."

"They're all morons," Ray said. Whatever he said, he clearly liked her, liked having a sister old enough to stand in for his mother. Stephen thought how useless Valerie was to him.

Ray carefully split the two sides of his Picaritas bag and licked the spice and salt from the greasy foil inside. "Where's María?"

"Wouldn't we all like to know. Momma's out shopping right now, she's furious, María was supposed to make dinner. I think her husband's back and giving her a hard time again about working here. This is it—Momma won't take her back this time. It's as bad as with Evita." She looked at Stephen, who looked away. "Maids," Charlotte explained. "Momma can't get one who'll really work *and* stay more than a few months." She turned her back to them and gazed out the window, which overlooked the pasture. Suddenly she leaned forward. "You guys weren't messing with Goldie, were you?" Her voice had turned harsh and witchy.

"We only rode him a little," Ray said. "He's getting fat." She shrieked, as if in rage, and Ray ran out of the room.

Stephen didn't know what to do. "We didn't really ride him."

"*I* know that. Goldie'd pitch you here to Sunday."

"Okay," he said. "I guess I better go find Ray." Ray was in the family room on the second floor, watching television. It wasn't as tall as a refrigerator, but it was bigger than any television Stephen had ever seen, more like a movie screen. The show wasn't much good, *Adam 12* in Spanish. It didn't matter. That evening, Ray had promised, they would watch a video. *Star Wars*, he said.

Stephen was thinking about guns when a short, stout woman came up to call them to supper. She ordered them to wash their hands, then stalked out of the room. "That's Zamira," Ray told him as they splashed around in the big, pink bathroom sink, fluted like a sea shell. Stephen used the egg-shaped, fragrant soap and was glad to get the horse smell off his hands. "She's not our regular maid," Ray said. "Momma must have got her to help with supper. A guy's here, a friend of Daddy's."

When they came down the stairs, Stephen could hear loud male voices, one of them southern, like Ray's mother, the other regular. Two men were standing with drinks in their hands in front of a huge, elaborately carved cabinet. One of them was tall and fat, with a full white beard that seemed to cover his face like a mask, almost no skin showing on his cheeks at all. He turned when Ray shouted, "Daddy!" and scooped Ray up with one arm, the other hand still holding the glass without spilling. The bearded man kissed Ray, then dropped him from a considerable height and directed his hard blue gaze at Stephen.

"Where are your manners, boy?"

He felt suddenly sick, paralyzed. Ray stepped forward and introduced him, and he realized that the man had been addressing Ray.

"Pleased to meet you, son," Ray's father said. He transferred his drink to his left hand and Stephen knew to step forward and shake his hand.

"Yes sir," he said, in answer to nothing. The hand was broad, paw-like, and seemed to swallow up his own hand.

"You call me Hank, hear?"

He nodded, held his breath until his hand was finally released, and drifted behind Ray, who was watching his father.

"You mostly stay out of trouble today?" Hank asked.

"Sure," Ray said.

Hank seemed to think about it for a moment, then grunted as if there were no point in pursuing the conversation any farther. The other man rattled the ice in his glass a little, and Hank refilled it from a square bottle. No one introduced the other man, but Stephen knew who he was, Mr. Richardson, the man who had owned the flower farm his father had come to Costa Rica to run. Richardson was as tall as Hank Pickett, but thin except for a paunch that pushed his white knit shirt out in front.

Stephen had met him twice. The first time was at the San José airport, where he had appeared after Stephen's dazed, exhausted family had finally gotten through customs and followed their mountain of luggage up to ground level and out through a crowd of expectant strangers in the unnaturally early Costa Rican night. He had been energetically friendly then, leading them to his car, organizing their luggage into an orange van, driving them to their hotel, and supervising the men who appeared from nowhere and lugged all of their belongings up to the cramped studio apartment where there was barely room for two beds and a small square table. Afterwards, he had taken them out to dinner at a brand new McDonald's, where they didn't have McNuggets, only chicken with bones in it, and the only milk available was hot. Not just not cold: hot.

The second time was at the Hoffmans' Escazú apartment, a few weeks later. He was dropping off some papers related to the transfer of the flower farm to Stephen's father, and he was sarcastic and insulting about everything Costa Rican. Stephen had never heard a grownup talk like that. Afterwards, his father had made a point to tell him that it wasn't true, what Richardson had said. He was just unhappy and disappointed. Ted had gone on and on about what a peaceful and good country Costa Rica was and how lucky they all were to be there, living peacefully in this safe place. Since then, though, he seemed to be changing his mind about how safe it was.

Richardson didn't seem to recognize him, scarcely acknowledging the boys' presence in the room. It didn't matter to Stephen. Aside from Richardson's bitterness that last time, he was not very interesting, and Stephen didn't think much more about him. Hank was the important one. But now he was ignoring them, too. Ray led Stephen into the kitchen, where Grace was supervising Zamira's grumpy, pot-slamming work. He couldn't tell whether or not they were arguing. The Spanish flying between them in tough little clumps carried obvious anger, but also companionability.

"Soon," Grace said absently when Ray asked how long it was going to be till dinner. "Go wash your hands."

"We already did wash them."

"Don't get dirty, then. I'll call you."

"Zamira already did call us."

"I said, I'll call you."

There was a concrete archway leading out of the back of the kitchen, then a brief tunnel of stone and vines curving around to the side of the house and leading to a patio surrounded by a low wall. The boys gathered small, hard fruit that had fallen from an overhanging tree and tried to see how far they could throw them from the patio down the terraced hillside.

"What's your mom mad about?" Stephen asked.

"She's just tense."

"She sounded mad. What were they talking about?"

"Daddy's friend." Ray checked his throw, looked at him, then heaved the fruit in a high arc toward a dry, bean-shaped pool on the terrace below them. It fell a few yards short, but bounced in. He made an explosion noise and watched while Stephen tried to match his throw. "You don't know too much Spanish, do you."

"I'm starting to get it more." Stephen's throw hit the rim of the pool and bounced over it.

Ray studied the result. "Pretty close. If these were ripe mangos or oranges or something, that would've been a kill."

"I don't think we could get an orange that far."

"How do you know what's going on in school?" Ray asked.

He shrugged. "Mostly I just do what the other kids are doing. We copy down stuff from the board. Tarea's easy. Also my main teacher sort of knows English. In English class, I tell *them* the answers."

Ray pried up a piece of loose concrete from the edge of the terrace. "Check out this baby," he said. He hefted it a few times, then heaved it like a grenade, stiff-armed. It landed in a flower bed about half way to the dry pool. He made the explosion sound, but in a half-hearted way. "Cement's heavier than an orange. I *know* I can reach it with a mandarina."

When they heard Charlotte call them, they went in to the dining room and sat down together at a long table. Hank and Richardson were already seated. Charlotte sat opposite of Ray and narrowed her eyes at him. Finally Grace came in and placed a big platter of brown, gravy-covered meat in front of Hank, then took her seat next to Charlotte. The table was already loaded with bowls of vegetables and mashed potatoes and fruit and flowers and more silverware than seemed necessary. Even in Cincinnati, Stephen's family ate with such elaborateness only a few times a year, and here in Costa Rica they used cheap plates from Mundo Plástico, and knives and forks and spoons even Valerie could bend.

Everybody grew silent, and Hank said a long, complicated table prayer that included Stephen and Mr. Richardson and Mr. Richardson's family and Stephen's family. Stephen felt his ears burn when he heard his name pronounced in that formal language, which scarcely seemed like English. Through the open kitchen door he could see Zamira's broad back bent over the sink. He thought it must be weird to have servants, weird to be religious. Weird but good.

The dinner was more relaxed than he had feared it would be. There was teasing between Ray and Charlotte, only mildly refereed by their mother, and Charlotte did Stephen the favor of including him in her criticism of little boys. He wished his parents and Valerie had been there to see him, his acceptance into this substantial household, this house big and solid as a fort.

Neither Hank nor Richardson talked much for a while, their eating serious and businesslike. When they did talk, the conversation was political. They referred to Ronald Reagan with a warmth and respect that made Stephen feel ashamed of his parents' frequent mockery of the first president he had known. Hank and Richardson seemed to regard Reagan as president, still. They spoke of "President Reagan," and called the real president "Bush" or "George Bush" or even "George," though he could tell that they liked him more than his own parents did. Hank and Richardson and Grace, too, when she was drawn into the adult conversation, spoke disparagingly of Óscar Arias, the Costa Rican president, who was a hero to Stephen's father and mother. He hoped his parents would never expose their opinions to Ray's family. His father and mother's politics was like their lack of religion, suddenly shabby and embarrassing.

After supper, Hank and Richardson left for the American Legion, and Charlotte took the boys up to the family room to watch *Star Wars*. An uproar of barking from outside interrupted the first scene, which was of endless blowing sand. Charlotte noticed his unease. "It's all right," she said, "Jorge's just let the dogs out. You should stay inside, though. They might not recognize you yet." He nodded, though it was grotesquely unnecessary advice. Dark had fallen during supper, it sounded as if it were still raining, and there were enormous dogs running loose. He would have gone out with Ray if Ray had said to. He would go anywhere with Ray. But nothing could have tempted him to go outside on his own.

During the movie, they had popcorn and Coke and then ice cream—great bowls of it they were allowed to dish up for themselves. Grace told them they had to be sure to take their dishes down to the sink before they went to bed, for Zamira had gone home. Stephen told them about the ants that had invaded the countertop of their apartment's kitchen when they had left some unwashed dishes out overnight. Ray was unimpressed. Everybody had ants, he said. Were they little or big? They were little, Stephen admitted, but there were millions of them, marching in endless lines like wavering pencil marks. "We have zumpopes," Ray said, "big leafcutters that can cut through aluminum foil. Do you have cucarachas?" Stephen didn't think so. His mother was always spraying inside the cabinets and along the baseboards, worrying about them. The apartment sometimes reeked for days with it. "We have cucarachas like *that*," Ray said, holding out his hands as if measuring a puppy. "Do you have scorpions?"

"Shut up, Ray," Charlotte said. "You're going to make him afraid to sleep here. You're so gross."

"I'm not afraid," Stephen said. He wasn't exactly sure what scorpions were, but even if they were some kind of snake, he wasn't afraid of them here. Not in this fortress, not with Ray beside him.

By the end of the movie, Stephen was exhausted, almost asleep, but when Grace had kissed them goodnight and sent them up the ladder to Ray's bedroom and ordered them to turn out the light, he came wide awake again. He had slept in bunk beds before, and Ray himself fell silent after only a few minutes of defiant whispering and flashlight signaling out the window from the top bunk, but it was impossible for Stephen to go to sleep. He was too excited to be there, too homesick, too full of new knowledge, too wired with ice cream and Coke, too nervous about getting down the ladder in the middle of the night if he had to go to the bathroom. There was a light on in the hall below, he could see the pale square it projected up onto the ceiling, but later on somebody might turn it off. He lay and stared up at the springs underneath Ray's mattress and reached his hand out and ran his fingers along the rough pistol grip of Ray's M-16 on the floor beside him. He felt as if he would never go to sleep.

He woke in the darkness, but he knew where he was right away. The square of light remained steady on the ceiling. There were voices from somewhere below, Hank's loud and unclear, Grace's soft. "Ray? Ray?" he whispered.

There was no answer, Ray must still be asleep. But then the bed creaked and a figure slipped over the edge and swung into the lower bunk beside him. He slid over against the wall. He couldn't see Ray's face, could only feel the warmth of his body next to him and smell his breath, sharp from a bag of Picaritas he had eaten after brushing his teeth. "What's going on?"

"It's Daddy. He's drunk. Did you hear him fall?"

"I don't know. Is he okay?" Stephen had never been this close to somebody who was drunk. His father never drank alcohol and sometimes acted displeased with Monica when she ordered a second glass of wine at a restaurant or opened a bottle at home. He had explained it to Stephen one time: his own father, the grandfather Stephen had never met, had been an alcoholic. He told Stephen not to worry about it, it wasn't his problem. And, no, Monica wasn't an alcoholic, he hadn't meant that, he was just angry and upset about something else entirely. It didn't matter what, it had nothing to do with him.

And now it was here, drunkenness was banging around in this house with him in it, him and Ray. Ray stayed in the lower bunk with him, narrating what was happening in the house below them. Grace waited until Jorge could come and help her get Hank up the stairs and into bed. Hank talked loud for a while, sometimes practically shouting, then he grew quiet. He must have passed out in that huge bed, that brutal Uzi nestled in the darkness underneath him.

That was it. Nothing else happened. Ray was still awake, murmuring beside him in the darkness, when Stephen found he couldn't keep his eyes open anymore. He closed his eyes and listened to Ray's voice and the silence filling the vast house below them. He would protect him, he was his brother. He would give his life for him. He was his brother.

CHAPTER THREE
BATMAN Y RATÓN MICKEY

MONICA WASN'T AN ALCOHOLIC, but once in a while she did need a drink. Like now, waiting for a taxi outside Super Anonos grocery store, with Stephen pushing Valerie in a shopping cart, pretending to be about to run her into traffic. Ted was out at the farm, helping Alejandro process paperwork on a shipment of chrysanthemums that had been rejected by Miami customs because of an insect. Not just rejected. Incinerated, all six cartons. Which left her to take both kids to a birthday party at the home of one of Stephen's classmates. It shouldn't have been a big deal, but she had never in her life looked forward to a party with strangers and wasn't at all sure why she was expected to stay at a fourth grader's party or that bringing Valerie would be appropriate.

Neither *Living in Costa Rica* nor *Key to Costa Rica* offered any help. When she had walked down to the hulera, the little rubber factory that was their closest public phone, to call and ask about Valerie, the boy's mother had insisted that the party was for all, of course the little sister should come, she remembered her from the eve of Independence Day celebration, what a precious girl. Did she like Mickey Mouse? Monica should tell her that Mickey Mouse would be there.

If a bunch of teenage girls hadn't been waiting to use the pay phone outside the hulera, she might have explored the question in greater depth. After she hung up, she considered asking one of the girls what the custom was, but she guessed from their cheap, flashy clothes and their slangy chatter that they wouldn't be much help. They might never have attended a party with Ratón Mickey. Stephen had told her it was going to be a Batman party, so she didn't understand that, either.

On her way back from the hulera, before going upstairs to the apartment, she had knocked on Eva and Pepe's door, hoping to get some advice from Eva, or maybe an offer to babysit Valerie. Eva wasn't home, but Pepe dragged her in, insisted on pouring her a Coke. He made her take a chair in the little living room, crowded with his amplifiers and audio recording equipment, and bustled around in the tiny kitchen, gleaming with brand new Hitachi appliances. A short, delicately-built young man, he was dressed in his usual black T-shirt and black jeans and was obviously grateful to be distracted from the hard, lonely work of becoming a pop star. He wheedled the party etiquette question out of her, thought about it for a while, then tried to remember if he knew anybody from the birthday boy's family. He thought he might have gone to high school with a girl related to the boy, a cousin. He might have dated her.

It was always hard getting out of a conversation with Pepe. He stayed home and tried to write music while Eva worked in his family's dress shop. The young couple had moved into the house just before the Hoffmans. A few weeks later, Monica had heard Eva calling for help, and had gone down and discovered that Pepe had left Eva locked into the apartment after an argument, the iron rejas making it impossible even to crawl out of a window. When Monica and Ted had talked to their landlord about it, he told them that a few years earlier a truck had knocked Pepe off his motorcycle. Some connections were missing, he had said, touching his head.

Pepe was learning English, but he was barely understandable, and with Monica, anyway, he always reverted to Spanish after a few sentences. "Monica," he said, when she was leaving, her etiquette question unanswered, "dime una cosa." It was his habitual opening—"tell me something," usually about some rock group she had never heard of, or her opinion of some garbled English lyrics he had written. He mostly asked Ted linguistic questions. "Ted, dime una cosa. ¿Qué quiere decir 'bitch'?"

"I've got to get back to the kids, Pepe," she said. If she stuck to English, she could usually tire him out.

"Okay, only say me when Ted go with me on the town." It was an idea that had come to him recently, and he now mentioned it whenever he saw one of them. "Just for the boys, you understand?" He winked awkwardly, the scar on his high forehead going white for a second with the effort. He was really very young. An adolescent, though he must have been 22 or 23.

"I'll ask him," she said. Don't hold your breath, she thought to herself, as the steel door of the empty attached garage creaked open.

That evening, Ted had been obsessed with the lost flowers, and she couldn't even ask his advice about the party, much less mention Pepe's question about boys' night out. They had burned the whole shipment, Ted kept saying, for one goddamn bug. There maybe were more, he admitted, but one would have been enough. They were going to bill him for the disposal costs, it was like making relatives pay for the bullet after they executed someone. And from now on, Alejandro had said, they would be checking his shipments with special vigilance. Just when things were starting to get straightened out. He sat up late that night, composing a letter of protest that would probably just make the situation worse, and left early Saturday morning to catch a bus into San José, walk halfway across town, then catch another one out to the farm in Heredia. It broke her heart, the prospect that another of his enterprises might be on the verge of failure. What would he do? What would they do?

After lunch on Saturday, Monica and the kids took a bus down to the big new supermarket in the commercial development close to the autopista, where they could catch a taxi to Rohrmoser, the classy neighborhood where Stephen's classmate lived. She wondered if there would be a chance of getting a drink at the party.

"See that store back there, the bakery?" Stephen was saying to Valerie, who had climbed out of the grocery cart. "Me and Ray can go in there and eat all the cookies we want."

"I know that."

"Any kind we want. Chocolate chip."

"Stephen," Monica said.

"Well, why does she have to come along? She doesn't even know this kid."

"Bernardo," Valerie said. "Bernardo, Bernardo, Bernardo—"

"Both of you, put the cart back and help me watch for a taxi." She had planned to catch one on its way back to San José, but none had appeared for a long time. She was beginning to worry about being late—even by local standards—when one of the red Toyota cabs spotted them from the far lane, honked, and whipped around in a dangerous U-turn. Of course, the driver said, he knew Rohrmoser very well. A half hour later, after a lot of backtracking and shouting questions out his window to pedestrians and ignoring Monica's suggestions, he found the address the invitation had given, a hundred and fifty meters north and four hundred meters east of the Instituto de Abasteceros, which turned out to be a nondescript, one-story building identifiable only by a small brass plaque on its door.

The street was lined with expensive cars. Monica whistled as they approached Bernardo's house, which was considerably grander than the Instituto de Abasteceros.

"Compared to Ray's house, this is nothing. Ray's got a indoor waterfall," Stephen said, but he stayed close to her as they waited for the wrought iron gates to click open in response to her push on the bell. Beyond the gate there was a narrow garden, dense with flowering shrubs, a flagstone walk, then the modern two-story house of tan stucco, imposing as an embassy, with a tall, arched double door of richly grained wood. A maid in black uniform let them into an atrium that was almost as lush with plants as the garden outside.

No one else seemed to be around. Music was blaring from somewhere, but music was always blaring from somewhere. Monica explained who they were, wondered if they had made a mistake in time or date. No, certainly not, the maid said. Might she lead them to the other guests? The maid's uniform had a deep, expensive sheen in the half darkness of the corridors she led them through, and Monica began to regret the casualness of her cotton dress, the perfunctoriness of her makeup. In the middle of the day, at least, and on a weekend, she felt stubbornly exempt from the expectations of fashion that seemed to have such a hold on Costa Rican women. A few days before, she had seen a woman her own age, mid-thirties, race downhill full tilt in four-inch heels to catch a bus. A hill steep enough that you breathed hard climbing it.

It was different in Nicaragua, Eva had said to her once. If she ever had the bad luck to go there, she would see that the Nicas dressed like rough soldiers. There was no refinement. It hadn't sounded so bad to Monica, who had brought down only one good silk dress, which she had bought at a consignment shop in Cincinnati. Some cotton prints, some slacks and blouses. With plans to work on her dissertation, she had felt she was somehow a graduate student again, she was entitled to be grungy if she wanted.

The maid was petite, and Monica felt tall and ungainly as she followed her, lugging Valerie through an inexplicable series of living rooms and patios furnished in chrome and polished wood and leather. Stephen's shoulder brushed her arm with every step. He carried the present that he had picked out after an agonizingly indecisive shopping trip through a huge toy store in San José. He had explained to her that he didn't know the boy very well, had hardly ever played with him on the playground, and wished Ray had been there to give him advice.

It occurred to her, when they finally reached the courtyard crowded with children, balloons with the yellow and black Batman logo everywhere, that she should have gotten something for Valerie to give Bernardo. He wouldn't know the difference, but the little girl might throw a fit when she realized she had arrived empty-handed. "Stephen," she whispered, "would you mind it if Valerie carried your present over to the gift table?" He looked at her in disbelief, and she shrugged. "Just a thought."

The present wasn't an issue, as it turned out. "Mickey Mouse!" Valerie shrieked.

"Where?" He sounded suspicious. He had been studying the milling children, looking for classmates he regarded even remotely as friends.

Monica saw Ratón Mickey then and showed him where to look. Big as at Disneyland itself, the cartoon figure bobbed and swayed among a bunch of younger children at the far end of the courtyard, half-hidden behind the spray of a fountain. Valerie pulled her toward them, then broke loose. "Val!" Monica shouted. "Valerie," but she was already swallowed up in the crowd of children. Stephen hung back. Something was wrong, none of his classmates were there, it was all little kids. A string of firecrackers sizzled from a different direction, and he spotted some boys he knew and ran in that direction, the real party. And indeed, life-size cardboard cutouts of Batman and Joker were standing there, characters from the movie that had opened that summer, Michael Keaton an unlikely Batman, Jack Nicholson as the Joker.

Monica had started to follow after Valerie when she felt a hand cup her bare elbow. She turned and found herself next to a smiling, strikingly handsome man. She was not to worry, he said, the little girl was among friends. Monica said that she didn't like it when the child ran off that way. He still held her arm. It didn't feel as awkward as she would have supposed. He introduced himself, he was called Enrique. He led her away from the children, leading as if in a dance, toward another doorway off the courtyard. He was a little shorter than she, and was wearing a linen guayabera shirt as soft and fine as silk. Unlike most Costa Rican men, he was clean shaven, and the absence of a mustache confused her judgment of his age. He could have been twenty, or forty, his skin a smooth tan above the pale blue collar of his shirt.

He brought her into a room full of adults sitting at round glass tables. After the midday glare of the courtyard, it was a little dark in here, but the room was high-ceilinged, beamed with the same lush wood as the door. Maids in uniform circulated among the tables with silver trays of hors d'oeuvres and glasses of wine. Everyone was dressed casually but expensively, the men in open-collared shirts, the women in dresses of brilliant, complexly colored fabric, sophisticated lines. Her black silk dress would have been wrong, but this cotton print was wrong, too. She self-consciously touched the scarf she had used to tie back her hair.

The room was loud with voices and salsa music from invisible speakers. People noticed them immediately and called out to the man, "don Enrique," "don Enrique!" They had been wondering about his disappearance, a woman said from a table near the courtyard. They had begun to feel abandoned. The man joked with the woman gallantly, and a little mechanically, Monica thought. She was sure that his friendliness toward her had been more genuine. When he introduced her to the seated guests, she couldn't remember having told him her name. Perhaps the maid had spoken to him. The men at the table closest to them stood and bowed slightly to her during the blur of introductions, and the women smiled extravagantly. Would she sit with them, one asked, though there was no vacant chair at the table. Yes, she must join them another said. They looked around vaguely, as if a chair might materialize any moment.

But Enrique took her arm again and led her through the room to a larger table, where he introduced her to his wife, Isabela, a woman of such fine-boned beauty that it was hard to see her clearly, as if something shimmered about her. She embraced Monica, exchanged cheek kisses with her, and produced a chair for her where there had been none before. The little girl was enjoying herself? she asked. And her son, that tall, handsome boy?

Yes, she answered, dizzied by the abrupt rush of graciousness, they were having a wonderful time, though in fact she had no idea what had become of them since they had disappeared into the swirls of children, the separate realms of Mickey Mouse and Batman. Enrique sat at the opposite side of the table. She was a child of great activity, he said. He had seen her playing at the civic celebration at Saint Mary's. A precious child, Isabela said, such lovely hair. Monica drank gratefully from the glass of wine that had appeared in front of her. She felt flushed even before the wine had had a chance to work.

Isabela introduced her to the others sitting at the table—her parents, her sister, several aunts, and two couples related to the family in a way that Monica didn't follow. The grandfather, señor Guzmán, was a wiry, stern-faced man, a fringe of white hair surrounding his darkly tanned, craggy skull, a sweeping, white brush of mustache covering his upper lip. He never spoke. His wife was more sociable, a plump woman with a seemingly inexhaustible curiosity about Monica's children and their reasons for being in Costa Rica. Hadn't the little ones been frightened to fly on an airplane? she asked. Didn't they miss their friends? What did they like most about this country? What was her husband's work?

After a few minutes, Enrique excused himself and moved to another table. There was a commotion of some sort from the courtyard, and señora Guzmán stood up and announced that she had to join them, the children, she was missing all of the fun. Her husband hesitated, then followed her glumly.

The grandparents didn't see much of the children, Isabela told Monica, though they lived only a few hours' drive away. Her father was a coffee grower near Gaúpiles, he didn't like the city. She excused herself and followed them.

The iridescent bubble of respectful attention and interest that had seemed to surround Monica collapsed abruptly. The aunts, the sister, the uncertainly related invisibly made a conversational hand-hold among themselves, a ring that left her on her own, though the men eyed her from time to time. She drank the rest of the very good wine in her glass and smiled aimlessly, sweeping the room for somebody she recognized, some parent who would return her gaze with recognition.

"Is Enrique he don't like." She turned and saw a pale, shaggy-haired man at the next table. He scraped his chair closer to hers over the polished tiles. "I am Arturo, brother of Enrique. We may speak English together. I prefer it."

Monica wasn't sure that she preferred it. Was he criticizing her Spanish? And there was an edge to the man's English, as if he had learned it under unpleasant circumstances. He seemed younger than Enrique, clean-shaven, but otherwise nothing like him. His black hair curled over the collar of a western shirt. The others at her table continued talking among themselves, his attention doing nothing to restore her brief popularity. She smiled and looked toward the courtyard entrance, trying to catch a glimpse of Valerie or Stephen. Or Bernardo, for that matter. Which one was he?

"You wonder why don Manuel don't like him," she thought the man from the next table said. It was hard to hear him through the music and clatter of the party. He leaned toward her. "Enrique believes is politics. Sure, but it's got to be more, no? Politics here is just sports, it don't mean nothing. Sports, sure, that do mean something. Very much something, you know what I'm saying?"

His large, prominent eyes fixed on her as if her agreement were important to him. The thought occurred to her that he was drunk. "I'm sorry," she said, "I don't understand." She decided to go look for Valerie, but then noticed that her glass was full again. She lifted it, and he reached over and touched it with his own.

"Salud."

She looked at him. "You're really his brother?"

"He would regard that as a nice compliment, your don't believing it."

She decided he wasn't drunk. And it was good to have somebody to talk to. She looked around at the expensively dressed guests, the maids circulating with silver trays. When her father was a congressman, her parents had belonged to a Georgetown country club, and that was the closest she had come to a scene like this. She said, "We thought we were putting our kid in a regular Costa Rican school, but everybody there seems to have money."

"The surprising third world."

She felt her face get hot. "No," she said, unsure what she was denying.

"I promise you," he said, "this is the third world, these ricos on top of a pile of povres."

Wasn't he a rico, she wondered. Or was this all coffee money, Isabela's family? "Well, the dress code is ritzy," she said. "I'm seriously underdressed."

He slid his chair back a little and looked her over with a directness that made her uncomfortable. He really seemed to be studying her $20 Target sun dress, her comfortable old sandals, the cotton scarf tying up her hair. "You are perfect," he said finally.

She gave a laugh that came out sounding high and crazy. Some people were looking at her. She swirled a coin of pale wine in the bottom of her glass, set it down, and decided to excuse herself and make her way out to the courtyard. There would be a piñata any minute now. She needed to know how Valerie was getting along, where Stephen was. She needed to find her children.

But a maid had just taken her glass and placed a full one in front of her. Feeling suddenly reckless, she turned to the man and asked, "Why no mustache? Your brother, either." He looked at her, and she repeated the question, which now seemed like someone else's question, but a good one, a fair one. She drank the excellent wine and tried to remember what he had said his name was.

He touched his upper lip. "That's what I thought you ask. Okay, for Enrique is very simple: because don Óscar have none, the leader of his party. For me, even more simple, that I look stupid with it. I notice this in L.A., in somebody bathroom, and boom, I shave him off." He extended a finger beneath his hooked, sharp nose.

She laughed again, more sanely this time. "That's where you learned English?" she asked. "L.A.?" It came out wrong, somehow, and she repeated it more carefully, "L.A." A city in California, where she had never been.

"I'm living many places in the States," he said. "L.A., Houston, Miami, New York. I prefer it so much. Y tú," he said, "where do you learn Spanish?"

"School. Junior year abroad in Madrid, another during graduate school."

Yes, he said, he had been hearing that, the Castilian accent.

She leaned back in the chrome and leather chair and recited a line from Lorca's *Blood Wedding*, pushing extra flannel into every *ce* and *ci*.

That's it, he said.

She remembered his name, Arturo, and met his eyes for a moment, then turned toward the courtyard. There was a casual movement toward the doorway, as if the children's party might be winding down. Stephen would be upset if he didn't know where she was. And Valerie? Where the hell was Valerie? She touched the hollow of her throat to see if she was sweating. She was, though it was cool in the high-ceilinged, shadowy room. She wiped her fingertips on a soft, thick napkin.

This glass would have to be her last. Then she would go find a telephone and try to call a cab. People were moving around more, getting up, changing tables, leaving and coming back. It made her feel a little dizzy, and she tried to focus on the man she was talking with, Arturo, who sat sideways to his own table, hands spread on his knees. He was wearing dark indigo jeans. And cowboy boots. Why did he prefer the U.S., she asked him. Costa Rica was peaceful and democratic and beautiful.

It was true, he said, the country was beautiful. But the democracy was a joke, men like his brother playing a game with men like Guzmán, a game of money and family and personal vanity. What could be accomplished, what was to be achieved?

She didn't know what. There was applause from the court-yard. Bernardo must be opening his presents. To abolish your army she said, that was an achievement.

That was from fear, he said. Costa Ricans were suspicious of each other, more than of the Nicaraguans, even. They were too nervous to let anybody have an army. "Listen, Monica," he said, "here's a story." He shifted his chair around a little more, so that they faced each other, almost knee to knee.

There was a man fishing with crabs on the beach, he said. Beside him on the sand, two buckets of crabs. A stranger observed the buckets and asked why one had a lid and one did not. Only one needed it, the fisherman said. In this bucket, beneath the lid, North American crabs. Without the lid they would climb one upon the other until they had reached the top, then they would pull each other up until all had escaped. In the other bucket were Costa Rican crabs. As soon as one crab seemed about to reach the top, the others would pull him back down.

He sat back, turned his hands palm upward as if he had made an irrefutable point.

She had heard the story before, about other groups. She didn't know about the Costa Rican crabs, she said. However, there would be a lot less pulling up by the North American crabs than he seemed to think.

Her husband, he said, the businessman now in the flower trade. He had come all this way to save the business of Cal Richardson, to extract him from the bucket of his own bad judgments.

It was for her father, she said. She thought for a moment, listening to the shrieks of the children batting blindly, ferociously at the piñata that must be hanging somewhere in the courtyard, Joker or Batman or Mickey Mouse leaping out of reach until everyone had a futile swing at it. She looked at the man's pale, lean face, his dark, too-large eyes. Did he know Cal Richardson? she asked.

He shrugged. They had done a little business. He too had tried to help him. "Hey!" he said. "Who's this?"

She turned and saw that Stephen had come up behind her. He hung back while she introduced him to Arturo, who rose and shook his hand. Then Valerie came running, holding a bag up in the air in triumph. She spilled it out on the table for their admiration—wrapped candy and small plastic toys and a clutch of superballs that Monica and Arturo had to move fast to keep from rolling off the glass. Their fingers bumped blindly as they wrangled the balls back into the party bag.

They rose, and she felt the floor tilt. She reached out her hand to steady herself and Arturo took her arm. They walked that way for a few steps, until she thanked him and took Valerie's hand. They went together to the courtyard, where the battered remains of a papier mâché clown hung in tatters from the bottom branch of some kind of ornamental tree. A regular clown, not the Joker. It was close to sunset, and a light drizzle was starting to fall.

"I walk you to your car," he said.

"I'm going to call a taxi," she said.

He picked Valerie up and led them past the crowd of parents and children milling around under the overhanging tile roof. Monica tried to get through to offer her thanks to Bernardo's parents, but Arturo put his free arm around her shoulders and drew her away. It would go on forever, he said, that clinging and gratefulness.

They found his car parked a block away. "Jesus!" Stephen said. It was a vast black Lincoln, not a stretch limo, but surely the biggest car he had ever ridden in. Stephen and Valerie sat in the back, sprawled there in the plush expanse, while Monica sat in front. The great car swung into the street with a rush of pure, silent acceleration. He didn't ask where they lived, just steered through the maze of glistening residential streets to the autopista and headed west.

He should take the exit after the bridge, she told him.

Stephen leaned forward and recited their address, which they had made him memorize in Spanish: from the hulera, three hundred meters east and one hundred meters south.

Of Escazú, Monica added. She didn't know how many huleras there were around San José. She didn't know what they made there—rubber door mats, those boots the school kids wore on the muddy playgrounds, campesinos' high black wellies? For her, it was just a place with a public phone.

Of Escazú, of course, he said. She shouldn't worry. He rummaged in a box concealed in the armrest between them and found a tape, popped it in. Marimba music. He smiled apologetically. Did she mind? A Guatemalan group, better than any in Costa Rica. "Is funny," he said, "a funny music, good for relax. The kids, I think they like it." He turned around and looked at the children in the back seat. "You like this? Is okay?"

She tensed, but the car streamed ahead into the rain and falling darkness as if it knew the way, too, the gorge cut through the hills for the highway its natural course. He straightened back in time to catch the exit that swept them up and around the overpass, past Super Anonos, and down into San Rafael de Escazú, the California-style mall of arched brick under construction and the exotic plant shop and the Benetton's and the exercise place and Grace Pickett's bakery and Mon Piks ice cream and Rosti Pollos with its racks of turning chickens and fragrance of wood smoke and the art gallery and the crêpe place a single blur of prosperity. They lived up the mountain a few kilometers, above San Miguel, she said, in the old part of Escazú. She felt vaguely embarrassed by San Rafael, full of North American and European pensionados.

Of course, he said, but swung the car onto a different road, one which fed into the main road like a tributary stream flowing out of the mountains. The Hoffmans had been in a taxi once that made the same mistake, and it had almost destroyed itself in the vicious potholes. A very ugly road, the driver had complained, and overcharged them five hundred colones when they finally arrived at the apartment. But the Lincoln smoothed the road like a miracle of accommodation, swallowing the punishment without fuss.

"God," she said, her irritation at being ignored soothed by the unearthly comfort, "this is so civilized."

He looked over at her.

His car, she said, it fixed the road. Then she told him something that had amazed them. A deep, broad pit had been dug in the road in front of their apartment, for some water line repair or something. When the workers quit for the day, they just chopped off a couple bamboo branches and stuck them in the gaping hole in the middle of the road and left. It stayed that way for weeks.

That was for safety, he explained, so people would see it and not fall into the hole. Those were responsible workers. Many wouldn't have bothered with the branches. But he understood her point, he added, most things here were not as they should be.

Not most things, she said. She understood about the roads, it was expensive to repair them, and people got along well enough.

What then?

She turned around in her seat, and in the illumination of tiny interior lights she saw that both children had fallen asleep—Valerie curled up on the seat, Stephen slumped against the cushioned door frame. She felt sleepy herself, and a little queasy. The bureaucracy, she said. Immigration, customs, ICE. They couldn't get their visas straightened out, equipment Ted needed was sitting in customs for lack of certification that nobody was able to explain but everybody insisted was necessary. They couldn't get a straight story about their request for a phone line.

He said nothing, and she suddenly felt angry with herself. She hated that whining tone, hated that he would think of her as one of those Americans always complaining about the inconveniences of foreign countries. She stared out the tinted window at a world a little darker than it really was, lights from the scattered houses they passed smaller and sharper than she was used to seeing. She told him about traveling through the Panama Canal with her parents when her father was in the State Department. At night the hills had looked like this, sprinkled with lights.

"What I'm wondering," he said, "why, with such connected father, why you don't pull that string and the embassy help you out."

"State was years ago, he's just a lobbyist now." She stared into the darkness. "But I'll bet that that was exactly what he thought when he invested all that money in the flower farm here, he assumed he had the pull to make it work. Cal Richardson was one of his old Georgetown buddies."

"What's his name, your father?"

"Michael Cheney. He was a congressman for one term, after State." She didn't know why she had added that. She never thought about his time in office without resentment, the most awkward and angry years of her adolescence, which was saying something.

"Michael Cheney. Mike. I think I know him."

"No," she said. It turned her stomach, really turned it, the confusion her father could bring down on her after so many years, just by being named. "It's a common name. He's not important. You might be thinking of Dick Cheney. No relation."

It was taking them a long time to reach the turnoff that would bring them back to the hulera road. Too long. They had missed it. They kept climbing. Anxiety churned beneath the buzz of all that wine. She thought she might be sick and leaned her head against the cold glass of the window. From time to time she caught a glimpse of little houses and sometimes big ones looking at them out of the darkness, then forest pushing a deeper blackness toward the road. How far could you drive into the mountains before the road turned to ox track, ox track to foot path?

The week they moved to Escazú, Ted brought home a detailed contour map he had bought at Universal—one of the two enormous office and school supply stores in San José—and spread it out on their table after supper and located their little road and traced with his fingers the disappearing dotted lines of trails leading up into the mountains. He had showed everyone in the family exactly where they were, put a pencil dot there, and where Pico Blanco was, the peak that loomed out of the mountains above them, where a plane crashed a few weeks later. On the map the contour lines snaked around it in tighter and tighter coils. When he tried to follow the mountain roads and trails, hiking by himself on Sunday mornings, he usually got lost, came back exhausted, but happy, as happy as she had seen him in a long time, strong and alive.

It was the same everywhere, she said. All bureaucracies stank, U.S. immigration certainly worse than Costa Rica's. Also customs. She told him about Ted's problem with the agricultural inspectors in Miami, the mess he was in because of one insect in a shipment of flowers. The car jolted a little as it veered onto a dirt road. She told him that he had missed their turn quite a ways back. Her voice sounded calm to her now, she clung to that calm as if it were a little life raft bobbing in the middle of the ocean.

The ones at the party, he said, his brother's friends, they were the problem. Not the dull faces at the agency windows who always tell you to come back the next day—something worse, ones into whose laps the piñatas poured. Look, he said, and dug into his jeans pocket and fished out a little, clear plastic envelope. Did she see this? He had found it in a bathroom before she got to the party. A child might have come across it, he said, one of her children. He held it up for her inspection. Cocaine, he said. He lowered his window, tore open the envelope with his teeth, and scattered its contents into the darkness, let it go. He left the window down. Cool, moist air rushed into the car, and she felt it ease her back into the seat, felt herself floating.

The rain seemed to be over. She couldn't remember when the wiper blades had stopped their rhythmic sweep across the windshield. The car moved more slowly, swaying and dipping in the terrible road, which tacked recklessly upward, throwing them glimpses of the valley glittering far below them before turning away again and again. They were far from where they should be, he had made a mistake, they were lost. Then the car braked, gravel slurring beneath its tires, and they came to a stop.

She choked off a cry. The lights of the entire central valley were spread out beneath them like an endless carpet of stars, the view from an airplane dropping out of the clouds at night, not something you should be able to see from solid land. From their apartment's balcony, some of the lights of San José were visible at night, and they had been to a restaurant in the mountains with a view that she had thought spectacular, but this was another thing entirely. She turned around in her seat to waken the children, as if the view were something happening, an event.

He stopped her with a hand on her shoulder. She should let them sleep, he said, they would come up here another time, they would enjoy the sight then. Now was for her. They sat there a while, the ocean of valley lights seeming to breathe slowly as veils of cloud moved across them from time to time. All quaintness, everything irritatingly inefficient or endearingly odd, the characteristic sweetness and struggle of the country seemed torn away, revealing something unearthly and terrifying and immense.

•

WHEN THEY ARRIVED at the apartment, he declined her invitation to come in and meet Ted, but he carried Valerie to the steps and waited for Monica to unlock the heavy sheet metal door to their garage before shifting the sleeping child to her shoulder. Sullen at being waked, Stephen nevertheless thanked him for the ride and said goodnight to him. Monica felt his thin, hot body as he pushed past her into the dark garage. She focused on that heat as she listened to him tramp up the wooden stairs to the apartment. She listened to the music throbbing from the other side of the house, the party guys entertaining, and wondered if Ted would come down before Arturo left. She said goodnight without quite looking at him, thanked him again for the ride.

He kissed the sleeping girl on the top of her head, pressing his face into her pale frizz, and then he kissed Monica on the cheek, lightly, politely, and she politely kissed him in return. His face was smooth and hard and cold from the night air. She would have shaken hands with him, she thought, as he walked back to his car, but her hands had been occupied holding Valerie. She still hadn't completely adjusted to the conventions of greeting and leave-taking here, the long exchanges of inquiries and good wishes, the disconcerting "adiós" upon meeting on country roads. She concentrated on Valerie's weight in her arms.

He backed his car perilously close to the ditch opposite the house and eased it around until he faced the long descent to San José, if that was where he was going. He leaned out his still-open side window. "I think maybe I can help about the inspectors of flowers," he said. "I know some guys."

"No," she said, "the problem's in Miami, not here."

"I know some guys," he said, as if she hadn't heard him the first time.

When the children were in bed, Ted brought some manzana tea in to her as she was undressing in the bedroom. "It's going to be all right," he said. "We've got it under control. We've worked out a new cycle of pesticides. I'm going to use some of my underemployed workers to do tougher soil checks, not just foliage. There's this testing procedure Alejandro's heard about."

She watched him as he sat on the edge of the bed, idly swirling the tea in the plastic mug, the flimsy bag probably disintegrating. Six years older than she, his blond hair combed straight back in a way that defiantly emphasized his receding hairline, he was still boyishly handsome, athletic-looking. His rounded German features conveyed a brooding intensity that was the main trait he had passed on to Stephen, who otherwise favored her side of the family—dark, tall, large-featured.

She turned toward the bedroom mirror to unfasten the hair scarf and closed her eyes. Valerie was going to look more like Ted, but Stephen had his bare-wire vulnerability to emotion. It was what had drawn her to Ted in the first place, and it was how she had explained his infidelity, his defenses were so frag-ile. At the same time, it made the betrayal crueler, for he must have known how she would feel, must have felt it himself in exquisite detail, must feel it still.

"Sorry to have been such a wreck this morning," he said. She heard the rickety wooden bed frame creak, the hollow sound of the cup being set down on the floor. He came up behind her and wrapped his arms around her, kissed the back of her neck. "Are you crying?"

She raised her hands to her face. He was right, her eyes were streaming. She shook her head. She felt his arms tighten around her.

"I'm just tired." She eased herself away from him. "I think I need that tea, now, my darling." She fished out the bag and dropped it into the wastebasket. Flecks of leaf floated on the surface of the tea. "It was so strange," she said. "Those people at the party were *rich*, Ted. You wouldn't believe it."

"Stephen told me about the car you got a ride home in. It was all he could talk about before he dropped off."

"That was Bernardo's uncle. The birthday boy."

"Speaking of cars, here's some good news. I had Alejandro swing by the repair place, and they swear it'll be ready next week." She sipped at the tea, and he said, "I know. But this time I think they mean it."

"Well, hallelujah." She thought of telling him about the party. But she didn't know where to begin. She hoped the tea would calm the headache throbbing at the base of her skull, the nausea stirring in her belly. She hoped the music from downstairs wouldn't be blasting much longer, and that she would be asleep before the party guys started any loud fucking in the bedroom that must be right below theirs.

He put his arms around her again. "Hallelujah is right."

CHAPTER FOUR

APPROACH TO THE CUMBRE

WHEN HE PICKED UP THE OLD SQUAREBACK, the reflective warning triangle required by law was missing from the luggage compartment. He asked for it, but nobody at the repair shop knew anything about it. He shouldn't worry, they told him, nobody had them, the police never checked.

Somebody had *his*, he pointed out.

He shouldn't worry, they kept telling him. He wasn't accusing them of stealing it, was he? Why would they steal it?

He didn't know why. The sunless shop in a semi-industrial, semi-wasteland area at the edge of San José wasn't a venue for productive discussion, so he paid for the repairs, grimly peeling thousand colon bills from the stack that represented the family resources for the next three weeks. He eased the car out of the corrugated metal building into the traffic racing back toward downtown San José and shifted uncomfortably in his seat, calculating the distance between colones in his briefcase and expenses lurking at the end of the month. He hated having to dip into the sheaf of notes before he could even get them home and divide them into various budget envelopes, record them in a ledger. Their reality was too frail even then. Dinero, plata, billetas, efectivo—he fingered the words like rosary beads, but they offered no comfort.

The money in dollars had been wired down to the bank in Escazú, a transaction that didn't always work, funds sometimes getting stranded in limbo as they floated electronically from Cincinnati to New York to San José to Escazú. This morning, when he had surrendered his bankbook and passport after waiting in line twenty minutes in the Escazú bank's upper lobby, he had done so with something like prayer. For the next forty-five minutes he had edged along penitentially in the second line, weaving back and forth through a rope labyrinth that filled the lower part of the lobby. He hadn't even read the newspaper he had brought with him, so focused was he on the success of his mission. Reaching the head of the line finally, he had given his name at one of the windows, and the teller had gone and talked to somebody in the upper part of the bank, returned with his bankbook and passport, and counted out a little pile of green American bills—hundreds and twenties. And he had felt personally blessed, beneficiary of a small miracle.

The exchange of dollars for colones was always an edgier and more profane transaction for him. It took place in the city, downtown, like business with a prostitute, and the uncertainty was more concrete—to be shortchanged, to be given a rate lower than the next guy might offer, to be arrested. Street exchange was illegal though open, the guys with their pocket calculators in the center of San José shouting "Dollars! Change Dollars!" at anyone who looked foreign. The tourist books warned against black market exchange, claiming the difference of a few colones a dollar wasn't worth the risk. But to change money at a bank meant still another long wait in yet another line. Further suspicious scrutiny of your papers. He once had a torn, scotch-taped twenty he had just received from a teller two windows over rejected in a bank. You would have to be crazy.

After getting the dollars in the Escazú bank this morning, he had crossed the shady old plaza, caught a microbus in front of the church, ridden into San José, then walked the ten or so blocks past shabby storefronts and the huge city cemetery to the busy downtown area, narrow sidewalks among the three- and four-story buildings crowded with lottery sellers set up behind card tables and country people with little pyramids of produce or sprays of herbs or homemade rat traps spread out on plastic sheets in front of government buildings.

In the heart of downtown San José, Avenida Central had been closed to automobile traffic, forming a pedestrian mall that now was cluttered with piles of sand and gravel, stacks of paving bricks, masons here and there on their hands and knees laying pavers around muddy holes that cratered the raw new plaza, one of the improvements supposed to be completed in time for the hemispheric presidential summit, now only a week away. The project had been going on for months and seemed barely half finished, but there was no sign of urgency. In approaching the cumbre, as in every enterprise, they held comfortably to the belief that what was necessary would be accomplished. On a futile trip to Migración a few days before, he had passed the old Bellavista fortress, now the Museo National, and saw workers patching bullet holes left over from the 1948 revolution and painting the stained and weathered concrete walls. Only on one side, though, the side from which the presidents would address the public and the international news media, who would gather in a huge new terraced plaza, which seemed even more hopelessly behind schedule than the other cumbre projects.

When he was approached by a money changer, Ted spoke with him long enough to get the rate, then crossed the street and got the rate from another guy. He walked around for a few more minutes, staring blankly at store windows, his briefcase handle growing slippery with sweat, before heading finally to the new, ten-story office building above the fancy downtown McDonald's. He took the elevator to the top floor, a sleek suite of rooms with no name on the frosted glass doors.

Richardson had recommended the place; this was the first

time Ted had tried it. It wasn't clear what business the firm conducted, other than buying black market dollars. Maybe that was it. He waited with his briefcase on his lap in an outer office while young men in short sleeve shirts and crisp slacks came and went. In a few minutes, one of them ushered him into a middle room, to an armchair in front of a large desk. A man in a gray suit, very smooth and scented, emerged from an inner office and spoke to him pleasantly in British English, but he left after a few minutes, and a thin, severe, pock-marked young man in aviator glasses and plaid sport shirt slid in behind the desk, accepted Ted's dollars, counted them silently, punched figures into a printing calculator, pulled a stack of thousand colón notes from a drawer, and counted them out for him with blurring speed and an incomprehensible mumble.

Uncertain as to the protocol, Ted hesitated after being handed the money, and the young man tore off the end of the calculator tape and gave it to him as a receipt. He checked the rate, a colón and a half better than what he had been offered on the street, and slipped the little piece of paper into his brief-case along with the bills, as if it were something other than the record of an illegal transaction.

The rate of exchange had begun to float upward for the past month, black market now up to around 83 colones to the dollar. The thousand colón bill was the largest available, and five or six hundred dollars translated into a significant bundle. The thou-sands were printed in red, with a bland portrait of somebody nobody had ever been able to identify for him—a far cry from the gorgeous, full-color five colón bill they printed for tourists, and less interesting even than the five hundred, which came in orange or purple. Still, the heft of forty or fifty of the thou-sand colón notes together was reassuring, and he was starting to get used to dealing in cash, even if it melted away all too quickly. The flower farm had a checking account, but it was still frozen. He wished he had asked Richardson more questions. The lawyer he had recently hired didn't seem to have a clue.

Monetary rituals completed, he had walked twelve more blocks to the garage where his car was being fixed, in a neighborhood of little furniture factories, vacant lots waist-high in coarse grass, decaying nineteenth century mansions, ramshackle warehouses, and rusting, corrugated tin repair shops, chickens stalking their back yards. Now he sat in his car at an intersection downtown again, leaning forward and twisting his neck to see the awkwardly positioned stoplight strung between La Gloria department store and the second story of a fried chicken restaurant. Still brooding over the stolen reflective triangle, he felt the old Volkswagen suddenly tremble and jerk until he shifted it into neutral. He didn't know if it was something to worry about. Moving again after the light changed and traffic lunged forward, the engine ran smoothly enough, but the mushy automatic transmission made it difficult for him to keep up with the violent rush of traffic racing from one stoplight to the next.

Calculating the money they had already sunk into the car, he missed a chance to turn onto the street he knew would bring him to the highway northwest of San José and then out to the flower farm in Heredia. He found himself caught up in noontime rush hour traffic in the middle of downtown San José, a maze of office buildings and banks and fast food restaurants and government offices and stores that was a nightmare to drive. His chest tightened. He leaned on the horn when a van taking a short cut between a service drive and a cross street came at him the wrong way, but the horn still didn't work, though they said they had fixed it. Voiceless in the traffic din, he was forced to swing right to avoid being mashed against a concrete road construction barrier.

Ted had walked all over downtown, but in a car, now, nothing looked familiar. He lost track of which direction he was going, whether he was on a calle or an avenida, craned his neck to read a street number high on the corner of some building, tried to visualize his map of San José, struggled to remember whether even-numbered avenidas ran north or south of the city's east-west axis.

Finally he recognized the cathedral and the tall palm trees of Parque Central, turned right again, and was about to head for a street he knew from riding the bus, which would take him west, to familiar territory, when he thought he saw Cal Richardson on the sidewalk half a block ahead of him. Stephen had claimed to have met him at the Picketts' a few weeks before, but Ted didn't know why he would still have been in the country. This guy really did look like him, though he had only gotten a glimpse of him in the crowd—tall, wearing a light blue tennis hat like Richardson used to wear.

When the man turned and started walking away, Ted sped up a little in the dense traffic, hoping to get a better look. But a bus cut in front of him, forcing him into the center lane. Caught in the traffic that swirled around the bus, he lost sight of him. At the next intersection, glancing up the block, he saw him again for a second, disappearing into a doorway. That was that, he thought. He would never know if it was him. But then he had to slam on the brakes to avoid a pickup truck pulling away from the curb, which left a parking spot miraculously open in front of him. He swung into it.

The doorway lead into a hotel, its cramped lobby dark and deserted, smelling of piss and beer-soaked carpet and fetid cigar smoke. He went to the desk, which was grilled like a bank window, but no one seemed to be around. Outside again, he saw that there was a bar a few steps beyond the hotel entrance. He might have gone in there, rather than into the hotel. The door of the bar swung open and a white-haired man and a young woman came out. The man held the door for him. "They been waiting for you!" he said. An American with a southern accent.

The woman said something to the man in Spanish, but he ignored her. Country music and the smell of barbecue drifted out of the door the man continued to hold wide open. Ted went in. There was a row of highbacked booths, a scattering of formica tables, a raised dance floor, and a stage littered with spotlights and mike stands. The music was coming from a round-topped jukebox at the end of the bar.

It was a big room, half-filled in the middle of the day, men, mostly, drinking and eating lunch. After walking past all the booths, he saw the bathroom doors, decorated with life-size cartoon cowboy and old West madam. He sat down at one of the tables and waited. A teenage boy came over with a menu and asked if he wanted anything. He asked in English, but he was Costa Rican, as was the bartender, probably, and a waitress clearing a table near the dance floor. The conversations he could hear were in English. So was the menu—ribs, chicken, hamburgers, steaks. On posters advertising Coors and Budweiser and Old Milwaukee, girls with breasts straining out of bikinis or pointing tautly from beneath unbuttoned shirts leaned forward, eager as cheerleaders.

He would have been embarrassed by this gringo bar if he had been with Monica, but right now it felt sweetly comfortable. He wondered what it was like at night. If he and Pepe ever had their boys' night out, maybe he would suggest this place, they could listen to some country music. Pepe was hungry for all things American.

The waiter shifted his feet. Ted ordered a hamburger and a Coke. Except for the accents of the help and the harsh traffic noises pushing in from the street, it could have been one of the bars across the Ohio his grandfather sometimes took him to when he was in high school or home from college— loose, grainy places where he had felt free for a few hours from his father's judgment. His grandfather was a piece of work— racist, full of raging self-pity when he was drunk, but funny and affectionate, too. He had died before Ted graduated from college, and Ted still missed him. He missed him now.

"How's it going then?" A man with curly, red-blond hair had come up to the table and stood there with a long-toothed smile. Stocky, sunburned, wire-rim glasses with tinted lenses.

"Fine."

He raised a bottle of Imperial in a kind of salute and asked, "Habla español?"

"Más o menos," Ted answered, cautiously, modestly.

The man sat down and set the bottle on the table. "I got to come here to practice my español. Only place anybody understands me." He extended his hand. "Stuart Fitzgerald. Me llamo Stu."

"Ted. Mucho gusto."

"There you go." He stared at his bottle, then slapped his hand to his chest and said, "Soy marinero."

Ted looked at him.

"Marinero! That's sailor. I'm a sailor. Retired a year ago. Merchant marine."

"Australian," Ted guessed.

"Kiwi. Sailed British registry, out of Hong Kong, mostly. Had a Chinese wife, died last year."

"Sorry."

He nodded, examined the label on his bottle, and looked up when the waiter brought Ted's hamburger. "Decent food," he said.

The fries were the usual white, waxy things, with the usual mayonnaise and ketchup glopped on top, but the hamburger was good, oozing fried onions. It tasted like home.

"Here long?"

"Couple months." Ted looked toward the back, where the men's room door now stood ajar.

"You aren't a regular, I know that."

"Never been before."

"Don't know where I'd go else." He looked around. "Quiet now, but it can get bloody bugass. You know what I mean?"

"I was looking for this guy, Cal Richardson."

"Cal, sure. Stayed next door."

"You live there?"

"Fuck no! I've stayed in some shit holes, but not no more.

Cal didn't mind." He lowered his voice suddenly. "Look at that. Look at that." He gestured with his head toward a young woman in tight spandex pants and cropped T-shirt who had just come in from the street and now stood looking around the room. "How'd you like a little of that there?"

Ted laughed uneasily. There was in fact something about those cropped shirts they were wearing these days, floating free over a woman's bare midriff, that just seemed to invite you to slide your hands up underneath them. "I'm a family man," he said.

"Course you are. Funny thing, so am I. Came down to C.R. to have some fun, enjoy myself with little Ticas like that, and what do you think I've got mixed up with? Bird almost as old as I am! Got grown kids! Can you believe it? Gets off work in a few hours and'll be down here looking for me. She's all right, tiger in the sack, you know what I mean? Talks English. But what am I doing with a woman almost my own age, when I can have something like that there?"

Ted picked up a French fry, set it down again. "You think it could have been Richardson? Guy wearing a blue hat, came in here a few minutes ago?"

"Richardson's a family man, too, you know that? Had his wife and boy down here. Last I heard, he's having trouble getting them all exit visas. Went bankrupt, I heard."

"When was this?"

"Fucking Immigration bastards. I've fought them myself, bloody fucking sons of bitches. Why don't we all just go down there with a couple automatic weapons and take care of it?"

"Canadians, they get ninety days on a tourist visa."

"Only thirty for you, right? Same for us. What fucking sense does that make?"

"Richardson has a kid?"

Stu mimed spitting on the floor. "Cunts drive you to the brink. Now I just go to Panama every few months, start the fucking clock over again. Got some nice places down there.

Sailed the canal a few times, back when I was a marinero for real."

Ted looked at his watch. Alejandro would be wondering where he was. He asked the waiter for the check.

"Your español's pretty good," Stu said. "I'm taking classes, but it's harder than I expected. Everybody says, `Spanish is a fucking snap,' but I picked up Chink quicker. See you down here again?" He gestured for another beer while Ted studied the bill.

"Maybe. Sure."

"Gets fucking bugass sometimes, Saturday nights. They got a contest, sometimes."

Ted counted his change.

Stu slowly waved one hand in an arc above his head, as if creating a banner there: "Great International Blowjob Contest, that's what they used to call it." He licked moisture off the lip of the beer bottle the waiter had just brought him. "Once, one of the judges locked himself in the head, refused to go on with it."

Ted laid down a few coins for a tip.

"Once, they had this three-way tie. Three girls, wouldn't allow no poufs in on it, you know what I'm saying? So there's a tie between these three girls. What do you think they did?"

He should just leave.

"Think." Stu's red face had gotten redder, though his voice had grown small. "Come on, what do you think?"

Ted shrugged.

The marinero leaned a little closer. "They had a blowoff, of course!"

•

THE ROADS UP THE MOUNTAINS northwest of San José were pretty good. Ted drove through Heredia and the old town of Barva. Thinking about Stuart Fitzgerald's story, he took a wrong turn onto a road that ended at the barred gate of a prosperous-looking finca. He made his way back to Barva and found the right road up to San José de la Montaña. From there it was steeper going, the old Squareback laboring in second and even first gear, but the surface was mostly new asphalt. Richardson had explained it to him: coffee growers and nurserymen and fruit growers had farms on the fertile slopes beneath Volcán Poas, and they got the road repaved every few years. There were stands of huge cypresses here, which some Germans had planted a hundred years before, windbreaks, but the wind pushed at him so hard anyway that the car rocked in its gusts. He leaned over to roll up the window.

He thought about the blowjob contest, what it would be like to be a judge, nothing mattering to you but technique. One of the things he hadn't told Monica about Elaine was how she liked to go down on him and how it made him feel—free, disconnected from himself in a way he imagined certain drugs might do. They had only gone to bed a few times before the guilt and worry proved too much for him and they broke it off, ending what was maybe never more than a stab at consolation after the solar energy business failed. Monica said it wasn't the sex, or not just the sex. The intimacy that had excluded her, something that must have happened before they had ever kissed. He had accepted this. They hadn't touched each other for the first couple months afterwards, then they started again, but still not often. It wasn't clear whether it was getting better or not between them. It should have gotten better by now. He flexed his fingers on the steering wheel, thought about the marinero.

Pulling into the long drive of the flower farm, he saw a white stake truck parked in front of the office. The bed of the truck was full of plastic barrels and wooden crates. Two men smoking on the extended tail gate greeted him politely, but looked blank when he asked what was going on. "Es mío," he said, indicating with a sweep of his hand the rows of arched greenhouses, the low cement building that housed the office and refrigerators and garage. What was going on, he asked again, and the older of the two men gestured ambiguously with his cigarette toward the office.

Es mío. It had never before occurred to him to say that the flower farm was his. It wasn't, really, though Monica's father had offered him a partnership in the business if he could keep it going and have it in the black within a year. He wasn't sure of his proper title in English, much less Spanish. Alejandro was the manager, gerente, yet he was Alejandro's boss. Jefe, he supposed. Soy jefe. The overseer was what he really was, which sounded horrible as soon as he said it to himself, not even wondering what it was in Spanish. What he really was was the accountant, and that was pretty good in Spanish, too—contador. But jefe was better. Breathy, a little menacing. Soy jefe. The farm wasn't his, but he believed he could make it his. He was an entrepreneur, after all. He wondered if Spanish used the French word, too. He could make it his own. Soy jefe.

In the office, Alejandro was talking with a heavy-set man in a denim jacket. When Ted came in, both men rose, and Alejandro introduced him as don Teodor. He had addressed him as señor Hoffman when they first met. Then, after Ted insisted, Ted.

Alejandro was in his mid fifties, had run his own flower farm, mined gold in the Osa Peninsula, had a milk distribution business, worked as a mason and general contractor. He had built the main structures of this farm for Cal Richardson and stayed on as manager, but Richardson had argued with him one too many times and he had walked off, waited for the business to fail. As he had warned, the tubing that Richardson had ordered for the arched supports for the greenhouse plastic had been too light, and some of it had collapsed in the ferocious winds.

Alejandro ran the day-to-day operations of the flower farm now, consulting with Ted on the planting schedule and cycles of fertilization and insecticide and fungicide spraying, though that was mainly a formality. Ted's horticultural background didn't extend much past an organic gardening supply company he had started once, and sweaty slave labor in his father's vegetable gardens when he was a kid. A decent welder, Alejandro had begun to reinforce the framework of the greenhouses. He took care of hiring and firing other workers and left Ted free to concentrate on straightening out the books, figuring out taxes and duties, making sure that bills were paid, looking for new marketing opportunities. Ana Rosa, the secretary, took care of routine invoices. She wasn't there, now, though her desk in a corner of the office was piled with papers that she always cleared before she left.

The man Alejandro was talking to was César something, from customs. He was delivering the generator and sprayers and rolls of plastic and soil sterilizer and chemicals that had been sitting in the customs warehouse from before Ted took over the farm. Some of it had been there for over a year, according to Richardson, who had left him a list of everything that had gotten hung up there, along with the bitter assurance that he would never lay his hands on it. The duties, he had claimed, had all been paid, and he had the receipts to prove it. In three months, Ted hadn't been able to get a straight answer about the impounded supplies and equipment and had begun to think that Richardson was right, he never would.

The customs man excused himself and left the office, and Ted asked Alejandro if that was it, all the stuff had suddenly sprung free from Aduana? What had happened?

Alejandro turned his broad, heavily-callused palms upward. It was a stroke of good luck, he said. Thank God. He didn't understand it, either.

They should get out there and unload everything, Ted said, before anyone had second thoughts. He dropped his briefcase on the desk and headed for the door, but Alejandro stopped him.

There would be something expected, Alejandro said, absently rubbing the corner of his heavy jaw. A tip.

Ted reached for his billfold. How much?

Two hundred and fifty dollars, Alejandro said.

Ted felt himself go cold. No, really, he said. The duties and fees had already been paid. Three men and a truck from eastern San José would cost about four thousand colones, he calculated, a little less than fifty bucks. That would be for private transport, and these guys were government employees. It was a government truck, government gasoline. Through the window he could see "uso oficial" stenciled on the truck's door. Four thousand colones would surely be enough for a tip.

He had been very clear about it, Alejandro said, two hundred and fifty dollars was what it would take. Otherwise they would drive the goods back. It was a lot, he agreed, but that was the way it worked. Ted was very lucky to have a chance at all.

He studied Alejandro's dark, square face. It wasn't really a tip, was it, he said. It was a bribe, correct? He sat down at the desk and found a ball point and a kid's school notebook he used as a scratchpad. Okay, he said, how much did he think the supplies were worth? With the duties, over ten thousand dollars, right? Alejandro nodded and Ted thought about it for a moment, doing calculations in the notebook. Richardson had paid too much for imported equipment, but that money was spent, and they needed the generator badly. They needed all of it. So he opened the briefcase and counted out twenty red bills—20,000 colones—and took the other 750 from his billfold. He recorded the amount, stuffed the bills into an envelope, and wrote "Aduana" on it, his pen making deep marks in the cushion of money. He handed the envelope to Alejandro and watched him hesitate at the door. What was the problem now?

Alejandro gestured vaguely, went out to the truck, and directed the unloading of the barrels and crates, matching their contents with bills of lading. Ted stayed at the desk, focusing on the columns of figures in the farm's official accounts ledger. Alejandro returned to the office in a little while, still carrying the fat envelope. They had been expecting dollars, he said.

Ted took the envelope and went outside and handed it to the heavy-set man. He had no dollars, only colones, he told the man. It was the currency of this country. Did the man know that he had given him the exchange rate of the black market? It was a full value tip that he had given him. He could go to the Plaza Nacional and buy his own dollars if he wanted.

The man looked at him for a moment, then smiled and shook hands with him, called him amigo. In the future, when he had such needs, he should ask for him, César Ruiz Castro. He had heard of Ted from a friend and knew he was a good man, a man to be trusted. He shook his hand again and said other things that Ted couldn't follow, the man's Spanish picking up speed on the freshly greased tracks of cooperation. Finally they all shook hands—Ted, César, Alejandro, the two workers from Aduana—and the truck drove away, leaving Ted and Alejandro standing in a garage heaped with packing materials, gleaming machinery, and barrels of chemicals.

Miguel and Roberto, two of the farm's laborers, appeared and began hauling the cardboard and excelsior and wooden crates out to the dusty area behind the buildings to be burned, while Alejandro double-checked the new inventory. Ana Rosa had returned to the office and was working at her desk, typing a contract proposal. On his way home, Ted would stop by Radio Gráfica in San José and fax the contract to a bouquet maker in Atlanta. He stood at the window and stared at the vaulted greenhouse shelters arrayed in orderly ranks on the slopes beneath the office, until he felt Ana Rosa's silence and turned around.

"You shouldn't worry about it," she said. "It's important that you learn the way." Though he knew from her employment records that she was forty years old, she dressed always in slacks and blouses, and with her short haircut and large round glasses, she could have passed for a college girl.

From the office windows, the scalloped profile of the greenhouse roofs looked like fish scales. They receded into a premature vanishing point, as if they covered the whole mountain.

She yanked the contract out of the typewriter and sailed it the few feet to his desk. "Your president will be here soon," she said. She liked to talk politics with him. "I think it's very bad, that you don't honor him."

"Okay, Ana Rosa," he said, "here's my plan. When they get here, send Bush and Ortega up into the mountains by themselves, let them work it out."

"Here in Costa Rica we don't admire Daniel Ortega so much."

Alejandro walked in, and Ana Rosa put another sheet of paper in the typewriter. She was shy around Alejandro. Was it all right? Ted asked him.

It was all right, Alejandro said. He stood there, polishing the horn-dark nails of his right hand with the thumb of his left. Ted had done very well, he said. He had been thinking about his question, why everything had been released so suddenly. Maybe it was just the time. Did he want to try out the new sprayer?

Ted went out to the storage barn with him, but after watching for a few minutes as he assembled the brass and stainless steel fittings and rubber washers, he walked down to the greenhouses, open structures of taut translucent plastic snapping in the sharp wind. Here and there the old plastic sheeting had deteriorated and torn, and there were great tatters flinging themselves around from the naked roof tubes. It wasn't a disaster yet, but he was glad that they had the new rolls of plastic.

He walked downhill from bay to bay of chrysanthemums, the smell of chemical fertilizers and pesticides sharp in his nostrils, the clear logic of the growing cycle calming him. The beds of mother plants, kept in a vegetative state by strings of electric lights that broke the darkness each night from ten to two. The rows of cuttings in the rooting areas, glistening with the spray of fertilizer from automatic misters. Bays of plants that had been allowed to go reproductive at calculated intervals, some starting to get a bit leggy, ready for debudding, others in bloom, purple, pale pink, yellow, deep orange, white, which would be harvested within a few days and boxed and shipped.

He looked for beetles, thrips, aphids, running his fingers from time to time through the frilled, dense foliage. The jacked-up regimen of pesticides would do the job, he thought, as long as the workers survived it. He wiped his hands on his trousers, then on the damp grass growing between bays, though that would have been treated, too. He would have to wait until he got to a faucet. Suddenly he felt an almost irresistible urge to rub his itching eyes, scratch his nose, and he resolved to order a case of neoprene gloves. He would like to try organic options. The industry might have caught up with the ideas he hadn't been able to get off the ground a few years ago.

The mature beds were beautiful. Chrysanthemums were autumn flowers for him. It was autumn now in Ohio, late October, and walking between the beds of stiff, furiously blooming flowers he felt an almost religious rightness, as if the flower trade had momentarily canceled his mistakes.

His mother had always planted flowers around their house outside of Cincinnati, away from the vegetable garden his father pushed farther and farther every year. Neither Ted nor his younger brothers and sisters had ever paid much attention to the flowers. It was sweet corn and tomatoes and peas and beans and cauliflower and peppers and finally even potatoes, thirty hills of them one year, that had held them in bondage until they could finally leave home, but he remembered her flowers now, a thin hedge of marigolds and snapdragons and firecracker plants and zinnias and chrysanthemums hugging the edge of the slab foundation his father had poured for the house that he had built with his own hands.

At the far end of the greenhouse shelter, he came to the less carefully tended area where he and Alejandro had begun to experiment with more exotic plants—spiky red and orange and yellow heliconias, ghostly pale green calathea, costus spicatus with its bright red nub of blossom protruding like an engorged clitoris—flowers from another planet, as distant from the homey chrysanthemum as sex was from housework. It was too early to tell if they would make it, or if he would be able to market them. Richardson had failed with carnations and then, more spectacularly, with roses, before retreating finally into chrysanthemums, where he had done almost as badly, making mistakes in insecticides and fertilizer, alienating his workers, ignoring the local market. Día de la Madre, August 15, a slow time in the States, might have made the difference between a rout and a decent profit for the month. Ted had begun buying tropical calla lilies from other farmers for consignment resale in the States. He wanted to try a variety from New Zealand he had read about in a trade magazine.

The erratic patchwork of the experimental plot offered none of the reassurance he found in the steady progression of the farm's main crop, yet he lingered there, pulling thready weeds from the loam, wondering if he could afford to build the more elaborately protective greenhouse a jungle flower required. Moving out into a bay devoted to some ornamentals that Alejandro had been raising on his own land before Ted hired him, he stepped into a stream of icy water running along the foundation of the structure. He squatted and rinsed off his hands, then studied the flowing water. At the lower end of the farm, the stream spread out into a grassy meadow, then disappeared into a grove of cypresses.

Tracing the water back, he found a length of old hose running away from the greenhouse irrigation system, connected to an open valve. He went to turn it off, but somebody had removed the valve handle. He returned to the garage, where Alejandro was still piecing together the new sprayer. Did he know that somebody had left a water valve open? Ted asked. They must be losing hundreds of gallons an hour. Did he know where a wrench was, to shut it off? He didn't know the word for wrench, just mimed using one.

Alejandro stood up, valve parts glittering in his hands like gold. It would be better not to shut it off, he said. It was necessary that the valve remain open, or the pressure would burst the pipes.

What pressure? Ted asked. This was just water, pouring out of an old hose.

It was from the water concession, Alejandro said. The farm had no well. Richardson had gone together with other farmers in the region and had a dam built higher in the mountains, with rights to use a percentage of the stored water. But he had used low pressure pipe to carry the water from the dam to the farm. When the water was running, it was fine, but if it was stopped below, two, three hundred meters of pressure would quickly build up and break the pipe.

Why couldn't they shut off the water at the reservoir? Ted asked.

Because the reservoir would overflow. The authorities checked it from time to time, and if they discovered that water was being wastefully spilled, they could revoke the concession or issue a fine.

But they were spilling the water right now out of the hose. It was running down the hill. What was the difference?

The difference was this, Alejandro explained: The authorities knew where the reservoir was and thus checked on it period-ically, a simple matter since there was only the one in many hectares of mountainside. But in this area there were many fincas, and on each finca there were many pipes, many hoses, many valves. If one of them was open, who would know it? Besides, from here it would be very inconvenient to have to go up to the reservoir every time they needed water.

Ted thought about it for a moment. It was still the rainy season, he said. What would happen in the dry season? Would they still have to let the hose run?

Alejandro said that in the dry season they would need the water, they would use all that they had a right to. And if the stream ran more fully than usual and they had to release a sur-plus, what did it matter? In a stream or in a pipe, the water ran down to the rivers, the rivers ran to the ocean.

Why hadn't the hose been spilling out water before? Ted asked.

Who knows? Alejandro answered. Perhaps they had been making use of the water at those times, or possibly some farmer farther up the mountain had been borrowing some of it for his own use.

They could do that, tap into the pipes?

It didn't matter, Alejandro said, the flower farm had all the water it needed. What happened to the remainder wasn't their concern.

Where was this reservoir? Ted asked.

Above, Alejandro said, gesturing vaguely over his shoulder.

Could he get there? He wanted to see it.

Alejandro shook his head. The road was kilometers away, and it was very bad, he would never make it unless he had a jeep.

Could he walk up to it?

There wasn't much to see, Alejandro said. He squatted and began fiddling with the new sprayer again.

Ted walked out to the back of the building, then along the upper perimeter of the farm, looking for evidence of a water line running up into the mountains. He found a path leading upward through the cypresses and decided that this was probably where the pipe had been laid. Where the path crossed a ditch, he could actually see the pipe, *a* pipe, anyway, gray plastic, and after a while, when the path disappeared and he had to cut over to a rutted ox track, he was able to follow the line with his eye until he could get back to it again. He climbed, sweat beading on his forehead, drying in the sharp wind. It felt good. He loved hiking in the mountains.

He was on someone's private property, he admitted to himself after crossing the third barbwire fence. He passed a cluster of shacks and waved to the children and old woman watching him from the grassless yard in front of them. It wouldn't be their land, though the dog barking and straining at the end of a piece of rope would probably not make the distinction if it got loose. There was a sewage smell, and the sweetness of vegetables or fruit rotting somewhere

He found the ox track again and stuck with it until he was out of breath and sat down on a boulder that forced the track to the edge of a slope too steep to hold more than the most wiry, desperately motivated scrub. Below, where the incline eased slightly, there was a small field of dark green coffee plants, which he hadn't crossed, yet which now lay between him and the flower farm.

The wind that had felt merely brisk a while before now cut through his cotton shirt and drove into him. High as he was, he couldn't see the main buildings of the flower farm behind the screen of cypresses, but the greenhouses beyond were mostly visible, touchingly small within great folds of the mountain. A skirl of smoke rose through the trees—the packing material being burned. He looked across the central valley, with San José sprawled between the two mountain ranges, and tried to pick out Pico Blanco, which rose above Escazú, where Monica would be trying to get Valerie to lie down for a nap, then maybe shuffling through her old dissertation notes, searching for the inspiration to get into it again, but more likely undressing and taking a shower in the midday heat before Stephen came home.

Ted thought about her long body under the drizzly, lukewarm spray. She had forgiven him for the sake of the kids, he understood that, and he had been wildly grateful. Still, was that really forgiveness? It was a question he could never ask her: will you forgive me for myself? For who I am to you, who you are to me, love of my life? He looked a little to the east of Pico Blanco for the enormous cross that was illuminated with electric lights and visible throughout the valley at night. During the day he could never spot it from their house, and he couldn't spot it now from here, on the opposite side of the valley.

Clouds were building in the east. He had to go back. He had lost track of the water line he had been following, if it was the water line at all, and he had some time ago given up on finding the reservoir. Alejandro was right. What difference did it make, as long as they got the water they needed and stayed out of trouble?

The clouds were blotting out the Escazú mountains. He had to get back down to the flower farm before the storm crossed the valley and climbed up to him. He felt like going on, though. Not looking for the reservoir any more, just climbing, climbing. Volcán Barva was somewhere up there, he had found it on a contour map while trying to pin down the exact location of the flower farm, and Volcán Poas, and the Cordillera Central running northwest on and on, through Nicaragua and El Salvador and Guatemala and Mexico and on and on and on. It wouldn't take much, he sometimes felt, to just start walking and keep on going. At this moment, tired as he was, that's how he felt. He felt like walking away into the endless mountains.

CHAPTER FIVE

A FOREST, PRONTO

CAL RICHARDSON SPENT THE EVENING at the American Legion in Escazú, watching delayed broadcast football on cable tv, Cardinals versus Saints, a game nobody in his right mind cared about. It was what they did here, pretending for a few hours they hadn't exiled themselves to this self-castrated little country. The men watching with him in the low-ceilinged, beery room were mostly pensionados, always fretting over the benefits that had lured them to Costa Rica, promises they could live like kings on their retirement incomes, tax advantages forever under attack by whichever party happened to be out of power at the moment. There was a minor embassy official. A couple guys he played tennis with, who had been doing pretty well in real estate until the Japanese moved in and started grabbing up the rest of the Pacific coast. A tourist from Chicago.

Some were vets, some weren't. All were excited about the presidential summit, including the tourist, whose travel plans had been screwed up by the government's decision to close down the international airport to commercial flights the day the presidents arrived.

Though Cal wasn't a vet, Hank Pickett had been taking him

to the American Legion so long that no one thought of him as a guest anymore. He had met a few other men of Hank's stature here. John Hull, who had had to leave the country on a medical excuse after the communists linked him to the La Penca bombing. Joe Fernandez, ex C.I.A. station chief. Richard Secord. Oliver North. Robert Vesco.

Tonight there had been only little fish, and even Hank had seemed futile and unfocused. He had offered the opinion that Ortega's rigged elections next year would finally bring the U.S. into Nicaragua in force, claimed that planning the invasion was the only reason Bush was bothering to come down for the summit. Yes! Great! they had all said, it was about fucking time. But nobody really cared, they kept their eyes on the game. They were just proud that the president of the United States was going to visit the tiny country they had chosen for their retirement or second career or sports fishing vacation.

They thought they had a stake here, even the tourist. Players in the American empire. He knew the feeling. He watched the little fish as if from another dimension. He must have appeared to them to be one of them—businessmen, patriotic Americans, heads of families. But his business was gone, his family was gone. He was a ghost hanging around without quite knowing why.

When the game was over, Hank offered to drive him back to his hotel in San José, but by then Hank was loaded and Cal decided to leave by himself. There had been a time when he would have been glad to die with Hank Pickett, but Hank wasn't that man anymore.

The bartender called a taxi for him—a brother or cousin probably, you couldn't count on getting someone to find his way to the Legion hall this late at night. He sat in the privacy of the back seat. Rain greased the darkness.

They wouldn't invade Nicaragua. He had gotten to know Bush a little while on Mike Cheney's congressional staff, even played doubles with him at Mike's country club a few times after Reagan brought him back to Washington to head the C.I.A. A decent guy, offering Cal fatherly advice on child-rearing, a father with his own disappointments. He wouldn't take on the communists. At the summit he would talk about freedom and democracy. He would make nice with Arias, and under the table he would throw the Contras some bone to keep them fighting what should have been his war, fighting for freedom. Washington insulated you, twisted you around until you couldn't remember why you were there.

Hank Pickett had fought the communists in Nicaragua before anybody had heard of the Sandinistas. But Hank had been in Costa Rica too long now. You had to respect the man he had been, but what made you a man was eroded here, leached out of you like calcium. Until everything collapsed, you loved it, it all seemed to make sense.

There was a bumper sticker plastered to the driver's visor, visible in the lights of the San Rafael strip. ¡VIVA LA PAZ! So Costa Rica had no army—so what? It just meant that they couldn't do their friends any good. They had an army of bureaucrats instead, quietly gnawing the guts out of you. Costa Rica tricked you with the mild climate, investment opportunities, decent standard of living, political stability, then commenced to chewing on you. Even the much-admired climate wasn't all that benign. There were storms that had flattened his greenhouses, ripped off the plastic, destroyed crops with rain that came down like an avalanche. There were avalanches. There were earthquakes. Poas was pumping so much sulfur into the atmosphere, they were getting acid rain on the volcano's slopes—industrial pollution without the industry.

As the taxi approached the Tiribi bridge, its headlights picked up a khaki-uniformed rural guard with a submachine gun slung over his shoulder, an umbrella protecting him from the rain. The guard on the other side was taking advantage of a bus shelter, his back against a post, visored hat pulled over his eyes. He might have been asleep. They both might have been asleep.

It was for the summit of presidents, the driver said to him, the guards, then lapsed back into silence when he didn't respond.

He knew what it was for. For the last few days he had been noticing guards posted at overpasses and bridges. The liberal government was scared to death of the bad press that would result from an act of terrorism. They kept changing plans for a security zone in downtown San José the day of the summit. As it stood now, there was going to be gridlock all around the central sector unless they declared a holiday. They would, of course, declare a holiday. Between the unions and the Catholic church, they had already whittled away three or four work days every month. What difference would one more make?

What difference did anything make? There was an obscure paramilitary organization here, but its idea of action was spray-painting denunciations of the governing Liberation party on the walls of abandoned buildings, and all those had been painted over for the summit. What could you do that would make a difference in a place like this? During the past few years, he had taken risks that were supposed to help the freedom fighters in Nicaragua, but he had been left empty-handed, deprived even of the awkward heft of his business. He thought about the empty bridge, the sleepy men guarding it. He thought about George Bush, his odd backhand.

It was approaching midnight, and not much was going on downtown in the rain. The taxi driver ignored stoplights, though he seemed to be in no hurry. He believed it wasn't necessary to observe them this time of night, Cal thought. Or maybe he really didn't notice them. They had a close call with a pedestrian trying to cross Paseo Colón, but the guy jumped back in time. He called something after them, not especially angry or abusive, just offended that they had not been more considerate.

Had he ever hit anybody? Cal asked the driver.

He was a very good driver, the man said. That guy back there was drunk.

When they got to the hotel, Cal paid the driver what he

asked. He stood under the sheltered entrance and smoked a cigarette, listening to the music whining from the bar next door. The whores that hung around knew by now not to bother him. They were friendly, but they had given up showing the phony interest with which they had once approached him.

"Staying dry?"

It was Arturo Aguilar, the pearly snaps of his shirt tinged red by the neon in the bar's window. Cal hadn't seen him in weeks. This is where they had usually met, though, and he felt no surprise at seeing him here now. Arturo owned a night club, and he had once invited Cal to be his guest there. It turned out to be a strip joint, and he had never gone back. Anyway, Arturo fit in better at this fake American country western bar, in his cowboy boots and jeans and shiny shirt. "Howdy," Cal said.

Arturo smiled his coyote smile. "You're looking very well, my friend."

"I guess I live right."

"Can I buy you a drink?" He gestured toward the bar.

"No thanks."

Arturo cocked his head, pushing that boyish charm at him. "You're living here still? I heard you were moving to another place."

"I'm tired," Cal said, though he wasn't tired at all. The nervous energy circulating beneath Arturo's pale, tight skin jumped between them like static. He didn't want Arturo in his room, there wasn't space enough for him, it had been contracting day by day, the walls had thickened like old adobe. He stared for a moment at the iridescent, mirror-smooth surface of a puddle, then led Arturo to the metal bus stop bench glistening next to the curb.

They sat there as if waiting for a bus, the welded slats of the bench making two cold, wet lines beneath their thighs. There should have been a third slat, but somebody had broken it off to keep people from sleeping there. Arturo made an ambiguous sound. "Your wife and son," he said, "they're okay?"

"They're fine. Thanks."

"Of course."

"I mean about the visas."

"Yet you're still here."

"They'll be fine." There was no life for him anymore in the States. He tried to picture Maureen back in her mother's condo in Orlando, Brian with his long legs thrust out from beneath a school desk, but it was hard, and it was hard to admit to himself that he didn't especially miss them.

"You got something to do here still?"

Cal looked at him. "I'm out of business."

"Yes," Arturo said, "you been set free. There's a story, maybe you heard it. This old dog is walking in the campo, hungry, hunting for a little dinner. He's too slow to catch rats or iguanas no more, and nobody feed him. Suddenly, boom! he step on something and feel a very bad pain in the leg. He look down and see that under the foot he has trapped a terciopelo, what you call fer-de-lance. The snake has bited him, but can no escape from his foot. 'Well,' say the dog, 'at last I get to taste terciopelo. They say is delicious.'"

A bus pulled up to the curb in front of them, splashing a little water from the flooding gutter onto their shoes. The door opened. Arturo waved the driver on, and they watched as it swung ponderously back into traffic and moved away from them. "I have met someone you know," Arturo said. "The wife of your successor in the flower business." Cal nodded, really starting to feel tired now. "You know she's the daughter of our friend Michael Cheney?"

Cal had first seen her years ago, during Mike's congressional run, a sarcastic college freshman. When he had met her this time, she looked as he remembered her—tall and gawky, with lots of black, kinky hair. Nothing like Mike. She had focused on her kids while he and Hoffman talked business.

"Very pretty and intelligent," Arturo said.

At first he had been bitter about Mike's turning the business over to his son-in-law, but with a little distance now, he felt mostly pity. Hoffman's problems were just starting. He stood up, the backs of his trousers pulling away from the wet metal with a queasy tug. "Good night," he said, and headed back toward the hotel.

Arturo was walking beside him, saying nothing, for a change, until they got to the door. "And soon, San José is full of presidents. Your Mr. Bush."

Cal held the door partly open, the stale smell of the lobby slipping past him into the wet brightness of the street.

"An important day," Arturo said. He lightly touched Cal's shoulder, looking up at him. "Really," he said, "you are looking very good."

"We're all pretty in the flower trade."

"Seriously," Arturo said, "I think it's true."

•

Two days before the summit, a forest of trees had appeared in the new Plaza Nacional. Cal walked among them now. Mangos, palms, robles, mimosa, water apple. Big, ten-inch-diameter trees that might have been growing there for years. He knew what had happened, what was going to happen. There was no fuzziness in his thinking, any more than there had been when he first found himself out of business, alone and childless, homeless, hopeless. He had understood everything at that moment—how Maureen had been able to turn her back on him after twenty-seven years of marriage, what a self-centered kid Brian had grown to be. Far from confusion, Cal's state of mind then had been one of intense clarity. And now he could see, as if he had been there, the way the trees' balled roots had been jammed into the brand new, pothole-sized planters. If they had roots at all. If they hadn't just been chopped out of the ground with hoes and machetes and hauled into the city and stuck into the unamended clay beneath the pavement. He saw their future, how they would survive a few weeks, at best, until the dry season arrived, when nobody would water them and what was left of them would die. How trash would collect in the gouged openings.

But what would the visiting journalists and politicians know about that? For them it would be a forest in the city. He walked among the trees and the crowds happy with the coming feriado, the free day when they wouldn't have to go through the motions of work. There were no peddlers. The black market money changers were gone, too, moved away from the plaza so their baying for dollars would be less insistently obvious to the international reporters swarming around the government center.

Within a few blocks of the plaza, he found the dollar buyers, along with people selling flags and balloons and souvenirs from folding tables or hand carts or plastic sheets laid out on the pavement. The merchandise lay there glowing with a strange beauty. He bought a handful of little American flags and a cheap nylon backpack with the Batman logo like a gaping, pointy-toothed mouth. He had lost his hat somewhere, and the sun was giving him a headache, so he turned west to the Mercado Central and wandered for a while in its dark maze. He found himself in the corridor of flower sellers, and bought a red, white, and blue bouquet of chrysanthemums, and held them before him like a torch as he twisted through the gloom.

He stepped out of the enclosed market, let his eyes adjust to the glare of sunlight for a moment, then walked across the street to Soda Cyrano, a little restaurant where he ordered a coffee and examined the flowers. Medium semi-incurve, Icecapade, probably. You could go with Blaze or Festival for the red, but these were dyed. You had to dye for the blue. They didn't look bad. He ordered a casado and ate everything on the plate—fried plantain, black beans, rice, overcooked beefsteak, even the piece of lettuce and crunchy slice of tomato. He didn't know why they didn't raise better tomatoes here. For a time he had toyed with the idea of getting into truck farming, but he was an exporter, he hated the idea of haggling with the local market. He paid, returned to the Plaza Nacional, and walked through the sudden forest, his footsteps as silent on the newly-laid paving bricks as if they were in a carpet of leaf mold, breathless with fertility.

The air throbbed with the rotor beat of helicopters ferrying reporters and security forces from the airport to landing pads on the roof of the Palacio or the Banco Nacional. As always, a heavy-set blind man sat on a bench and played amplified harmonica, keeping time with a stick rubbed against a ribbed club. Cal waited for a path to clear on the sidewalk outside La Gloria, where the tables of lottery ticket vendors half-blocked the way, as always. There had been a time when he hated the lotteries, envisioned himself tipping over their tables like Jesus in the temple, ripping the perforated, metallic printed sheets out of their hands, a time when he saw the wild hope for "el gordo," the fattened Christmas lottery, an even truer expression of what was wrong with the country than the insane, contradictory government regulations that made doing business impossible. Yet now he felt the sweetness of that hope.

By the time he got back to his room, he was exhausted, but he sat there at his little table until the push and blare of evening rush hour swelled in the rainy air outside his open window. Fully clothed, he stretched out on his bed and closed his eyes.

It was dark when he woke. He felt ravenous and was surprised to find that it was barely eight o'clock, he had been asleep for only an hour or two. Leaving everything on his bed, he walked a few blocks to an ASA cafeteria, brightly lit and golden, and ate a basket of fried chicken and French fries. The food was better at the country western bar, but he didn't want to meet Arturo Aguilar again. He had kind of liked Arturo, the way you kind of like a certain cramp in your muscles after strenuous exercise, pain that reveals you to yourself. But he was Hoffman's pain now.

Five years ago, he had thought he had it made. A flower farm in Costa Rica, his place in the empire, his loyalty to Mike

Cheney finally paying off. It wasn't really his, though, and they had used it, but that was all right, that was his soldiering. He hated drugs, hated that that was the weapon they gave him, but he had shouldered it when they said to. He had been a good soldier, and it wasn't his fault that Costa Rica had ruined it all. He wasn't to blame, but he didn't blame Arturo Aguilar, either. He blamed Mike—not that he had used him, but that he had thrown him away afterward, abandoned him in this backwater. This backwater that George Bush was about to visit. President of the United States. Whom he had aced twice in a single game. Who had shaken a fist at him in respect and mock anger.

He wandered down to the Plaza Cultural, bright as day, loud with a marimba band and racing children and the cries of souvenir vendors, tourists crowding in. It was the holiday already, as far as they were concerned. Everyone wanted to be here now, before the barricades went up and police would be everywhere. No one would get close to the presidents tomorrow, it would be all barricades and police downtown.

It was raining a little, but nobody seemed to mind. On a holiday, it didn't count. Well inside the rainy season still, the government had planned the main outdoor ceremonies for mid-afternoon, when you could pretty much count on a downpour. But it didn't *always* rain then, this time of year. Maybe it wouldn't. It was in God's hands.

He returned to his room and gathered his belongings into a single pile on the unmade bed. He put what he needed into the backpack, rearranged the rest into meaninglessly fussy order, and left the room without looking back. Along Avenida 2, police barriers were already stacked on the sidewalk, ready to be dragged across the calles.

There was a long line at the micro station across the avenue from paint-peeling Merced church, two busloads, at least, of people waiting to go to Alajuela. A few, probably, to the airport. He stood there in the darkness as patiently as everybody else.

He bought some potato chips from the powerfully built man who was peddling them, droning "plátanos, papas, helado," over and over. He wished he had something to drink.

By the time two buses had loaded and left, he was first in line as the next one worked its way into the cramped parking lot. He got on and took the aisle seat immediately behind the driver and waited with his things in his lap while the bus filled. He knew that almost every seat would be taken before somebody chose to sit beside him. Their week was over, they were going home to watch some television, put their kids to bed, make love, savor the long weekend, the flash of international attention. What did they have to do with someone like him? He was enormous, he felt he left no room, and was startled when a woman with a gym bag tried to push past his knees to the window seat. He sprang to his feet to let her in. Once they were settled side by side, he apologized for her inconvenience. He was going to get off early, he explained.

She nodded agreeably and averted her face. He looked past her at the oblivious jumble of cars below them as the bus swung out into traffic. He could smell the vague vinegar of her sweat after a day's work. She wasn't much older than Maureen, though probably a grandmother. What would his life have been like if he had been married to a woman like this, homely, content to ride the bus with a gym bag on her lap? Or like Grace Pickett, who stood beside Hank as soldier and soldier? He tried to think of all the marriages he knew anything about, from his parents' and grandparents' to the Hoffmans', and all of them were mysterious. Out of the corner of his eye he studied the woman's profile, rough, but with delicacy in the details of eyebrow, earlobe. He sat there in familiar silence with his momentary Tica wife, their bags resting on their laps as matrimonial as wedding rings, while the bus spiraled through downtown, rolled past the western suburbs, and picked up speed on the Autopista General Cañas toward Aeropuerto Juan Santamaría and Alajuela.

The bus pulled over now and then to let some people off. There were no regular stops, and sometimes he could not even hear anybody call out "¡la parada!" He imagined the passengers had long ago worked it out with the drivers. What he was looking for was the rising wall of lights from Hospital México, a place where he would know exactly where he was, where people must be left off from time to time. When he saw it, he leaned forward and spoke to the driver and stood to get out, but the driver motioned him to his seat again. They turned off the highway and looped down to the circular drive in front of the hospital. The woman smiled sympathetically, a burst of crinkles from the corners of her eyes, and blessed him, sent him off with God.

As he stepped down from the bus, he wondered what they thought, that he was visiting a sick relative, that he was sick himself? There was a generosity in the detour and the woman's stock blessing that moved him, and he found he couldn't take his eyes off the bus until it rose to the highway and passed out of sight.

The hospital stood behind him, vast and inviting, hundreds and hundreds of crisp, perfect beds murmuring, *Rest here. Let us care for you.* Somewhere on the far side of the highway, he knew, was Hotel Irazú, not one of the three judged fit to accommodate presidents, but probably loaded with journalists, functionaries. They hadn't announced where Bush would be staying. The Cariari had the best tennis courts, though, and was close to the airport. He slung the tight straps of the backpack over his shoulders and headed toward the highway.

The sky had cleared, and the darkness was thinned by moonlight and the glow of billboards that staggered up and down the highway connecting San José with the airport. Lights glittered here and there from the invisible bulk of mountains. He didn't want to be on the shoulder. He had seen the jeeps of rural guards weaving through the sparse traffic, and there would be others clustered around the Irazú exit. The coarse grass along the embankment was almost waist high, but he found footpaths worn into it, eroded at times but mostly smooth clay, rain-burnished, weaving along the contours of the land, carved out by the bare feet of camposinos, schoolchildren's shoes, clerks with jobs in San José, cows, goats, dogs. Where there was a half-finished development of some kind, commercial or residential, he could use the graded access roads, but mostly he stuck to the footpaths, which were at a comfortable distance from the highway and offered a sense of privacy. You could disappear into the tall grass if you needed to, and in many places the ditch plants were as tall as he was—elephant ear, queen of the night, wild bamboo, nameless shrubs. He was careful of the places where gray waste water ran in pearly streams. He watched out for cow flop. The air was dense with decay and night-blooming flowers.

In a car or on a bus, you felt that the whole trip out to Juan Santamaría airport was gently uphill, a slow rise to the plain at the edge of the mountain range north of the city. But gravity eased him along, and the ground he walked on gradually lost touch with the soaring highway. Headlights swept along above him in a stream of sound from engines and tires. In the south, above the dark mass of mountains sprinkled with lights, hung a more insistent light, which gradually grew larger, then split in two, until finally the plane took shape and sound and crossed the air ahead of him with a roar and disappeared again toward the airport to the north. In the south, another light grew visible.

As he walked, stumbling now and then but mostly making his way easily in the darkness, the salt of the potato chips scratched at his hunger. Thirst clotted his mouth and throat, and from time to time he squeegeed moisture off a broad, glistening leaf and sucked it from the blade of his hand. Sometimes there were houses and shops only a few hundred yards from where he walked, and he thought about leaving the ditch and climbing up to them, where he could find a pulpería or a soda still open for business, buy a box of juice or a bottle of water. He dried his damp hand on his trousers and flung his attention ahead of him as far as he could, set it like an anchor, hauled himself forward.

From Hospital México, it was about three miles to the Cariari. Halfway there, houses and the occasional street light fell away from the highway and the ground started to drop, losing the path in gullies and undergrowth. Now and then plastic bags of trash pushed at his ankles like bodies. He stopped and looked ahead at the bridge carrying traffic like tracer bullets into the night. Before him somewhere, invisible in the darkness, flowed the Rio Virilla. For five years he had crossed it several times a week carrying shipments of flowers or trying to retrieve lost packages, yet he hadn't been conscious that there was a river below, or that the bridge even *was* a bridge and not just another section of the highway, until he had driven the Hoffmans in from the airport and Ted had asked the name of the river. He hadn't known. A week later Ted told him, Rio Virilla. He had found it on a topographical map. And the river in the really dramatic gorge you crossed between Escazú and San José, by the dizzying old single lane bridge or the less interesting autopista bridge, that was the Tiribi.

Who the hell cares? he remembered thinking, choked with the bitterness of loss still rising around him. But now he was glad to know the name. Rio Virilla.

He kept moving down. The path didn't disappear, only became wily, dodging left and right to get down the increasingly steep slope. The highway, a sharper darkness overhead, grew remote. The lights that swept over it blurred the edges for a few seconds like a finger smudging glass. The hum of tires swelled and receded. He slipped, even the child's backpack unbalancing him, caught himself on invisible branches, slipped again, worked his way downward toward the water he could smell now, rank and soapy, but still couldn't see.

Breathless and wet with rain shaken from the trees and underbrush, he reached the muddy bank of the river. It was little more than a stream here, pushing against old concrete piers, gurgling through a mass of limbs and rubbish entangled in a wire fence. He felt the darkness pushing in on him. He was trembling with fatigue and hunger, his legs watery. It was time to stop.

He shrugged the backpack off his shoulders, bringing the straps away from his damp armpits, and felt the cool air on his back. He stood there with the straps hooked in the crooks of his elbows as if somebody were holding him from behind.

Deeper in the blackness underneath the bridge there was a shape that had nothing to do with the massive concrete columns that supported the bridge. He approached it, reached out his hand, and felt the fluted coolness of corrugated tin. It was a little shack, no bigger than a child's playhouse, three sides and a roof wired together with what might have been coat hangers, furred with rust. He let the backpack fall to the ground and squatted at the opening. After a moment, he crawled inside. There were some wooden pallets, two of them filling half the space. He lay down on the rough-sawn wood.

•

HE WOKE STIFF AND COLD, back aching, his damp clothes plastered to him, and a ripe, coppery smell wrapped around him. A clatter of parakeets swooped in a tight flock toward the surface of the river, then up again, their cries constant and mechanical. Looking out into the foggy half-light, he could see the scorched spot where there had been fires, and another sheet of corrugated tin, impatiens blossoming gaudily through the rust, which could be pulled up to close the opening of the makeshift shelter. Although he had hated the fuss and inconvenience, he had taken Brian on camping trips, once in the Ozarks and several times in the Indiana Dunes, and he remembered waking like this, sore, fog hanging in the cool stillness, Brian balled up in a sleeping bag beside him.

He had lost him to Costa Rica, as he had lost everything else. After their move down here they had clung to each other at first, the three of them, they had never been closer. But even while the isolation of language and foreignness held them most tightly, something had begun to tap at them, working on their hearts like a little hammer. If the boy had been sucked into the sea by the riptides at Manuel Antonio, he would not have been more hopelessly lost. If Maureen had been kidnapped and murdered. If an earthquake had shaken his farm off the mountain in a single huge shrug. He sat up, his stiff, greasy hair touching the metal roof, and looked at the river flowing a few yards away. Everything meaningful to him.

Though the sun had not risen yet, there was already a little traffic on the highway overhead. If he wanted, he could make it to the Cariari by breakfast time, have a nice slice of melon, some ham and eggs, coffee. They knew him, it wouldn't be a problem. He had played tennis there with the realtors. As his life was dismantled during the past three months, taken away piece by piece, his game had improved radically, he had never played so well in his life. Bush would be at the Cariari, he understood now—that was the message of those leaping kick serves, those crosscourt winners.

He walked to the river's edge and scooped up a handful of water. It ran clear and cold now. He stripped, stepped in, squatted carefully, and washed himself. Then he stood, naked, dripping, the water flowing around his calves, and studied the river. It wasn't going to be that hard to get across. A little ways downstream, the river was broken into manageable pieces by boulders and eroded chunks of concrete impaled with rusty reinforcing rod. He went back and retrieved the backpack, slipped its straps over his shoulders, gathered up his clothes and shoes, and started across, stepping from stone to stone, sometimes having to wade a little through thigh-deep water, but never having to backtrack.

On the other side he dried himself, put on his trousers and shoes and a clean shirt from the backpack, and found a path zigzagging up the heavily overgrown slope. From where the ground leveled out again, he could see rural guard jeeps parked at either end of the long, flat highway bridge, armed policemen standing around them looking sleepy and bored. He left the cover of riverbank trees and walked along a freshly scraped dirt road that ran parallel with the highway. A new housing development was going up here, lines of cement boxes awaiting roofs and doors, one of the hundreds of dreary urbanizaciones going up in Arias's last year of office, each already carrying his administration's boastful metal plaques.

In the distance beyond the new development there was a smaller bridge humped over the highway. He could see a jeep parked on the south approach to the overpass, and khaki-uniformed guards on either side of the highway beneath it.

It was a cloudless morning, the lines of green mountains to the north and south cut against the blue sky, the air sweet and cool. He walked a little farther down the dirt road, then away from the highway where a cluster of older houses met the new development. Two girls were hanging laundry on wires stretched between their house and a gnarled, half-dead mango tree, one of them teasing the other about something. A shirtless old man in a baseball cap sat in a lawn chair just inside an open garage and watched him approach. Otherwise, no one seemed to be out. When he reached the yard, the girls grew quiet. He greeted them and the old man. The old man wished him a very good morning.

Cal gestured toward the overpass. Was that the road to Heredia? he asked. Was that where it led?

The old man spat in disgust. The bridge over the highway was closed, he said. It was because of the presidents. The police wanted everybody to sit in their houses and watch television until the presidents were gone.

He was a nice, talkative old man, happy to have somebody to listen to him. He asked if he could get anything for him. A glass of water, if that would be possible, Cal said. The old man called out to one of the girls and ordered her to bring out a glass of water. The other girl pulled a dark leather folding chair from the back of the garage and set it up for him, then disappeared into the house with the first girl after she had brought out a glass of water.

The old man didn't even ask him where he was from, just launched into a denunciation of the government for interfering with the comings and goings of ordinary citizens. Cal sat there and let him rail on, a banana worker in the old days, a union man with nothing good to say about either of the major parties. He was a communist, a part of Cal's mind abstractly registered, though of the typical Costa Rican stripe, with little sympathy for the Sandinistas, either, nobody pure enough for him, comfortable in his discontent and powerlessness.

A helicopter throbbed overhead. Cal drank the glass of water, let the old man go on, and watched the bridge over the highway. Nobody came or went on it, cars or pedestrians, police or civilians. When it was time, he wiped the bottom of the sweating glass on his shirt sleeve, set the glass on the immaculate, red-waxed concrete garage floor, thanked him for his hospitality, slung the backpack over one shoulder, and left, not looking back when the old man offered to explain the quickest way to get to Heredia.

At the end of the long block there was a field with soccer goals, then what seemed to be a school—low, tin-roofed stucco buildings with covered walkways connecting them. No children were around, it was too early, and it was a holiday. Before long, boys and young men would be playing pickup games on the weedy field. Beyond the school there was a pulpería that probably did a good business selling junk to the schoolchildren, then the road that rose abruptly to cross the highway. Wooden barricades blocked the road before the overpass, and the jeep was still there, but no guards were visible. They were either napping in the jeep or socializing with the guards posted beneath the overpass or farther along the highway.

When a woman came out of the pulpería to sweep the sidewalk in front of it, he was already walking toward the barricade. He passed the jeep without looking in, skirted the barricades, and headed up the steep incline of the overpass. Somebody called for him to stop, one of the rural guards running toward him along the highway. Another voice shouted a question from beneath the overpass. He kept on, reached the middle of the overpass and stopped, looking west down the straight expanse of highway. A few cars swept along it, disappeared beneath him. In the distance, a caravan of three black limousines, tiny flags winking on their fenders, sailed toward him. He grasped the straps of the backpack and fumbled with the zipper. A helicopter soared straight down the highway, lower than the others he had been seeing, as if it were towing the limousines on an invisible wire.

A khaki uniformed guard was on the end of the overpass, then another. They were shouting something, running toward him. Their automatic weapons waved comically in his direction. The backpack's zipper stuck, tangled in the untaped threads of the seam, then let go. He reached into the bag, had to use both hands to fumble through the twisted contents. There was a thick popping sound, not from the ends of the overpass but from the highway beneath it, where a guard was running away from the overpass, pausing and turning now and then, trying to get a better angle.

The helicopter was above him and then gone, its string of funereal automobiles approaching him. He got the crunched flowers out, reached for the flags, and felt the sticks and stems explode out of his fingers. He dropped the empty little backpack into the air rushing ahead of the cars, rushing beneath him, felt the air around him suddenly excited and feverish, a blow to his thigh, his shoulder. A warm, rich taste in his mouth.

CHAPTER SIX

PAVO DAY WITH THE PICKETTS

It was late November when they became lovers, nearly the beginning of the dry season. Their timing was awful. The children's school year was ending, eliminating the reliably free mornings they had squandered for weeks in coffee shops and restaurants and long drives. Stephen was out at the Picketts' finca some days, and Ted was working regular hours now, really running the flower farm, but Valerie, without preschool, was relentless.

"I have to get away sometimes," Monica told Ted, and he managed to be home a morning or afternoon a week or took Valerie and sometimes Stephen out to the farm, and she would catch the bus into San José and meet Arturo for an hour or two and then fly out of there, spinning with lies. The first time, they had gone to a hotel, but later he had suggested the apartment of a friend who was out of the country.

The apartment was a nice, neutral place, clean, with a sky-light that leaked in the increasingly rare rains but otherwise flooded the living room and convertible couch with fierce sun-light. They were always rushed, hurling themselves into each other, and the brilliance of the room helped drive off the sense of doom she brought with her like another child. That the imperfections of her body were unambiguously illuminated here somehow helped, any honesty helped, and the shock of his hard, pale body against her dark skin, tanned from hours watching Valerie beside the pool of a little country club they visited as Pepe and Eva's guests or the fancy one Arturo took them to sometimes, was complete each time. She never closed her eyes, and afterward she often had deep, pulsing headaches from the glare as she would leap back toward her certified life, crash through a mirrored surface into obligation and family rituals.

Rituals such as celebrating Thanksgiving Day with friends. The Picketts had invited the whole family to come out for dinner, the first time any of them except Stephen had been there. On the drive to the Picketts' finca, Stephen was not much help in finding the way. Now and then he would say things like, "I remember a weird tree like that," or, "That wall doesn't seem right," or, "Have we gone over a bridge that rattles?" After twenty minutes, he was convinced that Ted had gotten them lost, and Monica worried that his squirming, heavy-breathing disgust and panic was going to push Ted over the edge. "Shh," she said, swiveling around in her seat, "just let Dad drive, we've got plenty of time," then had to quickly reach forward to keep the bunch of calla lilies propped between her feet from toppling over.

So far, Ted seemed to be doing all right. When Valerie screamed and leaped out of her seat and tried to twist his head to the side to see cows grazing in somebody's front yard, he just asked her if she thought that that would work on their lawn in Cincinnati. Monica kept waiting for the thrust of irony, hoping they would get through the day without it. She felt tender and protective these days, of Ted as much as of the children. The shock of Cal Richardson's strange death had left him moody and preoccupied. Distant. She treasured the distance now, though it also scared her.

Two policemen had come to their apartment the day after the presidential summit, looking for Ted. While Monica tried to keep the kids entertained with Monopoly in their bedroom, the police had questioned Ted about Richardson—an awkward business, between their incomprehensible English and his limited Spanish. Finally he had come and asked her to help, and she had left the kids in the bedroom, where they probably flattened themselves immediately against the door, trying to listen in.

Even she had had a difficult time explaining Ted's business relationship with Richardson. The police wouldn't say what had happened to him, only kept asking questions about him that Ted couldn't answer, and they seemed dissatisfied with what he did know, or with her translations. One of them kept trying to put the questions directly to Ted in English. The policemen were confused about Richardson's family, insisting that they were still in the country, Migración had no record of their exit visas having been processed. This lapse didn't surprise him, Ted had told her to say, nor would it surprise anyone who had had dealings with those idiots, but they had pressed him on it repeatedly until finally giving up and leaving.

Wondering what was going on and worried about Richardson's troubles screwing up their own, already-problematic visa status, they had considered speaking to a lawyer, but the one Ted had hired for the business didn't seem especially competent, and they didn't know anyone else they trusted. They had been treated dismissively at the U.S. embassy when they first arrived in Costa Rica, and they didn't want to make anything worse, for themselves or Richardson's family, either. A week later, a little article had appeared in the English language *Tico Times*, vague and untitillating in the middle of presidential summit excitement, reporting Richardson's having been accidentally killed after blundering into a security zone.

Throughout the questioning and the days afterward, a part of her had remained aloof from Ted, stiffened against him despite their mutual sense of emergency, their shared, anxious curiosity. She had sensed, almost physically smelled, something that made her want to hold him at arm's length. Later, she decided that what she had bristled at was the metallic stink of betrayal welling up in her own pores.

"What's the big deal?" Stephen said. "I've seen that many cows going right past our house."

"Not our real house."

"Our house *here*, stupid."

"That's enough!" she shouted. Lately, when Ted was quiet like this, she found herself taking on his touchiness as if it were a chore somebody would suffer for if it were neglected. As somebody would. As all of them had. He had accused her in the past of being oblivious to his emotional weather, but she never was that, only unwilling sometimes to expose herself to it. Now she watched out for it, more attentive even than during the terrible days when his affair was uncoiling itself before her eyes. She felt unfairly responsible for him, she had told Arturo, as if for somebody else's unwanted, destructive child.

She should do as the tortuga does, he had answered, who lays her eggs in the sand and then returns to the open sea, leaving the destiny of each to fate. "Is not possible for her to look back," he said. "Her life is in the blue ocean." Monica had stared at him, and he had added that it was metaphorical, of course. He wasn't talking about her leaving her kids.

Where was her life now? she wondered. She looked at Valerie and then Stephen, the space between them electric with resentment. "It's Thanksgiving," she said. "Let's see a little thankfulness. What're you guys thankful for?"

"Tío Arturo," Valerie said without hesitation, "and that I get to go to school, and orejas," a cinnamon pastry they got from their local panadería.

Stephen snorted. "School's over. And you're not in real school."

"All right," Monica said, "how about you, smart guy?"

"I don't know. Nothing." He met her disappointed smile defiantly. "What? I have to share my room with her, we can't make noise because of Pepe and Eva, the party guys' cigarettes are going to burn us all up, we got no tv, this crappy old car."

"How about Ray?" Ted asked, finally getting into it.

He was silent for a moment. "Okay, sure, Ray. Him and his family, they're about the only thing good about Costa Rica."

"Right. Let's forget beaches, oceans, mountains, rainforests. Democracy, peace, education." Without taking his eyes off the road, Ted recited the country's virtues. "Health care." He touched them like beads on a rosary.

"But Ray is special," Monica said, "you're right. We're all lucky you met him, Stephen. Otherwise, where would we go for turkey day? ¡Feliz día del pavo!"

"If we ever get there," Stephen said. "And, listen, I mean it, don't make fun of President Bush, okay? They like him. Ronald Reagan, either. Plus, they believe in God. They pray." He had been warning them about this for days.

"We'll try not to embarrass you," Monica said.

"I just hope *she* doesn't mess everything up."

"I think you'd better relax, buddy," Ted told him. He only called Stephen "buddy" when he was starting to lose patience with him. "Buddy" or "pal," his father's terms, she suspected.

"Mess what up?" Valerie asked.

"Nothing, sweetheart," she said. "We're all going to be on our best behavior."

The car wouldn't make it up the last, steep stretch of road, so they had to pull over and park on the narrow shoulder and hike up the rest of the way on the ribbed concrete tracks. Ted carried the armload of flowers. White calla lilies didn't say "Thanksgiving" to Monica, but they were one of his financial successes, and he was proud of them, even though they hadn't grown on his farm. When they came to the gate, Valerie slipped easily between the wire strands of the fence while Stephen wrestled the gate open far enough for his parents to squeeze through.

Barking broke out from near the house, and Stephen drew back behind Monica, but Ray ran down and assured them that the dogs were locked up. He and Stephen raced uphill, overtaking and passing Valerie, who cried out in anger or delight, flew after them like vengeance.

Grace Pickett met Ted and Monica on the front veranda of the big, Moorish-looking house and embraced them as old friends, though they had only met her a few times, when she brought Stephen back or picked up Ray at their apartment. She was that tanned, steely sort of southern woman, her dress elegant, her makeup and blond hair perfect. Ted presented her with the great bundle of flowers, and she oohed appropriately.

She apologized for the closed gate and their hike up the steep road. "One of our muchachos was supposed to be waiting for you all with the truck at the bottom of that bad stretch," she said. "Lord knows what he's found to do instead. I wonder why I even bother giving them orders. Why not just let them go ahead and do what they feel like?" She looked around. "And where'd that little angel disappear to in that pretty dress? Ray!" she shouted. "Get back here with those children!" Then, to Monica and Ted, "He talks of nothing but Stephen, Stephen, Stephen. He's got a million plans. I don't think he knows how to treat a little girl, though. His sister just bosses him. She's out with one of her beaus at the moment, looking at a horse. Ray! Get back here!"

"This is a beautiful house," Monica said.

"It has required a ruthless hand to get it into shape, let me tell you. An Iranian built it"—her voice dropped—"on drug money, so they say, and we got it for a song when he had to leave the country in a hurry. The things he'd done to the place!"

They went inside, and Grace went to find a vase big enough for the flowers. In the two-story atrium was the waterfall that Stephen had talked about so incredulously, a stream of water dropping along a wall of rounded stones. There was a colorful tile floor, the exposed massive beams of dark wood that was apparently a standard component of Costa Rican upper class architecture, high arched windows. The house was more vertical than Bernardo's family's, but like that house, the arrangement of space here didn't make any sense to Monica, who thought in terms of rooms for this or that purpose. She supposed it was for parties, receptions. She rarely entertained. Furnished with heavy, rococo furniture and Persian rugs, the place felt like a museum.

But the kitchen at the back where Grace led them was wonderful, with huge black ovens, polished counter tops, walls of white-painted cabinets, deep sinks. She could be a real cook here, she suddenly thought. Ordinarily a casual and unimaginative cook, she would be able to perform miracles of food preparation here. For the first time in her life, she felt the sting of house envy. Kitchen envy, anyway.

"It's my pride and joy," Grace said. The room was crowded with the aroma of roasting turkey, lardy pies, coffee streaming in a thin black line from a bolsa into a chrome thermos pot. Monica listened to Grace's detailed account of the kitchen remodeling that they had undertaken as soon as they bought the house, and kept expecting to see a maid. Stephen had given the impression that they had several of them. But none appeared.

A teenage girl, Charlotte, burst into the kitchen from the back door, ecstatic about a stallion she and Rodolfo had been to see, so focused on getting her parents to buy it for her that she scarcely noticed Ted and Monica. She went upstairs to change. Rodolfo came in and was introduced. He was a shy, handsome boy with curly black hair. When he shook her hand, Monica felt a contraction of breathlessness. His startling black eyes, hooded and unblinking, a face already carved into adult leanness. He might have been Arturo's younger brother. Curved, thin nose, pale skin. He might have been his son.

He couldn't stay for dinner, he announced regretfully, though Grace pressed him to. When he had gone, Grace told

Ted and Monica that he was the most promising of Charlotte's boyfriends. He came from an excellent family. Grace hoped nothing too serious would develop, though. She wanted Charlotte to get an education, learn a profession. That wouldn't happen here, she said, if she married young. She didn't seem very worried about it. Monica nodded stupidly, still feeling the heat of the boy's thin hand pressed into her palm. She wrapped an arm around Ted's waist and ignored his surprised look.

Out back, the dogs were barking again. Charlotte charged downstairs and raced through the kitchen, still in jeans and fringed white shirt, and burst out the back door. Grace and Ted and Monica followed her out. They could hear her screaming at Ray. They reached the patio behind the house overlooking a barn and corral in time to see her catch the halter of a palomino that was prancing and bucking in the middle of the corral, Ray clinging to its neck. When she had calmed the horse down a little, she grabbed for her brother's leg, but he slid off the other side and ran for it. Just outside the corral, Valerie sat on the back of a pony that was sleepily nuzzling a tuft of weeds, and Stephen stood holding the reins of a large white horse. He was watching Charlotte and the excited palomino in stiff horror.

Ray ran up the hill to his mother and was well into his defense argument before Charlotte could catch up with him. "It's that she's going to get a new horse," he explained. "So won't Goldie be mine, then?"

Grace kept Charlotte from grabbing him. "If I'm not mortified!" she exclaimed. "Both of you, get back down there and take care of your guests." She watched as the two of them scrambled back down the hill to the corral. Charlotte slapped at the back of Ray's neck a few times, but then she helped him and Stephen get up onto the white horse, settled Valerie more squarely in the pony's saddle, swung herself up onto the palomino's bare back, and led the others further down the long slope of mountainside.

Ted stared at them as if he couldn't believe it, as if his

children had been transfigured before his eyes. It was Stephen, Monica knew—they had never been able to get him onto even the dullest petting zoo pony, a great frustration to Ted, who apparently had ridden all the time during childhood summers on his grandfather's farm. When Grace headed back to the house, Ted stayed outside. Monica wanted to say something to him, but he was walking down the hill, trying to keep the children in sight. She prayed that he wouldn't ruin it somehow.

In the kitchen, Grace poured her a glass of wine, and she tied on a ruffled apron that Grace finally had handed her after she had insisted on helping. It made her nervous seeing Grace hustle around while she just stood there. Grace assigned her the whipping of mashed potatoes, and she stood there, watching the big KitchenAid stand mixer churn away over the slowly rotating stainless steel bowl. Now and then she poured in a little milk.

"I'm between maids *again*," Grace explained while replenishing her wine glass. Grace was drinking bourbon. "Man trouble, as usual, pigheaded husband too proud to have his woman work for us. He had some kind of a run-in with Hank. Just at the worst time, you can count on it. Holiday season."

"Where is Hank?" Monica had only met him one time, and he had been rushing, had barely stopped long enough to let Ray jump into the truck, though then he had gotten out and shaken her hand and thanked her for taking care of his son. He was a big man, at least twenty-five years older than Grace, she thought, a patriarch with white hair and full, mask-like beard. She had surprised herself a little with a flash of curiosity about what sex would be like with a man that age. She didn't think of herself as someone who thought about that sort of thing.

"He had to pick up some papers from our abogada," Grace said. "She promised by now we'd know about our Panama bank accounts. Fat chance. But he has to keep things stirred up or there'll be absolutely no hope. I'd like to twist that ugly rat Noriega till he can't even squeak."

Monica laughed.

"I mean it," Grace declared, though she laughed, too. "Hank can't even go into the country anymore, he'd get himself arrested. I'm serious, Noriega's declared him persona non grata. We think he might have thrown our Panamanian lawyer into jail. Or else *he's* got our money." She slid a pie, then two more, out of an oven and placed them on wooden racks. She checked the turkey, cut up vegetables, opened cans of jellied cranberries.

Monica stood there watching the mixer and wondered if the potatoes were smooth enough. She added a little more milk, then realized that it was too much, they were turning soupy. She wondered if you could add something, flour or something. Maybe they could be cooked down some more. She switched the mixer off.

Grace didn't seem to notice the potatoes dripping from the chrome beaters. She said, "Ray tells me you've managed to get yourself a phone?"

"Strange but true."

"Well, congratulations! Our poor old notice is still weathering on the wall. Six months since they assured me it was all taken care of. The time and money we've wasted!"

"I can hardly believe it myself," Monica told her. "We were getting nowhere, then this man shows up at our door, says he's leaving the country and do we want to buy his number?" She didn't want to tell Grace how much they had paid the guy for it, five hundred dollars American, plus around a thousand colones to ICE for the actual connection. The Escazú exchange was in heavy demand, and they thought they would be able to sell the number again if they needed to, but it had cut deeply into their budget, and Ted worried that a new exchange would be opened. He had heard rumors that there were plenty of numbers, only caught up in a bureaucratic logjam or corruption or technical confusion. It drove him crazy, the randomness and uncertainty of what should have been simple, obvious. And he didn't trust the seller, whose business card read "Creative Ventures," with offices in Tegucigalpa and Washington D.C., which sounded to him like the C.I.A. They had done it, though, and the phone worked, and now their landlord was saying he wanted to buy the number from them if they ever moved to a different exchange. Pepe and Eva were also interested. "It's what *I'm* thankful for," she said.

"I guess so! We've done everything, but this administration has it in for us, they won't give us squat. ICE claims they need to string new wire up the mountain to us. There's wires already! You can see them." She carried a stack of delicately painted plates out to the big dining room table. "Damn that man. And damn María for letting him push her around."

"My family had a maid for a while," Monica said, following Grace out of the kitchen. "Housekeeper, anyway, that's what we called her. Mrs. Lamke. She cooked, cleaned." She fell silent, wondering why she was telling Grace this, a woman she scarcely knew. She had always been embarrassed by that period of her life, when they lived in Georgetown, her father a rising though already middle-aged congressman, herself wildly unhappy about just about everything.

"Well, maids here are something else, I can tell you," Grace said. "I've been through six of them since we moved into this house, and they all have some *issue*. Zamira's the only one who's stuck with me, and she's so moody, I never know what to expect."

"This is the one with the husband?"

"That was María. Zamira's ill, otherwise she'd be here. If you're smart, honey, you'll stick with Nicaraguans, they appreciate what you're doing for them. Our muchachos are all Nicaraguan. Jorge, *he's* a gem."

Monica was about to explain how far they were from being able to afford hired help, much less needing it—muchacho, peon, empleada, servant, maid, whatever she had heard them called—when there was the bang of the front door being pushed open, and men's voices.

"There's Hank," Grace said, and pulled the turkey from an oven and wiped her hands on a towel and headed into the dining room to meet him. Monica followed, sheepishly glad that she, too, wore a cook's apron, however little she had earned it. Grace kissed Hank, stroked his smooth pink cheeks. He had shaved off his beard. Monica hung back and saw Ted in the doorway. They avoided each other's eyes at first, then she asked Ted how the kids were doing.

"Fine," he said. "You wouldn't believe it, Stephen's really riding, he almost seems to be enjoying it."

There was something irritating about Ted's amazement, but she knew what he meant. It *was* amazing, and she was grateful that things were going well. Still, she felt she needed to protect Stephen's happiness, maybe because she needed to protect her own. She went forward to shake Hank's hand and was caught up in his gruff, fatherly embrace. His massive body was solid and comforting.

"Miss Monica," he said, releasing her, noting the apron, "I hope my wife has not forced you into service!"

"I've just been ruining the potatoes." She found herself staring at his smooth-shaved face. He looked so different. Not just younger, but more focused, more present. She felt a blush rise up her throat, and she felt Ted watching her. Was this what it had been like for him, when he had first crossed the threshold of his affair, sex vibrating in the least expected frequencies? Had her gaze felt like this to him, sad and dangerous?

"I told the kids they should come back to the house," he said. "Did you know they mined gold around here? Hank says they still could." His maternal grandfather had been a lawyer in Colorado during the height of the mining boom, and once he had taken Ted to see an abandoned mine. Ted always spoke of it as if it were some glowing family heritage rather than a played-out hole in a mountainside, worthless payment for futile legal services.

"If they'd let me use cyanide," Hank said. "Any other way, it wouldn't pay."

Ray and Stephen came racing into the house. Charlotte followed a few minutes later, with Valerie.

They all sat down at the enormous dining room table. Hank offered up a long table prayer, mentioning everybody by name, and Stephen surprised her by joining the chorus of amens at the end of it.

"Cyanide," Monica said, as they settled into the meal. "I was reading about mining in the Osa—"

"My manager mined there," Ted said. "You can't imagine what they go through to satisfy the regulations."

"Dad—" Stephen probably hadn't been following the conversation, but he had caught the note of combativeness in Ted's voice and assumed the worst.

"Daddy's agreeing with Hank," Monica said. "Relax." She herself felt anything but relaxed. "So, how's business?" Grace asked, and Monica focused on the conversation of the children as Ted launched into an account of the ups and downs of the flower trade. She had it by heart—the sudden mysterious openhandedness of Customs, the experiments with exotics. Import duties. GATT talks. The gamble with local sales for Día del Muerte, when sellers of flowers lined the sidewalks of the great cemeteries, when it had poured all day, yet he had done all right.

Charlotte asked Stephen if he had gotten to the embassy to see George Bush during the cumbre, and he shook his head. Monica set her fork down on her plate, looking to steer them past the wreckage of that day. They had said as little as possible about any of it, but Stephen knew that policemen had come to talk with his father, he had had to be told the gist of it. She didn't know how much the Picketts knew. Hank was Cal Richardson's friend, she remembered Stephen saying. She wanted to talk with them about it, but not in front of the kids.

"We couldn't face those crowds at the Ambassador's place," she said to Charlotte. "How about you guys?"

"Mom went. She's chairman of Republicans abroad. I went to the beach with some kids I know. Herradura? It's nice, but sort of boring."

Stephen said that *they* had been to Herradura once, and Ray insisted that the best beach was at Jacó, and Valerie claimed that she knew how to swim now. Stephen snorted. Ray launched into a plan he had to get a boogie board for him and Stephen to use whenever they went to the beach together.

Monica was starting to feel safe, and then Hank's drawl rolled across the table to her. "Cal was a good old boy," he was saying.

"I've been thinking he must have gone crazy," Ted said.

Monica asked him to pass her the gravy and gave him a look.

"He was not crazy, I assure you," Hank said, "though what they put him through would have been enough to drive a man insane. They've been easier on you."

Grace looked at Monica and then said to her husband, "Darling, we require more white meat."

As he carved, Charlotte told them about the horse she had been to see with Rodolfo. He was a little expensive, she admitted, but she was certain that they could make it all back in stud fees. Or they could buy a few more mares, she knew somebody who was interested in selling some, and they could start their own line.

To Monica it sounded like what a horse-mad teenage girl could be expected to dream up, but Hank listened to her, asked serious questions, and promised to go with her to negotiate with the stallion's owner. Monica felt a stab of envy. Her own father had never listened to her with such attention, ever. Even now that she was a mother herself and had given him the grandchildren he expected, he seemed to hold her opinions in as little regard as he had when she was a girl. She looked over at Stephen, sitting proud and happily agitated beside Ray, and felt that she was beginning to understand what the Picketts meant to him.

The conversation turned back to the summit that had dominated the country's news for the past month, a circus starring George Bush and Daniel Ortega, Barco of Columbia crippled by the drug traffic in his country, Argentina's old soccer star, Carlos Menem, Menem's glamorous daughter. Monica was relieved to discover that she and Ted agreed with the Picketts about some things—that the summit was ceremonial, that the real decisions were worked out long before any of the presidents arrived in Costa Rica, that it was a good thing for Costa Rica to be thrust even briefly onto the international stage.

Neither Hank nor Grace seemed to be the rabid right-winger she had come expecting. They talked about schools and business and real estate, the bad situation in Panama, the horrible Noriega, their plans for the finca. Monica dutifully delivered her account of the comparative literature dissertation she had been working on since before Stephen was born, and admitted that by "working on it" she meant hauling her box of notes and drafts along when they moved. They talked about the Hoffmans' home in Cincinnati, and about Houston, where the Picketts were originally from, before they had moved to Nicaragua. Charlotte had just been born when they left the U.S. Ray was born in Costa Rica.

"Why'd you move?" Ted asked. "From Texas."

Hank cocked his big, florid face at the drumstick he was dissecting with the tip of the carving knife, separating the meat from the thin quills of bone. He exchanged a glance with Grace. "That," he said finally, "is a long story. Let us just say there was a difference of opinion between ourselves and the Internal Revenue Service."

"Hank was on the verge of doing harm to one of those fellas," Grace said. "I had to remove him from the aggravation, for the aggravation was not about to remove itself from him."

"How long were you in Nicaragua, then?" Monica asked.

"We bought a finca in seventy-two," Grace said. "It was paradise, I've never been happier. We owned a whole mountain, and a beautiful valley."

"Nicaragua was a great country in those days," Hank said. He laid the knife down and rested his meaty hands on either side of his plate. He and Grace looked at each other. "A great place to raise kids. Everybody was happy."

"We grew coffee, planted fruit trees," Grace said. "Charlotte helped me with the garden and the chickens. You remember those banties, sweetheart?" For a second she shifted her gaze to her daughter, who nodded vaguely, then locked it again into Hank's blue eyes. "I never worried about anything, even when he had to be away for days at a time," she said. "Everybody loved us, they looked out for us."

"Everybody was happy in Nicaragua," Hank said, "until the communists ruined it. Somoza was like a brother to me. A great and generous man. Tachito. Remember tío Tachito, honey?" he asked Charlotte. Monica studied the girl's face. She didn't think she remembered him. "We played golf, fished marlin and barracuda. I was with him once when he caught a twenty-foot freshwater shark in Lake Managua. Everybody was happy, before the communists."

"They turned the peons against us," Grace said. She looked at Monica, then Ted. "They turned squatters onto our land, set fires. A man who'd been our friend told me they were going to beat up Hank the next time he came to the village."

"They tried," Hank said. "I rode into town the same afternoon I heard about it. There were four of them. They didn't try it again."

"Daddy shot three of them!" Ray said.

Monica looked at Stephen, who seemed about ready to leap out of his skin. She said, "Why don't we have dessert so the kids can go run around outside?"

"Of course," Grace said, "the darlings have been so patient." She and Monica cleared the table and brought in the pies and whipped cream, and milk for the kids, and coffee.

When the children were gone, Grace suggested that they take their coffee into the living room, but Ted leaned forward and asked, "Did you really shoot those guys?"

"I had to," Hank said. "It was self-defense. And if I'd nailed the fourth bastard, excuse my French, it would have saved us a lot of trouble later on."

Grace said, "Things were quiet for a while, I thought it was going to be all right. Then the communists came back. They were starting to call themselves Sandinistas then, but they were the same bunch of thugs. They wanted our land."

"I killed nineteen men before it was over," Hank said, so quietly and calmly that Monica wondered if she had misunderstood him. "Had to."

Ted let out a breath that he must have been holding for a long time. "Jesus." Monica knew that he was trying to envision it, trying to imagine how it had been. She wanted to blank it all out.

"You know what they called him?" Grace asked. "El oso de la montaña. The bear of the mountain."

"Wasn't much of a mountain really," Hank said. "But that was the lowlands, any little hill they called a mountain. Nineteen of the bastards," he mused, not apologizing for his French this time. "They just kept coming for me, and our friends in Managua had their hands full, they couldn't help us anymore. I'd begun working with the C.I.A., but it was too late. Son of a bitch Carter. Nineteen seventy-eight, seventy-nine, it was all over. We got out with the shirts on our back."

"How I miss it," Grace said. "Costa Rica's been good for us, but it can never be the same, you know what I'm saying? The Ticos were taken in by the Sandinistas for a while, too. Then they wised up, but it was too late."

"It was too late," Hank said. He poured himself another scotch from the cut glass decanter Grace had brought to the table. He didn't seem drunk, but Monica noticed Ted watching him. She wished she herself hadn't declined the offer of an after-dinner drink, for the coffee was eroding the little buzz she had gotten from the dinner wine.

It was good coffee, at least. Arturo had explained to her the difference between what was harvested for export and what was sold domestically, and she sometimes thought she had learned to distinguish them. Once or twice a week they had gone to cafés in San José or little restaurants in the mountains while

Valerie was at preschool. The thought of her daughter enjoying the playground equipment had dimmed her guilt. Then they had stopped wasting time in restaurants.

She hadn't said anything to Ted about her excursions, waiting for him to ask about them, which he never did. He was usually gone most of the day to the farm or dealing with red tape in San José. Arturo had showed her how to pour from the little stainless steel coffee pitchers without it running down the sides or splashing all over—something Ted claimed was impossible. He would have liked to bring pliers with him to restaurants to reshape the pitchers' spouts. "Maybe that's the business I should start—miracle pitchers that don't dribble," he had said. He hadn't noticed her new deftness.

Grace said, "We were so happy, I thought we would live there forever. We never suspected what was going to happen. We hadn't discovered Nostradamus."

Ted gave Monica a look, and she tried to warn him with the brightness of her smile that he should let it go.

"In college I had a roommate who was sort of a Nostradamus nut," Monica said, trying to get in before him. "I don't mean nut. Enthusiast." She smiled at Ted.

"Honey, lots of people think it's nuts," Grace said. "But once you get into it, it's beyond question. Aviation, World War One and Two, the Soviet Union. And we're approaching World War Three, that's clear. Within our lifetime."

"1999," Hank said. "At the latest. Even I'll live to see it."

"And America and Russia are going to be allies. Against Red China and the Arabs. And who do you think is going to be the leader of the Antichrists? Khadaffi!"

"It's all there," Hank said. He had been slowly rocking back and forth in his chair, his massive hands pressed against the edge of the table.

Ted leaned back. "America?"

"He calls it 'Americh,'" Grace said. "Sometimes 'The Eagle.' Russia is 'The Bear.' We'll loan you our copy. It's all there—nuclear war, radiation, which he calls 'pestilential rain,' the Kennedy assassinations, Khrushchev, Grace Kelly becoming princess of Monaco."

Monica said, "It's pretty cryptic, right?" Walking a tightrope. "There's a lot of interpretation involved."

Ted laughed a little. "'Interpretation.'"

"We were skeptical at first," Grace said. "Who wouldn't be? It boggles the mind." She stopped, and no one said anything. "What we've come to realize," she said, "is how personal the prophecies are, there's individual meaning. There's the global meaning, but also individual."

Ted was staring down at his plate, maybe restraining himself, maybe getting ready to say something.

"Remember what they called Hank?" Grace asked. "Well, I was reading through *The Prophecies* a few years ago and it hit me: when the Bear makes an alliance with the Eagle, that was Hank starting to do work for the C.I.A.!"

"So," Ted asked, "is the bear Russia or is it Hank?"

Grace reached over and squeezed Ted's hand, held it there on the table. "That's exactly how we used to think," she said. "It had to be one thing or another."

"This or that," Hank said, "true or false."

"That black or white thinking," Grace said.

Monica knew how badly Ted was wanting to pull his hand free of her tender, iron grip.

"What's light?" Hank asked.

"Hmm?"

"What's light, is it a wave or is it a particle?"

"All right, I see—"

"What is it?"

"Okay, it depends on how you're looking at it. Sort of both."

"'Sort of both'!" Hank roared. "Exactly right. 'Sort of both.' And that's *science*, Ted, that's *hard* science. That's goddamn *physics*, excuse my French."

"So why should there be a single meaning for prophecies

written four hundred years ago?" Grace asked. She gave Ted's hand a squeeze and let it go. To Monica's relief, he said nothing. Sometimes he had the sense to shut up.

"She's been using Nostradamus to try and understand what happened to Cal," Hank said. "Tell them what you've found."

Grace rolled her eyes. "I'm just an amateur," she said. "I may be way off."

"Tell them what you goddamn found!"

"Hank! Well, the hard part's where to begin. He sometimes uses an actual name, like Hitler or Napoleon, but usually it's in a kind of code. I should get the book and show you." She sat there for a moment. "Anyway, with somebody like Cal, you have to find something in his background or appearance or something associated with him. I tried different things, but what seemed to work the best is what his business was. I looked for references to somebody associated with flowers. Here, wait."

In a few minutes she returned, carrying a thick, curl-edged paperback bristling with slips of paper. "Here," she said. She thumbed through the protruding slips and opened the book near the back. "Listen. 'In the year 1999, and seven months, from the sky will come the great King of Terror. He will bring back to life the great king of the Mongols. Before and after war reigns happily.'" She looked at them.

"Okay, I'll bite," Ted said. "Who's the great king of the Mongols?"

"That's simple—the Red Chinese premier, who controls Mongolia. Deng? Is that how you pronounce it? A year ago, it would have seemed ridiculous, wouldn't it, Red China seemed to be coming around. Then they have that terrible massacre, they're worse than ever."

"Could I see that a second?" Ted asked.

She turned the page. "Listen to this: 'The end of the wolf, the lion, ox and the ass, the timid deer will be with the mastiffs. No longer will the sweet manna fall upon them; more vigilance and guarding for the mastiffs.' When we were in Nicaragua, we got a puppy for Charlotte. He grew up into that great brute you heard barking. Well, when things were getting really bad, he saved our life. Some men attacked the house when Hank was gone, and Tracker and another dog drove them away. Tracker is half mastiff!"

"Okay—"

But she was paging through the book again. "Here, this seems to say that Khadaffi is the one in league with the Sandinistas. 'The powerless Prince'—that's Bush, I think, with a Democratic congress—'The powerless Prince is angered, complaints and quarrels, rape and pillage, *by the Cock and the Libyans.*' Do you know what Ortega's nickname is? El gallo, the cock! He goes on, about the powerless Prince, 'He is great on land, at sea innumerable sails.' There's going to be an invasion, in other words. If you ask me, Bush is finally going to crush the Sandinistas."

"Get to the part about Cal," Hank urged.

"We're in eventful times," Grace said. "'The wall in the East will fall.' That has to be the Berlin wall, which could go any day now. And he says communism—he calls it 'all things common among friends'—will be 'put far behind.' I think that's why Russia and America will be able to become friends."

"For the love of God!"

"Well, excuse me! I just find it all so interesting."

"Tell them about Cal before it's goddamn Christmas!"

She let the book fall open before her. "Since he was a florist, I looked for references to flowers."

"Grace—"

"Well, excuse me, Hank! I'm getting to it. Some of the verses are too difficult to understand, but some of them are clear as crystal. Here: 'The rose upon the middle of the world'—that's the summit, 'because of new deeds, public blood is shed; to speak the truth they will have closed mouths, then, at time of need the awaited one will come late.' Closed mouths is right! The government won't say a thing about it. There's references to bridges all over, where important things happen." She paged toward the front. "'Near a great bridge near a spacious plain the great lion with the imperial forces will cause a falling outside the austere city. Through fear, the gates will be unlocked for him.' The spacious plain and the falling is obvious. Outside the austere city, San José. The gates will be unlocked for him is a way of saying he will be killed, let into heaven, you know?"

"Could I see that a second?" Ted reached over.

But Grace didn't notice, paging around. "Here's an interesting one. 'From the useless enterprise'—That's Cal's business failure—'From the useless enterprise, honor and undue complaint, boats wandering among the Latins, cold, hunger, waves; Not far from the Tiber'—that's practically the Tiribi—'the land stained with blood and there will be several plagues upon mankind.' He got that right. AIDS?"

"This is all in translation, right?" Ted asked. He wanted to get his hands on the book so badly, Monica was afraid he would just reach over and grab it.

"Here's one that applies to Cal in the most uncanny way: 'The partner, solitary but married'—his wife was gone, you know—'will be mitred'—that probably means martyred." She smiled at Ted. "Listen to this, this is the key to what happened." She paged around, found it. "'In the conflict the great man who is of little worth will perform an astonishing deed at his end. While Hadrie sees what is needed, during a banquet he stabs the proud.' Hadrie is George Bush, who 'stabbed' Ortega at the banquet with his speech. What Cal was doing was warning him about the treachery of the Sandinistas, warning him not to abandon the Contras."

She continued paging around, her fingers ruffling through the book as if they could feel where anything of significance lurked. "See if this doesn't describe Ortega: 'The defaulter, dressed as a citizen, comes with the soldiers who are mostly outlaws, comes and takes over the king's power and estate.' That's exactly how they took over the country from Somoza.

Here's another of the flower references: 'Too late both of the flowers will be lost, the snake will not want to act against the law; the forces of the leaguers'—that's the presidents at the summit." She turned to Ted. "Does it surprise you Cal Richardson would be a martyr? Me too, I never liked him. It makes me feel ashamed."

"I don't get it," Monica said, despite her intention to leave the whole thing alone, to let it die down on its own as quickly as possible. "What's he supposed to have done?"

"He was on that bridge to give a warning," Hank said. "He died for freedom."

There was a long silence. Monica didn't know what to say. She looked at Ted, but couldn't read his expression. He truly had despised Cal Richardson. She had suggested to Ted that it had something to do with his father, or maybe even her father, and he had laughed at her. "The hell with you," she had said then, almost blind with anger and hurt.

The hell with you, she thought now. Work it out for yourself. She was abruptly bored with Richardson, with Ted, the Picketts, certainly bored out of her mind with Nostradamus. She felt a sudden fierce longing to see Arturo and tell him how fucking bored she was with all of them, herself included. Especially herself. Everyone on earth who wasn't him.

"What you have to remember," Hank said, "is that we've got this semi-communist faggot running the country, big peacemaker, Nobel Prize winner, he's not going to help the Freedom Fighters, and he's going to do everything in his power to keep anyone else from helping them. Ortega, Noriega, Castro—he's in their pockets. I know about them, and you'd better believe they know about me. They've come for me before, and they'll come for me again. I'll be ready for them, you'd better believe that."

"We got a M-16 *and* a AK-47 *and* a Uzi!"

They turned toward the doorway, where Ray and Stephen were poised like a pair of cats expecting to be driven off with stones.

"You!" Grace cried out. "Raymond Henry Pickett. How long you been lurking there?"

"Can I show them Daddy's guns? You don't have to get up, me and Stephen can bring them down."

Looking over Ray's shoulder, Stephen met Monica's eyes for a moment, then slid out of sight behind the doorway. He had long-standing instructions on what to do if one of his friends ever hauled out a gun and started playing with it: Run like hell, they had told him. Tell a grownup about it. When she had seen one of the party guys going into the downstairs apartment with a rifle a few weeks after they moved in, she had argued with Ted that they should find another place to live, but he had talked with their other neighbors about it, and Pepe had assured him that there had never been any trouble. Ticos never shot anybody, he said. Not that she trusted Pepe's judgment.

"I hope you know better than that," Grace said. "You're not to touch those things."

"If I ever catch you messing with those weapons, you'll be the sorriest boy in the country."

"He goes in there all the time, Daddy." Charlotte came out of the kitchen with a glass of Coke. "He knows right where they are."

"What is this?" Hank roared. "Every child in the world spying on us? Is this your idea of being excused from the goddamn table?"

"I just came down to get something to drink. *He's* been spying, though."

"Liar!"

"Where's that little angel?" Grace asked suddenly. Charlotte didn't have any idea, she thought the boys were playing with her. The boys looked at each other. They all got up then and scattered through the labyrinthine house and outside, calling, calling, and finally found her playing with Legos in Ray's crow's nest bedroom.

On the way home, Ted asked Stephen about Hank's guns,

but he had fallen asleep already. Valerie offered the observation that Ray had guns in his bedroom, lots of them.

"But those are toys, darling," Monica said. She looked over at Ted. "Right?"

"You won't let me and Stephen have even toy ones," Valerie complained.

Ted said nothing, concentrating on the treacherous road winding down out of the mountain darkness.

CHAPTER SEVEN

TED AND PEPE'S BUENA NOCHE

IN THE FIRST WEEK OF DECEMBER, the Hoffmans took a little vacation. They drove to the Atlantic port of Limón, then south on the coast road to Cahuita, where they found the cabina Arturo Aguilar was loaning them for the long weekend. They dumped their bags, changed into swimming suits, and hiked along the beach into the national park. A few hundred meters past the park entrance, they spread a blanket in the narrow rim of shade cast by the overhanging jungle. Valerie had an ear infection and wasn't supposed to go swimming. They had agreed that if Monica and Ted were with her, she could wade in the shallows. It would take both of them to keep her from flinging herself into the waves.

"After lunch," Ted promised. "Just let me have a quick swim, and after lunch I'll stick with her like a barnacle." Stephen was sulking, nursing his resentment that Ray hadn't been able to go on the trip with them, and Monica wanted Ted to take him out into the surf with him.

"It'll just make her jealous," he said, a good argument. Fact was, he needed to really swim, he needed to get way out there, away from it all, not standing around in a few feet of water, cajoling his son to get his face wet. Before they could lay any more claims on him, he ran down to the ocean and splashed in and dove and swam out through the breaking waves. In the smooth swells just beyond the breakers, he floated, and when the waves lifted him, he could see Monica rummaging in their big beach bag while Stephan and Valerie worked at building something in the sand. He swam farther out, until, when he turned and looked back, he could barely see them on the shore, specks in the shadow line where beach met green jungle.

It felt wonderful to stretch his muscles, to ache a little with exertion, moving powerfully among the endless waves. He was still trim and athletic, but he needed more of this sort of thing. He needed to start running again. He floated and swam until the beach itself was nothing but a narrow white line and the jungle looked more black than green. He floated and stroked lazily until he was beginning to worry about sunburn, then floated and stroked a while longer before finally heading back.

He swam steadily until he was out of breath, and then rested, treading water, let the waves lift him, and looked toward shore, the beach growing a little wider each time, the tiny knot of his family gradually becoming three separate figures. And then they became four figures, and then one of them raised an umbrella his family didn't have.

Treading water and scanning the beach spread out before him in the distance, he couldn't pick out his own family any-where, so he aimed himself toward the group with the beach umbrella, the closest thing to a landmark he had, and swam hard. When he was out of breath, he treaded water and checked his position. The group seemed no closer. If anything, the umbrella seemed to have shrunk. He swam again until he had to rest. He still had made no progress. And then the realization surged over him that he was caught in a rip tide. The ocean floor suddenly seemed miles beneath him, hauling him under.

He knew what to do. He had researched it before they vacationed in Costa Rica a few years ago, and before they had gone to a beach the first time he had given everyone instructions on how to recognize a rip tide. He had emphasized to them the need to relax and not exhaust yourself, the hopelessness of fighting the current, explained how to swim parallel to the shore until the invisible river rushing back out to the open sea lost its hold on you and you could make your way diagonally to shore. He had drawn diagrams and quizzed them—Stephen, who hated salt water and waves anyway, and Valerie, who couldn't swim at all without an inflated ring but was fearless, and Monica, who was a much better swimmer than he was.

He knew what to do, but his body refused to do it, obeying only its brute need to get back to them as quickly and directly as possible. Even though he knew the tiny figures gathered around the beach umbrella were not his family, he couldn't keep himself from swimming stupidly toward them. Straight in, as if there were a steel wire strung between their blue and white umbrella and the top of his skull.

A wave washed over his head and he choked on the fist of salt water shoved down his throat, fingers thrusting into his sinuses. He went down, thrashed back to the surface, gasped for breath. The wire held him pointed toward his false family. But it couldn't draw him in.

He wasn't really swimming anymore, just fighting not to sink again, and still he couldn't make himself relax, float, wait it out. He struggled and gagged on the salty ocean, waves pushing over his upward-straining face more and more often. The few other people swimming in the ocean, inside the breakers and unmolested by the current that for no good reason had seized him out of all the innocent objects in the ocean, they were as oblivious to his situation as if he had been a chunk of old, mossy styrofoam. He was too far out for anyone to hear him, even if he had had enough breath to shout for help, and he had no breath, he was out of breath, he was swallowing sea water, he was flailing far out in the ocean, he was drowning.

And then, for no good reason, he didn't even know it had happened, he found that somehow the shore was somehow rising up before him once more as he struggled hopelessly toward it. He swam a slow, awkward side stroke, all he was capable of now, toward what he eventually could see was a Costa Rican family having a picnic in the shade of their big umbrella, four adults and a baby, as it turned out. He stroked and stroked, terrified that the undertow that had arbitrarily let him go would seize him again, for good this time, drag him to oblivion, stroked until his elbow scraped on the gravely bottom, staggered up onto the hard sand and stood there on rubbery legs until he heard Stephen calling to him from far down the beach, and he saw them, Stephen and Valerie racing along the beach toward him. Monica stayed where she was, beach bag bulging with towels in one hand, the other shading her eyes. Even at that distance, he could tell how angry she was.

•

SHE WAS ANGRY AGAIN five days later, when he told her about getting caught in the rip tide. He was still peeling from his sunburn. "You didn't say a single word," she said. "You almost drowned, and you didn't say a single word about it. You let me complain like a goddamn bitch about making us wait so long."

"I didn't want to scare the kids."

"'Scare the kids?' Before Manuel Antonio the first time you went on so much about rip tides that Stephen was afraid to go near the ocean. And you waited a week to tell me? Jesus, Ted."

"I know, I'm sorry, Monica my darling. I told you now, anyway. Give a poor burn victim a break." He had spun it a little, actually, making it seem as if he had been caught in the undertow the whole time. "It's just that it was so ridiculous. I knew the right thing to do."

He waited for her to say it—knowing the right thing to do was never his problem. He could sense her considering whether or not to hit him with it. They were in bed, lying there in a darkness shaken by music and voices from downstairs. The night before, it had been the explosions of bombetas in the neighborhood, fireworks celebrating the Feast of the Immaculate Conception that had kept them awake. Tonight it was fiesta in the party guys' apartment. Around nine o'clock that evening a taxi had pulled up in front and dropped off two women. By the time Ted and Monica went to bed, a half dozen more cars had arrived, some filled with couples, some with just women or just men. Valerie was asleep by the time the music started, and Stephen was sleeping over at the Picketts', so at least that wasn't as much of a problem as it sometimes was.

"I'm going to have to take a nap or something tomorrow afternoon," Ted said. "We'll be out way past my bedtime tomorrow night." He turned over and eased his burned face into the smooth cotton of the pillow.

"'Tomorrow night.'"

"Pepe and me. I told you about it." He rolled onto his back again.

"Boys' night out."

"I'd just as soon skip it, but it's really important to him for some reason, showing me San José night life."

"He thinks you're pals, Ted. He thinks you're his amigo."

A few evenings a week, he and Pepe spent an hour or so practicing Spanish and English on each other. Sometimes they had actual conversations, but mostly it was trying to explain the nuances of slang. Ted had a little notebook filled with Spanish pachucos. Pepe never wrote anything down.

"I still can't get him to stop saying 'fucker man,'" he said. "I keep telling him, 'it's just "fucker,"' but he's always telling me what this fucker man or that fucker man did to him. Last time, he wanted me to explain exactly what "ass hole" meant.

"You should have told him, 'Pepe, amigo, an ass hole is someone who locks his wife in her own apartment.'"

He laughed uneasily. "Actually, he explained that to me. He said that after they had a big argument, she would sometimes run off when he was gone and leave the apartment door open so anybody could come by and steal his stuff. He was afraid she was going to do that."

"That's a wonderful excuse. I feel much better about it now."

"I'm not saying it's an excuse, I'm just saying there was a reason for it, he wasn't just being a jerk for no reason."

She put a hand on his arm.

"What?"

"I think the party's breaking up."

It was only a little past midnight, but the music had been turned off, and they could hear laughing and voices of departure from outside, cars being started, and then things grew quiet. But he could not fall asleep, and he knew by her breathing that she was also still awake. He rolled onto his stomach and draped an arm over her and stroked her a little in a friendly manner.

"I don't think so. Sorry, Ted."

"Okay, sure." He left his arm where it was for a few minutes, as if he really didn't mind. When he settled again on his back, he became conscious of sounds from downstairs, right below them now, a bed frame creaking, and soon rhythmical moans, a woman's voice. As it went on and on, he wondered if it was getting Monica at all turned on. After a while, he heard something that made him laugh out loud. "Did you hear that?"

"What?"

He moaned it out, "'¡Por favor!'"

"I didn't hear it."

The next time, she must have heard it. "Por favor." He whispered it. "Somebody's having a good time."

"You think so?" They listened. "He's mechanical," she said. "She's tired of it. She wants him to get it over with."

He said nothing.

She turned on her side and faced him in the darkness. "It's

the party guys, Ted. They give me the creeps. It's got nothing to do with you."

He rolled onto his stomach. He hated it when it had nothing to do with him. When it had nothing to do with him, he felt extinguished, not in the clear at all. A kind of half-assed death.

•

Though it was Saturday the next day, he drove out to the flower farm and spent almost six hours reading invoices and expense projections and contracts, catching up on research and correspondence. He walked with Alejandro up and down the bays of flowers and seedlings, comparing the effects of various pesticides they had been trying out, checking the canopies and supporting frameworks and the irrigation system. It was the dry season now, though they were still getting rain every few days, unpredictably, even in the early morning. It was El Niño, they said. Ted worried about the reservoir, the flimsy network of undersized plastic pipe, and the murky laws pretending to regulate water use.

He worked all day, and when he got home again he felt tired and virtuous. He had earned his night out. He took the family to the Pizza Hut in San Rafael for supper, and he didn't comment when Monica ordered a second beer with their suprema delgada, and afterwards he drove them to the Sabana Pops for ice cream. Back at the apartment, he helped the kids with their showers and tucked them into bed and made Monica a cup of chamomile tea.

"Thanks, sweetie," she said. "You know there's nothing wrong with taking a night off once in a while, don't you?"

"Now you tell me."

"I've *been* telling you. What do I have to do?" She was taking it too seriously. He raised his palms to her, making peace, and she asked, "When are you guys leaving?"

"He said nine."

"It's that now."

"He's never ready. I'll go down in about a half hour."

He waited for her to settle herself in their ragged old easy chair with a collection of Lorca poems she had recently dug out of her dissertation box, and then went into the bedroom to dress. Not sure what would be appropriate, he finally decided on dark trousers and a white oxford cloth shirt. He still felt self-conscious in the guayabera shirt Monica had bought him for his birthday. He went out to the kitchen and took two thousand-colon notes out of an envelope in the household bank drawer. Pepe had said that would be enough. He tucked the bills into his wallet, behind the photocopy of his passport, and slid his money belt, padded with two more tightly folded mil notes, through the loops of his trousers.

Pepe met him at the door with a mysterious, cautionary look, and led him back to the bedroom where Eva was sitting up in bed, watching television. Always carefully and stylishly dressed when he saw her, she was in a prim, long-sleeved nightgown now, her long, silky black hair spilled carelessly over the pile of pillows she rested against. A box of pink facial tissues was parked in her lap. She had a terrible cold, Pepe said, the poor little thing. He sat on the bed beside her and draped his arm comfortingly around her shoulders.

She sniffed, dabbed at her nose with a wad of tissue, and motioned for Ted to join them on the bed. He had never seen their bedroom before. The bed took up most of the room, with a narrow passage between it and a dresser holding the color television. He sat on the foot of the bed and started to commiserate with her about her illness, but then the string of commercials ended, and both Eva and Pepe focused on the screen. It was some sort of beauty contest from the U.S., the contestants' American voices beginning the answer to each idiotic question, then simultaneous Spanish translations that he couldn't follow taking over.

"Miss Hollywood," Pepe explained, without taking his eyes from the screen. He and Eva were watching the show with such intensity that for a while Ted thought they had some particular stake in it, maybe one of their friends or relatives was competing, or just a Costa Rican national beauty. But their interest was purely critical. Eva would make observations about this girl's big ass or that girl's face like a pig, and Pepe would agree or offer some other sort of criticism. After a while Eva asked Ted which one he liked the best, and he could only shrug vaguely. They all looked pretty much the same to him, blandly and conventionally beautiful in bathing suits that seemed to be made of shimmering, molded plastic.

Did he want a Coke? Eva asked, and before he could answer she sent Pepe to get it for him. He waited uncomfortably in the bedroom with the sniffling young woman and stared at the television. Ordinarily, it would have been Pepe ordering Eva around, demanding food or drink with an arrogance that seemed ironic, a parody of macho bluster laid on for the North American's amusement. And she would have been obeying him, though also with an air of irony.

Did he notice how thick that one's waist was? Eva asked when Pepe returned with the soft drinks. Ted watched Eva out of the corner of his eye, wondering how she could be so harsh about such imperceptible flaws, who was herself no great beauty, though attractive enough in nice clothes and makeup. Right now, she was notably without makeup, her face blotched and shiny with fever.

He looked at his watch. It was almost ten o'clock. The pageant went on and on, numbing him even to the oddness of sharing a bed with Pepe and Eva. They were so much younger than he was—that was the thought that pushed in at him. He wasn't of their generation at all. They were kids, twenty-two, twenty-three, and at forty-three he would have been an old man to them, except that his foreignness dumbed him down to a kind of awkward adolescence.

He had just about given up on boys' night out and was getting ready to excuse himself and return to his own apartment and go to bed, when Pepe left the room during a commercial break. He returned before the end of the commercials, cologned and freshly shaved, wearing a clean shirt. He watched one more contestant deliver her incomprehensible speech, gave Eva a kiss and tucked her in solicitously, murmurously, then directed him toward the door. Outside, when Ted started to ask about the delay, Pepe gestured for silence, still mysteriously anxious, until they had closed the doors on his pale blue Camaro.

"Is necessary," he said. "Is a *must*, you understand? We are having a bad argument, very very bad, so then I got to know, is okay? She's no being angry to me no more, you understand? Or, *bang*, some fucker man is walking off with my stereo. You understand?"

He nodded, glad to be moving, and decided not to correct his English tonight. It was boys' night out, not a language lesson. "I was starting to think you'd forgotten about going out," he said. "It was getting pretty late."

"Never! I never forget our date. Tonight I show you how we're really living in this fucker country! And is no so late. How do you say 'is early'? Un modismo."

"The night is young?"

"¡Eso! The night is young!"

Instead of heading down the mountain to San Rafael and then the highway into San José, Pepe popped an Iron Maiden tape into his deck and drove aimlessly around the dark streets of Escazú, music blaring. Here and there they saw clots of people standing around under street lamps, and he would slow down and try to see who it was. More often than not he would recognize someone and shout out the person's name, and they would exchange greetings or friendly insults.

"Here, in this place, the bitches are very hot," he said as they cruised once more along the town square. "Like California. I never see nothing like it!"

The music was loud, and Ted wasn't sure he had heard him right. "This place? Escazú?" Maybe he had meant that they *weren't* very hot, that it *wasn't* like California here. He knew what California meant for Pepe—the garden of earthly delights, a place where he had once fucked a teenage girl and the next day her mother.

"Mira," Pepe said, and stopped in the middle of the street. He pointed ahead, to where a couple were embracing in the shadows of a doorway. He turned off the headlights, maneuvered cautiously forward a ways, then flipped on his high beams and flooded the doorway with white light. The man and woman turned and peered blindly into the glare.

"What're you doing?" Ted waited for the man to run out at them and kick in their headlights.

But the man just stared, one hand shading his eyes, and after a minute Pepe hit the low beam and drove off. "I think I know that guy," Pepe mused. "What his name is? No recuérdolo. Anyways," he said, turning finally and heading downhill toward the freeway, "repeat to me, Ted, what is the correct pronounce of cocksucker?"

Ted told him, and grabbed at the dashboard as they raced down the twisting road into the now-mostly-deserted business district of San Rafael de Escazú. "Some fucker mans crash my side here," Pepe observed, pushing through the wrong end of an amber light at the bottom of the hill. "Uncultured people. They go to the fucker police, try to get money from my father. They say to him they take away my placa. He say to them they can go to hell, he no pay nothing."

Ted wondered how long ago this had been. "Did you lose your license?"

He shrugged. "They take it from me, they got to, for reason of respect, but not for long. We got a cousin in the government, he take care of it. My father damn mad to me, I got to talk him very soft for a while."

On the autopista he drove like a madman, but once they got into San José he slowed down and pointed out some of the night clubs on Paseo Colón. He stopped in front of one,

Club Panda, an ugly glass box building in which they could see people dancing on the second floor. It was upper class, he said, all kids. They didn't go in, however, and when a burly man in a suit approached them from underneath the night club's marquee, he drove on, north, to a dark, mostly industrial section of the city where there was plenty of parking in a lot surrounding what looked like a factory.

It was a club called Equus, though Pepe remembered it as being called something else when he had been in high school. It was his favorite club, he said. He made Ted follow a little behind him and keep quiet while he told the guard at the entrance a story that would allow them to avoid the cover charge. When they had been planning the expedition, Pepe had asked him if he didn't have some sort of official embassy documents he could bring along, "to open doors." Ted had forgotten about it, but it didn't seem to matter, for after a few minutes the guard waved them in.

The dance floor inside was dense with well-dressed teenagers, and a huge television hung above the entrance, deafening music videos writhing and flickering. There were a few tables on the periphery, and a bar at each end of the vast room. With Ted meekly following him, Pepe pushed through the crowds that roiled around the bars and every so often ran into friends with whom he would stop and exchange handshakes and kisses on the cheek and talk for a few minutes. Pepe and his friends weren't dancing. They held themselves aloof from the serious, clean-cut kids who were, and they seemed to regard the swirling masses from a bitter distance imposed by the few years that separated them from high school.

Pepe made no effort to introduce him to his friends. If Ted hadn't been afraid of losing him in the crowd, he would have wandered off on his own. He was about to try to push close enough to one of the bars to order a drink, when Pepe grabbed his elbow and mouthed to him that they were leaving. He didn't seem happy, he didn't seem like a man visiting his favorite club. In the parking lot, when he spotted some guys he knew sitting on the hood of a pickup, he stopped and made plans with them, something involving a band, but here too there was little feel of happiness, no more than there had been between him and the young people gathered in the streets of Escazú.

Pepe was mostly silent in the car as they drove off toward one of the eastern suburbs. Ted felt sorry for him, so nostalgic for a youth he had barely left. Ted had hated being a teenager, but he knew people who felt this glow surrounding those hormone-tormented years. It was strange and sad, he thought, but it was human, it deserved sympathy.

When they approached their next destination, Pepe cheered up, as if the lights of this more prosperous neighborhood cured some mood disorder. It was the Centro Commercial El Pueblo, a glittering aggregation of shops, restaurants, bars, and discos that Ted and Monica had seen advertised and talked of visiting, but never had. It had seemed too, well, commercial, in a North American mall kind of way. It wasn't the real Costa Rica, they had agreed.

He was glad to be here now, however. The little tour would tell him whether or not to take her sometime. Maybe there was a good restaurant. She had become quite the restaurant connoisseur down here, ordering with a confidence he had never seen in the States. In the past, she would dither, then order something familiar. Now it was pulpo, mariscos, pickled ayote. It would be nice to bring her here, to a new place he had discovered, give her pleasure.

The parking lot was full. They drove around and around, weaving between cars that had been jammed in where there was not enough space, parked at odd angles. Suddenly Pepe shouted that he saw an opening behind them, threw the Camaro into reverse, roared back, and slammed into a car that had materialized behind them.

Ted groaned. He had never had an automobile accident. At home, he carried zero deductible insurance, a talisman that had kept them all safe, including Monica, who wasn't the world's best driver. Here, he had gone for his car insurance to an agent recommended to him by Cal Richardson, a Texan who had managed to inspire confidence that he could lead them through the thickets of local legislation in the all-too-likely eventuality that some maniac would run into them.

A maniac like Pepe, who sat clutching the dead wheel, cursing quietly. After a moment he told Ted to stay in the car and got out and went back to inspect the damage. Ted swiveled in his seat and watched him shake hands with the driver of the other car. Together they stared down at the point of impact, pointing out this and that detail. Though the windows were down, he couldn't hear much of what they were saying over the noise of passing traffic and the distant boom of a disco. They talked with much shrugging and head shaking but no apparent anger. Cars that couldn't get around them just backed up and took another way through the crammed parking lot.

Eventually a policeman and a huge man in a brown suit came up from the direction of the commercial complex, and Ted felt a surge of dread, as if he had been implicated in some crime. But they just joined in the conversation for a few minutes, then strolled back to the buildings. When they were gone, Pepe opened the driver's side door and asked Ted how much money he had with him. Two thousand colones, he told him. Pepe waited, and Ted asked him whether he needed it. Yes, he was sorry, Pepe said. He took the two red bills, went back to the man he had run into, and talked some more. Finally they shook hands one more time, and Pepe got back in the car. It was nothing, he said, very minor. But he didn't want to stay here any longer, he was getting a bad feeling from the place.

"We're broke, anyway. We might as well go home."

"No, no," Pepe insisted, "the night, she is young." He drove this time to a darker, grittier neighborhood, only a few blocks from the glassy tower of the Aurora Holiday Inn, but here the streets were almost deserted, blank-walled, ominous. They parked on the street and walked back to a thirty-foot-high concrete building, windowless, with stubby crenellations like a darkly utilitarian fortress or prison. At its base, there was a heavy barred door, iron-sheathed, with multiple padlocks dangling from welded hooks. A little sign above the door read "V.I.P." The door was guarded by a one-armed man wearing a plaid suit from the fifties, something Buddy Holly might have worn. The man was heavy-faced, thick-necked, nothing like Buddy. The paper tickets protruding from between his fingers when he shook hands with them could have been razor blades.

Pepe wheedled and argued with him, trying to get them in without paying the cover. This was a very important guest from the U.S., Ted heard him say, it was an insult to make him pay. The guard listened impassively, and every so often he turned away to sell cover tickets to men who came up to the uninviting entrance in twos and threes. A vendor selling grilled meats and sausages on sticks leaned against the wall.

Finally Pepe told Ted that they would have to pay—three hundred colones apiece.

"Is it worth it? I gave you all my money at the accident."

"You don't got nothing?"

"Maybe a hundred colones, hundred and fifty." In his wallet, he had three hundred colones, plus some change. The two red notes folded tight and narrow in his belt were inviolable.

"Give me one hundred and fifty," Pepe said. "I pay the rest."

"Is it worth it?" Ted asked again, but then handed over a one hundred note and some aluminum coins. The fortress walls, the weight of the door, the half-dozen padlocks, the maimed guard—they made it seem that maybe something inside *was* worth the price, which, after all, he could see other men paying without objection.

Inside, Club V.I.P. looked like a long basement room, heavy pillared, with rough wooden booths. In the area closest to the door, a single morose, heavily-made-up woman occupied each booth. Pepe led Ted back to an unoccupied booth. Three drinks were included in the cover price, he told him. Pepe ordered a vino, and Ted asked for a Coke. When the waiter brought their drinks, his was a beer instead of the Coke. They were out of Coke, the waiter said. Ted shrugged, poured the beer into the glass. Pepe's drink came in a shot glass, a bourbon or something like that, not the wine Ted had assumed it would be. Maybe he had said fino. Maybe it was sherry or something.

The music in the narrow, oppressive space was very loud. One of the sullen women approached them. Pepe slid over to make room for her to sit down, and they started a conversation that Ted couldn't follow. He sipped at his beer and tried to look comfortable. After a few minutes, the woman must have realized they weren't interested in doing any business with her. She left, and Pepe tried to tell him something, but the music was too loud. They took their drinks and moved past the bar to a set of booths in the next room, farther from the speakers. Here there were women sitting four or five to a table, better dressed, more friendly looking than the ones in the first room. From time to time a man would join them, and sometimes a couple would leave by a stairs that must have led to rooms above the bar.

What did he think of them? Pepe asked, nodding toward a table a few yards away.

They were whores, right? Ted asked. Putas, prostitutas?

Of course. Some of them were very nice. In the States, did Ted go with prostitutes?

He shook his head. No, he was married, he said. He rubbed condensation from the beer bottle into the raw wood of the booth. He was a married man, he said again.

Of course, Pepe said. Sometimes, though, it was necessary. The waiter returned with another round of drinks, though Ted still had half a bottle in front of him. Did he know, Pepe asked, leaning forward, how hard marriage could be? Ted picked at the damp label of the beer bottle. It was very hard, Pepe said. About Eva, he was deeply troubled. Why had she married him, out of love, or for his family? It was a terrible worry to him. How could a man ever know the answer to that question, unless they were equals, or the woman was above him, which was also bad? Eva's family was nothing, whereas his own had land, position, a business. It was a mistake not to marry an equal.

Ted drank from the bottle, felt the cold rasp in his nostrils and throat, then poured the rest of the beer into his glass. When he looked around, a woman at one of the crowded tables smiled at him. She was not beautiful, but she had the most beautiful smile he had ever seen.

Did he know, Pepe asked, how many times, in a year of marriage, they had made love when he had wanted to? Only four times. Ted shook his head. He looked over to the table where the friendly prostitutes were sitting, but they were absorbed in their own conversation. The woman with the smile wasn't there anymore. Pepe repeated it. Four times, when only he wanted to. And he wanted to all the time, especially when he was worried about something and needed to relax. Before the babies came, he needed to know what her motives were. And could he talk to his father about it? Never! With his father he was still a child. It always had to be, "Yes, Papá, I see what you mean, Papá, yes, I'll try." He would never listen to talk about divorce, no matter how bad it was.

Ted started in on a third beer as soon as the waiter set it on the table in front of him. Pepe asked for another drink, but the waiter said only two of those were included in the cover. They argued about it for a while, then Pepe gave in and paid him. Ted kept thinking about that figure, four times, and the way he was able to bring it out of his pocket as easily as a bad watch, to demonstrate its defects. Ted had met Pepe's father, don Carlos, gray haired and barrel chested, who must have sired Pepe in a second or third marriage, the age spread was so large. Pepe at least wasn't looking to Ted as a substitute father figure, he was too young. He hoped so, anyway, for he could think of nothing to say about it.

Four times. After he had told Monica about his affair, they

hadn't made love at all for months. He had scarcely wanted to, he was filled with such self-loathing at how much he had risked for so little. He had been depressed, the solar panel business he had been so proud of was going under, Monica was preoccupied with the kids, and Elaine had been there beside him, suffering the failure with him, an unexpected, powerful intimacy. He couldn't imagine telling any of this to Pepe. He momentarily considered asking him how often *Eva* wanted to make love, but he let it drop. Total frequency of sex was not the issue, he understood that. Pepe's unilateral, unsatisfied desire was the issue.

Before long the conversation shifted from Pepe's marital grievances to the larger and more familiar subject of his musical ambitions. What were Ted's favorite groups? he asked, as he had asked on other occasions, and now, as on those other occasions, Ted had to fall back on groups that had flourished before Pepe was born. By the time he was in college, rock had lost its hold on him. He named groups he hadn't listened to in years. The Doors. The Rolling Stones. The Mothers of Invention.

When they had finished their third drinks, Pepe announced that it was time to leave. They had one more stop to make. Ted looked at his watch. It was almost two o'clock. A deep tiredness that had crept up on him during the past hour hit him heavily when he stood up, and for a few seconds he clung to the back of the booth for balance. He had to go home, he told Pepe. He wasn't feeling well. He would feel better once they were outside in the fresh air, Pepe said.

Surprisingly, it was true, and he waited, breathing in the crisp night air that was almost purged of diesel fumes this late at night, while Pepe argued with the impassive, one-armed guard about that third drink, then shook his hand and gave him a tip—it looked like sixty or eighty colones. "I'm broke," Ted reminded Pepe when they were in the car again. He shouldn't worry, Pepe said. Where they were going, he was known, they were all friends, it would be no problem. "She is so young, la noche," he said. "This place is a must."

They drove about ten blocks, closer to the center of San José than they had been before, and parked between buildings in a lot that was narrow as an alley, probably *had* been an alley until somebody built a concrete wall across one end to make a parking lot. Despite the hour, the streets here were still awake. A well-dressed couple with a toddler in a snow suit against the night chill. A cluster of teenage girls. Old men smoking on a bus stop bench.

A boy who couldn't have been older than Stephen offered to watch the car, and Pepe gave him some coins. He was strutting a little, now, and gestured toward the neon flourishes on the entrance of the night club where he was known, "Cherie," with a marquee and uniformed doorman and brass door studded with ornamental bolt heads big as noses.

A hulking, unshaven man in a sleeveless undershirt was talking with the doorman, and when Pepe tried out his visiting dignitary line, the man in the undershirt did something Ted had never seen in Costa Rica. He stepped up to Pepe, placed a hand on his chest, and shoved him, hard, so that he staggered back into Ted's arms. Ted himself almost fell backward with the sudden weight, but he managed to stay upright and held him until he was able to stand on his own. Pepe laughed and raised both palms toward the man who had pushed him, as if to show that no offense had been taken, but then he reached one hand into his trouser pocket and kept it there and stepped forward.

"Pepe, wait." This wasn't Costa Rica anymore, where machismo was a matter of hissing insinuations to women on the streets, arguments over politics or soccer that went nowhere and ended with handshakes. This was the weed-choked parking lot of road houses across the Ohio, where Kentucky boys and men with arms like sewer pipes settled things the hard way, where his grandfather one time pointed out to him a body bleeding on the ground in the calm between violence and the arrival of the police. When Ted had come upon a store in San José with knives and guns in the display window, it had forced a laugh out of him and he had told Monica about it that night and had never been able to find it again. It might have been a hallucination. "Wait," he said again.

Pepe took another step forward, and the doorman casually moved away from the man in the undershirt. Somebody pushed open the heavy door from the inside, spilling music out onto the sidewalk. The man in the undershirt said something, and Pepe said something, and Ted found himself standing next to Pepe, shouting, "Mira! Mira, goddamnit!"

Somebody laughed and stepped out of the doorway onto the mottled red carpet underneath the marquee. "'Mira, goddamnit'?" After a moment, Ted recognized him, Arturo Aguilar, his narrow face bleached silver in the buzzing streetlight. "Señor Ted, is that you, come to my club?" He was carrying a leather briefcase. He put an arm around the beefy shoulders of the man in the undershirt and squeezed and patted him and whispered something in the man's ear that made him grin. Then he shook Ted's hand, and then Pepe's, and invited them in. "I'm just leaving," he said, "but please, enjoy yourself." This was his dear American friend, he said to the doorman, who shook Ted's hand and then Pepe's.

Ted studied him as Arturo ushered them through the brass door. Over the past month, he had become tío Arturo, giving Monica and the kids rides, taking them as guests to swim at a luxurious country club his brother belonged to, loaning them his cabina south of Limón. Yet Ted scarcely knew him. They had only talked briefly two or three times, and he was embarrassed to have come so close to a fight in front of him.

"Is my place," Arturo said, with a little bow and sweep of a hand. "I hope it amuse you. But I got to go now, with permission." They were in a dim, plush corridor that snaked around toward the music and flickering light of the club. He shook hands with them again, squeezed Ted's upper arm, then was gone, the curving walls of the corridor swallowing him.

Ted stood there for a moment, then Pepe said something

and led him into the pulsing music and light of the club, a room with nice chrome and velvet chairs, six or seven glass tables, and lots of mirrors doubling the intimate space and scattering of customers. A man in a tuxedo directed them to the comfortable curl of a banquette at the back of the room. From here, they could see part of a small stage flickering with violet strobe lights, where a woman was dancing in front of a wall of mirrors that backed the stage.

How did he know him? Pepe asked, maybe bothered that someone else's connections had been the ones to open the door to this nightclub where he was known. Ted tried to explain it. He didn't know him well. A family friend. Was Pepe really going to fight that guy? he asked. He could still feel the pressure of Arturo's hand on his arm.

He was a certain kind of man, Pepe said, you had to watch out for your balls around him. He shifted over a little in the banquette to get a better view of the dancer, keeping time with the music by slapping his palm lightly on the polished surface of the table.

How did *he* know him, Ted asked.

He had bought some horses from his father, Pepe said. Formerly, this club had had an owner he knew very well. They were like this, he said, extending two fingers together. No sons of whores stood at the door in those days, giving trouble to decent people.

He cheered up when two attractive young women approached the banquette. They looked like college girls, younger and better dressed than the women at the V.I.P. Did he want an amiga? one of them asked Ted, surely a B-girl line, but he moved over to make room for her. She had a delicate, intelligent face and a mane of curly black hair. When a table opened up closer to the stage and Pepe herded them all toward it, Ted realized how small she was, barely reaching his chest. Her head seemed large for her slight body—another thing about her that made her look younger than she probably was.

By the time they reached the more advantageous table, the woman on the stage had removed her bikini top and was in the process of slipping out of the bottom. She danced naked for the rest of the song, then gathered up her scattered bits of clothing from the translucent, flickering floor and left the stage, to be replaced a few minutes later by another dancer who followed the same routine—one song clothed, then one during which she stripped and danced naked.

"My name is Cynthia," the girl sitting beside Ted informed him in the interval between music and dancers. He introduced himself and tried to make small talk, but after a few minutes it became clear that her English was not as good as her accentless introduction had promised, and they switched to Spanish. When the strobes flashed and the music started again and another dancer took the stage, it was not so bad, they could sit there and pretend it was too loud to carry on a conversation. The girl paid no attention to the strip show and focused on him, studying his face with a shy attentiveness. Every so often, she would graze his arm with her fine, manicured fingertips, as if mildly emphasizing a point.

Trying to ignore the excitement he felt for her, he looked around the room. A severely dressed old woman sat behind the gleaming bar. Otherwise, all of the women in the place were young and pretty, though none as pretty as the girl beside him. Most were dressed like her, in party clothes, though one blond girl, sitting by herself along the far wall, had on a gray jumper and white blouse that looked like some country's school uniform. Not Costa Rica's. Here, at her age, she would be in the sky blue shirt and navy trousers or skirt of a liceo student.

A few tables away from him sat a small, sturdily-built woman, maybe thirty years old, wearing an olive-green jump suit, almost military in cut, though the fabric seemed silky. She had a short, mannish haircut and wore fringed moccasins, which she occasionally rested on the table's edge or the lap of one of her companions. There were four men at the table with her. The oldest of them seemed in his sixties, big as a walrus, and now and then the woman kissed him in a friendly, amused way.

Cynthia put her hand on his wrist. She had been asking him something. He cupped a hand around one of his ears, as if she had to speak up, because of the music. Would he buy her a Coke? she asked.

He reached for his wallet. How much was it? He didn't have much money with him, he explained.

She said something to the young woman sitting on the other side of the table, next to Pepe, then told Ted seven hundred colones.

His arm went weak, as if something had banged the elbow nerve. He was sorry, he said, but he didn't have enough. Seven hundred colones, could that be right? Almost nine dollars.

Two hundred and fifty, she said, suddenly insistent, disconcerted, perhaps, at her bad judgment about him.

No, he said, really, he had almost nothing, looking to Pepe for confirmation, but he was watching the stripper. Cynthia looked at Ted, waiting for a real answer. They had been in an accident, he explained, and he had had to pay for damages, many thousands of colones. Did she understand? He was poor (he didn't know the word for "broke"), he just didn't have enough money with him anymore, even for a regular Coke, maybe.

The girl avoided his eyes. She had a brief whispered conversation with her friend, then asked him to excuse her please for a little moment and left the table. The three of them at the table watched another dancer strip, then the other woman excused herself, too.

Ted stewed in his humiliation, irritated with Pepe for having taken all his designated night-out money for the accident, when he himself obviously still had plenty. But Pepe clapped him on the shoulder and encouraged him to observe the new dancer closely. She was Black, her nipples large and purple when she removed the white frilly shirt she had been wearing. What did he think of her? Pepe asked.

He shrugged. What were they, he asked, the women on the stage? Meaning, were they all prostitutes?

"Bailadoras," Pepe said, they were dancers, thinking that he had wanted to know the word in Spanish. But what about this particular one? he asked, and before Ted had a chance to answer he said he thought she looked like a gorilla.

She wasn't, in fact, very attractive, compared to some of the women who had already danced, but he knew that that wasn't it. Pepe disliked Blacks, at least the Blacks of Costa Rica. In the United States, he had said, when Ted had challenged some racist remark, it was different, they were fine people, the United States Blacks. Here, they were uncultured. One of them had insulted him once. He was surprised that Ted took his family to the Caribbean beaches, there were too many Blacks there, you weren't safe. They weren't real Costa Ricans.

While the next woman danced, who seemed to break the rules by keeping her T-shirt and bikini bottom on for two songs and only stripped perfunctorily at very end of the third, Pepe asked Ted what shape of woman he preferred—"delgada, mediana, gorda?" "Mediana," he answered automatically. Pepe agreed enthusiastically, pleased that they were of one mind about this, and began assessing the various women who had stripped before them according to how perfectly they approached this ideal medium body. The woman dancing now was acceptable, though the deep golden color of her skin was still too dark for his taste.

The one Ted couldn't keep his eyes off, who almost made him forget his fiscal embarrassment, was the small woman in the olive-green jumpsuit. He kept watching her, she seemed so comfortable and funny. Pretty, though not striking in appearance, she joked with the men at her table, and in an interval between sets she jumped up on stage with the fat man from her table and did a brief mock dance with him, with much bumping of bellies and butts. Afterwards, she wandered around the club, talking with the employees and some of the dancers, who were sitting at a table near the far wall, dressed in their street clothes. Walking back to her own table, she shouted, "¡Guácala!" as one of the most beautiful dancers came out onto the stage, and then again from her table with the four men, "¡Guácala!," a child's word for disgusting, and the dancer laughed and stuck out her tongue.

He ached suddenly to be at the table with the woman in olive green, to have her put her arm around his waist—in friendship or love or simple amused acknowledgement, it didn't seem to matter, she was so comfortable and undemanding. He tried to concentrate on the beautiful woman who had finished her first song and was beginning the second, the one that counted. She danced gracefully, casually, as if she were among friends, and even when she was completely naked, not wearing even the high heels that most of the strippers danced in, she seemed to be at ease. The one who followed was not as pretty but danced more suggestively, caressing herself, writhing occasionally on the translucent floor, humping it, moaning. He tried to let himself be carried away by the act, but it left him unmoved, and when she bent far over backwards and thrust her shaved crotch ecstatically into the air, he felt nothing.

He thought about Monica, seeing her suddenly in the watery light of fatigue. She was mediana in figure, he supposed—his preference for that type expressed a kind of loyalty to her, he tried to tell himself. What would she think of him sitting here, watching women strip? He wouldn't tell her about it, though she maybe assumed something like this was a part of boys' night out. Elaine was definitely delgada, skinny, almost, though she made the most of what she had. He got up and went to the back of the club, to the men's room, where the urinals were filled with cracked ice, a nice touch. He went into a stall, slid the money belt part way out of his trousers loops, and transferred one of the narrowly folded mil notes to his wallet. Standing at the sinks, he looked at himself in the mirror, a decent-looking man with a receding hairline, sunburned face still peeling a little.

He came out of the restroom and stopped, the door hushing closed behind him. Two policemen were standing in one of the side areas of the club. Then he noticed two more, on the opposite side of the room, these with shiny braid coiled around their shoulders—officers, he supposed. He felt a hollowness in his stomach. It was a prudish country, you couldn't even find girlie magazines in the newsstands downtown. How could a strip club be legal?

But nobody was sliding toward the exit, nobody seemed to be alarmed. He made his way back to the table and watched the blond who had been wearing the school girl's uniform peel off a lycra swimming suit.

The woman in olive green was gone. He looked at his watch. It was three a.m. A gnarled, shrunken old woman had come into the club and was moving from table to table, selling roses in plastic wrappers. When she approached his table, Ted dug out his last two hundred colon notes and handed them to her. She handed him four of the roses, a fair price, if the flowers had been fresh. He figured they would be wilted the next day, but what did he know? He didn't know roses.

He had to go home, he announced, he was dead, he needed to sleep. Pepe, who had ignored the flower seller, agreed, and said he was going to pay their bill, but on the way, one of the dancers, the one with the shaved crotch who had given it her erotic all, spoke his name, and he sat down beside her and they got into a conversation. Ted watched them, then watched the policemen. They were probably off duty, doing private security work for the club.

There had been no dancers after the one who had been dressed as a school girl, and he had concluded that it was over for the night, when Cynthia came on stage and began dancing in a black lace bra and panties. He felt his heart tighten. He felt he shouldn't watch, he had forfeited the right. But he watched. Her body seemed to taper downward, from her large, delicate featured head with its flowing abundance of black hair, to fine shoulders and generous breasts, to a narrow waist and slight hips, the hips of a boy or a young girl.

She was into the second song, dancing in only her panties, when Pepe finally came back and got him. He rose and turned from the stage and followed him and didn't look back. It occurred to him, in the brief curve of corridor before the exit, that Cynthia, and the woman in olive green, and the crone selling flowers had been the only women in the club whose sex he had not seen. And the old woman behind the bar—he added her to the tally.

A waiter came after them and stopped them at the entryway. Pepe had not paid the bill. The waiter pretended that it had been an oversight. Ted thought that now Pepe really had no money—he had had three or four drinks in the club—but he went back and apparently paid. No one pursued him out onto the street when they finally left, anyway. No one knocked him to the ground, took it out of his hide.

He seemed preoccupied, had a bemused look on his face. Maybe it *had* been an oversight. The woman who had spoken his name, he told Ted in the car, she was a prostitute he had gone to before he married. He hadn't recognized her, but he remembered her now, she was very nice, a very nice girl.

Driving back to Escazú, he drove fast and aggressively, at one point barely beating a speeding taxi to a stretch of road that was narrowed to one lane by construction. Behind them, they could hear the taxi's brakes squealing to avoid the barrier. "Is very funny," he said. "In the club, I feel a little drunk. Now, when hands are on the wheel, not at all. Es increible, how sober I am in the car." It *was* incredible. Ted himself felt ponderously drunk, though he hadn't had a drink since the beers in the V.I.P.

In San Rafael, Pepe pulled into the Texaco station. Lights were still on above the pump island, but everything else was dark, the station clearly closed. He honked for a while, then lit a cigarette and got out and tried to get the pumps to work. Ted got out and followed him, as if he might be able to help.

Giving up on the pump, Pepe went over to a car parked right up against the building, blocking its entrance. He opened the car's door, and Ted could see bare feet. Somebody was sleeping or dead in the front seat of the car. Pepe shook one foot, then the other, until he managed to waken a boy about seventeen years old, wearing a greasy baseball cap, who went around and unlocked the pump switch. He wore a ring on every finger. He filled the Camaro's tank, joking sleepily with Pepe, and stuffed the bills he handed him into his jeans pocket.

In front of their house, Ted took the key from Pepe and unlocked and swung aside the heavy reja gate that protected the parking area. It was four-fifteen in the morning, birds were singing in the small remaining darkness. The air was cold and clean. "Good night, good morning," Pepe said.

"Buenas noches, buenos días," Ted answered, handing Pepe two of the roses. "Para Eva." He felt as if he had just tumbled to earth. He didn't know what anything meant, not friendship or betrayal, drunkenness or sobriety. Not flowers. Not money. Not women. Not men.

Before Pepe could work his key into his apartment's door lock, Ted turned back from his own door and said, "Pepe, dime una cosa." Back at the club, he asked, what was he going to try with that goon? Did he have a knife in his pocket?

Pepe straightened, squinted at him as the smoke of his cigarette curled across his eyes. After a moment, he smacked his hand flat against his pants pocket and laughed. "I don't got nothing there," he said. Only his courage.

CHAPTER EIGHT
APARTAMIENTO HOFFMAN

FROM THE BALCONY, she could see down the hill to where their street ran into the hulera road. In fact, she could see all the way across the valley to the blue mountains on the far side, some of which were volcanoes full of hot lava that would burn you to death if you even looked at it. But she was focused on the end of the street, which was where the Picketts' truck would appear, carrying Ray.

Because she was out on the balcony, Stephen was inside the apartment, pretending not to be anxious over Ray's arrival. She knew he was standing at the window of their bedroom, trying to pierce with his eyes the leaves of trees that would hide the truck's approach until almost the last minute. Willing the red truck to appear. She willed it, too.

Boby broke into an uproar, racing back and forth in the court-yard below her. She knew right away what was going on, even before she spotted the neighborhood dog who was crossing the street in front of their building. It was one of Boby's regular visi-tors, a cocker spaniel who squeezed easily through the bars of the reja, accepted Boby's greeting and inspection, then proceeded to his dish of meat bones and old tortillas and started eating.

Boby didn't mind, he always had plenty to eat. If the party guys had been around, they would have chased the little dog away, but they weren't home. Only Pepe and Eva's car was parked in the courtyard, and Eva loved all animals. Eva and Valerie loved Boby more than the party guys did, but he belonged to the party guys. They put out food for him and hosed down his place once a week, and the beautiful ladies who visited the party guys sometimes petted him, but mostly Boby had to depend on free dogs for entertainment, plus her conversation and the toys she dropped him once in a while. She would have played with him every day, but she couldn't go down into the courtyard. Eva and Pepe were nice to him when they came and went, and sometimes he escaped while they were getting their car through the reja gate. They never could catch him then, but he always came back after a few hours and would whine and bark to be let back into jail. He was too big to slip through the bars.

While the little dog ate and ate, Boby danced around her and sniffed at her bottom until she whirled and snapped at him, then she went back to eating, and Boby sniffed some more. He didn't do anything else to her, though he did to some of the other dogs who visited him. Valerie had learned a lot about dogs since coming to Costa Rica. She had seen them with jagged rows of teats hanging heavily from their bellies, and these, she knew, were mother dogs with puppies somewhere waiting to drink dog milk from those nipples. She had seen Boby and other dogs mounting each other from behind, and once, waiting with her family for a bus, she had seen a dog with what she thought was its tail stuck up another dog's butt, and had raced back and reported that to her family. She knew now that it hadn't been the tail, but the reality was even stranger, and she often thought about them, the two ordinary-looking dogs stumbling vaguely around, connected to each other by their private parts, not particularly upset, even though people were laughing at them. Another time she saw two dogs connected like that who were resting in the shade, facing in opposite directions, patient and apparently unconcerned. She had seen dogs fighting with each other in the streets, and once, in Cahuita, she had seen a big yellow dog, as big as Boby, lying in the mud beside a wooden walkway in the jungle. Flies were crawling over the dog, and later a man told them a snake had killed him.

She heard a horn honking. Immediately Stephen was out on the balcony with her, waving through the bars, then he ran back into the apartment and was outside on the road by the time the truck pulled up next to the building. Hank was driving, and Ray sat in the middle between him and Grace. Usually Grace was the one who drove Ray over for a visit or an overnight, or just Hank, and when both adults got out, she thought maybe there had been a change of plans, that Ray wasn't going to get to stay after all. But he climbed into the bed of the truck and tossed his backpack and rolled sleeping bag down to Stephen.

The little dog apparently had run away when the truck pulled up, and now Boby stood in the middle of his courtyard, barking mechanically. Monica came out to greet the Picketts. Valerie leaped onto the metal grillwork and shouted down to her, "Momma! Momma!," as if she had not seen her mother in a long time, and got them all to look up at her and smile and wave. She wanted to run down and join them, but there was something fine about watching them from above. She felt in charge, their queen. Stephen helped Ray carry his things into the house. She heard them pounding up the stairs and knew that they would come out onto the balcony before long, so she stayed where she was, her bare feet shivery when she jumped back down onto the smooth tile, her fingers clenched around the dusty metal of the reja.

Her father was still inside. He was working at the table, and she heard him say hi to Ray, but he didn't go down to talk with Grace and Hank, even though the boys were making so much noise he wouldn't be able to concentrate. She waited for him to ask them to keep it down. "Momma!" she shrieked again, adding a little more to the uproar. Monica ignored her this time. She was listening to something Hank and Grace were telling her.

Before she could scream again, Hank excused himself and disappeared into the building, leaving Monica and Grace talking beside the truck. He came up the stairs heavily, and entered the apartment, and then he must have noticed Ted. "I beg your pardon," she heard him say. "I can see you're a man hard at work."

"No, that's fine. It's good to see you."

"I just require the use of your telephone for a moment."

"Be my guest. Stephen!" he called out. "Keep it down in there!" And then he scraped his chair away from the table. "I'll give you some privacy," he said. He always did that when somebody was borrowing their phone, as if they were undressing.

"Ain't you I need privacy from," Hank said. "We know they got the bake shop phone bugged. Ever give us a phone at the house, *it* sure as hell will be."

He left anyway, and she crouched invisibly at the balcony door, watching Hank dial. Her father was a little afraid of Hank, she thought, much the way Stephen was a little afraid of Ted. Not because they had ever done anything bad. Just because. The way birds were afraid of even a friendly, nice girl like she was. She wasn't afraid of anyone. She didn't like it when Pepe insisted that she give him a beso on his stubbly cheek, but that wasn't being afraid.

She was sometimes a little afraid of tío Arturo, but that was different, too. She loved him and thought about living with him and driving around always in his wonderful car. What she was afraid of was that he loved her mother more than herself, and that he might someday take her mother to live with him and leave her behind. She didn't usually feel this way, only when she had been scolded harshly by her mother or had an earache or couldn't sleep because of noises. Really, she wasn't afraid of anyone.

He dialed and waited and then started talking Spanish to somebody. She smiled. It was exactly the way Ray imitated him talking to their servants. He persisted, though. He didn't go and get Monica to talk for him, as Ted had to do when he couldn't make somebody understand him over the phone. She couldn't understand what he was saying. She only recognized a few words—siete hombres, which she knew meant seven men, and importante, which meant important, and some boys' names, including Miguel, who was a kid in her preschool class. She missed Miguel and the rest of her classmates and especially el play, the school's swing set. School was over for the year, and she wouldn't get to go back until a long time after Christmas. Almost every day they walked past the playground, but the gate in the school's tall fence was locked now. She could have climbed over the fence, but there was barbed wire on top.

After Hank finished, he stuck his head into the bedroom where Stephen and Ray were playing, and he ordered Ray to behave himself. Then he went to leave, but as he was opening the apartment door he whirled around, even though he was so huge and white haired, and aimed a finger at her like a gun, so suddenly that she didn't have a chance to jump back. "Gotcha, little lady!" he bellowed, but he didn't pull the trigger or make the shooting sound. She didn't move until he was gone, thumping down the stairs. She wondered if he had known all along that she was hiding there, and she decided it was understandable that Ted was a little afraid of him.

Supper was always fun when Ray was there. They had perros calientes, which were hot dogs, and chips and carrot sticks and brownies that Grace had given them, and Ray kept telling crazy jokes that made Stephen and Valerie almost choke on their food from laughing. Ray turned to her once and criticized her for talking with her mouth full, which made her parents laugh with surprise and almost made her cry, but she drooled out some food on purpose, as a joke, and was able to forgive him, he laughed with such appreciation, and after supper he let her put on his old Super Ratón cape and mask with ears, which his mother had sent over for her.

The thing that made her feel really bad was later that evening, when Stephen asked if she could sleep somewhere else and give him and Ray some privacy. The two other times when Ray had had an overnight, he had just spread out his sleeping bag between Stephen's and Valerie's mattresses, and it had been fine. They had played cards and built garages and bridges from her Duplos, and she had not minded when Ray and Stephen had whispered for a while after Ted had made them turn out the light.

Ray was mostly Stephen's guest, she accepted that, but this was insulting, and when it became clear that her parents were inclined to accept Stephen's request, she destroyed the Duplo tower they had built and hurled several of Stephen's trucks off the balcony and tried to tear an ear off of the Super Ratón mask. Monica and Ted offered to let her sleep in their bedroom, in their bed, if she wanted, or on her own mattress.

She was too proud for that, however, and only accepted banishment from her own room when they agreed to let her do something she had always wanted to do—sleep outside on the balcony. Her father disliked the idea, she could tell. He thought that she should just do whatever he told her to do, but he couldn't think of any good reason once Monica had pointed out that the balcony was completely safe and the nights hadn't been too cold, and she could wear a sweat suit for pajamas, and it was as easy to move her light foam mattress out onto the balcony as anywhere else. They would leave the door open, and if it got too cold or if it rained (it hadn't rained in days), she could just come in and sleep on the couch.

Stephen was so grateful, he and Ray carried her mattress out onto the balcony, and he tucked in her sheets and blankets for her until it looked like his own bed, smooth and perfect, and brought her out some chocolate and cream Chiquis after her parents had kissed her good night.

It was almost as great as she had imagined it would be. She

turned on her side and watched the lights of the city in the valley miles below through a little opening in the trees, and when people walked by in the darkness she could see them and they didn't notice her up there. Boby barked at everyone who went past, as always, but now it was as if he were particularly guarding her, who was sharing the night with him.

The best thing, though, was something that Stephen should have been smart enough to figure out, that if you slid around to the narrow back part of the balcony, where the reja attached to the building, you could get close enough to the open window of the kids' bedroom to hear anything spoken above a low whisper. They were whispering like crazy when she got herself into position. She couldn't understand them at first, but it was exciting just to feel the buzz of their violated secrecy. Later, when they must have been certain that Monica and Ted were asleep, they got more careless, their voices rising until she could hear almost every word.

Mostly it was just the usual jokes and boasts and speculations that they shared even when they knew she was listening. Then there was a long silence, as if they had gone to sleep, but she knew they had not, and when they started talking again, she had wormed her way far enough behind the back of the reja to hear the remarkable thing that they had begun to talk about in tense, small voices.

They were examining something they never named, but she knew it was something that they shouldn't have had, for Stephen's words were strangled with frightened awe. "It's real?" he kept asking. He knew it was real, she could tell, whatever it was. She thought at first that it was some kind of animal, sleeping and motionless, like a snake she had once watched at a zoo. She knew he would never touch it, but then he said, his voice almost a croak, "Can I hold it?" And apparently he could, for after a moment there was a grunt of surprise. "It's heavy!"

"That's what I thought, the first time I handled this baby," Ray said. "Now I'm used to it."

And then she learned what it was, for she heard Stephen make the shooting sound, covertly but unmistakably, "pehw! pehw!" A gun. She wet herself a tiny bit, then got control of herself. It was very hard to stay motionless, however, in that awkward, cramped position. If somebody went by, they could see her there, glued sideways to the front of the building. But Boby would warn her in time.

"What are you going to bring?" Ray asked.

"You mean, besides the food." There was a long silence. "My dad has a machete," he said finally.

"A machete? Anybody can get a machete. Maybe I can get the Uzi. You can have this baby, and I'll have the Uzi."

"Won't your dad be taking the Uzi?" Stephen asked. Ray wasn't sure. "No," Stephen said then, "I'll take the machete. It's simple and silent." It sounded to her as if he had heard the phrase somewhere, and she liked it, too, and repeated it to herself, "simple and silent."

Ray finally judged the machete acceptable, and she felt proud of Stephen for defending it. It was all they had, the Hoffmans, in the line of weapons, and there seemed to be a point of honor in respecting it. She had been there when her father brought it home, acting embarrassed but pleased, and showed it to Monica. "What are you going to do with a machete?" she had asked, though not in a mean way, and he had pointed out the fancy handle carved out of cow horn into the shape of a cowboy boot.

"It's what you see camposinos using, everything from chopping down trees to trimming grass. And I like the sheath." He had run his hand down the carved, pale brown leather and then drew out the enormous, unpolished blade and hefted it a little. A sword, really. He wouldn't let either Stephen or Valerie touch it. "It was a bargain. Seven hundred and eighty colones, in this wonderful little shop in the Mercado Central full of harness stuff. Not even ten bucks. The old guy who shapes the handles, he picked this one out for me."

"It's really nice," Monica said.

"It'll be great for chopping weeds." He hacked some imaginary weeds. "God, the grip feels like it was made for my hand."

Stephen and Valerie had really wanted to hold it, and finally Ted let Stephen take it for a moment, in both hands, before taking it back. Ted only let her grab it while he was still holding onto the blade where it was dull down by the handle. She wasn't able to yank it away from him or convince him that she would be careful with it. A week later he had brought home a file with an equally fancy handle and a narrow, pointed sheath, like a dagger's, and he had used it to put a sharper edge on the machete. He kept the machete in the parents' bedroom where it was supposed to be safe. She knew Stephen wouldn't have any trouble finding it, though—there weren't that many places in one room where you could hide something that big. She herself knew exactly where it was: the top drawer in her parents' tall dresser. She wondered what Ray's gun looked like.

Ray and Stephen talked about other things after they had settled the matter of the machete. Food, clothes, matches. A tent. Horses. They were planning a trip, and nobody was supposed to know about it. When she realized this, she again felt an almost irresistible urge to pee. Pretty soon, she would have to go inside and go to the bathroom. She didn't want to miss anything, though. They talked about Hank and communists and guns and knives and drugs and Panama. She couldn't stop listening.

Gradually they grew quiet, and she must have slept a little, wedged between the reja and the house, for she was startled awake when Boby and a big stray dog in the road began to bark furiously at each other. She edged away from the now-silent window, went inside to the bathroom. Afterward, she found Ray's Super Ratón mask and attached cape hanging from the back of a chair and slipped it over her head, then stood for a while at the kids' bedroom door, listening. When she eased the door open, she could hear Stephen's soft wheeze, which meant that he was safely asleep. It was harder to tell about Ray, but she decided to take a chance and crept into the bedroom, dark except for their night light.

Ray's sleeping bag was not where her mattress went, parallel to the wall opposite Stephen's mattress, but turned so that the two boy's heads were right next to each other. Through the stiff eye holes of the mask, she examined their faces, Stephen's frowning slightly, Ray's blank and sort of dumb looking, his usual witty animation blotted out by sleep. She got close enough to smell his sour, milky breath—he hadn't brushed his teeth when they went into the bathroom to take care of that last task. She checked Stephen's breath, but it was minty.

With infinite care, she felt around for the gun Ray had smuggled into their gun-hating household, first under the folds of the sleeping bag, then in his backpack. She felt something hard beneath the lumps of clothes, but it was a metal race car that he had brought over the last time he visited. She checked under the pile of Ray's dirty clothes in the angle between the sleeping bag and Stephen's mattress and found only a bunch of hard fruits in his jeans pocket.

She had almost given up, had almost begun to lose faith in what she had so vividly pictured earlier in the night, when she wormed her hand carefully underneath the pillow Ray's head was resting on, her own favorite place for contraband, and touched cold metal. Her hand jerked in excitement, so that she was afraid she had wakened him. He just rolled over onto his other side, however, allowing her hand more freedom to explore the unseen shape—angular and mysterious, smooth here, rough there, both flat and round. Her hand found the hole of the barrel, and her finger briefly entered it, then retreated.

And then she found the trigger. Her pointer and middle fingers snaked around its curve. She held the grip steady with her other hand and pulled on the trigger, and she felt it yield slightly. She held it that way for a moment, pulling, until her fingers trembled with the pressure, then released it as gently as a breath and slid her hands out from under the pillow and slipped out of the room and closed the door. When she raised her hand to her real nose under the big nose of the mask, her fingers had a sharp oily smell. Just touching a gun marked you with its odor. She sniffed it some more, an interesting smell.

The gray cape trailing from her shoulders, she carried her powerful knowledge through the darkened apartment toward her parents' bedroom. She planned to enter and slide into their bed, and if they woke, tell them everything, and if they didn't wake, wait till morning to explode the bomb that would teach Stephen once and for all not to shut her out, not to treat her as if she were stupid and negligible as a baby. They would realize how competent and valuable she was, to have discovered something so bad they could never have imagined it. Monica would tell Arturo about what she had done, and no one would ever again think of leaving her behind.

She was stopped at the door of her parents' bedroom by the sound of voices. She stood in the dark hallway and listened, touching the big mouse ears to the surface of the door. They were fighting about something, though their voices were so calm and low, no one who didn't know them would have realized it. They thought no one could tell, but she could tell. She and Stephen always could tell.

She retreated from the door. She didn't want to go back out onto the balcony, so she curled up in the big fuzzy chair where her mother liked to read and drew her stockinged feet up under the thin fabric of the cape.

She shifted in the tickly, scratchy embrace of the chair and thought about Stephen and Ray. She was glad that she hadn't had the chance to betray their secrets. She almost cried, thinking about how close she had come. She felt shaken and relieved. She knew she couldn't go with them. It wasn't that she was a girl. She was just too little. She hadn't even been strong enough to pull that trigger, so how could she help them in a real fight? They should have trusted her more, she heard herself arguing, but hadn't she come so close to ruining everything for them? So how could she help them?

She hugged herself, wrapped herself more tightly around the clutch of things that she knew. After a while, just before she fell asleep, she realized she did know how. She would guard their secret and keep it safe. They wouldn't know about it themselves, what she was doing for them, masked, wrapped in a superhero's cape. Someday they would know. And then they would love her forever.

CHAPTER NINE

QUERIDOS AND STRANGERS

MONICA LAUGHED UNSTEADILY when she got out of the car in
front of Arturo's little house in the mountains.

"What?"

"Nothing."

"Querida, what?"

The whitewashed adobe walls with the band of pale blue
at the base. The faded tile roof, the rough wooden door, the
unsawn, whitewashed logs supporting a low porch roof. A
small-paned window, banana trees shading the dirt yard.
"It's— típico," she said. What tourist restaurants claimed to be.
She felt dizzy.

"You don't like?"

Of course she liked it, she said, reaching for the deliberate-
ness of a second language. She stood on the porch and looked
down onto a long, terraced slope, lush with coffee plants. They
were only a few kilometers from San José, but a ridge of mountains cut them off from a view of the central valley. This was
really where he lived? she asked. A watercolor you could buy at
tourist shops.

What had she imagined? he asked. He was leaning against

one of the rustic posts, his cowboy boots crossed in front of him. Arms folded so that she couldn't see his hands.

For a moment it was hard to speak. She had imagined something modern. His cabina in Cahuita, his friend's apartment. She felt the blood rush to her throat and cheeks, and she had to go to the door and rattle idiotically at the knob until he came over and unlocked it and let her in.

Inside, it was cool and dark. A few pieces of wood and vinyl furniture. Narrow kitchen with propane stove, stone sink, avocado green refrigerator. A small bedroom, windowless except for what light and air crept in around the rafter ends. Bathroom with tile shower, cálidor. The tall iron bed in the bedroom was covered with a worn chenille spread, neatly made. When she sat down, the creak of its springs gave her courage, as plain speech or old clothes do, and she began unbuttoning her blouse.

He stopped her. "We got time now. Something to eat first."

She rose and followed him into the kitchen and watched him take a salad out of the refrigerator, then two steaks marinating in a silky liquid, and a bowl of cooked rice. He divided the salad onto two plates, put the steaks in a pan on the stove, and seemed undecided about the rice. "Usually I eat it cold," he said.

"Cold is fine." She watched him arrange their lunch (somebody had prepared it, put it into the refrigerator) and had to lean with one hand on the low counter top. She was too far from home, she felt unbalanced, as if she were floating in space, and when he put the food on a porcelain-covered metal table that was exactly like the kitchen table her family had had when she was a little girl, she couldn't even sit down. She picked up the glass of wine he had poured for her, carried it into the dark bedroom, set it on a dresser, took off all of her clothes, even her watch, even her earrings, though not her wedding band, and crawled between the tight, cold sheets. (Somebody had washed and ironed the linens. Somebody had made the bed.)

It was ready, he called from the kitchen. The scrape of a pan, clinks of silverware on the porcelain table. Then he stood in the doorway. Was she all right? he asked. And she could no more answer than a boy drifting at the bottom of a swimming pool can answer the taunts of his friends, for he has dived too deeply, broken his neck. She has dived too deeply.

He sat down on the edge of the bed. The springs groaned, and he touched a cool hand to her forehead, like a parent checking for fever. She reached up and kissed him on the fleshy base of his thumb, kissed and then bit hard enough to make him narrow his eyes, though he didn't pull away. She kissed away the blood when it beaded up in a thin parenthesis, held her breath while he undressed, while he slid naked into bed beside her, while he reached inside of her, took her breath, gave it back to her again.

They had time now. Today they had a little more time. Ted was taking Stephen to Ray's house for an overnight, then driving out to the farm and airport, seeing a shipment off, and Valerie was at the national amusement park for a preschool classmate's birthday party. You didn't have to stay with them, it turned out. The birthday boy's parents had even picked Valerie up at the apartment, driving a new Toyota minivan that looked like the space shuttle, and would drop her off late that afternoon.

She had realized that after she did some quick Christmas shopping in San José, they could have three, maybe four hours together. The borrowed, neutral apartment with traffic sounds outside suddenly had seemed inadequate, and they were finally able to go to his own place in the quiet mountains. For the first hour she was not sure that she could stand it. Then it seemed that she would.

In the dim room she lay naked on top of him as if he were her naked shadow, her cheek resting on his bony cheek. Arms outstretched on arms, fingers laced together. His legs beneath her legs, her ankles against his ankles. Almost exactly the same height, they lay as if he were her shadow under the noon sun. They were breathing.

He wasn't inside her anymore, and the condom lay somewhere on the polished concrete floor where she had tossed it, but she could feel his short, thick penis pressed between her body and his body. Penises had little to say about the men they belonged to, she thought, who up until six weeks ago had been familiar with only one man's penis for over a decade. It was the sort of thought she had started to have when need had been taken care of and responsibility had not yet taken her by the throat.

There were other thoughts. That she was not paying Ted back, for instance, which is what she had been afraid of the whole time before she first went to bed with Arturo and for about twenty-four hours after. She wasn't paying him back, yet having Arturo for a lover somehow did free her a little from Ted's affair. It didn't free him, it just lifted the dead feeling from her heart a little. Which was lucky, for her heart was fully occupied now, not just with Arturo, who filled it himself, but with Stephen and Valerie in a new and frightening way, and Ted, too, and a dizzyingly blank future.

•

THEY SAT NAKED on towels laid over the vinyl upholstered kitchen chairs and ate salad and cold rice and warm steak at the porcelain table. It was the middle of the afternoon. A breeze moved from the open front door to the single, unscreened window at the back of the house, shaded by trees clinging to the abrupt slope. It was the best meal she had ever eaten, she said.

He said, at a four star restaurant like this, what else could she expect? She was quiet. He saw she was thinking about something, and after a few moments he asked her what it was.

The good meal, she said.

He thought about that, looking at her until she felt her nipples ache. About the meal, what? Before she had a chance to answer, he said he thought he knew. She was wondering who had prepared the meal and left it in the refrigerator.

Surely he had done it himself.

It was not so difficult.

She looked at him.

"Really," he said, "you are such something." What if he told her that he had a housekeeper who came and cooked for him and cared for this very little house, would that diminish her respect for him as a man of modern values?

He had done very well dividing the salad, she said. Serving the good meal. What was her name?

Yamilet.

A very competent woman.

Yes.

A señora with many children.

A señorita who lived nearby.

"Well," she said, getting up and taking her dishes to the sink. "I would like to lie down with you in your loud bed once more, señor. Then we have to go."

They lay under a sheet, the bed just complaining a little when they shifted positions in the dark room. Overhead, light ran like knives where the roof slope met the thick walls, but it stayed above, it didn't touch them.

"You're being very quiet," he said.

"Tell me something," she said. "After spending so many weeks talking and talking, how can I know so little about you?"

"You know everything that matters. That I adore you."

"You don't really live here, do you," she said.

"See, you know everything. Is my house, but no, I'm not here so much, is not always so convenient. Look," he said, propping his head on his left hand. His other hand rested on her hip, then slid down and began lightly playing. "I'm businessman who doesn't work too hard, with different businesses and guys to run them. I'm not so rich like my brother, but can afford this típico house to remind me I am Tico, and my nice car, and I have friends who open their house to me. I travel much. Because of you, not so much lately. What else? Parents dead, as you know. Unmarried all my life, truly."

As if swearing, he raised his right hand, then rested it on her again. She felt a finger nestle there, slide into her. He told her some other things. Or she dreamed them, it didn't seem to matter anymore.

When she woke, the blades of light had shifted overhead. She leaped out of bed and rummaged in the pile of her clothes for her watch and found she would barely have time to get home before Valerie was dropped off. He was already up and dressed. She shouldn't worry, he said, he knew a fast way through the mountains.

In the car, she brushed her hair and was putting on a little lip gloss when he slammed on the brakes and swerved to a stop, throwing her hard against the restraint of the shoulder belt. There were fallen rocks on the road ahead of them, some big as typewriters. Was she all right? he asked. She nodded, touching her collar bone and the side of her breast where the harness had dug in. He put the car in gear and eased it along the narrow dirt shoulder between the rocks and the sheer edge of the road. She glanced down the precipice falling away to her right before fixing her gaze on his concentrated face.

Once past the obstruction, he apologized. "Some say is sopilotes," he said. "Vultures. It's said that when they're hungry and nothing is dead, they drop stones onto the roads of the mountain and wait for some guy to crash."

When she smiled, he said, "Listen, querida, I tell you a story. One time the sopilotes are doing this thing, dropping stones, when one of them say, 'This is hard work, and some drivers is so excellent, he stop in time. Would it no be more simpler to drop the rock direct on cow or person?' And the others turn their long neck away from him in embarrassment, until one finally declare, 'We are no murderers. We are civil servants.'"

She put a hand on his shoulder. Even while joking he hadn't released the knot of tension in the corner of his jaw. She caressed the spot. "Mira," he said to her, pointing through the heavily-tinted upper portion of the windshield, a huge dark bird floating toward the next ridge, its long, blunt wings angled forward, its neck neatly tucked away between its shoulders, only the sharp beak visible.

She looked at her watch. Four-thirty. Valerie was supposed to be back before five. Would they make it? she asked him.

Yes, of course. He started speeding up, pushing the tight, badly banked turns his car seemed too big to negotiate. She wove her fingers into the thick hair curling over his collar and said, No, the vultures had had their chance already.

The road seemed to be still climbing. Now and then they would have a view of San José spread out far below, and once she thought she caught a glimpse of the cross that stood high in the mountains over Escazú. Then the road was unmistakably dropping, heading toward a steep gorge. There was something ahead, a roadblock with two jeeps and some uniformed men standing around, and beyond them a narrow bridge spanning the gorge.

More civil servants, she said, trying to joke herself out of the despair that was starting to settle onto her. He remained impassive as he pulled to a stop at the barricade. She waited for him to turn to her and make her smile, but his attention was somewhere else, taking in the jeeps and the men casually moving toward the car. They were in the familiar khaki of the rural guard, the police responsible for the countryside, except for three men in jungle camouflage fatigues such as she had never seen in Costa Rica. The men in camouflage carried automatic weapons.

He lowered his window, the brightness of the afternoon shoving into the car, casting everything into a yellow haze.

One of the rural guardsmen leaned over and greeted them politely, even deferentially, first him and then her. He looked at her curiously, and she thought he seemed familiar. But she didn't know any policemen.

Was there something wrong? Arturo asked. The man shook his head and assured them, no, nothing was wrong, it wasn't serious. He only needed to see their identification papers. Arturo gave him his driver's license, and Monica dug a much-folded xerox of her passport out of her purse. The guardsman made no effort to explain the barricade or their presence on the road, and when he had their papers he studied them for a minute and then walked over to where the others were standing.

What wasn't serious? she asked. What was going on?

For the first time since they had had to stop, he looked over at her. He smiled mechanically, his thin, wolfish face looking not quite like himself, and shook his head. He wasn't sure, he said after a few moments. It wasn't the guardsman he was worried about, they would just want a little bribe. It was the men in camouflage.

She thought that she maybe knew the guardsman who had spoken to them, she said. Maybe that would help. Maybe he was the parent of a child at Stephen's or Valerie's school.

He said, no, not those schools, did she know what a policeman made? Still, he said, he had noticed it, too, the man seemed to recognize her.

She checked her watch. In fifteen minutes, maybe less, Miguel's mother would be dropping off Valerie at home. Ted wouldn't be back for several hours, yet. What would she do? Eva and Pepe might be home, but more likely she would wander around, get interested in something, follow some passing dog. They couldn't take much longer, she said. He took her hand in a gesture of comfort, but he was preoccupied and distant and was showing none of the easy confidence that ordinarily surrounded him like a cloak broad enough for them both.

Several of the rural guards approached and asked him to come with them, they needed to ask him a few questions. She started to open her door as he got out, but the man said no, it wasn't necessary. She got out anyway and stood beside the car and watched him being led to one of the jeeps. It was Costa Rica, she kept reminding herself, they weren't going to hurt him. It was not El Salvador or Honduras or Guatemala. It was some bureaucratic thing, an opportunity to conduct some minor extortion. If only they would get it over with and let him take her home to her little girl.

She looked around. She had never been here before, and she recognized no landmarks, but they couldn't be too far from Escazú. If they had driven back to San José and then gotten onto the autopista, they would be home by now. But they couldn't be too far. She wished she had spent a little time with Ted's topo maps. There was no such thing as a road map for this sort of area. The gorge ahead of them was almost as deep as that crossed by the old Tiribi bridge. It probably *was* the Tiribi, only a different bridge. Far away, where the gorge twisted out of sight, there was a shack. Otherwise, she could see no buildings except for the distant flash here and there that must have been from an office building down in San José catching the late afternoon sun.

The guardsmen came back and asked her to step away from the car please. She moved to the side of the road and tried to explain about her daughter, that she had to get back at once, the child would hurt herself. Of course, they said, it would only be a moment, and they began to search the car. She walked toward Arturo, who seemed to be arguing with the rural guardsmen, including the one she maybe recognized, and the men in camouflage, but he noticed her and raised his hand, holding her off. A moment, he mouthed to her, raising his index finger.

All the doors were standing open. The big car looked winged. Her bag of Christmas presents was spread out on the ground, the toys arranged as if for sale by street vendors. One of the guardsmen went to Arturo and made him give him his keys and opened the trunk and removed some blankets and riding tack and a briefcase. She edged over to see what they were doing, until a man in camouflage blocked her way, made her return to the side of the road. They brought the briefcase over to one of the jeeps and handed it inside. She watched Arturo watching the men with his briefcase, and her heart fell some more, and she felt herself caught up by a kind of numb rage, against him, now, and herself for trusting him. She suddenly was certain he had drugs in that briefcase. She remembered the baggie of what he had said was cocaine, which he said he had found in the bathroom of his brother's house during the birthday party. Everything suddenly pieced itself together and she felt so stupid that even her panic about Valerie shrank to a kind of hard, nerveless tumor.

She had to pee. The mountainside here was rocky and eroded, but about fifty meters behind them, where the road turned, there was a cluster of small trees and brush. She walked toward the trees, and even when somebody shouted angrily at her, she kept going. Only when she heard Arturo call out her name did she stop and turn in time to see one of the men in camouflage starting after her, assault rifle raised in one hand. She had to urinate, she said, and turned her back on them and continued to the trees, which gave her little enough privacy, but by then she scarcely cared.

Her legs were trembling, and it took every bit of her long-ago, almost-forgotten camping experience not to wet her underpants. When she returned, Arturo met her before she reached the car, which looked butchered and desperate with its doors and trunk and hood flung open. The others were watching them, just out of earshot. He said, "Querida, I'm so sorry for this." He was focusing on her now, for the first time since they had been stopped. He said, "Never mind these guys. Believe me, they will no harm you." He held her then, and she started to cry. "They will no harm you," he kept saying, as if that had been her worry.

"God damn you," she said, "I have to get home. What's going on?"

"Listen to me," he said. "Is a mistake, but a little complicate. I think maybe you can make it go quicker."

She stared at him.

"Is political," he said, "what else? These guys got suspicions, and some person has put in the police computers I had involve with Cal Richardson, and because you also know him, they think they're onto a big something."

"That's who he is," she broke in. "He's one of the cops who interviewed us about Richardson. He was wearing a blue uniform."

"Yes," he said, "I think you're right. He get excited when he read your papers. All will be correct, but they're saying they got to take us to their station, could be hours. So I try to think about some how we can scare them off from us quick."

"'Scare them.'"

"Listen," he said, "most of these guys, they're just poor bureaucrats. You got connections to tell them, number one, we're okay, and number two, they have trouble from bothering you."

"Tell them who your brother is, he's connected like crazy."

He shook his head. "Connected, but to the wrong place. No, is your father, U.S. Congressman, State Department."

She felt like crying again, if this was his idea of what would help them. "He's just a lobbyist now. I have to get back *now. Now.*" She wanted to start running, to hurl herself past this whole clot of unbelievable stupidity.

"Querida, truly, Washington lobbyist is no so small to these guys. I hear his name down here, with respect."

What would they do if she walked past them and across the bridge and kept going? It was a bad dream, like the maddening runarounds she and Ted had had with Migración and Aduana and ICE and Salud. Only this was god knows where in the fucking mountains. She was with her lover now. These bureaucrats had guns.

"Say who you are, who is your father. They don't hear me. You must say them you are his daughter. Just say them who you are."

"I have to get back."

"Say them simply this: you are the daughter of Michael Cheney, of the company Vanderbilt and Wilson. He would no want you detained."

She stared at him.

He shrugged. "Or we just see how it goes." He turned and started to walk back.

After a moment, she followed him. She and Arturo walked back to the one in khaki who seemed to be in charge, and asked that he return their papers and not delay them anymore. She was the daughter of Mr. Michael Cheney, of Vanderbilt Wilson Associates, Washington, D.C. Surely they knew that he would not want her detained so idiotically, when his little granddaughter needed her.

The man looked blank. Big surprise, she thought. Then he said something to one of the other guards, who handed him the worn xerox of her passport. You were supposed to have the real thing with you, but if you lost it, it was hideously difficult to replace. A copy was usually enough, but here in the mountains, who knows? He looked at the page containing her Costa Rican visa, which gave her name as Monica Cheney Gireaux de Hoffman, which proved exactly nothing. She wanted to scream at Arturo.

The man did not appear to be scared, big surprise, though he also didn't laugh in her face. He walked over to a jeep and got inside and spoke on the radio. Two of the guys in camouflage came over, and one of them talked on the radio.

It was all just more delay, she thought. Nothing would be decided out here on a mountain road. Bureaucrats had enough trouble making decisions in the security of their own cubicles. They would have to go into San José, anyway. She could call Ted from there, though not until he got back from the airport, which would be an hour after dark.

What was going to happen to Valerie? She was a familiar figure in the neighborhood, everybody doted on her. But what if Patronato, the child protection bureaucracy, got hold of her? They could keep you from taking your kid out of the country. Ted had once read her a hair-raising article about it. What would it be like, dealing with them over an abandoned child? She had to get home. She had to get home.

She stood beside Arturo in cold silence, watching the charade of consultation and deliberation. She had to get home. The thought of her father being somehow helpful in this mess made her feel disoriented and puny. It physically sickened her. When she was a teenager in active rebellion against home and school, he had always been the one to make the phone call that gave her another chance. He had seen to it that there was always another school ready to accept her. He had paid the bills. And he did it all by remote control, a powerful man in a perfect marriage that ended neatly in divorce when the last child, Monica, left for college, where life finally started making a little sense. Things were better between them since her children were born, but she hardly ever saw him. When he had called to discuss the family's move to Costa Rica, he talked mainly with Ted.

The policeman she had recognized came over to them finally and handed them their papers. It was all right, everything was in order, they could go now. He hesitated and then asked her if she remembered him from a while ago, when he had spoken to her about an unhappy matter. She nodded numbly. Clutching her xeroxed passport, she turned away and headed back toward the car, which had magically closed itself into its former sleek, impenetrable form, her packages presumably returned to the back seat. Well, he said, he hoped that he had been of service in this matter as well.

He was asking for a tip, she thought, but she kept going, for she could not think about it, she just had to get home. His briefcase? she heard Arturo say. They had not yet returned his briefcase. She stopped and watched him go with the guardsman to the jeep that seemed to be their command center and felt a rush of anger over one more delay, then, in a kind of backwash, almost unbearable relief that there hadn't been drugs, that he was innocent. She only had to go home now. Valerie only had to be safe. Nothing else mattered.

"Little fling?" a voice said from behind her. One of the men in camouflage, who had appeared between her and the car. That's what it sounded like he had said to her, "Little fling?"

She was going crazy. "Cómo?" What had he said?

"What y'all doing out here with that joker?" he asked. "Having you a little Tico fling?"

An American. She stared at him. His heavy, good-looking face was deeply tanned, his black hair closely cropped, and he was holding his weapon pointing skyward as if any second its barrel would drop toward her. An American soldier. She said to him after a moment, in Spanish, what was *he* doing here? It was he who didn't belong here, she said.

She was able to turn away then. She got into the car, and waited for Arturo to return with his briefcase and start the powerful, luxurious American car and sail them across that bridge and through the beautiful mountains into the pleasant town of Escazú up to her own nice, middle-class apartment house, where her daughter either would or would not be. Had to be.

They didn't say anything for a while. Then she said, "One of them was American."

"The ones in jungle cloth," he said. "Advisors from Murciélago, a training camp close to the Nicaragua frontier. I wonder what they're doing down here. I think maybe something is going on."

She wanted to tell him what the man had said to her, but she found that she could not. Neither could she tell him she had been afraid he had drugs in his briefcase, nor about the coldness she had felt in him when he had been afraid, nor her impulse to abandon him like a bad dream. "Murciélago," she said. "Bat."

"They train civil guard there for catching drugs, that kind of thing. Militaries, truthfully. Very convenient to Nicaragua and our friends the Contras."

She looked at him.

"I speak as one loyal to freedom and democracía."

"How can you joke?" She couldn't remember hearing this tone from him, bitterness or weariness, she couldn't tell.

"Querida, is no joke more than any other here, a place where each one must invent some way to be serious. The Nicas always been that for us. I got many friends, Sandinistas, Contras, some one, then the other. The soldiers in jungle cloth think they got it simple. I promise you, is not simple. Still, I wonder what they're doing here. Something's going to happen."

•

SHE HAD BEEN RIGHT, they hadn't been far from home, only about twenty minutes. Even so, it was getting dark when they swung down from the southern mountains and arrived in front of the apartment house, an hour after she should have been there. She raced pointlessly up to her empty apartment, tried to think of somebody to call, then ran downstairs again and rang Pepe and Eva's doorbell and then even the party guys'. Nobody was home. She and Arturo walked around the building, calling Valerie's name, and had just gotten back into the car to start driving around the neighborhood when the white minivan pulled up. As soon as Valerie spotted Arturo's car, she shot out of the minivan and charged around to his door and yanked on the handle until he opened it and let her sit on his lap and pretend to steer.

Monica went over to the minivan and began the apology she had been preparing ever since they crossed the wretched bridge. Her best-case apology, Valerie somehow safe still with Miguel's parents.

The mother laughed and interrupted her. They had lost track of time at the amusement park, she said, everybody having so much fun, and then it took them longer than they had expected to have the birthday treats. She hoped Monica wasn't worried.

No, Monica said, of course not. Many thanks. A thousand thanks.

When the minivan was gone, she went over and took her Christmas shopping out of the back seat and broke the news to Valerie that Arturo had to leave, it was late. Valerie ignored her, continued to steer wildly through hairpin turns on the imaginary road. Only after he promised to come the next day to take them all swimming at his brother's country club could Monica manage to pry her fingers off the steering wheel and lift her off his lap. And while she was occupied with this struggle, she managed to touch him on the hand that still carried the marks of her teeth, on his hard cheek, on his hair, on his throat, on the sleeve of his shirt, on his chest.

Tomorrow, then, she said to him, and stepped back. Until tomorrow, she said, and could scarcely bear it when he looked away from her finally and pulled the door shut, as if her own greedy fingers were still clutching him, as if her whole body had to be torn away by force. And as the car moved out of sight down the hill, she wanted to hurl questions after him like grappling hooks. What should she do if the police came around? The one who remembered her from the Richardson business, he could return, he knew where she lived. And what if Ted found out? How could she bear it, what should she do? And would it be better to just tell him, as he had told her?

What sickened her the most about it was that Ted would think she was paying him back. He would be rageful, sarcastic, depressed for weeks, but throughout it all he would never doubt that she was balancing the moral equation. He would never believe how little he and what he had done had to do with it. It wasn't that he was a nonentity now—he loomed as large as ever in her life, she couldn't see past him. It was that Arturo existed in another plane entirely, not of equations but simple identity. Whose identity? She wasn't sure of that. She wasn't sure of much, she thought, as she carried the sticky little girl up the stairs to their apartment. But she knew necessity when it gathered her up in its arms. She knew what it meant to be alive.

CHAPTER TEN

TIROS IN THE DARK

THE LOUSY CAR BROKE DOWN even before they got to Santa Ana, overheating, smoke pouring out from under the hood at first and then snaking into the car itself through the vents in the dashboard. Stephen could feel rage boiling up into his head, thinking he and Ray might not be able to get to the fort and make camp before dark. Ted pulled over onto the side of the road, practically tipping them into the ditch, turned to him, and said, "Tell you what, Stevie, maybe we should just get out and let this sucker burn."

"Are you crazy?" he screamed, and felt like attacking him with his fists.

But Ted reached out a hand and put it on his shoulder, and said, "Sorry, I'm kidding, it's not really smoke. The radiator's boiling over. This stuff is only vapor. It's not really on fire."

"How do you know?" he demanded. "You can't see where it's coming from."

"The smell. But good point." He popped the hood lever and got out and lifted the hood, blocking Stephen's view. Stephen got out on the sloping lip of the ditch and scrambled around to the front of the car and saw that there was, indeed, no visible fire, and the smoke was thinning and blowing away.

"Something's keeping the radiator from working right. It was a bad thermostat before. Now I don't know."

"Can we go? Ray's waiting for me."

"We've got to let it cool down before driving again, or we'll get a real fire. We maybe should add liquid to the radiator, but I don't want to crack it. There's a store up ahead, isn't there? Let's get something to drink and see if there's a mechanic can help us."

He went to get his suitcase out of the back seat, but Ted told him to leave it and locked the car. "Why're you bringing so much stuff?" he asked. "Usually it's just your backpack."

He shrugged. "We might camp out."

"Really? Camp out? Good for you."

"That's why I have to get there soon, or it'll be too late."

"Do our best." Ted walked ahead of him on the narrow shoulder, and when it widened he tried to put a hand on his shoulder, but Stephen pretended not to notice and kept looking back at the car until the road turned and it was out of sight. Usually when they had car trouble Ted cursed and raged, but now, when it was Stephen who was being inconvenienced, he just accepted it. He thought about the suitcase he was bringing, and felt a kind of hard satisfaction that it contained his father's precious machete, wrapped in the leg of a pair of sweatpants.

The store was the abastecedor where the Picketts sometimes stopped to pick up dog food or a few groceries on the way to their finca. The owner recognized him. "¿Estefan, dónde está tu amigo?"

At his house, he was going there now, he answered. He hesitated, then introduced his father, who had come up beside him and seemed appropriately impressed by his familiarity in this foreign town. He showed him the chicks in wooden cages, and drank a Coke, and listened to Ted try to describe their car trouble to the store owner.

No, he heard the man say, there wasn't a mechanic around here now, though maybe at the filling station on the other side of town. Maybe the car would be all right now, the man suggested, and Stephen abruptly was certain that it was, and urged his father to go back and check. He didn't trust the old car's locks to protect his belongings, and he was struck by the thought of how unfair it was, how any least thing could wreck his most careful plans.

He was right about the car. It wasn't smoking anymore, and started immediately. When they approached the tiny filling station where the road turned and headed up into the mountains, he was afraid that Ted was going to stop and try to get a mechanic to work on it, but he kept on going on the winding, disintegrating road and only pulled over when the smoke started slipping out from underneath the hood again.

Ted eased onto the narrow shoulder and set the parking brake with a harsh crunch. "We couldn't drive up much further anyway," he said when Stephen moaned. "We can walk from here, can't we? Isn't that really steep stretch up to the finca just a few turns ahead?"

"Yes! We can walk it easy." He leaped out and grabbed his suitcase and started lugging it up the mountain, grateful for his father's unexpected reasonableness. He struggled a little when Ted took the suitcase from him, but he couldn't have gone far with it before having to stop.

It was hard even for Ted. "What do you have in here, bricks?"

He felt himself blush, imagining the heavy steel of the machete dragging earthward. "My warm jacket," he said. "Books." They both knew he meant comic books. "Stuff for when we're camping out."

"What, frying pan? Canned goods?"

He didn't want an answer, he was just teasing him. Stephen resisted the impulse to lash back. He already could be in trouble for taking the machete, so he didn't push it now. "Just some cookies and chips and juice boxes. Mom said I could."

"Okay, sure. I think it's great that you're going camping." He stopped after a while to rest his arm and checked his watch. "Oh, man. I'm going to have a close call." He had to pick up a shipment of flowers at the farm and take them out to the airport.

The good thing was that Ted couldn't hang around and get in a long conversation after they finally staggered up to the Picketts' house. He just said hello to Grace and gave Stephen a fierce hug and wished him and Ray luck, then headed back down the mountain.

Late as it was, afternoon already, Ray wasn't ready to go yet. He still had to pack his things, and he hadn't even cleared anything with his mother.

"I guess," she said vaguely when they presented the plan to her—to ride up into the forest reserve above the finca and spend the night camping out. They were careful not to specify when they were coming back, and she didn't ask. Looking at it fairly, Stephen guessed that she was thinking they would return in the morning—she mentioned lunch—but she never said anything for sure and really didn't seem to be paying very close attention to their preparations.

Grace and the current maid, a woman Stephen hadn't met before, were working on Christmas, sorting presents of used shirts and pants and dresses and underwear for poor families in the area. He didn't see anything in the pile he would welcome under his tree. The Picketts at least *had* a tree, though, a big one with needles like those in the United States, dense with glass ornaments and flashing with lights. All the Hoffmans had in their apartment was a little thing like a hedge bush, propped in a clay pot full of rocks to hold it up, with lights that Ted had rigged so they wouldn't flash on and off the way they were supposed to. Anyway, these stacks of clothes weren't the Picketts' own presents, which were bound to be great. The Picketts' own presents wouldn't appear under the tree until Christmas morning, Ray said. The Hoffmans had some wrapped presents around their little tree and would open them on Christmas eve. Stephen was hoping for a Game Boy, though his parents had warned him anything like that cost a fortune here.

Another thing was distracting Grace, he thought. She was probably worried about Hank, heading for the Panama jungle with a band of fighters. Nobody was supposed to know about that. He helped Ray roll up his much-washed sleeping bag and another, newer-looking one, for himself, and transfer as much of their combined pile of supplies as would fit into two army duffel bags. For privacy, Stephen thought they should do the packing in Ray's room, but it would have been too much work hoisting everything up through the ceiling trap door and then lowering them back down again, so they worked behind the long sofa of the family room, making sure that their weapons got in first, wrapped in layers of clothes. There wasn't much danger. Hank was gone, and Grace and the maid were pretty much ignoring them. Most importantly, Charlotte was away, who would have been the one likely to catch them. She was at some beach with the family of one of her classmates, celebrating the end of the school year.

They hauled the duffels down to the tin-roofed stable and cooperated in rounding up Mary, the big white horse that Ray was going to ride, and Davy Crockett, the pony, on which Stephen by now felt almost comfortable. Grace came down and helped them saddle up and fasten their camping gear to the backs of the saddles—a job that surprised him with its sheer sweaty difficulty. It was especially awkward with Davy Crockett, who kept twisting and struggling to step out from under the unfamiliar weight of the pack. Ray argued that Davy Crockett was too small. They should be allowed to take Goldie, since Charlotte by now had a new horse, the chestnut stallion that was watching them from the far side of the pasture.

Stephen was relieved when Grace refused. He had ridden Mary, that would have been all right, but he didn't want to be anywhere near Goldie. He was a gelding, Ray had explained that to him, which was supposed to make him tame, but while the new horse just kept his distance, Goldie tore from one side of the fenced pasture to the other in nervous bursts of energy.

Then he would trot up in a friendly manner and see what was going on, then tear away again, bucking and arching his neck, biting at the other horses across the corral fence.

When they were finally mounted and ready to go, the duffel bags slung behind them in bulky, professional-looking bundles, Grace pushed some loose hair back from her face and looked at the boys in a puzzled way, as if she hadn't been aware of what was going on until that exact moment, even though she had been helping them. She held the gate halfway open and said to Ray when he eased Mary toward the opening, "Why, you're leaving me, aren't you! I'm going to be all alone tonight."

"Momma," Ray said. "We got to get up there before dark."

"I know, darling boy. I'll have Luis come over and help me with the animals. You all have a nice time tonight. Say your prayers. Stephen, honey, you keep him out of trouble, hear?"

"Yes ma'am," he said, embarrassed and proud, and jabbed with his heels to get Davy Crockett moving. Even on the stubby old pony, he felt heroic. The feeling weighted him like armor as he followed Ray through the corral gate, onto the rocky track that swung around the back of the huge house, and up a trail into the rising forest.

It took them about a half hour to get to Ray's fort, a rectangle of broken, eroding concrete higher than their heads at some points, crumbled to below their waists at others, overgrown with brush and mounds of pink flowers. It was still sunny in the small clearing around the fort, but looking down into the valley they could see a great sea of shadow, imperceptibly rising. In a corner where the fort's walls were highest, Ray had dragged sheets of rusting corrugated metal for an open-sided lean-to. The other time Stephen had been up here, they had spent hours improving it, lapping the metal sheets so they would actually shed rain, fastening them together with wire, and building walls for the shelter with branches from a fallen tree.

The boys unloaded the horses and tied them with long ropes so they could graze on the lush grass of the clearing. They hauled their duffel bags into the fort, and Stephen had just begun unpacking things when Ray remembered that they had to take the saddles off. Stephen's good mood collapsed, fell to pieces around his feet. "Are you sure?" he asked. The thought of wrestling the heavy saddles off the animals was bad enough, but then they would have to face the worse job of getting them on again in the morning, this time without an adult to help. The pony's saddle was scaled down, but it still was heavy and awkward. He wished they had ridden bareback, the way they usually did, though then there would have been nothing to tie the packs to, and it would have been hard to stay on once the animals started scrambling upward.

Ray insisted. They got the saddles off and stacked in a corner of the fort without too much trouble. Stephen felt ashamed of his reluctance. Ordinarily, he was the responsible one, and it was disconcerting to think that he had had to be led by Ray into doing things properly. He had to trust him, for Ray knew things he didn't know. How could he, raised in a city?

He was learning things, though—how to ride a horse, how to play Nintendo. How to handle a gun. They had chips and juice boxes and white cheese for supper, nothing that needed cooking, but Ray always made a fire when he went up to his fort, and they had one going now in the darkness of early evening. Stephen had pulled up all the plants around the blackened fire spot and improved Ray's half-assed fire ring with rocks and chunks of concrete until there was almost no possibility of the fire spreading, unless it just leaped up into the branches of the trees growing out of the fort's old foundation, which he remained alert for. While Stephen poked and disciplined the fire with a long green stick, Ray unwrapped the revolver from a beach towel and showed him how to spin the cylinder, to make sure it was completely loaded.

According to Ray, it was a navy pistol, which seemed wrong to Stephen, though he didn't argue. It was old fashioned, an old West kind of gun that Ray had found in a drawer of his father's gun cabinet, along with a greasy box of ammunition, and it was so heavy that he had to hold it in two hands to aim it, one on the grip and trigger, the other grasping the long, squared-off barrel and loading lever like the forestock of a rifle.

In the twisting firelight, Ray aimed it this way and that, squinting down the barrel, then used both thumbs to draw the hammer back, then aimed again, at Mary's vague white shape at the far side of the clearing, at the heart of the snapping twig-fire right in front of them, out into the darkness. "If you fired it like this," he said, tilting the barrel upward a little over the dark valley, tiny lights twinkling, "how far do you think this baby'd shoot? A mile?"

"We're pretty high," Stephen said. "Maybe a couple miles." He imagined the bullet launched from the mountain on that journey, hurtling through the darkness like a tiny spaceship, arcing up and out and then gradually downward, downward, racing silently toward the fields and roads and little houses scattered on the foothills. Suddenly there was a flash of light and terrible noise from the gun barrel, which leaped up in Ray's hands and sent Stephen crashing backward off the log they were sitting on. When he scrambled to his feet, he smelled the tickly firecracker smell and saw Ray staring stupidly at the gun in his hands.

"God damn it!" Stephen said when he was able to speak, his ears ringing. "Why'd you do that for?" His voice in his own ears was thin and distant. He could no longer imagine the bullet speeding into the valley, it would have to have been blown into separate molecules by such an explosion.

Ray let out a shrill, strangled laugh. "I didn't mean to," he gasped. "It just went off. Jesus Christ!" He laughed in a more regular way and aimed the gun across the dark, glittering valley again, his left arm locked and rigid, his right forefinger wrapped around the trigger, and Stephen braced himself. Ray held the gun like that for a moment, his whole body stiff with excitement. Then he lowered it and rested it on his lap. "What do you think we hit?" he asked.

And then the image of the speeding bullet crashed back into his mind. "There are people down there," Stephen said. "You maybe killed someone."

Ray thought about it. "No," he decided, "I don't think so."

"You don't think so."

"It's too far away," he said reasonably. "This far away, a bullet can't kill anyone, it's just like if you threw a rock. It could break a window, I guess."

"I'll bet it could kill a person at any distance," Stephen said, still dazed and angry, but he hoped Ray was right. The darkness spread out before them was so immense, it did seem as if it would swallow anything as puny as a bullet without blinking. "Don't do it again, okay? Somebody's going to come up after us if they hear."

"They'll just think it's bombetas," Ray said. He turned the gun around till the barrel pointed toward himself, and offered it to him. "You want to try?"

"No!" he said, but after a moment he took the gun into his own hands and held it, the barrel still warm, as if alive. He didn't cock the hammer and he didn't touch the trigger. It wasn't so terrible anymore, however. Finally he gave it back, and Ray laid it next to his sleeping bag, where it would be within reach in case of trouble.

They were going to sleep out beside the fire, rather than in the fort's covered room, which was actually a little oppressive. They didn't think it would rain. Stephen unpacked his father's machete and drew it out of its sheath. The broad, thick blade gleamed in the firelight when he brandished it. The horn handle felt as smooth and curved as a tensed muscle, and the blade was flat and cold, its edge too sharp to touch. Stephen let Ray slash the air with it and behead some flowers, then took it back and returned it to the sheath and laid it next to his sleeping bag. After he was settled, he reached out and grabbed the sheathed machete and slid it into his sleeping bag.

"Ray," he said, once he had shifted around in the sleeping bag enough to feel familiar with the hard ground underneath him, "how do you think he's doing?" Meaning Hank, on his way to the jungles of Panama to look for one of Noriega's drug bunkers.

"He's doing good," Ray said. "He knows all the poisonous plants and snakes. Jorge's with him. Plus some other good fighters, from when we were in Nicaragua."

Stephen knew that Ray had been born in Costa Rica and had never lived in Nicaragua, but he didn't correct him. There were suddenly too many things he needed to know to worry about the past. "Why do they call it a bunker?" he asked. Ray had overheard Hank talking to Grace about the planned raid, and when he had reported it to Stephen, Stephen had been too dazzled to ask questions. He had been captured by Ray's plan—to meet up with Hank by riding through the forest reserves that Ray had explored with his father and get in on the action. The action itself was too remote and unlikely to worry him much, but he was starting to feel the burden of ignorance piling up on him.

"It's like a factory in the jungle, where they make the drugs."

"I know, but—"

"They sleep there, I guess. In bunks." Ray's voice in the darkness sounded strained, as if he were speaking to him from a great distance. Stephen squirmed his sleeping bag a little closer. The fire, which they had been feeding with dry sticks, was dying down, a thin glowing inside the fortress of rocks he had erected around it.

"You think Noriega'll be there?"

"Maybe. I'd like to get a shot at old piña face."

"Me too," Stephen said. "I'd cut him off at the knees." He could say anything to Ray in the dark—this was one of the things he had discovered about him. During the day, Ray would challenge his pronunciation of a Spanish or even an English word, he would argue with him about how to make a sandwich, but in the darkness, acceptance covered them. "You think we'll get there in time?" he asked.

"We're taking a shortcut over the mountains. By truck they have to go all the way around, almost to the ocean, it's a hundred times farther."

In the privacy of the sleeping bag, Stephen caressed the horn grip of the machete and thought about what it would be like to swing it at somebody, two handed, hacking into a man's leg the way he had once chopped at a young mango tree behind their apartment when Ted was gone and Monica and Valerie were lying down for naps. He wondered if it would stick in bone the way it had lodged itself in that tree so that he had had to yank it back and forth with increasing desperation to free it. It you hit the knee joint, he thought, it might go right through.

"Are you worried about him?"

"Why should I be? He's the bear of the mountains. He's already killed nineteen men."

"I think your mom was worried."

There was a long silence, the only noise a little crackle and hiss from the dying fire and the wind in the trees. Somewhere below them on the mountainside, dogs were barking in distant miniature. "It's that she thinks he's too old," Ray said finally. "She didn't want him to do it. He said he was going to get our money back from Noriega one way or another."

"How's he going to get money?"

"There'll be tons of money, from the drugs. He takes out the bunker, and then he gets to keep all the money they find there."

Takes out. Stephen knew what this meant, to take out the bunker. It meant to blow it to pieces. He loved the way it sounded. Take out the bunker. "How does he know where it is?"

"The C.I.A."

"Why don't they take it out themself?"

"He knows more about the jungle than anybody else. There's a million things can kill you in the jungle."

Stephen knew what the jungle was. It was like around Cahuita, hot and wet, where they had seen a dog that had been killed by a poisonous snake. This wasn't jungle where they were now. This was forest, which he preferred. He asked Ray a few more things, but Ray was getting sleepy and finally stopped answering, leaving him in charge of the darkness. It seemed to him that Ray was less worried about his father's going into a gunfight than he had been about his being drunk.

He tried to imagine his own father leading men through the jungle, his machete unsheathed in his hand. Except for one thing, it wasn't so hard. What didn't work was the other men, they kept fading away, leaving his father alone in the jungle. No matter how hard he tried, he couldn't get them to stay. He couldn't get to him, couldn't defend him against the poisonous snakes and deadly plants the jungle floor was writhing with.

He woke in the darkness, his face cold and damp, stars blinking through the moving branches of a tree. What had wakened him was thunder, rolling in the distance but getting closer even as he scrambled out of his sleeping bag and looked wildly around for the thing he had to do first. He started balling up his sleeping bag, which was awkward with the rigid length of the machete, and shouted for Ray to wake up, it was going to storm, they had to get their stuff under cover. Ray curled away from him. He shook him until he was awake. By then the thunder was almost on them, and he expected any second to be hit by the first driving shock of rain as they dragged their stuff toward the shelter in the corner of the fort.

And then the air around them shook and the ground shook and there was a violent roaring overhead, an airplane, then another, then another, all but invisible in the clear night sky. Stephen and Ray dropped the duffel bag they were carrying between them and stared up. It was terrifying at first, as if the unbelievable power of the planes would crush them or brush them off the side of the mountain like ants. After a while, it was just weird, to be standing, deafened and shivering, beneath a river of aircraft. When the cold night air started to get to them, the boys laid their sleeping bags out again, not under the corrugated tin, but close to one of the fort's walls and close enough to each other that they could touch, and lay on their backs, staring up at the miraculous violence in the sky.

Neither of them thought to ask the other what was going on, any more than shepherds discuss the heavenly host in the middle of a chorus. After it's over is when you start to ask questions, and this miracle kept on and on. Being boys, they were finally lulled to sleep by it, and in the morning the blue sky was unmarked and silent except for the scattered singing of birds and the shuffle and snorts of the horses grazing close by.

CHAPTER ELEVEN
TWO MONTEROS

THE LOOSE SASH OF THE BEDROOM WINDOW was rattling, and there was an unfamiliar heat on his scalp and neck and naked shoulders. The pillow next to him, when he groped his hand blindly across it, was warm as a living body. He buried his face in that animal heat.

He never slept this late. He always woke at five-thirty. Every morning he dressed in the dark and went out into the dark, silent apartment and started the water for coffee, the glowing coil of the stove burner his first light. He would spoon grounds into the deeply stained cotton bolsa and wait for the water to boil and boil, steam curling up from the kettle, its whistle gagged open with a fork or spoon. He would stand at the kitchen sink, staring out the window into the fading darkness and the ragged tops of their landlord's backyard banana trees. After ten minutes, he would pour the spitting, sterilized water into the grounds, watch it stream into the pan underneath the bag, and sit blank and thoughtless in the fortress of that stillness, until Monica and the kids got up and demolished it.

It must be ten or eleven now, wind kicking against the

house, sun blasting in. The sash rattled, there were voices from the next room.

He rolled over and felt the sun shove itself against his face, burning through his eyelids, burning the arm he flung over his eyes, a hot still breath on his chest. The sash rattled. He swung his legs out of bed and sat there, feeling the drug of oversleep swing through his brain like a tide.

After dropping off Stephen at the Picketts' yesterday, he had gotten to the flower farm and then out to the airport without further trouble, beyond having to stop and let the car cool down a few times, but after he was finished with the shipment and ready to go home, it wouldn't start at all, leaving him a long bus ride back from the airport to San José, and then a lonely wait for the last micro to Escazú, and then the micro ride, and then the trudge uphill the last kilometer from the plaza to the house. He opened his eyes and pulled on his trousers, looked for his watch. He could hear Valerie shriek about something and Monica shushing her.

Monica had been wide awake when he finally got home. She was freaked out, even after he explained the mundane problems that had delayed him. Lately, she was raw-nerved, tender. Maybe it was the approach of Christmas, electrified for her by the strangeness of its finding them here in the tropics. Usually she was pointedly unmoved by the holiday, which she claimed to have been overwhelming and rancorous when she was a girl. Ted's childhood Christmases hadn't been great, but he was more tolerant of the season and had always tried harder to accommodate the kids' raging greed. Now it was Monica who was taking the bus into San José several times a week to shop for gifts. As long as he had known her, she had hated shopping. Now cheap toys she had bought from street vendors jammed their bedroom drawers. Now it was she who remarked the posadas passing by on the road in front of their place in the evening, she who kept the kids up late, cutting out paper snowflakes.

He came out of the bedroom and found her on her hands and knees in the kitchen, spraying matacucaracha along the baseboards. The sharp smell of the cockroach killer made his nostrils curl and seemed to have settled into the coffee he poured himself. He wondered if she had let the water boil the full ten minutes. "You got in so late last night," she said to him, agitating the spray can's tinny rattle. "It's good you could sleep in."

"And now I've got to get out to the airport again and see if I can get the bastard started."

Valerie raced in from the balcony, hurled herself into his embrace, and sloshed half his cup of coffee onto the floor. "Yesterday I went on the *rides*," she sang, "and today I'm going *swim*ming," her voice lifting as if leaping out of clear water in a spray of light.

Holding Valerie in one arm, he set his cup on the sink and handed Monica a sponge for the floor. "You're taking her to the club?" There was a scruffy little country club twenty minutes' walk away from them, just beyond the village of Belo Horizonte, where Pepe and Eva were members. The Hoffmans sometimes went there as guests, swimming in the leafy pool, eating a snack on the patio or in the covered dining area.

Valerie answered him. "Tío Arturo's taking me to Bernardo's club. That boy in Stephen's class. The big pool."

"Is that right?"

"Yes it is right! Momma, isn't it?"

"That's right, honey." She sprayed into the rusty darkness underneath the kitchen sink, then slammed the door on the fumes.

"Isn't that out toward Alajuela?"

"I think so. Maybe." She had no sense of direction, never looked at a map unless she had to.

Valerie squirmed out of his arms and returned to the balcony. Ted was about to ask how things had gone for her at the amusement park birthday party, when the phone rang. It was Grace, calling from some noisy pay phone in Santa Ana to say that

Ray and Stephen weren't back from their camp-out yet, and she had to get to an appointment at the U.S. embassy in Pavas and wouldn't be able to drive Stephen home that afternoon as she had planned. Could Ted or Monica pick him up? They might be back already, she said, but she had to get to the embassy.

"Sure, we'll get him," he told her automatically. She hung up before he had a chance to think about how they would manage it. "You think we could run out to the Picketts' and pick up Stephen?" he asked Monica.

She blasted roach spray underneath the refrigerator and sat back on her heels. "What?"

"That was Grace. She needs us to pick Stephen up. You think Arturo could run us out there, and then drop me off at the airport? Stephen can go with you to the country club." He didn't know how come Arturo had so much free time during the day, but along with the rest of the family he had accepted it as a kind of natural advantage, like the mild climate—compensation for various inconveniences. It freed him to concentrate on the flower farm's unfolding demands, eased the pressure of constant responsibility for his uprooted family. Since the visit to the nightclub, though, he had started to think about him more.

When he had reported to Monica about his night out with Pepe, he had included the visit to Club Cherie and running into Arturo, but not the fight Pepe almost got him into—she already had a dim enough view of poor Pepe. He had told her there were exotic dancers, which she, indeed, had suspected would be a feature of the boys' night out. His story included the cops appearing after two a.m. and his thought that it was a raid, but he hadn't told her about the stripper who had asked him for that expensive Coke, nor the woman in the green silk jumpsuit, nor the fat man she had bumped and danced with, nor his envy and desire. He had given her the roses, which were wilting a little by the time she got up.

Valerie announced the approach of Arturo's car with a scream of pleasure and was out of the apartment by the time he parked. Ted and Monica followed her. Outside, between the reja and the great black car, there was a moment of confused formality and familiarity—embraces, kisses on the cheek, handshakes. Spanish and English. A thread of intimacy tangled among them.

"Yes, of course," Arturo said, shaking Ted's hand again. "All should be together on such a day as this."

Ted was the only one who had not yet ridden in Arturo's Lincoln. Monica got into the front, then half got out again, but Ted climbed into the back with Valerie, and Monica settled into the front passenger seat. Ted spread his arms over the seat back. "Well, they were right, this is quite a ship."

As the car pulled away, Monica said something in Spanish that Ted didn't catch. After that she ignored Arturo in a way that seemed ungracious, considering the favor he was doing them. She kept swiveling around and scolding Valerie—for being too loud, for bouncing, for standing up on the seat. He wished he had sat in front instead of her. He studied the dark hair curling over Arturo's collar, the sharp line of his cheekbone.

Arturo was wearing a white cowboy shirt, vaguely iridescent. Ted was glad that he had worn his sports coat. Nestled in the deep plush, cool in the air-conditioned quiet, he remembered the shabbiness he had felt at the school on the eve of Independence Day.

They sailed down the mountain toward San Rafael and the autopista. Arturo looked back at him and said, "Once again, good to see you. I hope you been well." He paid only intermittent attention to the road, seemed barely involved in steering the car.

"Very well. And you?" An interesting man. He liked him.

"Very well, thank you." Arturo concentrated for a moment on avoiding a motorcycle zigzagging up the road, dodging potholes. "And what do you think of your Mr. Bush today? He's showing us his strong hand, no?"

"Hmmm?"

Arturo looked at Monica for a moment, then back at Ted. "You've no heard the news? That Panama is invaded last night?"

"What? By us? We haven't seen a paper." A thrill seized him like voltage. "Son of a bitch."

Arturo told them what he knew from CNN. It was to install the government that had won the recent election, which Noriega had declared fraudulent and invalidated. Portly Guillermo Endara had been sworn in as president on a U.S. air force base. Noriega was in hiding, his Dignity Forces putting up sporadic resistance. There was bombing in Panama City. They were calling it Operation Just Cause.

"Thank god we're going to get Stephen," Monica said. "I wish he was here right now."

"Querida, don't worry. Is far away."

"What do you guys here think about this bullshit?"

"Ted." Monica looked feverish, her throat and cheeks flushed.

"Sorry," he said. "Pardon my French."

"Óscar Arias will deplore it, of course. Most Ticos will tell you they deplore it. War, bombers, is not our way, is not the way for this region. Everyone will say it: a bad thing. Very bad. Of course, behind the hand, Noriega is such a bad guy, we hate his guts. We're not sad to see him go. The Calderonistas, they'll be happy."

Monica was looking back at Ted, as distraught as if they were in the actual war zone.

"He's fine," he told her. "This is Costa Rica. We're in one of the safest places in the world."

"I'm going to go *swim*ming," Valerie sang uncertainly. "I'm going to go *swim*ming."

"You sure are," Ted reassured her, running his palm over her head. "We're going to get Stephen, then you can go swimming." He tried to imagine what was going on just a few hundred miles to the southeast, if bombs were still falling, if marines were coming in on amphibious vehicles or falling out of the sky beneath parachutes. What was Panama City like, anyway? He didn't even know exactly where it was, if it was on the coast, a more bustling Puntarenas or Limón, or inland along the canal. How could he not know that? He tried to visualize the map of Central America he had hung above his desk. "Bush," he said.

"Ted."

He leaned forward and massaged the base of her neck. Her skin was hot underneath his fingers, sweaty. After a minute he sat back and said, "I'll bet I know why Grace had to go to the embassy." Monica didn't respond. "She's getting dibs on the bank accounts Noriega tied up."

Monica said nothing. Maybe she thought it was indiscrete to talk about the Picketts' situation with Arturo there. It probably was. She stared ahead at the road raveling out in front of them, the landscape cooled by the deeply tinted glass. They were going a different way from the one he had learned, though not the long, fast way, either, on the autopista. He wondered how long it would take the banks in Panama to recover from Noriega and the invasion. He doubted that the Picketts would ever get their money back.

They swept through Santa Ana and swung up into the mountains, past the spot where he had had to pull over and park the fuming Volkswagen, past a smoldering pile of brush, through the gate that someone had left open, and up to the big Moorish house. Out of nowhere the Great Danes rushed the car, circled it, making that deep coughing thunder, then shot off down the road toward the open gate. Valerie was out of the car before he could warn her about the dogs, but they were already out of sight, anyway.

He followed Valerie to the swing set while Monica and Arturo went up to the front door and knocked. Once he had gotten Valerie flying back and forth on the swing, he joined the others as the massive door swung open. It was another one of the Picketts' workers, not Jorge, the one he remembered, but an old man. The señora was gone, he told them.

Yes, Monica said, they knew that, she had asked them to come for their son.

The boys were not here, he said. They had not yet returned. He gestured vaguely to the forested slopes rising behind the house.

Had they gone far? Arturo asked.

No, the old man said, he didn't think they had gone very far. There was a trail behind the house. Probably they had taken that trail.

Ted felt jumpy, purposeful. If he could show him the trail, he said, he would go up and meet the boys or find where they were camping and bring them down.

He loved hiking in the mountains that rose above the settled central valley, and even though usually you could not go many kilometers before coming upon cleared pasture, a house, cows plodding along the trail, steeply terraced coffee fields, he had found pockets in the mountains that seemed pure wilderness—cloud forest or jungle or desolate highland. Here, farther west, the peaks weren't as high as those above Escazú where he hiked, but he had studied the area on his topo maps and knew it was forest preserve, deeper, less likely to be interrupted by civilization. He remembered that gold mine that was supposed to be here. There were probably many of them, long abandoned. Indians had met Columbus with ornaments of purest gold. It had to have come from somewhere.

"I'll go with you," Arturo said.

Ted looked up into the wall of green that rose behind the house. "They can't be too far."

They were on horses, the old man said.

Ted shook his head.

"It's true," Monica said. "He told me they were going to ride up."

"I know. It's crazy, all the trouble I had trying to get him near a horse back home."

Arturo was talking with the old man. "He says there are horses we can use. You ride?"

Christmas was coming early. Ted's grandfather's farm, where he had learned to ride, was mostly rough, unprofitable hills; he could handle these slopes. He loved the idea of riding up into the green mountains. Monica was watching him, giving him some sort of look. Where were the horses? he asked the old man.

They easily caught the chestnut stallion, Ranger, but it took them a long time to corner Goldie, Charlotte's palomino gelding. The old man helped them saddle and bridle the horses. Without discussing it, Arturo swung himself up onto the palomino and bullied him into a weaving trot across the paddock. He was dressed for it, down to the cowboy boots that had struck Ted as a little ridiculous up until this moment.

He handed his jacket to Monica, shoved his left foot stiffly into one of the big wooden stirrups, and managed to heave himself up onto the chestnut's back without too much fuss. Valerie screamed that she wanted to go and tried to yank herself away from Monica, but Ted was too excited and concerned with getting the feel of the new horse to worry about consoling her.

It was fine, he discovered, wheeling the horse with a little pressure of his knees, passing at a walk through the gate, following Arturo and the old man, who led them on foot along the road that swept up behind the house to the trail that angled steeply back into the mountains. This was a much better horse than he had ever ridden. Charlotte knew what she was doing.

In a few minutes they were out of sight of the big white house, the air cooler with height and shade. Arturo was a few lengths ahead of him, moving up the mountain at about the speed of a man walking fast. Even from horseback, Ted could see hoof prints scuffed into the tawny clay of the trail, the palomino's prints laid over another set, the white mare's, he assumed, and a smaller set visible here and there, sometimes cut delicately into the center of the mare's prints, sometimes straying onto the grassier verge where the trail widened.

He tried to picture the pony, with Stephen's thin legs splayed along its sides. It hurt him a little, that he had never managed to spring this courage loose, that it was these Nostradamus-studying right-wingers who had done it. He urged the chestnut to move more quickly up the trail. It was a wonderful horse, strong, accommodating. His riding experience had been with casually bred, casually trained farm horses, and he had been taught to avoid stallions. His grandfather had had one for a while, a knotty-muscled quarter horse nobody in the county had had the skill or nerve to break properly. Ranger made him feel confident, power and knowledge flowing upward from its untroubled chest and shoulders and flanks.

Arturo moved to the side of the trail when he caught up with him. For a while there was room for them to ride side by side, their legs brushing roughly together now and then when Goldie lurched forward or hesitated, making more of the trail's difficulties than necessary. "You ride very well," Ted observed, glad he didn't have to deal with Goldie.

"And you." When Goldie leaned into the other horse, their stirrups creaking together, Arturo cursed him genially, almost absentmindedly. "This one," he said, "he always trying something. He makes me remember your amigo, no? Pepe?"

Ted pushed his horse ahead a few steps. "Pepe's all right," he said. "It was too bad, at the club, he didn't mean any harm."

"Of course, a very much all right guy. Only he's often trying something, is what I mean. His family raises very fine horses, you know that? Maybe that big one there, who knows?"

The trail switched back on itself, and both men had to concentrate on loose rock in the turn's elbow. "You've no been back to the club," Arturo said, once they were past the difficult stretch. "Always you're welcome, and Pepe, too. But maybe you think is not a place for a man such as you."

Ted felt suddenly uncomfortable. He ducked beneath a heavy branch that grazed Ranger's ears. He had to stay ahead now, for the trail had narrowed again, to little more than a gully washed between boulders and trees.

"Is very friendly, nothing is harmful. All is for relax. You don't like the girls? They're no beautiful for you?"

He didn't know what to answer. He just looked ahead, focused on the trail in front of him. It was hard to carry on a conversation talking over his shoulder, and he wished that he had let Arturo keep the lead. He couldn't change places now, though. Anyway, they must be close to the boys' camp. Every time the trail turned, he expected to see them. He listened for their shrill voices, Ray's manic laugh. He concentrated on the rhythm of the horse beneath him and tried to gather the morning into some kind of order, but it kept scrabbling away from him—a nagging dream, Panama, the Picketts, his stranded car, and Stephen, and Monica and Valerie waiting for him, and Arturo.

He listened for the boys' voices, but heard only the clop and scramble of the horses and Arturo's conversational swearing at Goldie, and the wind pushing through the treetops. Suddenly the trail opened into a brushy clearing, with the foundations of a ruined house that could have been the fort Stephen had talked about. "Stephen!" he shouted. "Stevie! Ray! Come on, we've got to go home now."

Arturo moved around the edge of the clearing. Ted dismounted awkwardly and stumbled and fell back into the cushion of impatiens that crushed damply beneath him. He still had a hold on the reins and must have yanked Ranger's mouth painfully, but the horse only snorted in surprise and took a few steps toward him, then began snuffling around in the succulent vegetation.

He tied the reins to a sapling and climbed over the vine-smothered wall where it had decayed into a reef of crumbling cinder block. There were trees growing inside the foundation that were already as big around as a man's leg. He found a fire ring, the ashes carefully smothered with dirt, and stuck his head beneath a lean-to of corrugated metal.

He found Arturo standing at the place where they had entered the clearing. "They've gone on," Arturo said, showing him where a path branched off from the trail, ferns and brush broken by the horses.

Ted walked up the path a few hundred feet, shouting for the boys, before he returned to the clearing. While he stood there, gazing blankly into the forest that had swallowed his son, he felt Arturo's hand slide down his back. He turned, and Arturo brushed his shirt sleeve and the seat of his pants.

"Is from the chinos," Arturo said, taking Ted's elbow in hand and brushing again at his sleeve. There were cheerful splashes of magenta on his cotton shirt. "The flowers you fall in." The impatiens.

"Shit." He brushed at the pollen he could reach, but stepped away when Arturo offered to help. "Never mind," he said. "I have to figure out what to do." He looked to see what time it was, but he didn't have his watch. Chinos. Why chinos?

"We got to follow them."

"How long do you think?"

He shrugged.

Ted thought about Monica and Valerie waiting for them. He said, "You'd better go back and tell them what's going on. I'll catch up with the boys. The trail's easy to follow." He saw Arturo looking at him as if he would get lost or something, and waited for an argument. He wasn't sure he wouldn't get lost, without a map.

But Arturo shook his hand and untied the palomino and swung himself into the saddle. It shocked Ted, a little, that he would leave him there so readily. He felt lonely when Arturo disappeared down the trail. He wished he had eaten breakfast, brought along an orange or something. Well, he would catch up with the boys and eat some of the junk they must have packed, and lead them back. He hoped they had clean water. He walked Ranger over to the ruined house, and used a part of the wall as a step to get himself onto the horse.

The trail was narrow and less well defined than it had been, but it was not hard to follow. The ground was soft enough to leave hoof prints here and there that guided him through a little meadow a mile or so beyond the ruined house, and he entered the trees again more confidently than when he had set out, urging Ranger to a pace that was surely fast enough to catch up with the boys. Stephen, after all, was riding a Shetland pony. And Stephen was Stephen, always cautious, if not actively afraid. He called to the boys until his throat felt bruised, listened for a response. There was nothing, just the forest that swallowed up his shouts and gave nothing back but the cries of unseen birds and the drone of insects.

After a while, the trail grew so steep that he had to dismount and lead the horse past the worst of it. Where a stream bed tangled itself into the trail, the banks of the wash were cut deep into the brown earth, and he could only go forward. He stopped for a moment where the clear water pooled, letting Ranger drink. Trying to ignore his own thirst, he studied the hoof prints that were pressed into the silt. When he found the print of a boy-sized tennis shoe, he dropped to the ground and studied it. It was Stephen's, he was sure of it, walking beside the pony. Ray must have been still on horseback.

Stephen's footprints seemed like a promise that he was not out of reach, and Ted mounted again and urged the horse forward as fast as he dared on the wet, treacherous ground, calling out, certain that he was within earshot. He called until his voice broke, but there was no answer, no clink of harness or breathy laugh or neigh from horses pushed into unfamiliar territory.

And then he discovered that he had lost the track. He stopped and looked around. He had to go back, following his own trail, until he found where the boys had left the stream bed and entered the damp forest again. Before he left the stream himself, he got down and scooped up water in his cupped hands. This far up in the mountains, the water was probably all right, but it was hard to get the first swallow down his abraded throat. It burned, but then it was wonderfully cold and loamy. He dropped to his stomach and pressed his face into the little stream and drank his fill. For a while afterwards he kept having to spit out particles of sand.

He followed the new trail as it wound into the mountains. Sometimes there was no path at all, just ferns and succulents broken by the careless boys and their horses. He stopped at a ridge that gave him a view of the meseta behind him, but it was too far away to make out the civilization that he knew sprawled along its floor. He glanced at his bare wrist, then tried to judge the angle of the sun. He had expected to be back with the boys by now, and he wondered if Arturo had taken Valerie to the fancy club for swimming, and if Monica had recovered yet from the sense of personal emergency that seemed to have seized her when they had heard of the Panama invasion.

He himself had felt energized by the news, though now it was just a story. Now the only real things were the mountains, the loose-strung trail, the horse that was miraculously willing to carry him, and the fleeing boys somewhere ahead of him. His buttocks and thighs were getting sore, but he felt unaccountably happy.

He thought he had been climbing all this time, but when the trail splashed for a while along another stream bed, he found that he was descending, and almost as soon as he noticed that, he noticed a wire fence slumping along between posts with leaves growing out of them, and then a cleared field, and two men threshing something in a big tarpaulin. Somehow the forest had spilled him out of itself, and he could no longer see tracks. The air was filled with the sweet smell of burning grass. Somebody was burning off a field somewhere, though he could see neither fire nor smoke.

He rode toward the threshers. Had they seen two boys on horses? he asked. One horse big and white, the other little? He didn't know the word for pony. One boy dark haired, the other blond? He used the strange Tico word for blond—macho—only half trusting it. Had they seen them?

The men gestured ambiguously and one of them said something that Ted couldn't follow. He thought he was saying there was a road beyond this field, leading down the mountain, he should go that way. He rode in the direction they had indicated and found what seemed to be an old ox cart trail, little more than some ruts cut into the coarse grass. There were hoof prints of cattle and horses, going in both directions. Stephen and Ray might have followed this path back down toward the central valley, looking for a little town, a pulpería with a phone. He wouldn't have, though, if he had been them. He would have kept going.

Not stopping to let Ranger graze or to stretch his own aching legs, he headed in the other direction, climbing again, now and then encountering a line of rusty fence or a pasture long ago burned into the forest, or a few cows, but no human beings after the threshers, no planted fields, no houses, and increasingly rugged terrain. He wasn't tracking any more, he barely attended to the hoof prints sometimes visible in a stretch of eroded slope. He just kept moving.

He entered a pass carved between towering bald rock face and impenetrably forested mountain side, so deep he couldn't see the sun, and the narrow slice of remaining sky was such a profound blue, he felt he could almost see stars. When a long-nosed coati appeared suddenly on the trail no more than fifty feet ahead, stared at him for a moment, then shambled off, monkey-like, raccoon-like, he was unsurprised, neither pleased nor shaken. And the vultures that hung like flakes of black ash in the sky seemed to have nothing whatever to do with the solid earth he crept along, the animal kingdom to which he belonged. He kept going.

CHAPTER TWELVE

THREE MUJERES

After Ted and Arturo turned their backs on her, riding away, Valerie ripped herself out of her mother's arms and ran back to the house. Ignoring Monica's call, she went in and climbed a narrow, dead-end staircase that rose past the waterfall to a little balcony. She pried open a window and crawled out onto a shallowly pitched stretch of roof, from which she could see the corral and sloping pasture and the finger of forest that hooked down from the mountains and curved around the finca's open land. There was a river hidden in those trees, she knew. On Thanksgiving Day she had ridden the pony named Davy Crockett along its bank, behind Charlotte on the golden horse named Goldie and ahead of Stephen and Ray, who were riding double on the white horse named Mary.

She had discovered this vantage point when she was looking for Ray's tower bedroom after Thanksgiving dinner. His room had turned out to be on the other side of the house. From where she was now, she could see across to its narrow windows, though she couldn't get to it. She had tried before, and had almost slid off the corrugated metal roof.

The part of the roof where she was sitting was less steep than the part she had tried to cross that day, and she had no problem sitting or even walking around a little here, as long as she didn't get too close to the edge. At the edge, where she could look straight down three stories to the stone patio, something seemed to tickle her inside her stomach. But there were thin wires running from nails in the roof to a towering television antenna behind her, and she had found that she could always grab hold of one of these if she started to feel scared.

She didn't feel scared now. She felt angry, not so much at Arturo and her father, though they were deserting her when they should have been taking her to the pool, but at Stephen, whose adventure was selfishly ruining her plans. It would serve him right if she told. She maybe would tell, despite her secret promise, but she was angry at her mother, too. She watched her walking slowly back up from the corral, her eyes on the ground. If she looked up, she was going to see Valerie high on the roof, high as a bird might have been, watching her with the indifference of a flying bird. But she didn't look up. She disappeared into the house and left her alone in the blue sky.

It was getting hot. When she shifted position, she could feel the heat from the red painted ripples of the metal roof, even through her sandals. She had her swimming suit on under her sun dress, but still she had to tuck the skirt of the dress underneath her to keep her bottom from feeling fried, and she couldn't press her hands down for more than a second. She was getting sunburned, that was for sure. Nobody had thought to plaster her with sunscreen before they left the apartment, and since they had gotten here, nobody had thought about her at all. It wouldn't be her fault if she turned red.

She studied the trees concealing the river gorge, and now and then thought she could make out the flash of water from beneath the mass of green. She remembered the muddy banks and the water rolling and twisting within that shadowy depth. It made her thirsty. Using the guy wires for handholds, she crept back up to the window, crawled inside, and wound down the stairs past the waterfall to the first floor. She expected to meet her mother or Grace or the servant, but the living and dining rooms were deserted, huge and dark with the massive furniture. The bright kitchen was empty, too, but she felt better there. She climbed up onto the counter beside the sink and drank directly from the faucet, as she had seen Ray do when no adults were around. It was good water, she supposed. She couldn't have done this at their apartment.

Probably she should ask her mother about the water. Wiping her lips, she went out onto the patio full of plants, came back in and checked the rest of the downstairs, then went up to the second floor, where most of the bedrooms were. Monica was in the family room, watching the enormous television, and she jerked up in surprise when Valerie touched her on the neck.

"Oh, baby, where were you?" she asked, taking her onto her lap and hugging her.

It wasn't a question worth answering. She settled herself in her mother's arms, however, and allowed herself to be cuddled. She stared at the television. An army man was talking from behind a cluster of microphones. "It's about the fighting in Panama," Monica explained without being asked.

Panama was where Stephen and Ray were going. She watched the screen with interest, but it was just the soldier talking and someone asking questions, no pictures that might have included her brother or his friend. Still, she was pleased to be watching television, and she was glad that Ray had that gun and Stephen had that machete. They could defend themselves when they got to the war. She decided that she would never betray them, and wondered what else was on.

After a while there was a commercial, and her mother lifted her off her lap, got up, and walked over to a window. "I'll be happy when we get Stephen back," she said. "Of all the times for him to be gone."

Valerie had the remote control hidden in her lap now, but

she didn't know how to work it. If her mother left the room, she would see what she could do. The commercials ended, and the show returned to reporters talking, and then outside to some city street that looked to Valerie like San José, with noise in the background that made it hard for her to understand the unseen man talking in an excited voice. When the camera looked down the street, there was smoke in the distance, and a woman running.

It was Panama, but Valerie knew that she wouldn't see Stephen and Ray riding down these streets. She could just tell, it wasn't a place where there would be horses. It also didn't look like much of a war. The woman she had seen was wearing a dress and the men who appeared now and then were dressed in regular clothes. They weren't fighting, they were just running. When the show switched back to the reporters, she slid off the sofa and left the room without Monica noticing she was gone. She stopped a ways down the hall, aimed the remote through the wall to where she thought the television was, and pressed a button, then another, then all of them, but nothing happened. The voices talked on as if she didn't exist.

She found the ladder leading up to Ray's room, climbed up holding the remote in her teeth, and settled into the jungle of toys and scattered clothes and pillows. The fort of Legos that she had made on Thanksgiving Day was still partly intact, but she ignored it in favor of Ray's futbolín on the floor, which she played by twirling both the plastic handles of one team and the metal rod ends of the other, spinning the red and blue men. Then she turned her attention to a slot car setup she didn't know how to work, and then a collection of dinosaurs that she assembled from all over the room, and then a gun belt with bullets in loops of leather. The first gun she found didn't fit into the holster, but then she found what must have been the right one. She wrapped the belt around her waist and fastened the big silver buckle with difficulty, not getting it quite right, and took some shots out the narrow window overlooking the valley. She shot into the line of forest and imagined the bullets splashing into the river hidden beneath the dense branches.

There were windows on three sides of the room. She shot through each of them in turn. Suddenly there was a man on horseback riding out of the forest above the house, and she shot him before realizing that it was Arturo, on the golden horse named Goldie. He was alone. Her father didn't appear. Neither did Stephen or Ray. She watched Arturo ride down the slope until she couldn't see him anymore, near the house. She climbed down the ladder, ran past the television room without saying anything to her mother, and raced down the stairs to the front door. The old man, whom she hadn't seen since her father and Arturo had ridden off, was taking the reins of the horse and Arturo was approaching the house. She didn't run to meet Arturo as she usually did, but waited for him to reach the steps where she was standing.

"La pistolera," he said as he picked her up and carried her inside. Where was her mother?

"Are we going swimming now?" she asked.

"Valerie, no, sorry."

"When the boys get back from Panama?"

He looked at her. "Where is your mamá?"

She buried her face in his shoulder and wept, a little surprised at the heat of her own tears, the genuineness of the sobs that shook her. She wasn't really so concerned about going swimming anymore—having the run of Ray's house was more fun—but still she felt sadness welling up inside her like a flood, she didn't know why. She felt him bend over her, his face pressed against the top of her head for a moment and his arms hugging her deliciously. She had never felt so sad, so wonderfully sad. But when he stepped into the house and called out, "Monica! Monica!" she tore herself out of his arms and ran into the kitchen and hid there behind the pantry door.

He didn't follow her. When she slipped out of the kitchen, she saw him go upstairs. She kept out of sight, but followed at a safe distance and was just reaching the top of the stairs when Monica came out of the family room and they hugged each other in a way that startled the anger right out of her. They weren't just hugging, they were kissing, too, and Arturo was petting her mother's hair. And then they stopped kissing, and Arturo said something that Valerie couldn't hear, and Monica said, "We should call the police. What if they're lost?"

"No," Arturo said. "I'll go after them, is easy to find horses, even in the forest. You know how it is with the police."

"Hikers died in the mountains."

"They're fine, querida."

They talked for a while more in low voices Valerie couldn't understand, kissing and petting each other in a way that made her burn with jealousy and interest. Finally Arturo pulled free. He passed Valerie on the stairs before she had a chance to take cover, and then came back and sat beside her, his arm around her. "Now I go to Panama to get those damn boys, okay?"

"I don't think Hank needs them."

"No, I don't think so neither." He hugged her and ran downstairs, where the old man was putting some things in a big woven bag. Arturo took the bag outside and tied it to the saddle and got up on the golden horse again, which bucked and danced around as if it didn't want to obey him, pretending it wasn't glad.

"I can go swimming as soon as you get back," she called from the open doorway, but he didn't hear her and headed up the mountain without giving her a backward glance. She drew her gun and fired a few shots after him, not trying to hit him or Goldie, but it was too late anyway, he was gone, more gone than before. His beautiful car stood uselessly in the driveway, staring up at the house. She walked over to it and got into the stuffy back seat, then climbed over into the driver's seat. The pistol jabbed her in the side when she landed, but she didn't cry, just knelt there and steered for a while and made loud motor sounds. She saw her mother come to a window and look down at her, but nobody came to make her get out.

It was stifling hot. The car windows would not respond to the buttons that ordinarily moved them up and down with a purr. They were like sunglasses, making everything outside look dark and cool, but inside, the plush of the seats was radiating a breathless heat. It was uncomfortably quiet, too, and suddenly she felt as if she were running out of air, and threw open the door and jumped out and ran down the hill to the empty corral and past the barn and through the long grass of the pasture.

By the time she reached the trees, she was out of breath and it felt as if the gun were stabbing her in the side again, though actually it was just flopping against her leg. She sat down at the edge of the woods and looked back up at the big white house and the forested mountains rising behind it and other, more distant mountains looking over them, gray as rain clouds. They weren't clouds—the sky pinched in by the mountains was a bright, clear blue, and the sun was beating down.

Beneath the trees, it was cool. She found the muddy trail along which they had ridden on Thanksgiving Day, and followed it until it reached the bank with the river racing past. She could hear things singing and calling out to each other. The wind rustled high overhead, but down on the forest floor where she was standing the air was poised and motionless.

She removed her white sandals to keep them from getting any dirtier than they already were and felt the cold mud of the trail squeeze up between her toes, the brown, smooth coldness curling through. When the trail grew rocky, she wanted to put her sandals back on, but decided it would be a good idea to rinse her feet in the river first.

She unbuckled the gun belt and hid it beside the trail before making her way down the bank. There she found a place where the river broadened and swept into a pebbly bay that she could wade in. She watched the mud lift from her pink and white feet in little puffs of smoke that gradually thinned and disappeared, and then her feet themselves disappeared as she reached the deeper, colder water that made her gather up the skirt of her sun dress to keep it from getting wet. Her sandals dangled from her other hand, now and then trailing a little in the water that kept pushing her, urging her along through the splashes of sunlight on the dark water that seemed like something she could gather up in her hands. Butterflies folded themselves like sails on the muddy banks and then rose dizzily into the still air and flickered in and out of the shadows.

The river bottom was no longer firm beneath her feet, but silky, sucking gently at her ankles as she glided farther and farther out into the exciting water. Her dress was soaked by now, and clung to her bathing suit. When she let the skirt go, it floated around her waist as if she were spinning in a dance, a ballerina. She spun like a ballerina, lost the bottom, slipped beneath the water and tumbled and lost track of up and down and opened her eyes and watched butterflies of light dart around her and the water tumbling her in a rude way that made her feel like crying but she was swimming she could swim and bumped something with her knee and got her feet underneath her and stood up, gasping, then lost her balance again and sat down, but the water here only came up to her chest, even sitting, and she stood again and waded to the bank and pulled herself up, and then she did cry, for she had lost her sandals, the river had taken them.

She cried for a while in the cool secret shade where nobody could hear her, while the river lapped apologetically at her feet, until finally she lost interest in her grief and climbed the bank and retraced her way back up the trail, following her own perfect footprints facing the other direction. The sun, when she reached the edge of the woods and started up through the pasture, felt good on her shivering skin, and her hair was almost dry by the time she reached the house.

The Picketts' red truck was parked next to Arturo's car. This meant that Grace was back, and that Valerie would be stepping into a house that was no longer hers, she was only a guest again. She found Grace and Monica in the kitchen, having something to drink. They stared at her when she stepped into the room, and she collapsed on the floor in tears.

"Here, here, honey pie," Grace crooned, "I have just the thing for you." She swept Valerie up in her arms and carried her into a bathroom where she had never been before. There was a bathtub. Not just a tiled shower stall, a real bathtub. Grace ran water into it, and while it filled, she and Monica peeled off Valerie's sun dress and swim suit and sponged off the worst of the mud at the sink. When the tub was sufficiently full, Monica lifted her in, and she lay back like a queen in the warm water and let her mother wash her hair while Grace went to find some clean clothes that might fit her. Her skin bore the white shadow of her sundress and sandal straps, while the rest of her glowed pink.

"What happened?" Monica asked when Grace was gone.

"I fell in some water."

"Well, I can see that." She didn't pursue it, though, when Grace returned with some neatly folded clothes—underpants and shorts and a T-shirt—which she laid on the closed toilet lid.

"These old things of Ray should about fit you," she said. "I had them all out and ready to go for Christmas presents. Merry Christmas, sweetie."

Monica dried her off with a thick, soft towel and helped her into the clothes. They didn't look like Christmas presents to Valerie—the colors were faded and the shorts were frayed a little around the elastic waistband—but she thanked Grace anyway. She didn't mind that they were boy's clothes, though she had started complaining about wearing Stephen's hand-me-downs. Nobody asked about her sandals.

They all went back down to the kitchen, where Grace made lunch for them—cheese sandwiches and chips and fruit. Grace poured Valerie's milk into a stemmed glass matching the ones the adults were drinking from. It was very elegant, and she worked hard not to spill, while Grace told Monica what she knew about the invasion of Panama. She had gone to the embassy to talk to somebody about Hank. "He left yesterday to clean up one of Noriega's drug bunkers on the border, and do you think anybody bothered to tell him all hell was going to break loose, we were about to invade the country? No, they did not, not a word, the little embassy morons. I've had it with them, I've just had it up to here."

"What did you find out?" Monica asked.

"Not a damn thing. Nobody would see me, they're all going crazy."

"*You* must be going crazy. You must be worried sick."

"You bet I'm worried, he could be in a war zone and not even know it."

"Oh my god." Monica seemed about to cry, which made Valerie start crying.

Grace pulled her onto her lap and reached over and took one of Monica's hands. "It's not that bad," she said. "He knows what he's doing. It just makes me so mad that they wouldn't tell us anything, exactly the people who could help them out the most. Southern Command has a general in charge who doesn't trust anybody on his staff who speaks Spanish. What kind of idiocy is that?" She transferred her to Monica's lap and brought out a box of cookies.

"I wonder what's taking them so long to bring the boys back," Monica said. "You think they could be lost? Should we be doing something? I've just been sitting here."

"That mountain's Ray's back yard," Grace said. She put some cookies on a beautiful plate with golden decorations on its rim and set matching, smaller plates in front of Valerie and Monica.

"They're just little boys."

"Arturo and Ted will find them."

"Arturo is my tío, I love him," Valerie said.

"Is that right?" Grace said.

Monica hugged Valerie, a little too hard, then set her on a chair of her own. "Do you know him?" she asked Grace, studying the broken halves of a cookie as if thinking of fitting them back together again. Valerie had already eaten one and taken another.

"A little," Grace said. She smiled suddenly at Valerie. "I can see how you'd be taken with him, darling. He's a very handsome man."

"Oh, I don't know," Monica said.

"He is handsome, and you know it." Valerie felt her face burning with loyalty. "You love him, too."

"Oh ho!" Grace laughed, on Valerie's side.

"She does! She kisses him!" Valerie was laughing now, pleased with herself.

"We all love tío Arturo," Monica said.

"Kisses him! Kisses him! Kisses him!" She knew she was going too far, but she couldn't stop herself, it was like spinning around and around until you're dizzy and just waiting to fall. "Kisses him!"

"All right, that's enough, missy," Monica said, and loomed up and grabbed her. "She's exhausted. Is there someplace I can put her down for a nap?"

Valerie went limp in her arms, let herself be laid down in Charlotte's bed upstairs, and buried her face in one of the fancy pillows and pretended to go to sleep until they left. She gave them time to get downstairs while she went around the room, examining Charlotte's pretty things, and then crept down the steps and slipped unseen behind the kitchen island. The dishes had been cleared from the table, which was now piled high with stacks of clothes and small boxes. Monica and Grace were wrapping the things in Christmas paper.

"How do you stand it?" Monica was saying.

"If only those sons of bitches would support him."

"He seems to be in good shape."

"For his age, I know. Honey, I tried to talk him out of it. He shouldn't be helling around in the jungle, with a little boy at home only nine years old, who needs a daddy. 'Needs his daddy to be a man,' he says, and that was that."

"Jesus, Grace."

"He'll be all right. I know he will." She was wrapping up some kind of small toys, matchbook cars, Valerie thought. There were shoals of these in Ray's room. She wondered if maybe she would be given one.

While Grace picked up another toy, Monica was wrapping folded clothes, like what Valerie was wearing. She held up a tiny sweatshirt. "This is sweet," she said.

"I thought I'd given away all the baby clothes, but then I found another stash. That was Charlotte's."

"Did Charlotte have any toys when she was my age?" Valerie asked, coming out of hiding.

"Why, hello, darling, that was a mighty brief siesta."

"Did you sleep at all? Never mind, I know you didn't."

"Come on up here, sweet girl, and help us wrap Christmas presents."

She got up on a chair next to Grace and picked out a little fire engine and asked, "Who are all these toys for?"

"Poor kids," Grace told her. "There's families around here have five or six kids and hardly a toy among them. Can you wrap presents?"

"There must be a lot of kids for all these toys."

"There are. Here." Monica slid a square of wrapping paper across the table to her. "You'll be up to your ears in toys in a few days, believe me."

"I really like this truck," Valerie said, but she placed it on the piece of paper and wrapped it as neatly as she could and taped it thoroughly and placed it next to the pile that already threatened to overflow the table. "Who do you suppose will get that truck?" she wondered aloud. "It will make some kid very happy."

When they were done wrapping, Grace said, "Well, shall we go out and play Santa?"

"I should stay here," Monica said. "They could be back any moment."

"It's easier if you keep busy. I learned that a long time ago."

"I'll help you!" Valerie shouted.

"Good! Monica? They get back before us, Luis will be here. Come on, we won't be gone long. I need your company."

Valerie was a little disappointed when her mother agreed finally to go along, but she sat comfortably on the bench seat between them in the truck and nobody bothered her about wearing a seat belt. Her face and shoulders were hot, and the breeze from the windows felt good on her skin. They lurched down the mountain road and drove into a town, where Grace had to do a little shopping at a store that had turkey chicks and chicken chicks in cages, and stacks of greasy looking bundles that Grace told her were banana leaves, for holiday tamales.

"Those women lined up," Grace explained to her as they left, "they're waiting to get their corn ground in the molina to make tamales. They wrap them in those leaves." A dozen or more women and a scattering of children were waiting in the hot sun, buckets and bulging cloth bags beside them. All she could see of the molina was a half door, over which a boy was hoisting a blue plastic bucket. Behind the door, it was too dark to see anything. "I make a mean tamale myself," Grace said. "Do you like tamales, darling girl?" She didn't know, but she suspected that she wouldn't like any food wrapped in leaves.

Grace drove them over bad roads back into the hills, stopping in front of houses that mostly looked like shacks, slapped together from rusty corrugated metal and old boards. Valerie helped Grace carry presents up to the house, Grace would talk with the grownups for a few minutes while the kids milled around the presents in a restrained frenzy, and then they would drive to another shack. She had a hard time believing that the people really lived there. After a few times she stayed in the truck with her mother while Grace brought up the gifts.

Grace made no comment about this. She had big shopping bags that she used to carry the presents, and she didn't really need help. At one of the last places, though, she hugged the woman who came out of the door carrying a baby, and then gestured for them to come in from the truck. "Go on," Monica said to Valerie, "she wants you," but when Valerie was halfway up the path, Grace gestured again, that they should both come.

The woman bent down for a beso from Valerie and then introduced a cluster of children who gathered around her, and led them all inside. Valerie clung to Monica. She had caught the woman's name, María Luz, but the kids were all mixed up.

It was dark inside, with just one small window, and light coming in through cracks between the boards. There was a concrete floor, a table and chairs crowded into the half of the room that served as kitchen, with stove and sink and refrigeration and table, and a couch and dresser and a few extra chairs in the other half. Something was cooking on the stove, filling the house with a warm smell. There was a small television on the dresser, with a soccer ball on top of it made from the little cards with flags on them that came in bags of Picaritas. Valerie and Stephen had a collection of these cards at home, and she knew they were for soccer teams, but it had never occurred to her that they could be pieced together to make such an interesting thing. She would have liked to lift the ball off the television to get a better look, but there were too many people in the room she didn't know.

A boy reached over her head and turned on the television and tuned it to a soccer game, with tiny gray players moving around on a pale green field. Some other kids and a few adults came over to watch the game. She held her ground in front of the dresser for a few minutes, then edged out and tried to get to her mother, who was in a corner of the kitchen talking with Grace and María Luz. The bag stuffed with presents seemed to have disappeared.

Through the open door she could see kids out in the dusty yard playing soccer with an empty plastic Coke bottle. She went out on the rickety porch to watch. Only boys were playing, though some of them were smaller than she was, and she thought maybe they would invite her to join in. She was barefoot, but so were most of the players.

An older girl joined her on the porch and said, "Good morning. My name is Jessica."

"Hi." She waited for the girl to say something else, but she just stood there, smiling. "Do you live here?" Valerie asked. "We brought Christmas presents for the kids who live here." The girl looked at her. "I helped wrap them."

"How are you?" the girl asked.

"Good." Valerie was starting to feel put upon. "Do you live here?"

The girl said something in Spanish that Valerie didn't catch at first, but when the girl repeated it, she understood, the girl was asking what her name was.

"Valerie."

"Valerie, qué linda." The girl stood there for a moment, as if she were thinking about Valerie's name. Finally she said that she knew the señora, doña Grace, very well, and also her husband. She said that her father was with him in Panama.

Valerie was not impressed. Her brother and her friend Ray were in Panama, too, she answered. The girl nodded. Somebody screamed, and they turned and saw a boy kick the plastic Coke bottle through the branches of a mango tree in a high, tumbling arc.

CHAPTER THIRTEEN

THE WILD FRONTERA

THEY WEREN'T SURE when it was that they had crossed into Panama. Stephen thought that it must have been when they entered a forest of cedars that cut across the mountain slope. The air was cooler there and smelled different, and the ground was silky with fallen needles beneath the towering, straight trunks. Their voices took on a strange resonance, and even after they had passed into pasture land again, the mountains felt foreign to him, more foreign than Costa Rica was. Ray had actually been in Panama three or four times before, though only in Panama City, where his family flew periodically for shopping and to revive their visas. He thought that it had been later, when they had scrambled up from a river bed and entered tangled jungle in which they could barely make out the trail. This just felt like Panama, he said, and Stephen was too inexperienced to argue with him.

What they knew was that the danger was greater now. Anyone they met could be an enemy, there was no way of knowing. Ray remembered soldiers in green uniforms guarding Panama City government buildings with machine guns, but they both understood that you couldn't count on that.

Guerrillas dressed any way they wanted to, and anyone could be a communist without letting you know until it was too late. Early in the morning they had crossed a deserted highway and then passed through a little village where dogs and barefoot children had chased after them and a woman had watched them from a darkened doorway. That was still Costa Rica, they agreed. Now they would have to go around any village. Stephen worried that they wouldn't notice in time.

They ate whenever they felt hungry, which was pretty much all the time. They had plenty of chips and bananas and packaged cookies, which Ray preferred to those from his mother's bakery, but they wished that they had brought more juice boxes. They had a canteen, which Ray filled at clear-running streams. Stephen refused to drink this water at first, but it didn't seem to bother Ray, and after a while Stephen put aside his caution. There was medicine for parasites, Ray said. Water didn't kill you. You wouldn't know it to hear Ted and Monica talk.

By midday his tail bone felt bruised and his legs were cramped and chafed. Often he chose to go on foot, leading Davy Crockett and doing about as well keeping up with Ray as he did when riding the fat old pony. The trail deteriorated as it moved more deeply into the mountains, and sometimes Ray had to lead his horse, too, though he would always try to stay mounted, driving her to keep going until she stumbled or refused to go on at all. Then they would have to backtrack and find an easier way.

The landscape was gradually getting more rugged, yet occasionally they came upon stretches of passable dirt road, and then they could make good time and Stephen wished that he had a real horse, not just this pony who had once seemed plenty formidable to him, but was incapable of more than a brief, stiff trot. Even that was uncomfortable, though, and he secretly preferred the thin tracks winding through the rocks, where he and Ray struggled on equal terms.

Ray had some allergies, and from time to time that morning

his stream of talk was interrupted by sniffling and fits of dramatic sneezing. They had been smelling smoke for a long time before they reached the crest of a ridge and saw it rising in several brown plumes from the valley below. Stephen thought that maybe this was what was setting him off, but Ray said no, it was pollen. His campfires never caused a problem.

As they descended into the valley, they found a road almost good enough for a car, and rode side by side in the worn tracks separated by grassy strip, Mary adjusting her pace for the slow pony. Neither boy had thought to bring a hat, and the sun pressed down on them, and sometimes the dirt road before them seemed to shimmer before breaking into another long switchback. Far below them they could make out a few people working in the intense green of a coffee field dropping from terrace to terrace.

Although it was afternoon, still, Stephen felt sleepy, tired of riding, tired of chips and cookies. He was even a little tired of Ray, who was bragging again about how many communists his daddy had killed, and what he would do to the enemy once he joined up with Hank and his men.

"How are we even going to find them?" Stephen asked. He had been toying with this question most of the trip, but Ray always seemed to know the way, and it had seemed wrong to question it, as if he didn't really want to get there. He *didn't* really want to get there, he was barely able to admit to himself. He didn't expect to, any more than he expected a mango to really blow a hole in a wall when he or Ray flung it like a grenade.

Ray's father owned real guns and really used them, really had killed men, was attacking a real drug bunker—these were adult facts, as real as divorce or being fired or getting cancer, things that had happened to the parents of kids he went to school with. But for him and Ray to join a real battle, he didn't believe that. He had asked the question out of fatigue and irritation, not because he wanted an answer. He didn't ask the real question: Would they ever be able to find their way back?

Uncharacteristically, Ray shut up in the middle of a story

and rode in sulky silence for a while, digging his heels into Mary's vast sides harder than usual, so she surged ahead a few yards. Finally he let Stephen catch up with him and said, "I got us this far, didn't I? I found the way to Panama."

Panama was a whole country, but Stephen couldn't deny Ray's accomplishment. He was sorry that he had challenged him, and he ached from even the brief, cold silence Ray laid on him. "I just want to know when we're getting close."

Ray nodded and started over telling about how he had learned to shoot a gun and how much bark he had once knocked off a tree with a single shot. Then abruptly he broke off and ordered Stephen to be quiet, though Stephen hadn't been the one talking. They stopped the horses and Ray pointed ahead to a field where two men were doing something to a wire fence. There were more men on the far side of the field, and one of them seemed to notice them, and shouted something, and the men at the fence looked up. Ray slapped Mary on the rump and yanked her big, calm head toward the mountain.

Stephen thought that they were going to retreat the way they had come, but Ray urged Mary off the road and up a pasture slope toward where the trees began again. Stephen turned to see what the men in the field were doing. One was walking toward him, calling out something. He felt a contraction of dread seize his stomach and banged his heels against Davy Crockett's sides and grabbed mane and willed the startled pony up the hill after Ray.

Ray approached the line of trees before Stephen was halfway up the hill, the long, coarse grass making it feel as if he were moving through water. He screamed at him, panicking at the thought that he would disappear into the woods and lose him, but Ray kept Mary at a trot just within the shadow line, every now and then jerking left as if to enter the woods, but then continuing on the outside. Stephen followed in an erratic curve up the hill, trying to intersect Ray's dodgy flight, and was close enough to see that there was an old barbed wire fence guarding the woods when Ray jumped off and dragged Mary through a narrow gap left between two posts, a third post hanging loosely from the ends of the wire as a gate that could be pulled aside.

Stephen reached the gate before Ray had remounted. He got the pony through, and only then dared to look from the shadowy woods back down the bright mountainside and saw that they were not being pursued. Sobbing, he hauled the loose post back into position and hooked it to one of the fixed posts with a loop of rusty wire that was apparently meant to serve as a latch. "Why did you leave me like that?" he cried.

Ray said, "Those were communists."

Stephen had no answer for this, though it didn't seem like an adequate explanation.

They rode deeper into the woods, found a trail and followed it as it wove its way farther and farther up the mountain. When they came to a place where the trail decayed into gully pressing against a cliff of almost shear rock, they cut back across an open field where cows watched them suspiciously. They found another trail, climbed around the side of the mountain that seemed to have suddenly loomed up to frustrate their progress, passed in and out of dark, muddy stretches of forest that alternated with open fields, avoided a meadow where a lonely shack and scattering of lean-to sheds guarded the rutted path, and found themselves in a wild notch between mountains steeper and more forbidding than any Stephen had ever encountered. Even with this fat pony under him and Ray Pickett beside him, he felt alone. He ached with homesickness and bruises from the saddle.

The sun had been hot overhead only a short time before, but it seemed like evening here—not the quick slide from afternoon to night that he had gotten used to in Costa Rica, but a kind of permanent condition, as if they had fallen into a well. They agreed that they didn't want to go farther in this direction. They had to get back to the trail they had been following earlier, before this gloom turned to real night. They turned their horses and urged them to hurry, anxiety buzzing like insects. They found a trail and followed it upward until it turned at the lip of a gorge, and then turned again.

And then the trail opened onto a shelf of rock overlooking a huge valley. It was like nothing they had ever seen before, an ocean of forest or jungle sweeping away from them on and on until disappearing finally into the shadows of mountains blue with distance, and more mountains beyond those. They got off their horses and stared out onto that green immensity.

"We were both wrong," Ray said after a while.

Stephen knew what he meant—*This* was Panama. This was Panama, monstrous and impossible.

Ray was sniffling, and at first Stephen thought he was crying. He had felt like crying himself many times that day, but not now, he didn't know why. He wondered if he should tell him about the line of snot that was running down his upper lip, just missing the corner of his mouth. "You need a kleenex or something," he said finally, gesturing toward his nose, and Ray took care of it with the back of his hand. "You worried about your dad?" Stephen asked. He knew they would never find him in Panama.

"It's just allergies," Ray said.

Without discussing it, they turned their backs on Panama. They led the horses off the ledge and onto the rocky trail, walked side by side where it was wide enough. They passed back through the dark notch, now even darker and colder than before, got lost where the trail branched confusingly among eroded, sloping shelves of rock, then found their own tracks printed in soft earth.

They felt better, now, after the grim shock of Panama, and they made a game of spotting the tracks, distinguishing Mary's hoof prints from Davy Crockett's, Stephen's Converse from Ray's Reeboks. After a while they could do it from horseback, though sometimes they had to get down and search for a clear trace, and sometimes they had to guess. Ray claimed that his father had taught him to track any kind of animal, and when they disagreed, Stephen gave in and went the way Ray said.

It didn't really matter. They were heading home. Ray's laugh shook through the canopy of forest like the cries of monkeys, and Stephen felt some of the exhilaration with which he had started the journey. He was tired, sometimes feeling himself drift off as he rode along an easy stretch of trail. When they stopped to drink from a stream and rest on the bank, he felt sleep pull at him. But knowing that each step narrowed the distance between the alien and the familiar kept him going. The horses grazed on the soft grass.

He retrieved the chip bag that Ray had tossed onto the bank and crunched it into his duffle bag. While the duffle was open, he drew out the machete. "I think I need to keep this baby handy," he said, just for the fun of it, keeping the adventure alive, and tied the leather thong of its sheath around his waist. It made it a little hard to get into the saddle, but once he was up, it hung nicely along his leg, bumping against the stirrup with an authoritative weight when he got the pony moving up the trail. Ray hauled out the old revolver and fussed for a while at the lack of a proper holster, eventually jamming the gun under the rope securing his duffle to the back of the saddle. It wasn't a great arrangement, but he practiced whirling around and drawing it. He took the lead on the trail, giving Stephen a better view of the move.

They were climbing through dense forest when Stephen thought he heard something from the trees ahead of them. After going through the tiny village that morning and running from the workers in the field, they had encountered nothing but a few isolated farms, and they had met nobody on the trail itself all day. Before he could warn Ray, the trail turned and a dark, heavy-set man on foot appeared, and then another, both of them dirty and rough looking, carrying wooden boxes, about the size to hold a basketball. The boys said nothing to them, just moved their horses to the side of the trail to let them pass, and the men kept their unfriendly faces down, acting as if they didn't even see the boys.

The boxes had handles on top and openings in the sides covered with mesh. As the second man passed him, Stephen saw movement within one of the boxes, a tiny green creature flickering in the darkness, and minute cries. A third man appeared, carrying a long bundle wrapped in canvas. Like the other two, he was dressed in dark, filthy clothes. His face was covered with terrible pock marks. He turned as he passed Ray, and Stephen thought that he had noticed the revolver thrust into the ropes behind Ray's saddle, and then he looked straight at Stephen with small, expressionless eyes, and Stephen had to look away, pretending to calm the sleepy pony by patting its neck.

As soon as the men were out of sight, Ray drove Mary up the trail fast. He was waiting at the next turn, looking wild and afraid. He had the revolver resting on the saddle in front of him, and was poised as if to take off again. "You know who that was?" he hissed.

"Who?"

"Noriega! It's Noriega!"

"Who?"

"Noriega! The third guy! Piña face!"

"How do you know?"

"I've seen a million pictures of him."

Stephen felt sick. Ray was serious. It wasn't like before, with the communists, just a guess. "How could it be?" he asked. "What's he doing here?"

"How the hell should I know?"

"They have birds in those boxes."

"So?"

"What should we do?"

"I don't know, get away."

"He saw your gun, I think."

Ray looked at it as if somebody else had just now placed it in his hand.

"We have to tell somebody," Stephen said.

"Did you hear that?"

"What?"

Using both hands, Ray aimed the gun's barrel past Stephen's head, ready to shoot the first thing that appeared behind them.

"Just get going!"

Ray kicked his heels into Mary's sides and got her scrambling up the trail. He was holding the cumbersome pistol in a way that made Stephen fear he was going to accidentally blow a hole in the horse's neck, but he had to concentrate on getting Davy Crockett to move and didn't dare cry out a warning. He kept thinking about what Noriega must have in that long bundle. Weapons.

The trail was overgrown, and he soon lost sight of Ray and Mary ahead of him, though for a while he could hear them crashing through tree branches and brush. As those sounds faded, the pony gave up its pretense of hurrying and settled into a slow climbing pace, no matter how furiously he thrashed the reins and kicked at him. He thought he could make better time on foot, but he was afraid to leave the pony behind, so he got off and tugged him up the trail.

They were easy to follow, anyway, Mary's hoof prints churned into the slippery clay. At times he felt he must be close, the prints were so sharp and deep, and he risked calling, but he heard nothing in return.

He plodded on. In the deep shade of the forest, it felt as if he had been alone forever, and he was glad he had at least Davy Crockett for company. He couldn't tell how long it had been since Ray had abandoned him this second time. It was late afternoon. He pushed from his mind the question of what he would do if he lost the trail of hoof prints. What he would do when night fell. It kept him moving. That, and the thought of the horrible men with their cages of birds. The flash of green in the dark box, the miniature head and beak, the eye like a microscopic bead of fire was somehow more terrifying than even the bundle of weapons.

Finally the trail broke into the open, where the dark, dank smell of forest was replaced by the sweetness of burning grass. He was at the upper end of a broad, sloping field studded with stone outcroppings that cast long shadows across the ground. He could see for miles, down to where the slope eased and became green with cultivated fields patched irregularly against the hills. In the distance far below him, there was a sweep of perfect green and a big house of blazing white. For a second his heart leaped, but then he saw white columns reaching to the second story. It seemed even larger than the Picketts' house and had a shallowly-pitched green roof. It looked like a hotel, or a president's house. A long wall snaked across the hills below it, punctuated here and there by little towers with green-tiled roofs that matched the house.

The forest loomed darkly behind him, scary, but a place to hide. He was about to start riding along the edge of the trees, when he heard a voice from far down the slope. After a moment, he spotted Mary's white shape behind one of the masses of stone, and Ray looking over the top.

Crying with relief, he made his way down the hill to him through the thin, drifting smoke. He slid stiffly off the pony when he reached the rock pile. Ray crouched among the rocks. "It's like a fort," he said. He was trying to dislodge a stone from the main cluster of boulders.

"It's getting dark," Stephen said. "We have to get to that house."

"What if it's Noriega's?" Ray asked. Neither of them believed it was, though it was grand enough. They were pretty sure that they were in Costa Rica now, and started making their way down the long, rough slope. It occurred to Stephen that the enormous house might be abandoned, or unfinished, like the witches' house that Arturo had shown them one day, a men-acing concrete shell of a mansion overlooking a road in the mountains close to Escazú. What if, when they approached it, this house was like that one, haunted with emptiness that let the sky shine through from the other side?

When an eroded gully blocked their way, they rode along the edge of it, looking for a place to cross. It was like a river, though, winding endlessly, its sheer sides pushing them farther and farther away from their destination, until they couldn't see the house anymore. The smell of burning grass was heavier, starting to sting. Then they could see the house again, farther away than before. Between them and the house, a line of smoke stretched across the hillside.

When they turned to get around the gully from the other side, they saw something in the distance above them, an army-green truck, still far enough away that they could barely hear its engine, though they could see that it was bouncing and lurching over the rough ground.

They rode behind a pile of rocks and dead trees. Ray cocked the revolver. They watched. The flat windshield reflected the sun in brief flashes. The truck zigzagged among the invisible rocks and ditches. Then it seemed to leap and swerve and something flew off the back and a man they hadn't noticed clinging to the bed dropped to the ground and seemed to be running straight toward them. Noriega's man. Ray wheeled the mare and headed off in the opposite direction, into the loose, brown curtain of smoke.

Stephen shouted after him. He peered back over the rocks at the truck, which had stopped. Then he pounded his heels into Davy Crockett's sides, heading fast downhill to where he had lost sight of Ray and Mary.

As he approached the wall of smoke, the pony jerked and stopped, refusing to go any farther, snorting and whinnying and yanking its long-maned head back and forth against the reins. From here, Stephen could see the actual fire, a line of thin flames working toward the gully, devouring the long, coarse grass, bursting into blasts of denser smoke when it hit some richer fuel.

He was sick with horror. He looked back, and could no longer see the truck. Maybe it had gone off a different way, maybe he could go back now and get to the woods. While he was still desperately trying to decide what to do, he heard a shot, and then saw Mary's pale form emerge from the smoke, galloping flat out toward him. She was riderless.

He screamed, "Ray! Ray!" Mary circled above him on the slope before approaching, wild-eyed at first, but then seeming to be calmed a little by seeing Stephen and the pony, though whinnying and tearing off in sudden bursts when the smoke swung toward them. He slid to the ground and crept closer to the smoke that boiled now along the lip of the gulley. He called and called, hearing only the shush and snap of the fire, and he couldn't see anything, his eyes burning now, streaming with tears. He put his hands over his eyes like a visor and ran straight into the smoke, and gagged, and staggered back. He stared around. The horse and pony had moved farther away.

He had to do something. Ray was in there. Noriega was closing in. Without deciding to do it, he ran to the lip of the gully and leaped and slid and rolled to the bottom, the sheathed machete tripping and tangling him before he could get to his feet again. He scrambled forward along the sand and gravel, thirty or forty yards, maybe, until he reached a cut in the sheer side and moved up it until the smoke rolled above his head. He crawled and clawed his way up the ditch. The smoke started to choke him again, thrusting itself down his throat, gagging him. He heaved. He fought for enough air to scream out Ray's name, then started wriggling his way toward where he thought he must be, keeping as much as possible to the twisting labyrinth of erosion, where he could breathe better close to the raw earth, though even here sometimes he gagged. He saw something ahead of him, and he shouted but got no answer. The smoke was choking him.

He slid back down in the ditch a ways where he could breathe and unfastened the awkward machete from around his waist. He tossed it aside, then retrieved it and drew it from its sheath and drove its blade into the smoldering grass above him so it stood up and he could find it again. He breathed a few times deeply, sucking air out of the sand and clay, and then charged out of the gully toward where he had seen something, and threw himself to the ground, shouting, "It's me! It's me!" He wriggled forward over the coarse grass, imagining what it would feel like to be shot, and found Ray lying motionless, twisted oddly, pistol jammed into the elastic of his shorts.

He grabbed him under the arm pits and managed to move him a little. The smoke rolled around them, cleared, rolled in again, as he gradually dragged him toward what he hoped was the gully. It seemed he had gone too far, he must have gotten turned around, but then he saw the white handle of the machete, and pulled and pulled Ray's surprisingly heavy body toward it, until finally he felt the crumbly edge of the gully, and slid backward into it, dragging Ray after him. He propped him up, trying to help him breathe. He scrambled back up and retrieved the machete. Smoke rolled overhead.

CHAPTER FOURTEEN
UN CUENTO FOR BEDTIME

GRACE AND MARÍA LUZ stood beside the stone sink, talking about what Hank had wanted for breakfast before he left, how many times Guillermo had reminded María Luz to get word to his boss that he wouldn't be in to work. They talked about what a bad man Noriega was and how long it would take to restore order in Panama, and they never mentioned the mercenary raid on a drug bunker. They never mentioned the chance that they were widows.

Monica listened to them and said nothing. It wasn't her conversation. What she needed to talk about was something else. Anger and guilt and confusion and desire. A fear so complicated she couldn't see whether it crouched behind or ahead of her. She stood there in María Luz's tiny kitchen as if mute or ignorant of the language, feeling jealous of Grace's friendship with María Luz, who was pretty and funny and seemed to handle effortlessly the crowds of children who surged in and out of the dark, ramshackle, painstakingly clean little house. There had to be something feudal in the relationship between the Picketts and this family, she thought, feudal or colonial, and she wished she weren't just another gringa, helping the

North American patrona deliver Christmas gifts of castoff clothes and toys.

She excused herself for a moment to check on Valerie, whom she found talking with an older girl outside on the porch while a bunch of boys played some loud, wild game in the deeply shaded dirt yard. She wanted to pick the little girl up and carry her back inside, but Valerie seemed absorbed in her own conversation, so she left her and made her way back past the knot of children and older men watching soccer on the little television. Grace and María Luz were standing as they had been, talking. They were holding hands. She felt hot with shame. They were friends. Their lives were connected.

María Luz smiled at her and motioned for her to join them in the privacy they had declared in the crowded little house. How beautiful Valerie was, she said. And she had a son, also?

Yes, she said, he was with his good friend Ray. Which of these children were hers? she asked, and María Luz pointed out the girl talking with Valerie outside on the porch, who she said was fourteen, and two little boys playing on the floor, toddlers, twins. Her baby girl was taking a nap in the bedroom. She identified other people in the crowded little house—her grandmother, her sister-in-law nursing a baby on a sagging couch, an uncle, two aunts, cousins, nieces and nephews.

Were they all here for a Christmas party?

They were just visiting, María Luz said, but there got to be so many, it had become a party. It only needed balloons. She had some somewhere, she thought. She went to the refrigerator and took out a bowl and filled plastic glasses with juice and gave them to Monica and Grace. She handed her a second glass, for Valerie. While Monica started off to find her, she met a woman who had just come in, carrying a covered dish of something steaming and fragrant. María Luz introduced her as her mamá, and called out to everybody that they were about to eat, and people started pressing into the kitchen area. They filled plates with pasta from a huge pot on the stove, and arroz con pollo, which is what María Luz's mother had brought, then drifted with their plates back to the television or outside. María Luz went to look for those balloons.

Valerie came in with the older girl. "Do you want a refresco?" Monica asked her.

"Sí, gracias," she answered.

Monica laughed—neither of her children would ordinarily speak to her or Ted in Spanish, even phrases they knew well. She saw Valerie's face harden, insulted, and she stroked her hair apologetically. Did she want some spaghetti? she asked.

"Spaghetti?"

It was a little different from what they had at home, she told her. She thought she would like it, and went to get her a plate. With Stephen, she wouldn't have been so sure, he would go hungry rather than eat something he felt suspicious about. She was grateful that she didn't have to deal with him right now. She felt ashamed of the thought, but she couldn't help it. Things were crowding against her too hard, she had nothing to spare.

Stephen was okay, she was sure of it, she couldn't worry about him right now. He was, after all, merely camping out with his friend in what was essentially his friend's back yard. Ted had gone to find them, Arturo would lead them back. Nobody she loved was in Panama, where people were being shot and bombed and burned to death today.

Today was something she didn't have to worry about anymore. She and her baby were in this safe, good place. The danger was yesterday and tomorrow, where her life was already careening through the darkness on unmarked roads and she didn't know who was going to be hurt, but someone would be. It was tomorrow and yesterday she had to worry about. Yesterday when she had been utterly alive. Something shimmered still in the absolute center of her, the moment when he took away her breath, the moment when he gave it back to her again. How could she live without that?

And the wild ride through the mountains, the vultures, the roadblock. His fear, the way it led him away, and how she could not be sure exactly who he was when it turned him loose again. That deferential policeman and that horrible American soldier. When she had thought about it afterward, trying to grasp the nightmare familiarity she had felt, she realized that it was as if her father had reached out his hard hand, had found her, had found her out.

Yesterday, after Arturo left, she had put Valerie to bed and undressed and stood under the feeble spray of the cálidor, soaping herself, waiting for the panic to drain away that was pooling around her naked feet. Stephen, at least, was safe with the Picketts, she had told herself, just as Valerie had been safe all along with her classmate's minivan-driving Tico family. She had let the hot drizzle wash over her body, listening for the apartment door to open and Ted's stockinged feet to creak across the floor.

Finally she had gotten out of the shower and dried herself. She went to bed, and lay awake for a while, and got up and set the already boiled water on the stove for tea. She discovered that she wanted a drink, and went and searched through the storeroom over the water pump, hoping to find some forgotten six pack or bottle of wine. She considered going down and asking Eva, but she didn't think anybody was home. She thought about the bar down the road from the hulera, La Uvita, The Little Grape, where she had seen workmen drinking in the evenings but had never gone in. It wasn't a place where a woman would go, but she had thought about it while her manzanilla tea brewed in twice boiled water.

She had carried the steaming plastic mug to the kids' room, sat down on Stephen's neatly made mattress bed, and watched Valerie sleep in her little nest of toys and clothes and stuffed animals. Flushed, exhausted from the day of rides and junk food, the little girl was sleeping with arms and legs recklessly flung out from beneath the tangled sheet like a bird struck down in flight. She had set the tea down and stretched out on Stephen's tightly tucked comforter and for a moment allowed her body to remember the shape of Arturo's body, its exact pressure. Without that pressure she felt her life would spill helplessly out of her. She had slipped in and out of dreams, got up again, went out into the living room, and curled up in her big armchair. When Ted finally returned, she had just woken from another nightmare and stared at him almost without recognition.

Would she be able to help with this task? It was María Luz, with a handful of limp balloons. She distributed them, and the women started blowing them up and knotting their ends and tossing them to the little children, who leaped after them, shrieking. What did this mean? María Luz asked Monica, handing her one she had just blown up. The balloons all had advertising on them, in English. This one showed a stethoscoped cartoon doctor approaching a bloated, smoking furnace. It carried the name of a Chicago plumbing and heating company and the caption, "A Cure For Your Gas Problems." Monica explained the pun and then what a furnace was, and María Luz laughed and repeated the joke to her mother. They had Monica translate the other balloons, but none was as good as the gas one.

"We should probably be getting back," Grace said.

"Yes," Monica said, in a sudden spasm of guilt. "Stephen'll freak if he doesn't know where I am." She didn't want to leave, however. She felt safe, as if these particular people had been assigned the task of keeping her from harm, keeping her from doing or suffering harm. So when María Luz invited them all to walk over to see her uncle's new house, she agreed, and took Valerie by the hand, and followed the others down a dirt path through the trees to a neat, cinder-block house perched above a stream.

The children swam there, María Luz said. Valerie and her brother someday should come and play. The uncle, a tall, quiet bachelor only a few years older than María Luz, showed them into the house, which seemed to Monica stark and underfurnished, with white-painted stucco walls and smooth concrete floors gleaming with red wax. A jigsaw puzzle picture of a jaguar was the only decoration on the walls. Everybody complimented the uncle on the jaguar, saying how lifelike it was, as if he had painted it rather than just put the pieces together. He had a Christmas tree in the corner of the living room, a little cedar that could have been the twin of the one in the Hoffmans' apartment, but richer in ornaments and strung with lights that flashed on and off when he plugged it in for them.

María Luz and her relatives were proud of the house, proud of its newness and solidity, and proud of the uncle, an engineer who had worked for a time in the United States and knew some English, though he was too shy to try it out on his visitors. As they were leaving, María Luz cleared her throat in the night air and launched into the "ABC" song, which she said was the only English she remembered from school. She got Valerie to join her, and laughed when they discovered they had conflicting versions of the last line—"Tell me what you think of me," and "Next time won't you sing with me?" She drew her daughter to her, and asked her to sing something, and the girl's clear, sweet voice accompanied them along the dark path, a song full of longing that Monica recognized from the passing Christmas posadas they had watched from their balcony.

Back at her own crowded, shabby house, María Luz insisted on showing them her husband's motorcycle, a lean, dented Suzuki that was chained up in an attached shed as if it were a dangerous animal. Guillermo was a mason, she said. She patted the dusty saddle bags he used to carry his tools, and was suddenly unable to speak. She looked away, a hand covering her mouth.

May he be safe, Monica said, jarred by her pain.

"¡Ojalá!" María Luz answered, God grant it, and embraced her as if Monica's husband, too, were in the jungles of Panama, tangling his fragile life in a conflict of drug traffickers and mercenary soldiers, maybe caught in the avalanche of the invasion.

"Ojalá," Monica said.

The few lights of the house disappeared almost immediately as they drove away through the trees, bouncing along the bad roads, weaving back toward Santa Ana and then up into the mountains. Valerie was asleep in Monica's arms. "Thank you, Grace," Monica said. "I'm very glad to have met her."

Grace said, "This whole area once belonged to her family. It got divided up over the years, sold off. They rent that house."

"She's wonderful," Monica said.

"She is. She was a girl working for me when she got pregnant with Jessica. Thirteen years old. I never knew who the father was, but she learned about birth control after that, let me tell you. It's common, ten or twelve years between a first child and the rest of the kids. I wish you could have met Guillermo. He's a little younger than she is, a very sweet young man."

What's he doing raiding a drug bunker in Panama? Monica wanted to ask. Did Hank teach him to fight? Did he get him on the C.I.A. payroll, too, or does he just pay day wages for a young father to risk his life with him, maybe help him kill somebody? She studied Grace's profile, dimly lit by the dashboard lights, looking for a sign of the violence that must have touched her.

Then she gave up and gazed out at the passing darkness. If there was something unholy in this family, she wasn't able to follow it past the hard edge of their politics, which is where Hank's soldiering probably lived. Grace was a better woman than she was, braver, did more good in the world, loved more faithfully. Monica thought of her father, whom she had feared and despised most of her life, who must have loved her mother once, who loved *her*, though with some kind of knotted energy that bit into the flesh. For him, it was all politics, love and power included. How much had she learned from him? How much could she have learned from these people, if she had met them sooner?

They were on the last, steep part of the road to the Picketts' finca. Grace was quiet—absorbed in the difficult driving, or thinking about her scattered family. Surely by now the boys would have been brought back, would be playing in Ray's room or watching television. Monica stroked Valerie's hair and tried to picture Ted and Arturo across the kitchen table from each other, talking about—what? The invasion? Politics? Not her, though she had the two of them hopelessly tangled in her heart's ropes.

What could she do? She had a right to passion. Not just safety, not just partnership. Not just her children, even, though they were as necessary to her as breath. Didn't she deserve more than that? And did she deserve Ted's hurt, edgy love, his decency that somehow had not been touched by his affair, though it had broken forever something between them, had broken something in her?

She couldn't think about Arturo. She never could think about him, really, any more than she could think about her own blood, on the move in every part of her body at once. She could think the word, "blood," but it didn't seem to have much to do with the thing pulsing within her, surprising her once a month with cramp and flow that had no more to do with what kept her alive than the word itself did. The word "blood." The word "Arturo."

The Picketts' house was blazing with light when it swung into view above them on the black mountainside. Monica got out and opened, then closed the gate. After they parked, they could hear the dogs barking thunderously. She hefted Valerie out of the truck and followed Grace inside. She knew at once that the boys weren't back yet, though Charlotte was home from the beach, listening to music from a boombox on the kitchen table and eating salad and potato chips. Her newly-permed, newly-blond hair was pulled back in a pony tail, and her skin was burned the color of rose gold. "Where were you?" she cried out as soon as she saw her mother. "They dropped me off and it was like everybody'd been abducted by aliens. Luis said you'd been gone for hours."

"Shh," Grace said, gesturing toward Valerie, who hung limp over Monica's shoulder.

"Oh the darling angel! She's so sweet! Momma, I had the best time! We stayed at this new place that wasn't even built the last time we were at Jacó, and it is much, much nicer than Club del Mar. You guys should go there, Monica, Las Palmas." She jumped up and hovered over Valerie as if she were about to snatch the little girl away. "She's so cute! Can I hold her?"

Monica was about to hand her over, but Grace said, "We need to let her sleep, honey. Come on." She led Monica to a little side room off the kitchen that she had never noticed before and helped her settle Valerie on a narrow bed against the wall. There was only one small window in the room, yet the barking was louder here than in the kitchen. Grace didn't seem to notice it. Anyway, Valerie was used to sleeping with dogs barking all night outside the apartment, Boby challenging every dog that walked past on the road.

Charlotte followed them in. "God, I can't believe what a great time I had. There was this boy that Susana knows, Álvaro, and he is so nice—"

"Darling girl," Grace interrupted, "I want to hear absolutely everything about it, but not at this moment, all right?"

"All right." She took it gracefully. They had a nice, comfortable relationship, Monica thought. She couldn't imagine that she would get along that easily when Valerie was seventeen. "Where's Ray? Daddy's not back yet?"

"Ray and Stephen are camping."

"How about Daddy?"

"He's not back yet, honey."

Charlotte fished for the crumbled chips at the bottom of the bag. She was wearing a man's white shirt with the sleeves rolled up and the tails knotted above her navel, and tight, faded jeans. "Álvaro says we invaded Panama last night," she said. "Is that right? Is that what Daddy's doing?" She didn't seem worried.

"We don't really know what's going on," Grace said. "I'm thinking maybe I should go into Santa Ana and try to call Rawlie Edmunds at the embassy again and see if he's heard anything."

"If we invaded them, does that mean we'll be getting our money back?"

Grace shook her head. "We don't know what it means. I just want to find out about Daddy, that's why I have to call." She looked at Monica. "Do you want to drive down with me? Charlotte can entertain Valerie if she wakes up."

"They'll be back any minute," Monica said.

"Charlotte can get them something to eat, and we'll be back in just a little bit. Your husband can handle things a little while longer."

"I'm extremely responsible," Charlotte assured Monica. "If she wakes up, we'll have fun." She saw them to the door as if she were their hostess, and stood on the steps with her arms folded complacently. As they walked down to the truck and got in, the thunder from the dog pen behind the house swelled in volume. Charlotte shouted at the dogs, then called out something to her mother.

Grace was already backing the truck around. "Could you hear what she said?"

"Something about the dogs."

Grace leaned out the window and shouted, "They'll be fine!" and headed down the mountain.

"A new boy," Monica said.

"Oh, yes."

"Poor Rodolfo."

"Rodolfo will be all right."

"I liked him."

Grace looked over at her for a moment. "I liked him, too," she said. "Nice boy, good family. He has that bony handsomeness, doesn't he? It's a type that makes me nervous."

Monica remembered the electric shock of his handshake and wanted suddenly to defend him. "I don't think I believe in types."

"Oh, there are types, all right. And I know Rodolfo's type. Nice boy that he is, he can't help it." She looked at Monica again. "Arturo Aguilar is that type, wouldn't you say? If you believed in types?"

She felt her stomach tighten, as if against a blow. Then she laughed self-consciously and looked out at the passing shadows. "I don't," she said after a moment. "I don't believe in them."

"He doesn't make you nervous."

"I didn't say that." This time the laugh came more easily. She felt something ease, as if a deep, habitual cramp were relaxing its grip. It had to do with Grace being on her side. "You know, Valerie this afternoon," Monica said. "She was playing, but she wasn't all wrong. I'm very grateful to him. He *has* been like an uncle to the kids."

"He's many things to many people."

"What do you mean?"

"Nothing. It's hard to explain."

"I'd like to know what you meant." The tension was in her guts again.

"Well, I don't know, but he seems to bring out...." She stopped, groping for something.

"The worst in people? That's not true at all."

"No," Grace said, "not at all, not the worst, at all." She thought about it. "Their longing. Their heart's desire."

"His type? His type does this?"

She seemed to want to drop it, but Monica refused to let her off the hook.

"Cal Richardson," Grace said after a moment, "I think he changed when he started doing business with Arturo. Not necessarily for the worse, but look how he ended up. Even Hank—I don't know."

"Arturo's type affects him too?"

"Forget it, please. He's been kind to you and your family."

They drove in silence, the jarring mountain roads giving way after a while to smoother asphalt. Monica waited for the pounding in her chest to grow quiet. It was stupid enough. Blackness still pushed in around the beams of the headlights, until they started passing a few scattered houses. "Grace," she said, "I need to know something. Do you think he could be involved in anything illegal?"

"I don't think you should worry about that."

"It sounded like you were warning me off."

Grace pulled over to the side of the road where it widened at the edge of the village. "You just have to be careful. For everyone's sake." She waited, and when Monica looked away, she put the truck in gear and drove on to the pulpería in Santa Ana where they usually made calls. The store was closed, though, and the phone in the square was out of order, but they found a liquor store open, which Grace thought had a pay phone.

Some people were standing around outside the open door. Inside, a three-man marimba band was setting up. The store seemed to stock mostly beer, which filled a cooler and was stacked in cases along one wall, with a small set of shelves behind the counter lined with whiskey and bourbon and a few dusty bottles of Chilean wine. Even with the musicians set up in the angle between the counter and the other wall, there was room for people to listen and maybe dance. She couldn't tell whether the space had been specially cleared, or whether this was the regular arrangement. A very tall, very thin old man, dressed in a frayed yet elegant gray suit coat and vest and tattered blue jeans, stood swaying beside the marimba, as if the music had already begun.

While Grace went to make her call, Monica asked the man behind the counter for two Bavaria's, and then was afraid, momentarily, that it was a breach of decorum, that they had blundered into a private party, but the man opened the beers for her and told her the price and invited her to stay and enjoy the music.

A teenaged boy, sixteen or seventeen, was lounging on a stool behind the counter, looking amused and disdainful as the musicians started to play. After a few minutes, he went to the back and turned on a radio tuned to a rock music station,

Radio Uno, she thought, which pulsed unpleasantly against the cheerful sweetness of marimba and guitars. She expected the owner to rebuke the boy and make him turn off the radio, but he didn't seem to notice, and the musicians played on as if there were a wall protecting their music from the intrusion of Kiss.

She carried the bottles to the front of the store, where she could listen to the live music with less distraction and wait for Grace to finish her call. By the time Grace hung up, Monica had finished the first beer and was starting in on the second. "You want me to get you something?" she asked, but Grace shook her head.

"Rawlie's in a meeting, but the girl said he'd be out soon. I gave them this number. We can wait a few minutes, can't we?"

"I guess. Sure. You think they're back yet?"

"Who knows?"

"It's been dark for hours. How could they find their way in the dark?"

"They'll find a road. Otherwise they'll have to camp another night. The boys won't mind."

"If they found them. They could all be wandering around in the mountains by themselves, couldn't they? I keep thinking about those German hikers."

Grace touched the bottle in Monica's hand. "Is that cold? Maybe I will go get me one."

Monica followed her. "I just can't get my mind around it," she said. "I can't get a picture of them out there. It's like they've gone to another planet." She felt herself starting to slide into the kind of numb panic she had felt that morning. The beer was helping her knotted stomach a little, but not enough. "Maybe we should call the police to search for them. Arturo said—" What had he said? She couldn't remember. She asked for another Bavaria.

"Trust me," Grace said, "we don't want the police in on this. We just have to wait for them." She looked at Monica, and then put a hand on her arm. "We have to wait," she said. "We have to wait for them."

Sliding. She was still sliding. Grace didn't have a tight enough grip. Her hand was cool and dry and strong. But it wasn't enough.

"¿Señorita?" She turned. It was the tall old man, shabby and formal looking at the same time, his long gray hair combed back in smooth wings. Would she care to dance? he asked. He was almost toothless, and he formed his words with great care, fitting them around the two or three long teeth that saved his gums from total emptiness. She looked at him blankly, trying to remember something, and he repeated the invitation.

"He's asking you to dance," Grace said to her, as if she hadn't understood. "He's harmless, I think. I see him around, doing odd jobs for people."

"He's not harmless," Monica said. "We know that. No one's harmless." And then she smiled and took his hand and let him lead her gracefully in circles on the improvised dance floor, his shoulder thin and sinewy beneath the coat's padding, his hand light as bird's wing behind her back. When the song was over, he bowed to her, and everybody clapped. He thanked her again for the honor of the dance. As the musicians began another song, the old man quietly asked whether there were a few extra coins for some refreshment, and she said yes, of course there were, and found a hundred colón note in her purse and pressed it into his mottled hand. He bowed to her again, gracious and aristocratic, and stood talking with her for a few minutes about the evening and the music and the beauty of her dancing before excusing himself and going to the counter.

Grace's friend from the embassy never called back. They waited another half hour, then left. "How are you doing?" Grace asked, on the way up the mountain again.

It was a real question. She thought about it. There was a long silence, broken only by the jolt and rattle of the truck on the rough roads, the snarl of the engine. "Grace," Monica said finally, "I'm sorry I got pissy with you."

"I understand."

"No."

"Yes, I do." Without taking her eyes off the road, Grace reached over and squeezed her hand. "How bad is it?"

She gave up then, let go her end of the rope she had been clinging to to hold herself together. "It's pretty bad," she said. "I'm not sure I can stand it."

"You'll be surprised what you can stand," Grace said.

•

OUTSIDE THE PICKETTS' HOUSE the Land Cruiser was parked a little ways from Arturo's Lincoln. Monica felt light-headed, simplified somehow, as if she had been fasting, rather than drinking. The dogs were howling with a new mournfulness, it seemed, a confused, anxious music rather than the eager racket they usually made.

The elderly servant met them at the door, and they found Hank lying on the kitchen floor, his pants pulled down and his broad buttocks swathed in bloody gauze. Grace cried out and ran to him.

He pushed himself up onto one elbow and gave her an awkward kiss when she flung herself down next to him. "Hell of a homecoming, ain't it?" he growled, and then he noticed Monica standing in the kitchen doorway. "Forgive my ungentlemanly posture," he said to her, grimacing with pain. "I'm afraid that at the moment I cannot rise." There was a liquor bottle on the floor beside him, and a tumbler half full.

"What on earth?" Grace asked.

"It's that fool Princess. I was half way to the door, and she came flying around the house and attacked me before she recognized me. I don't know how she got out. They were all out, tearing around loose. For a second I thought Tracker was going to go after me, but he just slammed into that idiot and they went down in a heap. By the time he hit her, I think she realized what she'd done."

Charlotte rushed in with a pile of white towels and explained all over again what had happened, sliding past the issue of how the dogs had come to be running loose.

"Do we need to get you to a doctor?" Grace asked.

"Well, take a look. I'm not in a position to judge, but I think we can handle it ourselves."

As Grace carefully removed the gauze, Monica went in to check on Valerie, who seemed not to have moved since they had left. She sat on the edge of the bed and stroked the little girl's hair so lightly she could barely feel the tickle on the palm of her hand. At least he's back, she thought. At least he's not lying dead in the jungle. She wondered if he had been wearing those double-knit slacks and sport shirt when he was on the raid, or if he had changed afterward, from fatigues or something. Maybe it all was just a story, after all, something for the American Legion. She heard him grunt in pain, and then Grace ordering Charlotte to bring in their medicine chest, then water running.

Grace stuck her head in the door. "It's not too serious," she said. "I'm going to clean it up and take a few stitches."

"Do you need any help?" Monica asked, and was relieved when she said no, she had had plenty of practice.

"Also, it's something that girl better learn. What could she have been thinking?"

It didn't take very long. Afterward, they helped him move to a long leather couch in the living room, where he could rest on one side and drink and curse the stupidity of young dogs. "Where's Ray?" he asked suddenly. He nodded when they told him about the camping trip, and Ted and Arturo's going after them, and didn't appear worried. Mostly he kept talking about the dogs, and what a fool he had been to turn and try to get away. "Offered the ignoramus my most undistinguished feature," he said.

"It's quite distinguished, dear," Grace said.

"Compared to Southern Command, though, the dog's a genius," he said.

Grace said, "I couldn't believe when I heard about it and

they hadn't warned us. What happened? Did they manage to get word to you finally?"

"They did not. They surely did not. Haynes personally commissioned the job, and he didn't think to tell me a God damn thing, pardon my French."

"Maybe he didn't know about it," Grace suggested.

"How could he not have known about it?" Hank roared. "He's goddamn C.I.A.!" He sank back on the couch in disgust, then pushed himself up again and took a drink. "You could be right. *I* wouldn't want them to know if I was trying to surprise somebody. Somebody else managed to leak it, though, if it wasn't them."

"Is everybody all right? I was just with María Luz."

"Sheer luck," he said. "We got as far as San Vito and hit washout, and hiked in, and found the factory. We wondered why there didn't seem to be anybody around. And when we went in, what did we find? We found not one God damned thing. Just benches and empty shelves and trash. We didn't figure it out until we got back to the Cruiser and the muchacho we'd left watching it said some kids had come by and told him there was an American invasion going on. *They*'d all heard about it the day before, they said. Noriega's apparently holed up in some church."

He finished his drink, and Charlotte poured him another one. "Does this invasion thing mean we'll be getting our money back?" she asked him.

"Maybe, unless somebody drops an atomic bomb on the banks," he said. "I put nothing past them." He drank, and lapsed into disgusted silence. Monica was settling back in one of the huge old leather chairs, trying to think of something to say, when he startled her by asking suddenly, "You say Aguilar is helping find those boys?"

"He and Ted rode up after them," she said. "I was sure they'd be back by now." Grace was looking at her.

"He's a horseman, I'll give him that," Hank said. "Your Ted, is he a horseman?"

"I don't know. He rode when he was a kid, apparently. He seemed to be doing okay." She had never seen him on a horse before in her life.

"What horses are they riding?" Charlotte asked, a question that seemed to have just occurred to her.

"Arturo has Goldie, Mr. Hoffman is on Ranger," Grace said. "The boys have Davy Crockett and Mary."

"They took Goldie and Ranger? They took my horses, and nobody asked my permission?"

"You weren't here, sweetheart," Grace said.

Hank waved his hand dismissively. "They'll be all right, don't get worked up about it. They're horsemen, it's an honor for a horse to be ridden by a real horseman."

Charlotte didn't seem to think it was an honor for her horses to be ridden by anybody but herself, but she kept quiet about it after that. When they heard crying from the small room off the kitchen, she offered to go check on Valerie, but Monica was already up and on her way. The moaning and growling of the dogs was loud in the little room and may have been what woke her. Monica took her on her lap and cuddled her on the hard bed. "It's all right, baby," she murmured. "It's just the dogs."

"What's wrong with them?"

"One of them accidentally bit Mr. Pickett on the butt, and I think they feel real bad about it."

Valerie sat up. "On the butt?"

Monica smiled. "He's okay. It wasn't too bad." Anything having to do with butts amused Valerie. But instead of laughing, she wailed and thrust her face against Monica's breast hard enough to hurt. "No, sweetie, it's okay, it was just an accident, and he's okay, Grace fixed him up." She cried and cried, though, and it seemed as if the dogs increased their mournful din in sympathy or shame.

Finally she calmed down, though her body was still racked with a sob from time to time. She straightened, and blew her nose into a tissue Monica had dug out of a pocket and held for her, and listened to the barking of the dogs, which had shrunk to a kind of mournful, mechanical jabber. "They sound like gooses," she observed.

Monica listened. "They sort of do. When did you hear geese?"

"At my home," she said. "My real home. Remember when Daddy woke us up? I was outside in my nightie and I couldn't see anything, I could just hear them in the sky."

She remembered. It was spring, a few months after Ted had told her about his affair. He had gotten them all out on their deck, and they had stared up into the darkness, and listened to the heartbreaking music of what must have been an enormous flock of wild geese on their way north to Canada, following the Ohio River.

She laid Valerie back down on the bed. "Do you think you can go to sleep, now? We're going to spend the night here, and in the morning Daddy and Stephen will be back."

"Will you stay in this room with me?"

"Scrooch over."

They settled themselves on the narrow bed. "Good," Valerie said. "Now, tell me a story."

"Oh, God, baby, I'm too tired."

"I really need a story."

"Just close your eyes."

She started to cry.

Monica stroked her hair. "Let me think." She lay there, trying to think, but the only thought that came to her was that if she were quiet for a while, maybe Valerie would fall asleep. She didn't fall asleep, though. Monica could feel her alertness quivering in the dimly lit room, while her own buzzy tiredness dragged and dragged at her. "What should the story be about?" she asked, too sleepy to be ashamed of her lack of imagination. Even her tongue was heavy, though that might have been the beers.

There was a long silence, a drifting. Then she heard Valerie say, "a goose."

"A goose. Okay." She roused herself, propping herself up on an elbow. "Once upon a time there was a goose." She pushed the sentence out. "And this goose had a problem." She looked down at Valerie, who looked back at her. "What do you suppose her problem was?"

She thought about it for a moment. "She was lonely."

"That's right, she was lonely. And who was she lonely for?"

"Her children."

"Yes, for her children. Why do you suppose she was lonely for her children?"

She sat up.

"Okay," Monica said, "sorry. I'll tell it. Lie down and let me think." She couldn't think, she was too tired.

"Once upon a time there was a goose," Valerie recapitulated helpfully. "And she was lonely for her children." She lay back down.

"Yes, she was lonely for her children. They had all gone out one day, over the hill and far away."

Valerie made an irritated noise. "That was ducks." She didn't want her to cheat.

"They'd all gone out, and hadn't come back, and sad mother goose went out searching for them," Monica said, unable to start over. "She called to them in her dogish voice, honking and honking, but they were nowhere to be found."

"It was dark," Valerie murmured.

"It was dark, a very dark night, and she flew over mountains and jungles and cities, but she couldn't find them." She listened to her own voice, as if from another part of the room. She heard herself telling the story, she was barely in the room at all. "The goose asked everyone she met. She asked a horse, but he hadn't seen them, and she asked a dog, but he hadn't seen them. She asked some crabs on the beach, but they didn't know, so she flew out over the ocean, until she thought her wings couldn't beat any more, she was so tired. But she found a turtle swimming in the ocean, who let her rest on her back. They floated, and the goose asked the turtle if she'd seen her children. And guess what?"

The dogs had grown quiet, except for an occasional yelp or whine. She adjusted the blanket around the sleeping girl's shoulders and stretched herself out, let her own head settle onto the pillow beside her.

The turtle hadn't seen her children, but she had heard them. They were flying so high, just under the stars. And the goose said, Then that's where I have to go, even though she was already so tired, she couldn't feel her wings anymore. And she flew for hours over the black ocean, until she heard their voices, and she flew faster and caught up with them under the stars and she said, Thank God I've found you, my darlings. But they didn't say anything to her, they just flew on, and she asked them, Where are you flying to? But they didn't say anything. And she asked them again, where were they flying to? And they said, To our heart's desire. And where is that, my darlings? she asked.

There was no answer, only the small rocking of the girl's breath in sleep. The whole house was quiet. There was nothing but silence, inside and outside. Your heart's desire, where's that? she asked. She kept on asking and asking, until finally they said, Can't you see? And she looked and saw the great V of them, flying together beneath the wild stars.

CHAPTER FIFTEEN

LA CORDILLERA, FOLDING AND

UNFOLDING

MOUNTAINS DENSE WITH FOREST pressed in on him. Here and there in the almost perpendicular walls of green rising hundreds of feet overhead, veiny trunks were visible, robles or estraques, their muscles bunched against gravity and wind and common sense. The coati had disappeared. It hadn't been afraid of him, it just had had someplace to get to.

He touched Ranger's sides with his heels. The trail edged its way nervously along the pass where the earth crumpled into cordillera, folding the land back on itself, then back again, then back again. Horse and rider moved forward into what appeared to be absolute, untouched mountain wilderness. Then there would be a line of rusty fence threaded into living tree trunks, or a shed clinging to the slope, or charred tree trunks. Once, the rusting hulk of a bulldozer sinking into the earth. But always the mountains looming above him.

A hard wind pushed into his face. Except for the threshers, he had met no one the whole ride, and now saw nothing on the trail, which was too rocky here to leave prints. He pushed on, though the ache of riding so long was awful. At the narrowest parts of the pass, the sun was behind the mountains, the sky looked hard as lapis, as if poised to send an avalanche of darkness crashing down on him, though it was barely midafternoon.

And then the trail broke abruptly into the open, and a valley stretched out below him into a blue, infinite distance. Wild, green, unbroken. He watched a vulture float in that sky, a flake of ash, then lost sight of it. He had to go back. He couldn't go any farther. The boys had surely found their own way home by now. He was more lost now than they probably had ever been. He slumped forward, feeling the ridge of mane rough against his forehead. He stroked sweat from the horse's hot, veiny neck.

Retracing his way through the steep pass, nothing seemed the same. He came upon a meadow, with grass that looked as lush and even as a palace lawn, though close up he saw it was at least a foot tall, wind blowing it in waves like wheat. A stream seemed to cut through the middle of it like the ragged part in a careless child's hair. He let Ranger graze for a while, but he didn't have the energy to dismount. He was about to urge the horse forward toward the stream when he saw something. There was something, another man on horseback, shadowy on the far side of the meadow, smaller than he could have been: it wasn't a meadow, it was a moor. Before he could think to rein him in, Ranger whinnied and surged forward, lurching drunkenly as his hooves sank into boggy ground, which sucked and released them with the sound of huge obscene kisses.

In the distance, the other horse jumped sideways, its whinny lifting and sailing toward them, barely reaching. The rider hurled it down the bank and across the stream and up the slope, a white shirt flashing when it caught a shard of sunlight, and a golden horse making the most of the open ground, plunging and dodging.

He held the reins slack in his hands and let Ranger carry him forward until Goldie and Arturo reached them. Goldie whirled and took a nip at Ranger's shoulder, and Ranger jumped to the side, lost his center, went down, spilling Ted onto the soft ground and shoving down hard on him like a huge hand. The horse rolled and staggered to his feet again, groaning, leaving Ted half-buried in the cool, spinning earth.

He found himself reclining against Arturo's lap, Arturo holding him, pressing a plastic bottle against his lips, dribbling water into his mouth and down the front of his shirt. His back and trousers were soaked from the damp ground. Arturo handed him the bottle and brushed his palm across his forehead, smoothed his hair with finger tips cold and hard against his sunburned scalp.

"My friend," Arturo said, "you should wear a hat."

He lay there, breathing in and out. He could have lain there forever. But after a few minutes Arturo eased him forward till he sat upright, and said, "I got to help that horse now."

"Oh, man, he's hurt?" He struggled to his feet and stepped unsteadily toward Ranger, who faced him a few yards away, swinging his beautiful head back and forth. Ted felt like weeping, he stretched out his hand to the wonderful horse. Charlotte's horse.

"This one," Arturo said. "This estúpido." Goldie was standing farther off, apparently calm, tearing at the thick grass. "He turned the leg wrong when he try that bite, I felt it. Venga, hombrón, estúpido," he crooned. When he reached the horse, it jumped a little but didn't try to run off. Ted took Goldie's reins while Arturo worked his way down the right rear leg until the horse reached suddenly back at him with bared teeth. Ted grabbed the reins closer to the bit. "Not too bad," Arturo said. "I fix her a little so she don't swell so big."

"Can he be ridden?"

"That big one will carry the two." He dug his hand into an oozing hoof print and scooped up some foul-smelling muck and eased it onto the injured leg, smoothing it around as if creating the animal out of black clay.

"Do you know where we are?" Ted was sure they couldn't get back to the Picketts' place before dark, much less find the boys. He was so tired and sore, so happy to have Arturo with him again. He hadn't realized how lonely he had been. Now he only wanted to lie back down on the soft ground. The boys could camp out another night, if they weren't back already. They probably were back already. They probably were sitting in front of the Picketts' monster television this minute, with Monica and Valerie and Ray's sister and parents. It was all right. He felt a deep, unaccountable contentment. They could spend the night under the stars at the edge of this remote highland moor.

"I think a road is not so far away," Arturo said.

Ted squatted stiffly and watched him work on Goldie's leg. "I haven't seen a road for, I don't know, hours. How did you get ahead of me?"

He wiped his mucky hands on the long grass. "Is because of this, señor Ted. You are following where they have been. I go to where they are going."

"I lost the trail somewhere. They must have cut back."

"You did very well. Is just I got more information. Do me this favor, get a blanket from the saddle and make ribbon."

He found the blanket and tried unsuccessfully to tear it. It was like felt, a sort of stadium blanket. Finally he used his pocket knife to hack off a strip about six inches wide, which Arturo wrapped around the muddy leg, tucked in, then smeared with more mud. "You know this area," Ted said.

"Where they go. This is the place I think, but I find you instead. They're someplace other. Now, if you're able."

Arturo wanted to help him get up into the saddle again, but he wasn't ready for that yet. They set off on foot, leading the horses, and made their way over the boggy field down to the stream. Swirls of black silt still hung in the glassy water where Goldie had splashed through. They followed the motionless stream without crossing it, Arturo's wiry figure leading the palomino shimmering in the directionless light. Ted followed, his feet moving through the tall grass and over the uncertain ground, and the big chestnut horse followed him.

"Arturo, dime una cosa." How well did he know this area? he asked, offering his awkward Spanish as if it were flowers. What was it, he asked, a national park? Wilderness? He felt himself babbling.

Arturo slowed and let him walk up beside him. He jerked the reins when Goldie reached across them to nip at Ranger again. The stupid horse hadn't learned a fucking thing, he said, and then put a hand on Ted's shoulder. "Sí, yermo," he said, wilderness, but he shouldn't worry, they would find a road soon enough.

The trail was getting narrower, making it impossible to walk side by side. Arturo found a break in the press of forest that had closed in on them and pressed ahead into its obscurity. Barely able to see in the deep shadows, Ted followed the thud and clump of Goldie's hooves, the flash of white tail. The trail was climbing again, winding up the sharp incline into the droning forest, little more than a track scribbled through the perpetual evening. Where the forest thinned again into still another sun-struck, windswept meadow, he caught up with Arturo, who was checking Goldie's leg.

Ted stretched out on the uneven ground. As he watched Arturo work, he rummaged through his skimpy Spanish, piecing together sentences in his head. Arturo glanced at him over his shoulder. How had he gotten ahead of him? he asked again.

He believed he knew where the boys were going, Arturo said. He had been heading there when they met.

Where did he think they were going?

South. So he was able to go directly to this pass, Arturo said, which the Pickett boy would know was the only way south.

"What made you think they were going south?"

"From Valerie."

Ted stared at him in confusion.

"She's little, nobody notice when she's around. She hear things."

"She doesn't know what *south* means."

Arturo came over and sat down beside him. "What she say is Panama," he said. "Panama from there is south, then east."

"They think they can ride horses to Panama?"

"They're boys."

Ted shifted his weight, testing his legs and backside.

"Is bad at first," Arturo said.

"I haven't ridden in twenty years. Your body toughens up after a while, I know that."

"It get worse before it get better."

He groaned, struggled to his feet, and untied the reins that held Ranger to a greasy-feeling bush. "Any idea where they are now?"

"I think you're right. They have turn back."

"Can we find them?"

"I think so."

"It'll be dark soon."

"I have told to Monica, we find the boys, bring them back to her."

It was strange to hear him say her name. "She'll be so worried."

Arturo looked up at him. "I think you love her very much," he said.

He didn't know what to say. It had been a long time since he had taken it for granted. "Why do you say that?" he asked, studying the oiled leather reins curling in his hands.

"Because she is worth it."

He looked up into a sky turning cobalt in its deepest center. She was. He had never loved her well enough. "Here," he said, "get up. I'll ride behind." He leaned against the big horse's side. Arturo came over to him and didn't argue, just put a hand on his shoulders, then swung himself up into the saddle. He walked the horse over to a rock that Ted could use as a step and reached his hand back to help him haul himself up onto Ranger's broad haunches. It was awful, the skirt of stiff leather behind the cantle jammed underneath his crotch. He grabbed onto the rolled edge of the saddle's back and concentrated on settling his body into the movements of muscle and bone.

Arturo looked back at him. "Can you do it?"

He nodded. He hoped so.

Goldie snorted, then limped after them as they crossed the bare outlook into what seemed like sheer trackless forest. In a few minutes, they struck a dirt road no worse than the one that ran past the Hoffmans' apartment in Escazú. "Where did this come from?"

"I think is the road for us to find these boys." He pointed down to a slurry of hoof prints and tire tracks in the dirt and pushed Ranger into a trot.

The road turned back on itself, climbing again. They slowed to a walk. Then it dropped again, to a gorge that swallowed the road and drew it deeper into the forest, then opened onto a field trashy with blackened stumps. There were men clearing brush with machetes. One of the men saw them. He straightened and watched them. After a few moments he called out to the other men, and started walking toward the road.

At the far side of the burned field there was a kind of encampment, a slum of corrugated tin and pressboard and wooden shacks gaudy with blue and faded-orange tarps, huddled against the wall of forest. Dogs barked, and out of nowhere a little mongrel charged the horses and barely missed being crushed by Goldie's disgusted trampling. Somewhere, somebody was playing loud rock music. Its throbbing rose and fell against the backbeat of an unmuffled gasoline engine, and the air was sharp with the smell of kerosene and wood smoke and cooking meat. Some kids were playing soccer in the road. Men and women came out into the dusty paths that wandered among the shacks. A woman watched them, ignoring the chicken that was dangling by its feet from one of her hands, struggling now and then in a mechanical, abstracted manner. In her other hand there was a broad-bladed knife.

Ted looked around, saw wires strung between naked tree trunks looping among the shacks, catching their roofs in a crazy tangle. The road they were on ran through the middle of the settlement. Beside it, gray plastic pipe protruded from the ground here and there, leaking a little at the joints, where dark pools of mud snaked into the dust. He saw a shed with a rusty awning and a woman standing in the shadows before mounds of vegetables and fruit.

"Where are we?" he asked. "What's this place?"

""Is nowhere," Arturo said. He urged Ranger ahead. "Is all reserva, nobody allow to be living here."

A man shouted something from a doorway and Arturo stopped and turned. The man was huge and dark, naked to the waist, his great belly hanging over khaki trousers. From one of his thick fingers an assault rifle dangled by its trigger guard, pointing backward, looking puny and cheaply made.

Arturo swung out of the saddle and embraced the big man (he looked puny, too, in the big man's arms), then reached up to help Ted dismount. Ted gripped his hand, slid off the horse, and felt as if his body were shattering beneath him. Arturo caught him and helped him stagger a few steps and introduced him. Ted wasn't able to follow it at first. The man's name was Héctor, he got that, and heard himself described as Arturo's very good friend, a businessman in the flower trade, and then he lost the thread again. Ranger and Goldie were snuffling for grass tufts beside the road. Kids were patting the horses, offering them bouquets of weeds.

Héctor led the men into his makeshift squatter's house. It was cool and dark, earth-floored. Suspended from the ceiling was a mylar fold-out snowflake, big as a basketball, glittering red and gold and green, exactly like the one Monica had had him hang from a light fixture in their apartment.

Ted felt fatigue and hunger swirl through him. He wanted to just collapse here, safe in this village that had taken root in the wilderness, this house, shelter for the night that seemed to have been gathering weight over his head all day and couldn't hold off much longer.

A girl about Stephen's age brought them glasses of something milky with black seeds at the bottom, and they sat down on a plastic-upholstered sofa. Héctor went out again, leaving them alone in the room, except for a teenage girl who was playing with a baby in a doorway.

"They're wait for some guys to come with a truck," Arturo said. "Héctor hear the boys are near a finca across this mountain, and these guys will take us." Ted wondered how the squatters could know about the boys. The little girl came back, this time with plates of rice and black beans and tomatoes and fried plantain. Ted ate everything, his tinny fork scouring the plastic plate.

"You want more?" Arturo asked. Ted said he was fine, but Arturo spoke to the teenage girl and she shouted something to the kitchen. This time a woman came in and retrieved Ted's plate and returned with it filled with food again. She wiped her hands on a faded, flower print apron and stayed with them, talking with Arturo.

Ted half-listened for a while, then realized she was talking about the invasion. It was difficult to follow. When the baby started to cry, the woman told the girl to take care of it, but then she followed her to the next room, and he could hear her singing something, and the baby continuing to cry. He didn't know whose baby it was, the teenage girl's or the woman's.

He balanced his empty plate on his knee. "Does she know what's happening?" he asked.

"She say Noriega is hiding. She say a lot of killing."

Ted leaned back, resting his head against the corrugated metal wall, and closed his eyes. "She's Panamanian," Arturo said.

"What does she think about it?"

"She and Héctor, they're refugees from Noriega's sapos."

Toads. A little miracle of stray knowledge. "So she's happy about it."

"Not happy, not unhappy. Just a new set of stooges. The story of Panama."

"He wasn't worse than anyone else?"

"He's plenty worse, believe me." He got up and went outside, and Ted could hear him talking with somebody. When he returned, Ted asked him what time it was, but he didn't know. Arturo sat down beside him on the plastic couch and rested a hand for a moment on his knee. "I'll tell you a story," he said. "There was a young guy, upper class, what they call in Panama rabiblanco. White ass. This guy, this white ass, he's very good looking, a sexy guy, but he's serious. Medical doctor. He talk about Noriega and the drugs, very public, very brave, sexy man. He goes to Nicaragua and fight against Somoza with the Sandinistas, then he fight with the Miskitos against the Sandinistas."

"Pastora." Ted wondered if that was who he was talking about, Eden Pastora.

"Is with Pastora and the Contras for a while. He goes to the jungle, to the Miskito indios, and he fight with them against the Sandinistas. And all the time he's thinking about Panama. He's sometime in Costa Rica with me, in my own house, my guest, and then is a coup in Panama, and he decide to go home.

"Is no secret. He thinks he's so famous, he'll be okay, he just get in the bus to go home. At the frontier they take him from the bus. They bring him to a place, and they start to do very bad things to him. They beat him and they cut him here and here—" He touched Ted on the inner thighs, two quick strokes, "so he can't close his legs together. He knows what they do, a doctor. They beat him till his balls grow big, they push a sharp wood up his ass. Other very bad things. They keep putting him in cars and taking him to different towns, sometime in Costa Rica, sometime in Panama, doing very bad things to him in these different places, so his blood drop in the dust of different towns, all day, and at last they have a man who is cook take a knife and cut the living head from him and they put his body in a mail bag and throw it in the river like garbage."

Ted was trying not to hear. He was fighting the urge to press his hands against the places Arturo had touched, the places on his inner legs that already felt like they were on fire, it was too much.

"I learn about this ending from Héctor. He's from the poor, once a soldier in Noriega's guard, a trusted man, but he know the coup leaders and is afraid what the sapos will do to his family. He comes here, to Costa Rica."

"He'll go back now?" Ted asked. His inner thighs, the muscles and tendons of his groin burned. It had to get worse before it got better.

"Who knows who will be the next ones in power? Héctor is serious. But many, many hands are in the bowl. Colombia and Nicaragua and U.S. and Cuba and even my neutral Costa Rica, and they are all wanting to keep on making the money of drugs and politics. Many businessmen, many militaries, many politicians. I think it would surprise you, Ted my very good friend, the ones who got their hands in this bowl."

"It wouldn't surprise me. We know what North and his buddies were up to."

Arturo looked at him. "Those guys, yes. Still, I think it would surprise you." He stood up and went outside.

Ted was going to follow him, but he stayed there on the sofa. He just wanted his boy to be safe. He didn't want anything else. He folded his palms between his legs and clamped them there. He wondered if Hank really worked with the C.I.A. They should never have let Stephen be alone with the Picketts. They had to have been out of their minds.

He went outside to find Arturo. Night still hadn't fallen, only the blue had thickened some more over the bowl of mountains. The horses were grazing at the edge of the burned-over field, where the men had returned to their dull, rhythmic hacking of machetes against blackened scrub. It was a settled place, a real community, no more temporary-looking than a dozen villages he had come across in the hills above San José.

In the ditch beside the road, three cows moved slowly toward him, an old woman plodding behind them, touching them now and then with a stick to keep them moving. The cows didn't seem to see him, though the woman murmured adiós as she passed by. The banana trees growing between some of the houses must have been planted there by the squatters. They looked to be ten years old, at least. There were even a few cinder block and cement buildings, though most of the houses were made from old lumber and corrugated metal and sticks. There were flowers growing by the doorways.

Arturo was standing in the shade of an enormous tree that must have been left from the original forest. He was talking with Héctor and two other men, and when he saw Ted he walked over to him.

"They're getting fuel, then we go."

"How about the horses?"

"They care for them here."

When the truck appeared, it was moving fast, billowing dust, an old army transport vehicle with no doors on the cab and a flatbed in back with some crates pushed up against the cab, roped in. A small man with an intense, pock-marked face was driving. Héctor introduced him, Sánchez, and another man, Juan Carlos, who jumped out. Héctor helped Ted and then Arturo into the cab, and Juan Carlos scrambled up onto the bed. They lurched into motion before the man had a chance to settle himself completely. The driver shouted something out the door. Ted turned around and saw that the man had managed to wedge himself among the crates. He looked like a tough guy, with handsome, broad face and hooded eyes. He was peering into one of the crates as the truck roared along the fields and into the forest rising behind the village.

Ted felt as if he had been plunged without warning into deep, fast-running water. He hung on to a greasy canvas strap overhead and tried to make himself narrow and steady so that he wouldn't knock Arturo out of the doorless cab. He reached his right arm around Arturo's shoulders and clutched the edge of the seat back. The driver's hand on the long floor shift pressed into his knee at every gear change. Tree branches whipped against his knuckles.

At first the road was not too bad, but as they wound their way up the mountain it deteriorated. They did not slow down much, just crashed ahead through a barely-visible crease in the forest. From time to time the driver did slow, and leaned out the open side and consulted with the guy in back. He spoke with an accent that Ted found practically impossible to understand.

"Are these guys Panamanian?" Ted asked. Arturo didn't respond. Ever since the truck had started up the mountain, he had seemed to be drifting, sinking into the roar of the truck. Ted had to put his mouth almost against his ear to be heard. He felt that thick, fragrant hair against his face.

Arturo pulled himself out of whatever place he had gone to. "Indios," he said. "Bird collectors." The forest's green blur lashed at them.

Poachers.

When the track broke out of the trees and clawed along the edge of a bare, eroded precipice, he forced his gaze down into the shadows and ridges of the valley, but it was too far below them. There were vultures, almost at eye level, floating over the valley that twisted into the vast green forest. He couldn't tell if it was the valley he had entered before Arturo found him, or another one. As they pushed forward, it kept changing, now narrow, cramped into a river gorge, now flinging itself out in a vast blanket of green. Then the truck plunged once more into the forest and the large world collapsed in a crush of shadow and slashing branches.

Had he seen the boys himself? Ted managed to ask the driver.

Of course he had, the man said, swinging the huge, almost

horizontal steering wheel violently to one side, then back in the other direction in great sweeps as the trail wound through the forest.

Two boys?

Yes.

On horses?

The man laughed and said something incomprehensible. Then he said, one was not much of a horse—scarcely a goat. It seemed to Ted like a cruel remark. Stephen had been riding that pony.

They broke into the open finally and followed an actual road for a while, zigzagging down the slopes of a bare, eroded ridge toward some hilly grasslands. They were so high, and the country here was so thoroughly deforested, they could see for a long, long ways. A curtain of smoke hung farther down on the mountainside. As they worked their way down the mountain, they caught the pungency of burning grass. Ted looked for the workers who might be burning off the field, who might know about Stephen and Ray, but he saw no one. The smoke might have been from smoldering, isolated brush piles, though he knew you couldn't assume anything. They might have just quit for the day, letting the fire burn.

Arturo had not emerged from his silence. Ted swayed against him as the truck pounded over the rough road that ran along the upper edge of a broad, sloping pasture. Was this the finca they thought the boys were headed to? Ted asked. Did he think they would be able to help?

It was possible, he answered. Anything was possible.

The road angled down the open slope for a while, then changed direction. As the truck skidded through the switchback and started to gain speed again, there was a sudden frantic pounding on the roof of the cab. Without slowing, the driver leaned out perilously and shouted a question to the man in back. Before he could answer, the truck hit something, as if a mine had exploded beneath them, slamming them to the side and sending the truck swerving onto the rutted pasture slope.

Ted looked back. The man who had been riding in the bed had disappeared. One of the crates was tumbling along the ground behind them until it struck something, and a handful of green flecks burst into the air. The driver managed to stop the truck, and Ted thought they were going to go back for the other man, but Arturo pointed ahead and the driver started forward again, jolting across the open field. Ted saw it then, maybe a half mile farther down the mountain, between them and the line of smoke: a white horse galloping away from behind a pyramid of rock and brush, its rider crouched over its neck like a jockey. Ray. Disappearing into the soft pall of smoke.

Dodging boulders and sinkholes, the truck beat its way down the slope that had appeared serene and smooth from a distance. Ted was just deciding that maybe he could make better time if he jumped out and ran, when the white horse galloped back out of the smoke, riderless. Arturo pointed to something else, harder to see in the yellow angled light—the long-maned, long-tailed pony. Like the white mare, it was saddled and bridled, its reins dragging on the ground. The pony seemed to startle and ran a few yards before stopping. Now it was studying the fire, or something in the fire.

The driver was having trouble steering through the network of erosion. The truck braked, skidded to the lip of a gully that was deep and wide enough to have swallowed it. While the driver struggled to throw it into reverse, Ted saw a movement behind the rocks. He pushed his way over Arturo's legs and stumbled down from the truck and started running. "Stevie!" he shouted. Headlong, his lungs burning with the smoke, coughing.

He still couldn't see any flames, only the dense blur floating over the ground and the shimmer of mountains hanging in the sky. When he got to within fifty yards of the rocks, the pony trotted away for a few paces, keeping its distance, watching him. He ran to the pile of rocks where he thought Stephen was hiding from the fire that must seem to him like the end of the world. He pictured him so clearly, crazy with fear behind the rocks, that he could hardly believe it when he found nothing there but an empty Picaritas bag stirring fitfully in the hot wind.

"Stephen!" he shouted, scrambling as far as he could up the side of the rock pile, but he couldn't see anything, and the smoke took his voice away. He slid down, found the gully deepening into arroyo where he must have fled. He scrambled down its sides and breathed in the sweeter air and moved awkwardly along the loose earth and rock as it snaked up the slope, away from the fire. It was probably the same gully that had stopped the truck. If he had stayed up there, he could have intercepted Stephen already, grabbed him, held him until the fear and confusion faltered, as he had held him that rainy night at school, Independence Day lanterns glowing.

The gully turned and turned again, narrowing until he could step out and see the whole hillside, the fire behind him and the truck circling farther up. He started running across the trails of erosion. The crêpe paper farol burning. Stephen trapped in the circle of the crowd.

Smoke hung more densely now around the pyramid of rock when he reached it again and slid down the gully's side and started picking his way forward, down toward the advancing fire. That circle in the school hall, the fire in its center. Soon he had to drop to all fours to suck air from the rock and eroded clay. That dance of panic. The fire sent a tide of darkness flooding above his head.

No. Not panic, he understood suddenly. Stephen had fought his way *into* the circle. Into it. He had fought his way into the circle where the fire was. He had been trying to put it out. He had been trying to save them.

Ray was in there, he knew that now. The horse wouldn't have run back if they had gotten through.

He couldn't see in the gully, the smoke was thicker, or night might finally have fallen. He clawed his way up the collapsing side and looked toward the drifting line of smoke, where he now could see actual flames licking here and there. The smoke wasn't as dense as it had seemed, but he couldn't draw a full breath without gagging, and the wind kept pushing the smoke forward. He heard something, a gunshot, maybe, a single dull crack. He couldn't tell where it came from. Then another. A gunshot, he was sure of it this time. Somebody was shooting a gun.

He crouched at the edge of the gully, sheltering his face in the crook of his arm. He tried to call out, but the smoke had done something to his voice. He looked back, peered into the smoke, and heard another shot. This one he could sense cutting through the ruined air that swirled around him. He ran crouched over, sucking at whatever oxygen hung close to the parched ground.

He heard a voice. He moved toward it, stumbled, fell to his knees on the hot ground, groped his way forward. His eyes were streaming, he peered through the shimmer and smoke. He stood and moved toward where he thought the voice had been and stepped into nothing, pitched forward into space, landed hard, his outstretched arms collapsing, his face skidding against earth.

He got to his knees, believing his face was on fire, but when he pressed his hands to it, it was wet and sticky. The stickiness felt like fire. He crawled forward into the grumble of the fire that seemed almost over his head. He edged forward. It was dark down there in the gully, he could barely see the rim, then he saw a shape in front of him. He stretched out his hand, tried to speak.

There was a glimmer of movement and a whisper, something alive in the air above his head, and the sound of scrambling in the loose earth, then nothing, he was gone, he was losing him again. He staggered to his feet and took two, three steps forward. A figure was there before him. He lurched forward, pressing his hands to his streaming eyes to clear them.

Something struck the side of his knee and his leg collapsed

beneath him and he went down, suddenly sick with pain, and looked up and saw him a few feet away, holding a machete in both hands, like a baseball bat or an ax. Braced.

"Stevie." He dragged himself forward, trying to refuse the pain, and wrapped his arms around him and sank to the ground with him. He held him that way, shaking, and saw something. He groped until he felt the other boy, his bare arm, thin and still, and gripped it. He gripped it and didn't let go until he thought he felt a pulse quiver beneath his fingers.

"Ray."

"He got knocked out."

He reached over and felt Ray's damp forehead, the swollen knot. The boy jerked, the whites of his eyes flickering in the disappearing light. The smell of vomit. Stephen was crouched next to him. When he put his arm around him, he was shaking wildly, he thought that he might be having a seizure. The wound in his leg was roaring, it made his whole body feel electrified and weak.

"I didn't know it was you," Stephen said. He laid something in Ted's hand, a big, old-fashioned revolver.

"Jesus."

"I ran out of bullets."

He looked at him.

"I used your machete. I'm sorry."

He touched as close as he dared to the raging in his leg. Not very close, but even there his pants leg was soaked with blood. He couldn't move it. He vomited into the reek of vomit that cut through the smell of smoke.

•

It was dark. The fire had burned past them and was faintly visible in flashes of sparks and the vague glow moving on up the mountain. One of the Indians—Juan Carlos, the one who had been riding in the bed—found them and shouted. Arturo and the driver were apparently still in the truck. Juan Carlos and Stephen dragged the still-stunned Ray out of the gully, then returned for Ted. He tried to help them, clawing at the rocky cut, pushing with his good leg.

When he came to, he was lying on the warm, charred ground beside Ray. Ray was breathing. Juan Carlos had torn off a sleeve of Ted's shirt and tied it around the wound on his leg. The night was chilly on his bare shoulder and arm. The lights of the truck swung first in one direction, then another, weaving slowly toward them from the far side of the field. Far below, there were floodlights of a house that must have been visible before night fell, though he had missed it. The lights made nothing clear from this distance, just blurred the air a little.

When the truck reached them, they loaded Ray and Stephen into the cab, with Juan Carlos on the running board blocking the door to keep them from falling out. Arturo and the driver hauled Ted up onto the truck's bed, braced him against the back of the cab in an opening among the remaining crates. Arturo settled himself beside him and knocked twice on the roof of the cab. The truck jerked into motion.

Ted watched the distant flicker of the grass fire on the invisible mountain. A faint piping sound floated above the roar of the engine. The pain was horrible, it had somehow spread to his calf and thigh. He spasmed on the ridged metal truck bed. Arturo put an arm around him, cushioning his back from the metal of the cab, his hand warm on Ted's bare shoulder.

"Is very bad, I know. At the house they got something will help the pain. They'll bring a doctor for you and the boy." He studied the bulky bandage. "The bleeding is control, I think." They were driving parallel to the line of the fire and turned onto a road, which would take them down to the big house.

"How'll we get back?" His voice was raw in his throat, he could barely get the words out.

"Somebody at the house drive you. They got a phone, you'll call her, she don't worry no more."

"Picketts, no phone."

"Then she got to trust this night I say her the truth, I send you all back to her. Only hurted, I'm very sorry for that. She'll no forgive me."

"Send us."

"I think maybe I stay with my old friend Héctor for a while. I been missing him a long time."

Ted tried to think. "Horses."

"Señorita Charlotte's fine horses. And the old one and the little one. Somebody bring them back." Arturo was quiet, watching the road unwind behind them. "Maybe I'll go some other place for a while. I been thinking about that. Maybe Panama, what do you think? You think that would be interesting?" He was trying to distract him, Ted understood.

Well below the fire, now, they had escaped the haze of smoke. A few stars were visible. Ted said nothing. He hoped Arturo was right about the plantation house having drugs, for the pain had continued to swell, engulfing his whole leg now, muscle and tendon and bone and skin, ankle to groin.

It was going to get worse before it got better, he remembered Arturo saying. Well, it had gotten worse. It had gotten a lot worse. He closed his eyes and moved his fingers a little, edging them to the bulky bandage, which was spongy now with blood that continued to pulse from his leg, pooling around his foot in the cool darkness. Arturo was wrong about the bleeding, he thought dreamily, though he had been right about everything else. He couldn't seem to move or speak anymore, but he was aware of the bouncing truck bed, Arturo's arm cushioning his back.

A thin, high, piping song.

ABOUT THE AUTHOR

Lon Otto is the author of *A Nest of Hooks* (University of Iowa Press), winner of the Iowa School of Letters Award for Short Fiction; *Cover Me* (Coffee House Press); and *A Man in Trouble* (Brighthorse Books). His fiction is in a number of anthologies, including *Flash Fiction* and *Flash Fiction Forward* (Norton), *American Fiction* (New Rivers), *Blink* and *Blink Again* (Spout Press), and *Not Normal, Illinois* (Indiana U. Press). He has also published the letterpress chapbook *Water Bodies* (Coffee House Press) and the craft e-book *Grit: Bringing Physical Experience Into Imaginative Writing* (Writehorse). He lives in St. Paul, Minnesota, is Professor Emeritus at the University of St. Thomas in St. Paul, and has taught for many years in the University of Iowa Summer Writing Festival.

www.ingramcontent.com/pod-product-compliance
Lightning Source LLC
Chambersburg PA
CBHW050759190726
48285CB00005B/1729